To Dream Anew

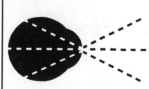

This Large Print Book carries the
Seal of Approval of N.A.V.H.

To Dream Anew

Tracie Peterson

THORNDIKE PRESS

An imprint of Thomson Gale, a part of The Thomson Corporation

THOMSON

™

GALE

Detroit • New York • San Francisco • New Haven, Conn. • Waterville, Maine • London

THOMSON

GALE

LIBRARY OF CONGRESS CATALOGING-IN-PUBLICATION DATA

Peterson, Tracie.
    To dream anew / by Tracie Peterson.
        p. cm. — (Heirs of Montana ; 3) (Thorndike Press large print Christian romance)
    ISBN-13: 978-1-4104-0292-9 (lg. print : alk. paper)
    ISBN-10: 1-4104-0292-4 (lg. print : alk. paper)
    1. Women pioneers — Fiction. 2. Ranch life — Fiction. 3. Montana — Fiction. 4. Large type books. I. Title.
    PS3566.E7717T6 2007
    813'.54—dc22   2007032946

Published in 2007 by arrangement with Bethany House Publishers.

Printed in the United States of America on permanent paper
10 9 8 7 6 5 4 3 2 1

To my Saving Grace Church family.
You've all been so supportive
and loving,
a wonderful representation of
what the body is all about.
Thank you for your love.

CHAPTER 1

Dianne Chadwick Selby sat straight up in bed. Panting, she put her hand to her mouth to stifle the scream that threatened to break free. She threw back the covers and ran to the cradle at the foot of the bed. Her six-month-old son, Luke, slept peacefully. His closed eyes and even breathing offered some solace to her frayed nerves.

Looking back to the bed, Dianne was equally relieved to see her husband, Cole, deep in slumber, ignorant of the terror in her heart.

Dianne drew a deep breath and sat down at the foot of the bed. The dream had seemed so real. She could almost hear the screams and cries of the people who were under attack. There had been a great battle. Soldiers and Indians. Even Cole and Lucas had been there.

"Something wrong?" Cole asked in a

groggy tone. "What time is it?" He yawned and glanced at the window.

"I don't know," Dianne admitted. She got up and looked outside. "There's a hint of light on the horizon. Probably a half hour or so before dawn."

"Sure comes early this time of year," Cole said, moaning softly as he sat up.

"Are your ribs still sore?" Dianne asked, pushing aside the images from the night.

"Yeah," he admitted. "That horse has a mean streak a mile long."

"He definitely didn't take to the saddle," she said, remembering the strawberry roan gelding. She smiled and went to get the liniment from the mantel. "Here, let me rub some more of this on. Koko said it would do wonders." Her aunt was especially gifted with healing remedies. Koko was half Blackfoot Indian and had learned many medicinal remedies from her mother. Her knowledge had been a blessing to this family on more than one occasion.

Dianne rubbed the ointment across her husband's back and side, drawing her hand gently over the bruised ribs. She loved this man more than life — would give her life for him. She thought of her dream and shuddered.

"What's wrong? Why were you up? Is

8

Luke all right?" Cole took hold of her hand and stilled her ministering. He stared long, searching her face as if to find the answers there.

"I had a nightmare. I dreamed Zane was in a battle. A horrible battle. There were bodies everywhere. Dead soldiers and Indians. Then without warning, we were in the middle of it too, and the Indians were attacking here at the Diamond V."

Her uncle's ranch lay in the lush Madison Valley, along a river also named for the country's fourth president. Uncle Bram had loved this land as much as she did, but now he was gone — killed by a grizzly attack. It seemed only yesterday he had been telling Dianne of his great plans for the Diamond V.

Cole rubbed her hand gently. "It was only a dream."

Dianne shook her head and gripped his hand. "But there are so many threats of Indian attacks and conflict. Zane's regiment is moving to the Little Big Horn River, where they plan to help move the Sioux and Cheyenne back to their reservation. What if something goes wrong? What if the Indians stage an uprising?"

"Nothing will go wrong. Your brother knows how to take care of himself. Not only

9

that, but the army is well aware of what's going on. They are trained to handle these kinds of matters."

"But there's always the chance that something could be missed, overlooked."

"Dianne, it was just a nightmare."

Luke stirred and Dianne glanced to the cradle. "I couldn't bear it if anything happened to you or Luke. Or any of the others, for that matter."

"But we have to trust that God has it all under control," Cole said with a lopsided grin. "Which is a heap better than taking on that load ourselves."

Dianne smiled. "I know you're right. I just can't help fretting."

Cole pulled her into his arms and together they fell back against the bed. He nuzzled her neck with kisses, leaving her happy and contented with the attention.

Luke began to fuss, then to cry. Dianne watched her husband rise up and look to his baby boy. "Traitor," he murmured. Then looking back to Dianne, he shrugged. "Another time, I guess."

She laughed and pushed him aside as she went to tend their son. "At least he's sleeping through the night. Koko's children didn't do that until they were nearly a year old."

"Hard to believe our little guy is already six months old. Seems like only yesterday he was born." Cole got up and stretched and winced.

"Maybe you should take it easy today," Dianne said as she changed Luke's wet diaper.

"There's not much time to rest on a ranch this size. I can't believe the way the herd has grown. It's a blessing, but it also means more work." He began to dress for the day as Dianne took her place in the rocker.

She forced herself to relax as Luke began to nurse. She knew she would only frustrate him if she let herself remain tense and her milk wouldn't let down. Still, the images of the night lingered in her thoughts.

"Trenton told me he was going to take a stab at that roan today," Cole said, buttoning his shirt. "Your brother is quite good at breaking those green mounts."

"Trenton seldom has the chance — or desire — to talk to me, it seems," Dianne said sadly. "We used to be so close. Zane and Morgan had each other. They had a special bond because they were twins, you know. . . . I could never get in close to either one of them. But Trent . . . he was different. He cared about what I thought and talked to me long into the night when

11

we were young."

"He's a grown man now," Cole offered. "And no doubt he lived a good deal in his time before joining us here. A man changes. Can't be helped."

"Women change too," she murmured, knowing in her heart she was far removed from the young woman who had arrived homeless and parentless on the Diamond V.

Cole leaned down and kissed Dianne's forehead. "I'd better get to work. Ring the bell loud and clear when breakfast is ready."

"No doubt there's already a pot of coffee brewing on the stove," she said with a grin. "Probably biscuits baking in the oven too. Faith is always good to sneak over and see to that." The former slave was a faithful friend and worker on the ranch.

"She and Malachi sure make our days a whole lot easier. We'd all go hungry and have shoeless horses if not for them." Cole went to the bedroom door and opened it. Looking back, he smiled. "You two make a man proud." He didn't wait for a response before heading out.

Dianne shifted Luke and smiled at his greedy feeding. He was such a little butterball. He watched her with dark blue eyes that never seemed to miss a single thing. If

Dianne frowned, he frowned too, and if she smiled, his grin was bigger by far.

The dream still haunted her, however. In spite of this peaceful moment and Cole's obvious love, Dianne felt cold inside. She closed her eyes and saw the battlefield once again. No doubt she was merely recalling the vivid descriptions written up in the newspapers. Journalists seemed to have a flair for the dramatic and graphic.

But what if the dream was a forewarning? Didn't God do things like that? Joseph was warned in a dream to take Mary and Jesus and escape Herod. Other people in the Bible had dreams that helped them to survive.

But this dream offered no promise of hope. It only showed complete destruction. Dianne shuddered again and Luke stopped nursing, looking up as if to ask what the problem was.

"Oh, my sweet baby boy," she said, stroking back his tawny hair. "I pray it was only a bad dream and nothing more." He gurgled and smiled in response.

Dianne laughed, but the joy was only momentary. Prayer would see her through the day, but hard times were coming. Gus, their foreman, said the winds were blowing up a change, and frankly, Dianne wasn't at all sure she liked the sounds of it.

Later that morning Dianne and Faith made jam. It promised to be a hot day, so they hurried to get the task out of the way before the sun would make everything unbearable.

Faith's children, Mercy and Daniel, played quietly in the corner while Luke slept in the front sitting room. Faith rubbed her bulging abdomen and smiled.

"This one sure is a kicker. Can't hardly see how we'll make it to October. I'm bettin' this baby comes early."

Dianne shook her head. "Each time has been different, hasn't it?"

Faith nodded and re-secured a red bandanna around her head. "Guess carrying babies is as different as the babies themselves. Leastwise it's been that way for me."

"My mama indicated the same thing," Dianne said, remembering her mother's words, "although she did say they all had one thing in common."

"What was that?" Faith asked, giving Dianne a curious look.

"She said they all wore her out."

Faith laughed and stirred the cooking jam. "That's true enough. But it's a joyous burden to bear, don't you agree?"

Dianne did agree. She loved little Luke

more than she could express in words, and she looked forward to having more children. She wanted a whole houseful — like it was when she was growing up.

"Mmm, smells good in here," Cole said as he came through the back door. "Any coffee left?"

"Now, Cole Selby," Faith began in a scolding manner, "you know there's always coffee to be had in this house."

He grinned. "Well, there's always the chance it could run out."

"Maybe when that strawberry roan of yours sprouts wings and flies," Faith said, putting down the spoon to get a cup of coffee for Cole.

"I think maybe that roan did grow wings," Dianne teased. "At least it sure seemed Cole was flying pretty high yesterday when that beast finally managed to let loose of him."

"Now, if you're not going to be nice to me," Cole began, "I won't tell you the surprise."

Dianne noted the amusement that danced in his expression. "What surprise?"

"We're going to Bozeman City for the Fourth of July celebration. We'll leave in a few days."

"Truly?" Dianne questioned. This would allow her to get over to Fort Ellis and see if there was any word from her brother's regiment. Not only that, but the festivities might be precisely the thing to get her mind off of her worries.

"Truly." He threw her a look that suggested he knew what she was thinking. "I figured we couldn't be missing out on the country's centennial celebration. A lot has happened in a hundred years. Lot's happened in the last fifty years. Anyway, I also figured it'd be the easiest way to put our minds at ease. I'll take you over to the fort first thing and we can ask about Zane."

"There's bound to be supplies we can pick up as well," Faith offered.

"For sure. That town's grown up quite a bit, and it'll be interesting to see what all they're offering." Cole took a sip of his coffee. "We'll take a couple of wagons and buy what we need. I've already talked to Malachi, and he's pretty excited about making the trip."

"You don't think the trip would be too hard on Luke, do you?"

Faith answered before Cole had a chance. "That baby is made of tougher stuff than you give him credit for. He'll be fine. The trip will probably do all of us good."

"What about the ranch?" Dianne asked.

"Are you looking for excuses not to go?"

Cole asked after downing the last of his coffee.

Dianne shook her head. "Not at all. I just wondered if you'd made provision for that matter."

"You don't see me as being very capable, do you?" He was smiling, but there was something serious in his tone.

"I know you're capable," Dianne said, trying to choose her words carefully. "I just didn't know if you'd thought this through or if it was more one of those whimsical things."

"I'm hardly known for whimsy," Cole stated matter-of-factly. "We'll leave a small crew to keep an eye on things, but I figure this is a good way to cut the boys loose and give them some time away from the ranch. They'll enjoy the holiday and help us get things freighted back here afterward."

"Sounds like a perfect plan to me," Faith said, lifting the heavy kettle from the stove and placing it on the wooden counter. "This is ready to strain."

"I'd better get back to work," Cole said, putting the coffee cup in the sink.

Once he'd gone, Faith turned to Dianne. "He's a good man, you know. You can trust him to think things through. Besides, Gus isn't going to let him make a bad decision."

Dianne shrugged, knowing she'd been careless with her words. "Cole hasn't been doing this very long. I worry he'll overlook things."

"And if he does, he'll make that mistake only once. We learn from our mistakes," Faith said in a motherly tone. "Least we do if we're allowed to make them."

Dianne sighed. "Sometimes it's hard to let him have free rein. I guess because of working with Uncle Bram for so long, I feel like this place needs my attention."

"You've had these issues before. You've struggled with trusting Cole to do his job on other occasions."

Dianne shook her head. "It's not a matter of trust, but rather training." She always justified it this way to herself. Cole often did things differently from Uncle Bram, and it made her nervous. It wasn't that she didn't believe Cole capable, but only that he might not realize why things were done a certain way, and end up causing them more trouble than help.

"You worry too much."

"That she does," Koko announced as she came into the room.

"Well, I simply feel that Uncle Bram gave me a responsibility to see to this ranch and its success."

"But he'd also want you to relax and let others do the jobs they are capable of. Cole is a good man, the same as Bram was. He'll make wise decisions."

"Cole's planning for us to go to Bozeman for the Fourth of July celebration. Will you bring the children and come too?" Dianne asked, hoping to divert the discussion.

Koko shook her head. "I don't think so. With all the Indian trouble, it would probably be wise for me to remain here. No sense causing anyone to be uncomfortable."

"I wouldn't worry about making the townsfolk uncomfortable," Dianne declared as she helped Faith with the jelly jars. She was glad to have the focus off of her treatment of Cole.

"I wasn't so much worried about the townsfolk," Koko admitted. "I didn't want the children hurt."

Dianne thought of nine-year-old Jamie and six-year-old Susannah. Both children bore some of their mother's features, although each were more white than Blackfoot. Society surely wouldn't see them that way, however, and Koko was right about the tensions and ugly attitudes toward those with Indian blood.

"Well, what can we bring you back?" Dianne finally said, knowing that she couldn't make the situation right. She met her aunt's expression and offered a smile.

Koko nodded as if sharing unspoken information with her niece. "There are several things we could use. I'll make a list for you before you go."

The smell of something rotten and foul was the first thing that caught their attention.

Colonel Gibbon's forces moved forward to join up with George Armstrong Custer's ranks along the Little Big Horn River. Their objective was to quell the Sioux and Cheyenne and see them returned to their reservation to the east, but the smell and deadly silence distressed every member of the regiment.

Zane felt a chill run up his spine. The sensation did nothing to ease his fears. For days there had been rumors and disconcerting messages from his superiors. One infantryman had come to tell them that some of Custer's Indian scouts had been found. They spoke of a horrible battle in which every soldier was annihilated, but surely that couldn't be true.

On the other hand, he heard more than one man complain that they were heading out on another wild goose chase, and just as the first thought didn't ring true, Zane didn't feel this to be an accurate statement either.

Sweat dampened his skin and ran a stream down his face. He could feel it slip beneath his collar, leaving him sticky and uncomfortable. The temperatures were near the one hundred mark. Funny how that at the first of the month they had marched in snow. Most of it hadn't lasted much longer than it had taken to fall from the sky and hit the ground, but in places the white powder had accumulated. Zane tried hard to remember how he'd hunkered down in his wool coat chilled to the bone, but it was no use. The heat of late June now threatened to bake him alive.

He could see in the faces of his comrades that he wasn't the only one to bear the harsh elements in discomfort. The dust and sweat made striping streaks on the faces of the soldiers, almost as if they had painted their faces Indian style, for war. Especially those in the infantry. They marched long hours in the dust. Day after day they walked in a cloud of their own making, then struggled at the end of the day to scrape the earth from their bodies.

Zane knew their misery. Infantry life had never really agreed with him. Now, however, as a newly appointed lieutenant, he was at least given the choice of riding if he wanted. Some officers rode, others did not. Zane was known to be a good hand with a horse — his background on the Diamond V preceded his transfer into Colonel Gibbon's forces. The ranch was a good provider for army horseflesh, and his superiors seemed bent on keeping Zane happy, lest the supply be cut off.

The horses were acting strange, and that, coupled with the awful stench, made everyone uneasy. They would probably come up on a buffalo jump or some other place where a mass butchering had taken place. The smell of death always made the horses nervous. Zane tried to calm his mount, but the animal continued side-stepping, as if to avoid what was ahead.

Without warning, a pale-faced rider came flying over the ridge. His horse was lathered from the strain, and the man appeared to barely keep his seat on the animal. Zane's horse reared slightly and whinnied loudly as the rider came to a stop not far from where Colonel Gibbon sat atop his own mount.

The man, really no more than a boy, leaned over the side of his horse and lost the contents of his stomach. The action took everyone by surprise. Without looking up, the man pointed behind him and shook his head. The words seemed stuck in his throat.

"What is it? What did you find?" Gibbon asked impatiently.

"They're dead, sir. Custer. His men. Every last soldier — dead."

CHAPTER 2

And so they were.

Zane could only stare in dumbfounded silence at the bleached and bloated bodies of men who were once soldiers. *Where was God when Custer and his men met this fate?*

Scenes from the Baker Massacre, where the slaughter of the Blackfoot tribe took place some six years earlier, came back to haunt him. *Where was God then?*

Zane could scarcely draw a breath. The scene was unreal, too horrible to even allow the images to settle in his mind. Burial duties were all that was left them now. There was no great battle in which to prove their bravery or manhood. Bravery this day was shown by the ability to witness the massacre at the Little Big Horn and not give in to insanity.

"Sir, how could this have happened?" the raspy voice of one of his newer recruits asked. The man paused in his construction of a litter for the wounded as Zane stepped closer.

Zane looked to the man and shook his head. "I suppose it was bound to happen."

"Beggin' the lieutenant's pardon," the man began, "but how can you say that? The U.S. Army should never have been caught by surprise like this. How could they have been ambushed without warning?"

Zane heard the disbelief and horror in the man's voice. He felt a certain degree of it himself. If it could happen to someone like Custer, it could happen to anyone.

"I have to believe that if they'd been prepared, this would never have happened." Zane tried hard to sound convincing. The truth of the matter was, he wasn't that certain of his words. The territory around them was wild — untamed and unsettled. The Sioux, Crow, and Cheyenne knew it better than the soldiers could hope to. That's why they used Indian scouts. How could he convince this soldier of something he couldn't completely come to terms with himself? "It's a matter of preparation — of training," Zane added softly.

The man nodded. "I suppose the Indians are long gone now."

"The report indicates they've moved on down into the Big Horn Mountains."

"I suppose we'll give chase." The soldier looked at Zane, seemingly to pull the truth from him.

"I cannot honestly say. I've not been given any orders except to make litters for the wounded and see them safely on their way to the steamer, *Far West,* up on the Big Horn River."

As the sun dipped below the horizon, Zane longed only for a bath and the ability to blot out all that he'd seen that day. The Sioux and Cheyenne had mutilated most of the dead, believing they were somehow denying their enemy wholeness for all eternity. The wounded were another story entirely. Their misery and fear seemed contagious. Zane longed for word from the couriers who'd gone out days before in search of the *Far West.* They were feared dead, but General Terry, the overall commander, held out hope that they would return, and because of this they were soon to move the wounded to safety.

But could safety be found on Indian land? Every man among them wondered if another ambush awaited them upstream. Every noise, every crack or snap of a twig brought men to attention, guns in hand.

For a long time Zane sat on the riverbank staring blankly at the water. *It's senseless,* he thought. *I figured to be a peacekeeper, not a killer. I believed it was right to serve, to give of myself to the country that had already given me so much.*

"I thought I was honorable."

But there had been no honor on the banks of the Marias when Major Baker had led the soldiers in a massacre of innocent Blackfoot Indians. There had been no honor when they'd turned the sick and wounded out into the snow and forty-below temperatures.

Other images came to mind. Other encounters and campaigns. Other hurting, frightened people.

It's not worth it. I can't make this right in my own mind. . . . How can I defend it to anyone else?

All around him his men were eager to hunt down the Sioux and Cheyenne responsible for the Custer massacre. Men spoke the name Custer with the same reverence used for God. The man who had at one time been mocked by some and revered by others was now elevated to sainthood in the eyes of many. With every body buried and every new body found, the men saw nothing but the blood-haze of their anger.

They wanted justice for their fallen leader and comrades.

No, they wanted revenge.

These thoughts haunted Zane throughout the next day and the day after that as the wounded were moved out. The irrepressible heat refused to abate. The high temperatures and searing sun made tempers flare and set the men against one another. At times, Zane had found it necessary to break up fights, yet he couldn't bring himself to be too hard on the men. They had seen sights such as no man should ever have to see. They had come here innocent in some ways — boys who were seeking adventure. They would never be innocent again.

"Sir! Come quick. They'll kill her for sure!" a young private called to Zane as he ran toward him.

Zane jumped to his feet. "What is it? They'll kill who?"

The private gasped for breath. "We found . . . we found a squaw and papoose. She's Sioux, and well, you know the boys ain't feelin' too friendly toward 'em right now. Especially 'cause the women were the ones doin' most of the mutilation."

"Take me to them. Hurry!"

They turned and ran back the same direction the private had come from. *What am I to do with a squaw? What is she doing here still? Her people have long since moved out.*

28

Or had they? Maybe it was a trap. *What if, like Custer, we find ourselves suddenly attacked by thousands of Sioux? What do I do then?* The questions ricocheted through Zane's mind and his heart sounded a furious beat in his ears as he approached the circle of blue-coated men.

"Put a bullet in her and be done with it," one man said.

"No, torture her. Torture her like she done to our men."

"What's going on here?" Zane asked in his most authoritative voice.

The men parted at the sound, and Zane stopped in his tracks to see the young woman, tiny babe in arms. She stared at him in wild-eyed fear. Her long hair was sticking out in disarray around her face and shoulders. She was filthy, caked in dust and blood. She'd been wounded, hit in the head and cut on the arms. The baby began to cry.

"She's a Sioux, Lieutenant," the man at his left finally answered. "We found her hiding in the thicket. Her and her brat."

"She's probably waiting to kill us in our sleep," another man called out.

Zane walked forward, watching as the woman cringed and pressed herself back against a tree trunk. "She's hurt. Get the doctor."

"Beggin' the lieutenant's pardon, but the doc is busy with wounded soldiers. He can't hardly be stoppin' to take care of some enemy squaw."

Zane eyed the man hard. The anger he felt inside threatened to boil over and play itself out in a fist to the man's smug-looking face. Zane turned and looked at the men around him. "So we are to be no better than them? Is that it? We've resorted to openly killing unarmed women and children?"

"You saw what they did," a grizzled sergeant reminded. "Them Sioux women picked the bones of our dead. They made it so some of the men wouldn't even be known to their mothers. They killed wounded men if they found them still alive."

"Did anyone catch this woman in such acts?" Zane questioned.

"No, but she's got blood on her hands!"

"She's got blood on her face as well. You'll notice she has a head wound." Zane turned to the sergeant in particular and pressed the question again. "Did you see her mutilate any bodies?"

"No, sir," the man answered in a clipped tone. "Didn't see her try to help any of them either."

"From the looks of it," Zane said, getting

30

a better view of the baby as the woman shifted it in her arms, "I'd say she was probably giving birth during the battle. Looks to me that maybe one of our soldiers tried to kill her — maybe even while she was laboring. Takes a brave man to attack a woman giving birth." Zane felt torn. He knew these men were angry because of their fallen comrades. He understood their rage, but it grieved him to see that they'd become nothing better than savages themselves.

"Now, I want you," he said, turning to the sergeant, "to go get the doctor. Bring him to my tent." Zane didn't wait for a response but instead turned to one of the other men. "Take her to my tent; it's just up the ridge. Put her in there and get some hot water so the doctor can treat her wounds."

The man nodded but looked none too happy, while the sergeant trudged up the path in no apparent hurry. Zane drew a deep breath and turned back to the woman. He stepped closer, relieved to see that she made no attempt to retreat further.

"Ma'am, this soldier is going to escort you to my tent. A doctor will come and see to you and the babe. Do you understand?"

She stared at him for a moment, then nodded. The soldier approached and looked back to Zane. He appeared hesitant as to what he should do.

"Go with him, ma'am."

For several seconds no one moved, then finally the woman stepped out. She held the baby tightly and let her gaze dart from man to man, looking ready to fight anyone who dared to approach.

Another lieutenant reached out to touch Zane's arm. "Zane, do you really know what you're doing?"

The woman's head snapped up and she eyed them both hard. Just as quickly she looked away and clutched the child ever closer.

"I'm doing what any decent Christian man would do. No one touches her," Zane commanded, looking to his men. "Do you understand? We will not lower ourselves to the standards of savages. I will personally deal with any man who breaks this order. Understood?"

The men grumbled affirmation. A couple of them cast disgruntled comments to the air, but Zane wasn't sure who had spoken and decided to let it go. He could comprehend their anger — their frustration. But he also knew these men and knew that most of them would never be able to live with themselves if they harmed this unarmed woman. He wanted more than anything to

32

tell them that. To explain that he knew their hearts were burdened because of the previous days. He wanted to let them know that he understood their anguish and the need to avenge their fallen comrades. But he couldn't. In that moment, Zane knew they would not hear him — they would not respect him. And right now, he needed their respect.

"Get back to your duties," Zane commanded in a gruff tone. "If you have trouble following my orders, try to imagine telling your wives and mothers of your desire to murder a new mother and her baby. Try to picture how they would react to such thoughts."

He turned and walked back up the path to where his tent had been erected. He wondered if the doctor would refuse the request to help. He worried that the woman would die in spite of their care. Then he worried that if she lived, someone would seek to kill her and the baby.

He waited outside his tent, hearing the baby cry from within. The doctor finally came some thirty minutes later, looking apprehensive as he approached Zane.

"I understand you have found a wounded squaw and her infant."

"Yes, Captain. I would appreciate it if you

would attend to them. They're inside my tent."

The man, older than Zane by a decade, looked at the tent momentarily. "Wouldn't it be better to just let them die?"

"I don't know, sir," Zane replied. "Would it? Is that what Christian men are called to do?"

"This hasn't been an easy situation. I've treated Indians before. I'm not averse to it. However, I have wounded soldiers to deal with and no one is going to take this interference kindly."

"I'm asking you to see to her. I think she just gave birth. That baby didn't look very old. She may well die anyway, but at least we will have done the honorable thing."

"Even if *they* didn't — is that it?" the doctor questioned.

"Exactly. I can't help what they did or didn't do. I can only stand before God with my own deeds."

"Very well. I'll see her."

Zane waited outside the tent for what seemed an eternity. He could hear the captain talk to the young woman in broken Sioux and slow, methodic English. Her answers were muffled and Zane had no way of understanding what she might be saying.

Pacing back and forth in front of the tent,

Zane tried not to notice the men who watched him. They were curious to say the least, but they were also angry. Angry at him for interfering with their chance for revenge. Still, Zane couldn't imagine the barely-eighteen-year-old Thom Martin taking a gun to the woman, even if she were Sioux. He couldn't see Sam Daden scalping the squaw — especially after he'd spent his first day helping the wounded by throwing up every time he ate something. Then there were Joe Riddle and Will Vernon. They both talked tough and held a great deal of anger for the losses on the battlefield, but Zane didn't think killing a woman and baby to be in their capabilities.

"Lieutenant, I'd like to speak with you," the doctor said as he emerged from the tent.

"Yes, sir?"

Zane could see that the captain looked perplexed. He rubbed his jaw and shook his head. "You were right. The woman gave birth just a few days back. Her head wound is more superficial than dangerous, and the baby is in good shape, although born a bit early." He glanced back at the tent and then returned to eye Zane. "I'm not sure what to think. I guess I'd rather you take a look for yourself."

Zane shifted his weight. "What do you

35

mean, sir?" His brows knit together. "If you don't understand, how am I supposed to help?"

"The woman isn't Sioux."

"So is she Cheyenne?"

"No. She's white."

Zane thought he'd misunderstood. "White?"

The doctor gave a deep sigh. "That's right. As I washed her wounds I realized she wasn't Indian at all. She's as fair as either of us. Speaks English perfectly well."

"Come to think of it, I spoke to her in English and she had no trouble understanding," Zane remembered.

The doctor shook his head. "She said she was taken hostage by the Sioux. The baby is the result of being raped by a Sioux warrior. Seems she hated the tribe as much as we do, but she loves that baby."

"What do we do?"

They moved toward the tent. "Come with me."

"Yes, sir."

Zane followed the doctor inside. He turned to secure the flap and give them more light as evening set upon them. This accomplished, he turned and beheld the woman for several moments. His eyes widened at the sight. She was clean now, her dark brown hair smoothed back from her face and flowing freely down her back. She watched him with the same intent interest with which he watched her.

"It can't be," he whispered.

She was the spitting image of Susannah Chadwick — his mother.

Without thinking, Zane realized the truth. "Ardith?" he asked, remembering his feisty ten-year-old sister who'd disappeared so many years ago in a swollen river. They'd all believed her to have drowned.

The woman eyed him critically. "I knew it was you. But I didn't know which one of the twins you were until that soldier called your name. I told the doctor you were my brother."

He felt awash in emotion. She had often called the twin brothers by their combined names to save time and effort. He used to get mad at her laziness, figuring that everyone could tell him from his twin, Morgan. Now, however, it would sound wondrous to his ears.

"It's really you, Ardith." He went to her and knelt beside her. "I can't believe you're alive. We searched up and down that river — miles and miles." He felt his voice break and choked back tears. How could it be that she was here — alive, after so many years?

"Pawnee found me," she offered. "They pulled me from the river. I don't remember it, though. I was sick for days after that." She closed her eyes. "It wasn't so bad with the Pawnee. They tried to find the wagon train once they knew who I was, but you'd gone ahead too far. They never caught up." She opened her eyes and fixed them on Zane's face. "A few years after that, the Sioux stole me away in a raid."

"I can't believe it." He reached out to touch her, but she recoiled. Her action startled Zane. "I'm sorry."

She shook her head. "It's been hard." She looked to the sleeping baby and then back to her brother. "It's been very hard."

Zane looked up to the doctor. "Is she going to be all right? Is she healthy? Can she travel?"

"She's in good physical condition," the doctor stated evenly. "I can't imagine her mental state being as good, however. She's had to live among the Indians and face unspeakable things. Death would probably have been better for her."

Zane shot up and came nose to nose with the captain. "How dare you! This is my sister you're talking about."

"She was your sister. Look at her now. Do you really want her back in this condition?"

38

Zane bit back an angry retort. Squaring his shoulders, he never blinked. "She's my sister, and that baby is my niece or nephew."

"Yes, but where can she live? Who would take her in now, knowing that she's lived among the savages? Civilized people aren't going to think much of what she's been through. They'll worry that her experiences will somehow taint them. Where can you possibly hope to find refuge for her — for this child who will so clearly be of Indian ancestry?"

Zane knew the answer immediately. "Our sister, Dianne, will take her with open arms. She lives on a ranch in the western part of this territory. I'll put in for a leave immediately and take Ardith and the baby to her."

The older man put his hand on Zane's shoulder. "Do you know what you're doing? Are you certain your sister won't be horrified?"

"I'm certain. She'll only see that the lost has been found. She'll only know that her sister has come back from the dead."

CHAPTER 3

The streets of Bozeman seemed strangely void of activity that Fourth of July. Dianne felt rather let down, and had it not been for her excitement at seeing all the stores and knowing the possibility of a wide selection of goods, she might have lost interest in their arrival altogether. Gazing down the street, Dianne wondered at the contents of each building. Many had chosen to replace earlier wooden structures with brick. It reminded her of towns back East.

"Bozeman has certainly grown," she said under her breath.

Having lived in the territory for nearly twelve years, Dianne had missed the bustle of the city. She'd almost forgotten what it was like to be in a big town, and she'd definitely forgotten what it was to have a multitude of choices in supplies and goods. Bozeman City wasn't all that large, but it was by far and away the biggest town in this part of the territory, and the shopping looked promising.

"My, but it is exciting," Faith declared as they maneuvered the wagons on Main Street.

Dianne and Faith had chosen to ride together so Faith could help with the children. "Cole said there were very nearly ten general stores and a variety of specialty shops. There's even a milliner, and I definitely intend to take advantage of that. My hats are all so old. Why, this bonnet I'm wearing is near to bare threads," Dianne said, pulling her team to a stop as Cole motioned her to the side of the dirt street.

He rode up and smiled. "I doubt there's a single shop open today, but tomorrow we'll purchase everything we need. I'm going to go ask where we might camp for the night. We don't want to get ourselves in trouble on our first night."

Dianne nodded and took the reins he handed her after dismounting. "You should probably let Malachi know what you're doing since he's driving the other wagon."

"I'll let him know, Dianne," Cole replied, his tone clipped. "I had already thought of that. Just figured to tell you first."

She bit her tongue. It seemed nothing she said was ever quite right. On the other hand, why did she doubt that he'd think to tell Malachi? She'd once again proved she lacked faith in his ability. Yet she honestly didn't feel that way. Did she?

"I can't believe the children all fell asleep. They were so excited about coming to the big city," Faith said with a chuckle. She rubbed her rounding abdomen. " 'Course, this one didn't sleep much."

"I hope the long ride wasn't too much for you," Dianne said, unable to hide her concern. "I slept well enough last night. The sound of the river rippling along soothed me. Were you comfortable?"

"We were fine. Mercy was a bit frightened sleeping outside and all. I might have her sleep in the wagon with Daniel and me tonight."

At ages five and two — Daniel's second birthday was today, in fact — Faith's children wavered between absolute daring and total fear. Faith had told Dianne that it was simply the way children were at that age.

"Mercy positively insisted on sleeping out under the stars with her papa," Faith chuckled. "There was no convincing her otherwise."

"She never fails to amaze me," Dianne said, grinning. "She's so ladylike sometimes, and other times she's like a prairie storm."

"That's for sure. Still, I'm real pleased with the way both of them handled the trip." Faith looked away, shaking her head. "Those babies have traveled farther in their short lives than I ever hoped to in my growing up years. I was an adult in full before I set out more than five miles from the plantation."

"Did your owner never take you anywhere with him? I thought slaves often traveled with the family."

"My master never traveled much at all. Never saw any need in it," Faith replied. "If something had to be done, he usually sent one of his men to do it. I used to dream of traveling to faraway places and seeing the world, but I never figured it'd come to pass. Sure never figured to be in Montana Territory like this."

Dianne reached over and patted Faith's hand. "It's wondrous, this life God has brought us to. There are times when it feels like just yesterday we were struggling across the plains — worrying about sickness and having enough water." She felt a pang of sorrow at the memory. Dianne always avoided thinking about the wagon train trip that had brought them west — the images were so bittersweet. Ardith was lost to the river, and Betsy had died from a mule kick to the head. They hadn't been long in the territory at all when Dianne's pregnant mother, Susannah, had died as well.

"You're thinking about your family, aren't you?" Faith asked softly.

"I can't help myself. There are times when I still expect them to come through the door. Sometimes when I'm alone I swear I can hear Mama calling me. I know it's not her, but it seems so real that it makes me miss her all the more."

Dianne shifted and shook her head. "She wasn't always . . . disturbed, like you saw her on the wagon train. Her dependence on laudanum no doubt affected her mind. She was a good mother, though I sometimes longed for more affection from her. It was just her way."

Dianne pushed the sorrow from her mind and forced a smile. "I know I'll feel better when I see Zane — or at least hear from him. Morgan sent a letter last week, but I've not had any word from Zane in so long. The rumors about the Indian wars leave me worrying something fierce over him."

"You're bound to hear something soon. Just be patient and enjoy the holiday. Freedom is such a precious thing."

"Indeed," Dianne agreed. She glanced up to see Faith grimace. "Are you all right? Are you sure the trip wasn't too hard on you?"

Faith laughed. "I feel just fine. A little ride to town didn't hurt us any."

Dianne shook her head. "It was more than a little ride." She eyed Faith to detect any action that might contradict her statement.

"I'm fine, Dianne. Stop worrying over me like a mother hen. I'm tired — I'll admit to that. Baby's kicking hard too, but nothing more. I'm too excited about the celebration."

Cole returned about that time, looking somber. She couldn't imagine what had happened to dampen his spirits.

"Dianne Selby, isn't it?" a feminine voice called from the boardwalk.

Looking down, Dianne met the smiling face of Portia McGuire. No, she'd married Ned Langford. She was Portia Langford now. Portia and Ned had accompanied Trenton when he first arrived in Montana. "Why, Mrs. Langford, it's nice to see you again. Is your husband nearby?" Dianne looked past the woman to see if Ned was anywhere in sight. Her brother Trenton often spoke fondly of Ned; the two had been friends long before the man had married Portia McGuire. Trenton would be thrilled to know Ned was in town. Dianne turned to Cole. "Look, Cole, Portia Langford is in town. I was just asking her about her hus-

45

band." She turned back to Portia and waited for her response.

Portia frowned and put a handkerchief to her face. "I'm afraid my dear Ned has departed life on earth."

Stunned, Dianne looked to Cole, willing him to speak. "We're sure sorry to hear that, Mrs. Langford."

"I blame the Grant administration," she said, startling them all.

"President Grant?" Faith asked.

Portia looked at her rather hostilely. "I'm not in the habit of answering the questions of Negroes, but yes, President Grant. Had he not demonetized silver, leaving gold as the standard for banking, silver might have retained its value. Instead, so much that my dear Neddy worked for was no longer worth much of anything."

Dianne could not tolerate the woman's condescending tone. "Faith is a good friend, Mrs. Langford. I would appreciate your treating her civilly."

Portia's eyes narrowed, but her voice was smooth and sweet. "I do apologize. Things here in the West are simply so very different from life in the rest of the country. It's a much less refined land, and the manners follow suit by nature of the setting."

Dianne's temper was getting the better of

her. She opened her mouth to retort, but Cole had already begun to speak.

"Excuse me for askin', but I don't understand what role the devaluing of silver played in the death of your husband." He pulled his horse in closer as two wild riders went barreling down the street in an obvious race.

"My husband took his life," Portia said, dabbing at tears. "He couldn't bear that we were to be without financial means. Why, his poor father took to his sick bed upon hearing the news and with Neddy's death . . . well, he like to have suffered an attack of his heart. He's better now, however. I am at least blessed to report that much."

"I am sorry about your husband," Dianne said, shaking her head. It was only then that she noted the young woman's attire. A rich plum foulard draped Portia's hourglass frame in a most stylish creation. She hardly looked the part of grieving widow, with exception to her handkerchief.

"I came back to Bozeman to make amends with my father," Portia said, tucking away the lace-edged cloth, along with all reference to Ned. She straightened. "The army is away from the fort. I've been at the hotel for the past two days, sick with a blinding headache, so I've had no time to find out if they've returned. I was just setting out for answers when I caught sight of you."

"We hoped to see my brother Zane, as well as celebrate Independence Day with the rest of the town," Dianne offered in explanation of the reason for their presence. "The army rode out earlier in the spring, and we haven't had word since. They were in pursuit of the Sioux and Cheyenne, as I understood it."

"What's *she* doing here?" Trenton asked as he walked up alongside the wagon.

"Trenton, I didn't know you were here," Dianne declared. "I thought you were busy running errands for Cole."

"I was," he replied, still eyeing Portia with caution. "Where's Ned?"

Portia stiffened. "He's passed on."

Trenton stepped closer to the woman. "What did you say?"

"I said he's dead." She looked up and stared him hard in the eye. "He killed himself."

Trenton was notably upset, but he held back his reply and looked to Dianne. "I'm afraid there's more bad news. That's why I came to find you." He held up a piece of paper for Dianne, Faith, and Cole to see. "There's been a big battle over the mountains to the east. Along the Little Big Horn River."

"I didn't have a chance to tell you," Cole declared as Dianne eyed him accusingly. "I only heard it myself a few minutes ago, and I came right back to tell you."

Dianne dropped the paper, not able to read the words. "Zane?"

Trenton shook his head. "No one knows. They weren't in the opening battle, as you'll see in that report. General Custer and all of his men are dead, however. Colonel Reno has lost a lot of men as well. All told, some three hundred fifteen men are lost. The article says General Gibbon joined Reno and the Indians left, but . . ."

"But what?" Dianne asked, unable to bear the thought of a battle that killed over three hundred men.

"They're sure to pursue the Indians. No one can just let them go — not now."

Dianne felt the joy of the day slip from her. Her shoulders slumped forward as she closed her eyes in sorrow. "He *has* to be all right. Oh, how could this have happened?"

"It happened because we've stupidly settled this part of the country instead of leaving it to the savages," Portia declared.

Dianne opened her eyes and glared at the woman. "Your own father is among the troops. I thought you said you came here to make amends."

"My desire to make amends with my father has nothing to do with the army and its mistakes," she replied defiantly. "I care about the man, not his job."

"Since when do you care about anyone but yourself?" Trenton asked sarcastically.

"Since Ned died and I realized that life is too short to let anger stand between myself and others." She pulled the handkerchief back out and dabbed her eyes again. "I've been attending church, and I've come to realize the error of my ways."

"Well, it's too late," Trenton answered in anger. "Ned is gone. You can't make that right."

Portia broke into sobs and buried her face in her gloved hands.

Dianne felt compassion for her. "Trenton, that was rather harsh. You mustn't say such things just because you're hurting in your loss. The important thing now is that we need to find out the truth of what's happening with the army."

"Better still," Cole said, his voice bearing his concern, "what's happening with the Sioux and Cheyenne?"

The centennial celebration of America's

freedom from the English was a muted affair. People were afraid. Custer was dead — the very man whom many had hoped to elect that year to the presidency.

Rumors ran unchecked and Dianne had to admit her fears were bordering on silent hysteria. Inside she felt herself coming undone, like a knitting project unraveling before her eyes. Luke had struggled against sleep because of her unrest. He'd finally settled down for the night, but try as she might, Dianne couldn't seem to do likewise. Nor could she find any solace in her husband's words.

She kept thinking back to her dream, knowing it had been a forewarning of things to come. Perhaps the Sioux and Cheyenne would cross the mountains and wipe out white settlements as they went. They had tasted the blood of victory and were no doubt driven to continue their rampage.

"You need to rest," Cole whispered. They'd made their bed inside the wagon at Dianne's insistence, but the shelter gave her no more comfort than if they'd been outside.

"I can't sleep. I keep thinking of what's happened. You read that paper. It talked of the battleground looking like a slaughterhouse. That the dead were mutilated."

51

"Stop. It won't do you any good to keep rehashing the details," Cole admonished. "We have to trust that God is watching over Zane and keeping guard over the remaining soldiers."

"But God didn't keep Custer and his men from harm. Maybe He won't keep Zane safe either."

Cole tried to pull Dianne into his arms, but she resisted. "I can't simply forget that, Cole."

He sighed. "Then stay awake all night."

The baby slept peacefully at the head of their makeshift bed. Dianne knew Cole was only trying to calm her fears, but she couldn't lie to him. She had no desire to be in his arms when the rest of the world had gone completely mad.

"I'm so afraid," she whispered.

Cole reached out again and this time she let him pull her close. "I know you're afraid," he replied. "I wish I could make it all seem right again."

She buried her head against his shoulder. "I wish you could too."

CHAPTER 4

The next morning Dianne and Cole sat in silence with Faith and Malachi. Mercy and Daniel played beside Faith, while Dianne felt the need to cradle Luke in her arms.

"What are we to do?" Dianne finally asked.

Cole shook his head, hard pressed to know the answer. He knew he couldn't share all the news he'd been told; it would be enough to send them all into a panic, and Dianne had a tenuous hold on her composure already. Rumors were overtaking common sense, with terrible tales of Sioux and Cheyenne being sighted in the pass just east of town.

"I'd feel a sight better iffin' the army was back at da fort," Malachi said in his deep, soft voice.

Cole felt the same but hesitated to comment. Dianne was already fearful of the situation. Especially how it might affect her

53

brother Zane.

"Well, it seems the threat is real enough to take precautions," Cole said, trying his best to sound nonchalant.

Trenton rode up about that time. He tied off his horse in a hurry and came to join the others. Cole tried to warn Dianne's brother with his eyes to use discretion in what he shared.

Trenton caught his look. "Stores are open. I'd say if we're going to get supplies, we should do so right away. People seem to be stocking up."

"Probably wise," Faith said softly.

"No doubt it's for the best," Dianne agreed.

"Army isn't due back for some time," Trenton added. "We might as well head home and wait it out there. It might be a month or more."

"Those were my thoughts as well," Cole said. "Let's go ahead with our shopping and then head back to the ranch." He hoped Dianne wouldn't question his decision. It seemed of late she had no confidence in his choices. He wasn't sure why she continued to second-guess him; sometimes she went so far as to actually change his decisions and directions — right in front of the men. It put the ranch hands in a precarious position, uncertain to whom they owed their loyalty, and Cole's leadership suffered.

"Do you think we'll be in danger on the trip home?" Dianne asked. She stared down at their baby, and Cole knew her biggest concern was for Luke.

"I think we should be fine. The only sightings of Indians have been to the east of the pass."

Her head snapped up. "There've been sightings?"

Cole felt like kicking himself. "Well, there have been *rumors* of sightings. You know how folks are around here. Their imaginations are running wild. They're scared and jump at every noise."

"My imagination is working plenty hard," Dianne admitted, her eyes wide with fear.

He reached out to gently stroke her cheek. "I know. That's why we'll head home as soon as we have what we came for. We'll all feel better in the comfort of what's familiar."

"I'll go with Malachi and get the work materials we need," Trenton suggested.

"I'll stay here with the children," Faith offered. "That way you and Cole can go together."

"But you were looking forward to shopping every bit as much as I was," Dianne protested.

Faith rubbed her stomach and shook her head. "I'm thinking it best for me to stay here and take it easy."

"Well, give me your list, then," Dianne said, returning her gaze to Cole. "Will you help me?"

"Of course. We can go arrange for everything, then take the wagon into town and load it on our way out."

"Stay away from the east end," Trenton warned. "It's pretty seedy down that way — a lot of brothels and saloons."

Dianne lifted Luke to her shoulder, patting him gently. "Why does someone always have to come and spoil a place with such things."

"Seems like they're always on the east side of town too," Faith added.

"My daddy always said that was because it was where folks entered a town and the first place they stopped for refreshment," Cole threw in. He tossed back the last of his coffee and got to his feet.

"Why couldn't folks come in the westward way?" Dianne asked.

"You have to remember that until the continental railroad went through, most folks were traveling from the east to the west. Not a lot of traffic going in the opposite direction. Guess that's why they got established that way. It was probably just too much trouble to move them afterward."

"I suppose so," Dianne mused. "Too bad, just the same. I'd love to have a town where there weren't any shady dealings going on at all."

Faith gave a laugh. "Well, if I remember right, we're supposed to see Jesus return in the east. That'll put them that need Him most that much closer."

Dianne laughed. "I suppose you're right."

Cole felt encouraged by his wife's amusement. It seemed she'd done nothing but cry and worry since learning about the battle yesterday. Cole hated seeing her so tense, so troubled. He would have given almost anything — even wasted time shopping for female doodads — to see her happier.

"We'd best get a move on," Cole said, dusting off his pants.

Malachi, a barrel-chested man who had to weigh at least two-hundred fifty pounds, jumped up from the ground with the agility of a wild cat. He reached out his hand to pull Faith to her feet, prompting Cole to do likewise for Dianne.

She clutched the baby close as Cole pulled her into his arms. "I know you're worried, but we'll have a nice time together. You'll see." He leaned close and kissed Dianne on the forehead. She stiffened, looking up at him as if he'd lost all reasonable thought.

"I won't have a nice time until I know about Zane," she said sadly.

Cole shook his head. Only moments ago she'd actually laughed, and now she had returned to her morose outlook.

"Now that's no way to be," Faith insisted as she reached out to take Luke from Dianne's arms. "The good Lord didn't climb down from His throne last night. He's still sitting there watching over all. He'll still be sitting there tomorrow as well. You need to give Zane over to His care."

"I did that a long time ago. Just as I'm sure other mothers, wives, and sisters gave over Custer's Seventh Cavalry. But I'm afraid He might not have any better answer for me than He did for them. And sometimes that's very hard to understand."

"I know Faith would enjoy this material," Dianne said, trying hard to get in the spirit of shopping. She held out a length of the twilight blue wool. It reminded her of the sky moments before night overtook the last bits of light. "It's very soft."

"Why don't you go ahead and get it," Cole said. "Winter's coming on and it would probably be good to have. It's not particu-

58

larly feminine, so if you ladies decide against it, you can still use it for making shirts for the men."

She nodded. One thing was true: Cole had never begrudged her the right to spend money as she saw fit. *Of course,* she thought, *I could argue that it's my money to begin with.* The thought tightened itself around her heart. *Uncle Bram left it all to me, with the provision that I would see to his family. That will always come first. Cole must understand that.*

But there was no reason for her to doubt that he did. Dianne shook her head. Why was she having such doubts about her husband? He'd never shown Koko and her children anything but the highest regard. He'd even taken Uncle Bram's only son, Jamie, under his supervision to teach and train. Watching Cole with Jamie always gave Dianne an image of how he would be with Luke.

"I think I'll get the entire bolt. Koko would like this material as well."

"Good idea. Did you find boots and shoes for the kids?"

Dianne smiled. "Yes. I gave footprint drawings for Mercy and Daniel, as well as Suzy and Jamie, to the clerk. He found everything we needed."

"Are we nearly finished, then?"

"I think so. I'd like to pick up a few baubles for the kids. You know, some little presents to take back."

They finished shopping and headed back to the wagons down the busy walkway. Dianne clung tightly to Cole's arm. The town no longer seemed quite so friendly. Dianne constantly glanced to the mountain range east of Bozeman. She'd heard talk in the stores that the townsfolk believed the mountains would act as a deterrent to attack. She could only pray that their thoughts would hold true.

"I had hoped to introduce myself," a man declared, standing directly in their path.

Dianne looked up to the owner of the voice. The man's expression seemed void of emotion. He swept Dianne with a look that went from the top of her head to the toe of her boot, then settled on her face. "I'm Chester Lawrence."

He said the name as though it should mean something to her. Dianne looked to Cole, then back to the older man. He scowled. "I know you're the Selbys from the Diamond V."

Cole revived from his momentary surprise. "Yes. We are." He extended his hand. "You'll have to forgive my lack of manners. We didn't get much rest last night."

"Worried about Indians?" The older man's tone seemed mocking.

"I suppose any time such a massacre takes place, it gives a fellow cause for concern," Cole replied. "By the way, the name's Cole. And this is my wife, Dianne."

"Heard tell you inherited the ranch from your uncle," Lawrence said without any apparent concern for overstepping the bounds of propriety.

"Yes," Dianne said softly. "I did."

"Well, if you're looking to sell, I'd be happy to give you a fair price. I'd buy the cattle and all."

Dianne looked at him oddly. "Why would you ever think we'd be interested in selling?"

"Well, everyone has their price. My missus and me, along with our children, plan to make this territory our home. We intend to have the biggest spread in these parts, and since we aren't all that far from your boundaries, I figured we'd see about buying you out."

"Well, I'm sorry Mr. Lawrence, but we've got no interest in selling," Cole said before Dianne could offer her thoughts.

Just then a woman joined them, her arms full of packages. "Take some of these, Ches-

61

ter," she commanded.

Dianne waited for an introduction. Chester Lawrence seemed to understand. "This is my wife, Cynthia," he said, taking the parcels from his wife's arms.

"Pleased to meet you," Cynthia said without smiling. "Are they the ones?" she asked, turning to her husband.

Lawrence laughed. "Yup, they're the ones, but they tell me they have no thought to sell."

Cynthia gave a snide laugh. "Chester's pretty much used to getting what he wants. I'd suggest you rethink the matter."

Dianne didn't care for the woman's tone, which bordered on a threat. "I'm sorry, Mrs. Lawrence. We have no thought to leave the territory. We have built a good life on the Diamond V and intend to continue doing so."

"Mrs. Selby! Mrs. Selby!" Portia Langford called from across the street. She stepped into the rutted street and attempted to cross between two freighters, barely making it across before a pair of racing youth came down the street from the opposite direction. "My, but it is a busy place," she said, putting her hand to her neck.

The Lawrences watched her with moderate interest, causing Dianne to offer introductions. "Mr. and Mrs. Lawrence, this is Mrs. Langford."

Portia eyed them critically, then smiled at the man. "I'm pleased to meet you both. I do apologize for the intrusion, but I was most desperate to speak with the Selbys before they left town."

"What is it?" Dianne asked, curious to know what would have caused the young widow to seek them out.

"Well, I wondered . . . that is . . ." She paused, looking uncomfortable. "You know that I've come here to see my father. They tell me at the fort that he may well not return for at least a month."

"Yes, we heard the same thing," Dianne admitted. She hated the long wait but knew that nothing could be done about it. At times like this she could only pray that Zane would retire from the army and leave fighting Indians to someone else.

"I wondered . . . if you might allow me to impose upon your hospitality," Portia continued. "I can scarcely afford to stay at the hotel for a month."

Dianne, noting Portia's discomfort and feeling sorry for the woman, didn't even bother to consult with Cole. "Of course you may stay with us. We've plenty of room."

Portia reached out and squeezed Dianne's

arm. "I just knew you'd say yes. Your kindness has always been well known to me."

"Are your things at the hotel?" Cole asked.

"What little I brought. I can have everything ready within half an hour."

"That's good. Go ahead and ready your things. We'll be by to pick you up in about forty minutes." Cole then turned to the Lawrences. "It was good to meet you, but we're in a hurry and need to rally our group to collect our purchases. Feel free to come by sometime for a visit. Folks out here need to make friends of their neighbors. We'll be glad to get to know you better."

Chester shook his head. "Ain't lookin' for friends, Mister. I'm lookin' to buy your land."

Cole chuckled and Dianne recognized that it was forced. "Well, I'm sorry Mr. Lawrence, Mrs. Lawrence. We aren't of a mind to sell. We'll be happy to extend neighborly hospitality, however. You're welcome to come see us anytime."

Dianne was content to keep quiet on the subject. Chester Lawrence made her uncomfortable. He seemed to leer at her in a manner that was almost suggestive, yet there was really nothing wrong in his behavior. *I'm being silly,* she thought. *It's no more than the strain of worrying about Zane and the Indians.*

Portia drew her out of her thoughts. "Mrs. Selby, I'll see you soon. Thank you again."

Dianne could only nod.

Cole took a firm grasp on Dianne's arm. "We'll be seein' you," he told the Lawrences. Dianne forced a smile and nodded in affirmation of her husband's words.

Chester Lawrence muttered something, but Dianne couldn't hear him well enough to know what he was saying. "What a strange man," she murmured.

"A dangerous one, too, if I don't miss my guess," Cole replied.

Dianne shivered. She felt the same way. "I suppose some folks don't know what it is to be friendly and simply settle down to the way things are. He seemed like the kind of fellow who doesn't like taking no for an answer."

"Just mind yourself if he comes calling," Cole replied. "Make sure you keep plenty of folks around. I don't trust him, but I don't want to accuse him falsely. He's done nothing to us yet."

"Nothing but demand the ranch."

Trenton approached them from the opposite direction. He looked like a man with a purpose. "Cole, we've gotten everything loaded with exception to whatever you and Dianne bought."

"We'll load up Faith and the children and head back through town. We can make stops on the way. Oh, and we need to make room for Portia Langford."

"Why?" Trenton asked, his voice low.

"Because she doesn't have the funds to wait a month at the hotel until the army returns to the fort. She's here to make amends with her father," Dianne replied. "She's asked for our hospitality, and I feel there's no reason not to extend it in Christian love."

"I don't think she worries overmuch about Christ."

"Trenton, that's a mean thing to say."

Cole interrupted the sibling argument. "I just remembered something. Trenton, would you take Dianne back to camp and get everyone loaded up? I'll only be a minute."

Dianne stared curiously after her husband but said nothing. She then looked toward the mountains and whispered, "I wish the army were back."

Trenton put his arm around her. "I know, but it's going to be all right. You'll see."

"But I worry about Zane. He's been through so much already. What if he doesn't make it?"

"I've endured a great deal too, and it didn't do me in," Trenton said as they began walking toward their camp. "Dianne, I know I haven't been very forthcoming with all that's happened in my past, but it hasn't been pretty. I went through some times when I thought I'd lose my life."

"Why are you telling me this now?" Dianne asked. She looked up into the face of her brother, noting the pain in his expression.

"You've been through some bad times too," he continued, as if not hearing her question. "We've survived. Zane will survive too. He's tough, and he knows how to take care of himself."

Dianne shook her head. "I've often wished you'd never stayed in New Madrid. It feels like we lost our closeness after that. And now it seems that too much has happened . . . that we'll never have it again."

Trenton sighed. "I know. But I'm not the same man. Like I said, the past was ugly and it tainted the boy you knew. You have no idea how much I longed to join all of you. Things weren't what I thought they'd be at all, and the worse things got, the more I longed for home."

"But you should have come here then," Dianne declared. "You could have easily worked on a wagon train and paid your way west in labor."

"I wish I had. Unfortunately, it wasn't that easy." He smiled down at her. "Let's not dwell on the past. My only reason for bringing it up was to encourage you. Zane is strong. He'll get through this."

Dianne squeezed her brother's arm. "Will you ever share your past with me? Can we ever regain the closeness we used to have?"

Trenton shook his head. "There's nothing there worth sharing. Nothing at all."

CHAPTER 5

The heat of late August and the lack of news from Colonel Gibbon and his men made for testy spirits on the Diamond V. Dianne settled into her routine, caring for Luke and overseeing the household alongside Koko, but her mind was ever on Zane and the threat of Indian attack.

News had come that the Sioux and Cheyenne had escaped to parts unknown. The thought filled Dianne with grave concern. If the Sioux headed for the Big Horn Mountains, as was suggested, it wouldn't be that difficult for them to travel west and up through the Yellowstone area. It would be simple to continue north through the Madison River valley. The thought left her sleepless at times.

Six-year-old Susannah Vandyke clattered the dirty breakfast dishes as she helped her mother begin to clean up. Dianne's nerves were already stretched taut, and when a glass fell to the floor and shattered, she jumped up from the table.

"Koko, please just leave the dishes and the broken glass. I'll take care of it."

"Susannah should clean up the mess she's made," Koko countered softly. Turning to her daughter, she instructed, "Go get the broom and dustpan." The dark-eyed girl, who looked very much like her mother, nodded and hurried from the kitchen.

Jamie, Koko's nine-year-old son, got to his feet. "Uncle Cole, do you think the Sioux will attack us?"

It was the last topic of conversation Dianne wanted to hear, yet at the same time it was the only thing on people's minds.

"I don't know, Jamie. I guess there's probably more concern about other tribes hearing about what the Sioux did and trying to imitate it."

"Why?" Dianne asked, sitting back down. "Why would peaceful tribes begin to fight?"

"Because it worked for the Sioux and Cheyenne," Cole replied matter-of-factly. "I've already heard rumors about problems on some of the reservations. If they think an uprising will return them to their old way of life and restore the buffalo to the plains, then they might rise up to make a stand."

Susannah returned with the broom and

dustpan, and Koko instructed her on how to best clear the mess away. Dianne wished they'd all go about their business so she could ask Cole the questions on her heart. She didn't want to frighten the children.

When the little girl finished her work, Dianne said, "You did a wonderful job, Susannah." Dianne then looked to Koko. "Please. Go ahead. I know you have plans to go down to the river and teach the children about the plants and herbs." Koko seemed to understand Dianne's urgency.

Koko took the dustpan from Susannah and motioned for her son. "Come along. It's time for school."

Dianne waited until they'd gone before turning to her husband. "Do you think we should make some kind of hiding place? I mean, there are the children to consider, and if the Sioux come this way . . . well . . ." Her words trailed off.

"I don't know that it would help us much. If the Sioux have remained together, that would mean there are thousands of them," Cole said, pushing back from the table. "If they make it to this valley, there probably won't be anyplace to hide. Several thousand people can cover a lot of territory. Honestly, I think there's a bigger threat from some of the other tribes. Some of the area men are planning to meet the day after tomorrow. I guess we'll discuss what kind of protective plan we can form at that point."

"We've never had to worry about the Indians before," Diane said. "I mean, with Koko's brother traveling freely with the Blackfoot, we've generally known safety. Other tribes knew we were sympathetic and friendly. Why, we've even traded cattle with them."

"Times are changing." Cole grew thoughtful. "Seems we've been having our battles with the Indians since first coming west."

Dianne wondered if Cole was remembering the time he'd been taken by the Sioux and later by the Blackfoot. He never spoke much about that time, and once when she'd asked Koko's brother, Takes Many Horses — the man responsible for rescuing her husband — about it, Cole had merely admonished her to let the matter rest and ask no more.

Dianne gave a little shudder. "They're getting desperate."

"Yes. And desperation makes people do things they'd otherwise never attempt. We've seen enough of that out here just trying to make our way. The Indians have seen their entire way of life changed. The buffalo and elk aren't nearly as plentiful. Settlers are fencing off the land and building towns. The Indians have no place in any of it."

"And reservation life isn't really any life at all," Dianne commented. "Not when you consider the freedom the tribes have enjoyed for generations. Freedom to roam at will."

Cole heaved a sigh. "The government will win this one. We've seen it over and over in history. They'll round up every last Indian until they have them all contained where they want them. They did it in the eastern states; they'll do it here as well."

"But at what cost?"

"That's always the question, isn't it," he more stated than asked. "Look, I'd better get to work. I can't say it would do much good to dig ourselves a hole to hide in. Caution, I guess, is the best answer. I'll post some men several miles out in each direction. They can let us know if Indians appear to be moving this direction."

"And then what?" Dianne asked, knowing the answer wouldn't be good.

"Then I guess we'll run in the opposite direction. We'll head to whatever town is closest and warn them as well. I'll make sure we have our fastest mounts here in the corral. Maybe you should figure out a way to pack Luke Indian-style or some other such way so you can both ride a horse instead of a wagon. A wagon ain't gonna move fast enough for much of an escape."

"All right," Dianne said, meeting his eyes. "I won't lie and say I'm not frightened, but I think I'm more scared for Zane. I just wish we could have word."

Cole smiled. "I know, but it's times like these that we have to trust God more than ever. You've helped me to learn that. We can't put our trust in appearances."

His words warmed her heart. "I know you're right, and I promise to try harder."

"Good morning," Portia Langford declared as she swept into the room.

Dianne got up from the table, as did Cole. "Good morning," Dianne greeted. "There's some breakfast warming for you on the back of the stove if you're hungry. You know the way to the kitchen."

It was the same routine most every morning. The rest of the household was awake and fed long before Portia even managed to make her way out of bed. The woman was clearly used to being done for instead of having to do for herself, but at least now she seemed to understand that no one had time to wait on her.

Dianne couldn't help but grin when she thought back to those first few days when Portia constantly complained about the need for a maid.

"I'll just have some tea, thank you," Portia said, moving off toward the kitchen.

"When all of this is settled," Cole said softly, "I do think it would be wise to hire a cook and housekeeper."

"We've been talking about doing that since Uncle Bram first built this house," Dianne replied. "Koko and I really don't feel the need. Sure, it's a lot of work, but Faith is good to help with the cooking from time to time, and sometimes Charity comes over to help with the housework."

"But the children are needing more and more attention. Koko has her hands full just trying to school Jamie and Susannah. One day it'll be the same for you with Luke and —" he paused with a grin — "any other children we might have."

Dianne felt her cheeks grow warm but said nothing. Cole came to her and pulled her close. Kissing her long and passionately, Dianne temporarily forgot about the Indians and other conflicts. This was the only place she truly felt safe.

"Please be careful," she whispered as Cole pulled away.

"Stop worrying. Everything will be all right. You'll see." He left then, passing Portia as she came back into the dining room.

"They always say that," the older woman murmured.

"Say what?" Dianne asked as she began picking up the dirty dishes.

"That everything will be all right. Every man I've ever known has always said the same thing. 'Don't worry, Portia, everything will be all right.' But it never is," she said sadly.

Dianne felt a chill run through her body. "We must have hope."

"Hope doesn't get you very far at the deathbed of someone you love." Portia's words were laced with a bitterness Dianne couldn't begin to understand.

"I've lost many people I loved," Dianne began slowly. "It's never easy."

"Now I may lose my father . . . and then what?" Portia questioned. "I have no one else. No one at all."

"What about Ned's folks? You mentioned when you first came here that they're still living. Couldn't you go back to them?"

The dark-haired beauty shook her head. "Hardly. They were never very kind to me. They felt Ned could have done better for himself. Imagine that. I was a rich widow. I certainly didn't need the Langford money to see me through. Yet they still thought Ned had lowered himself to marry me."

"I'm sorry to hear that, Portia. There's no accounting for how some people feel. You simply have to face it and go forward."

"If my father doesn't return, I'll have to figure out some way to go forward. I can't remain here forever."

Dianne got the distinct impression Portia was hoping she would contradict her. But where the widow was concerned, Dianne had always felt uneasy. She knew Trenton didn't like Portia at all, and she respected his opinion — he had spent more time with Portia than anyone.

"Well, there's no use in fretting," Dianne said, gathering the last of the silver. "I need to go see to these. If you should get bored, we'll be doing some canning today and later some laundry."

"In this heat?"

Dianne smiled. "The vegetables won't wait until it's cooler. We've set everything up outside so as not to cause the house to grow too hot. You're welcome to come and lend a hand."

"I know nothing about it," Portia said, focusing on her tea.

"Well, maybe it's time to learn. Then when your father returns, you'll be very useful to him."

"I can hardly imagine he'll see it that way."

Dianne shrugged. "You can never tell what a person will think or feel until you give him a chance."

Two days later the canning was nearly done, without any help from Portia. Dianne wiped the outside of a jar of tomatoes as she considered what was to be done about the very idle Mrs. Langford. It was one thing to be a guest staying only a few days, but the woman had been with them for nearly two months, and her inability to help around the house was taxing. Dianne supposed the only way to make a change was to simply assign Portia some duties.

"She won't like it," Dianne muttered.

"Who won't like it?" Koko asked.

Dianne looked up at her aunt. The woman looked very much like her Blackfoot ancestors today. She had chosen to wear a simple dress of deerskin and her hair was plaited in two long black braids. "I was thinking that we should assign Portia some jobs around the place."

Koko smiled. "You're right. She won't like it."

"I've never met a woman who liked to sit around idle as much as that one. She doesn't even read or sew. She just sits there staring out the window or rocking on the porch."

"She gives a fair try at complaining," Koko teased.

"No trying about it. That woman has complaining down to an exact form. She knows very well how to get under the skin of anyone around her."

"Listen," Koko said, cocking her head. "Riders."

Dianne exchanged a glance with her aunt and fear gripped her heart. Riders these days weren't always the welcome kind. Dianne moved for the shotgun that leaned against the house. "Go be with the children."

Dianne edged to the corner of the house and immediately exclaimed, "Zane!"

She turned to Koko. "It's Zane, and he has a young woman with him."

Koko came and joined her. "Maybe he's taken a wife."

"I suppose that's possible. Come on. Let's go greet them."

Dianne was so relieved to see her brother again that she completely forgot about the shotgun in her hands.

"I hope you aren't intending to use that on me," Zane said good-naturedly. "Especially since I brought you a wonderful surprise." He slid from his horse and Dianne rushed into his arms.

"We've been so worried. We heard about the battle at Little Big Horn. We weren't sure whether you were dead or alive." She pushed away and studied Zane for a moment. "You aren't hurt, are you?"

"No. I'm just fine." His expression was quite animated. "I have a surprise for you."

"So you've said." Dianne looked past Zane to the young woman who sat with head bowed atop the back of a sorrel mare. She wore a cradleboard on her back.

Zane left Dianne and helped the woman down from the horse. He brought her gently to where Dianne stood. "I hope this doesn't come as too much of a fright, but God has given us back something very precious."

The woman lifted her face and Dianne gasped. It was like staring into the face of her mother. She felt lightheaded and was afraid she might faint.

"It's Ardith, Dianne. I found her. Or actually, God brought her to me."

The two women locked their gazes. It was as if they searched each other's eyes for answers to a decade's worth of questions.

"I can't believe it." Dianne's eyes filled with tears. "Ardith, is it really you?"

"Yes," the woman whispered. "I'm not the same girl you used to know, but it's me."

Dianne pulled her sister into her arms and cried. "This is too wonderful." A million questions circled around her thoughts of praise. This was truly too much to have even hoped for. She recalled the days after Ardith had fallen into the flood-swollen Platte River and was swept downstream. They had searched and searched but never found any sign of the girl.

Ardith had been ten years old, and the loss to their family had been acute. Dianne pushed such thoughts aside as she continued to hug her sister. How could it be that she was here after all these years? How could she have survived?

It took some time to compose herself again, but when Dianne pulled away, she could see that Ardith had been crying as well.

"Come on. You must be exhausted. I'll set you up in our spare guest room. We have another guest in the room next to yours, but we have plenty of space, so never you mind." Dianne knew she was rambling, but the words just seemed to bubble out. "Koko, will you help me get some bath water ready for Ardith?" She turned and looked to her aunt. "This is our aunt, Koko Vandyke."

Ardith looked that direction as well and recoiled. She backed up, terror in her eyes.

Dianne didn't immediately notice, but Koko did.

"I'm your Uncle Bram's widow," Koko offered. "Didn't Zane tell you about me?"

Ardith looked to Zane. "You said she lived as white."

Dianne realized that Ardith was upset by the Blackfoot dress and style their aunt had chosen. "Koko is half Blackfoot. Sometimes she wears this manner of dress," Dianne offered. "Especially when we're doing hard work."

Ardith shook her head. "I hate the Indians. I hate them all. I don't care if she did marry Uncle Bram. I want nothing to do with her! Nothing!" She turned and hid her face in Zane's chest.

Dianne looked to her brother. "It's a long story," he said softly. "I found her as a hostage among the Sioux. She's suffered a great deal."

Just then Dianne spotted the infant in the cradleboard. She had shocks of black hair and her skin was ruddy. There was no doubting that the baby was Indian — probably Sioux. Dianne looked back to Koko, but found that the woman was gone.

"I'm so sorry, Ardith. I didn't know. Come on. Let's get you upstairs and let you rest. Can I help you with the baby? I have a little one myself. Did Zane tell you?"

Ardith lifted her head. "He said you had a boy."

Dianne smiled. "That's right. His name is Luke. What's your baby's name?"

"Winona. Her name means 'giving.' "

"What an unusual and beautiful name," Dianne said, looking over Ardith's once again bowed head to meet her brother's eyes. She saw a hint of understanding there. Ardith had come back to them, but she was very fragile and extremely wounded.

That night Dianne lovingly dressed her niece in a flannel gown — probably the first the child had ever worn. She then wrapped the baby snuggly in a warm blanket. Winona was very small but seemed healthy. Ardith had told them that she was born nearly a month early by her accounts.

"The constant travel and battle brought it on," Ardith said, watching Dianne from the bed. "I'd already lost another baby that way."

Dianne looked up, unable to hide her frown. "You had another child?"

"It wasn't born alive," she said, looking away. "It was sometime last year. I didn't want it anyway."

Dianne was shocked by her sister's words.

"What of Winona?"

"She's the only thing I'm living for. She gave me a will to live; that's why I called her 'giving.' "

Coming to the bed with the baby in her arms, Dianne tried to figure out what to say next. "Can you talk about your time since leaving us?"

Ardith reached up and took her daughter. "There are some things I will never speak of. They would serve no purpose."

Dianne sat down on the bed beside her sister. "I came after you that night in the camp, when you had gotten so upset. I knew you felt abandoned."

"I was selfish. I didn't want Mama to have another baby. After I fell in the river, all I wanted was to find you all again. I prayed so hard. I told God I didn't care how many babies Mama had, I just wanted to go home." Ardith fell silent for several moments, then continued.

"The Pawnee found me. They were kind to me. I was sick for some time, but they nursed me back to health. I couldn't tell them where I belonged. I wasn't even sure where we were. As time went on, I couldn't even remember much about where we were supposed to be traveling. I remembered some things, but others were just clouded memories. Bits and pieces of people and places.

"Among the Pawnee, I stayed with a man and woman who had three daughters, and together we helped each other. I taught them English and they taught me the Pawnee language, as well as skills for staying alive. As my memories faded and my understanding of where I might find you completely slipped away, I learned to be content with my Pawnee family."

"What happened to put you with the Sioux?"

Ardith shook her head, her brows knitting together. "There was a raid. Many of the Pawnee were killed. My adopted family was murdered. The Sioux held this band a grudge. Apparently there was some sort of war between the two tribes, and we were caught up in it. Several of the women and children were taken to be slaves. I was one of them."

"How old were you?"

"Fourteen. As best as I can tell. Zane told me I'm now twenty-two."

"Yes, you'll be twenty-three on the first of September. That's just days away."

Ardith shrugged. "I thought maybe I was older — I lost track of the years, and the Sioux certainly weren't concerned. I was put to work helping with the children. I learned to speak Sioux rather quickly."

"But they treated you much worse than the Pawnee?"

Ardith shrank back against the pillows. "Yes."

Dianne reached out and took hold of her hand. "I'm so sorry. You don't have to talk about it."

"I won't speak of some things," Ardith admitted. "I can't. We were beaten and starved at times. After a couple of years I was traded and things got even worse. I was given to a man in marriage — a marriage I never recognized or wanted. He raped me." She looked up at Dianne. "I won't say more."

"Was he Winona's father?"

Ardith looked at her sleeping child and nodded. "The other baby too."

"Where is he now?"

"I'd like to believe the man died, but I know he didn't. I saw him ride off after the massacre. He's probably with the others planning some new war on the white man. They hated us for coming to their land, for pushing them off and killing the buffalo. They despised our insistence that they accept our ways — that they live on reservations. Most of the young men were deter-

mined to kill every white man they met."
She paused. "Walks in the Dark felt that
way."

"Your husband?"

"He wasn't my husband!" Ardith nearly
screamed. Winona stirred and puckered her
face as though she would cry. Then just as
quickly, her countenance calmed. "He was
nothing more than my attacker. My tor-
menter. I prayed daily he would die. I hope
he's dead even now. I would take great
pleasure in knowing that he suffered as
much as I did." Her face contorted.

Dianne was startled at the hatred in her
sister's words. Ardith obviously possessed a
deep hatred within her, yet it amazed Dianne that she clearly loved Winona.

"Well, it's getting very late. You and Winona need your rest. Would you like me to
put her in the cradle?" Dianne pointed to
the little bed.

"She probably wouldn't sleep there unless
we wrapped her very tightly. She's used to
the board."

"I understand," Dianne said, smiling. "I'll
leave you to do as you think best." She got
up and moved to the end of the bed. Paus-
ing there, she added, "Ardith, I'm so glad
to have you home. I thought you were dead
— lost to us forever. I know Zane has told

you much about the family, but if you ever want to talk about Mother or Betsy or anything else, please know that I'm no delicate flower. I've endured a great deal, and I promise I won't fall into a feminine faint over anything you might tell me."

"Zane told me you were strong. He said you were probably stronger than all of us rolled together."

Dianne shook her head. "No, I'm not that strong, but God is. That's where I draw my strength." She smiled. "I'm not always very good at it, but I try to keep my focus on Him."

Ardith said nothing, and Dianne took that as her cue to leave. "I'll see you in the morning. Sleep well."

CHAPTER 6

Ardith Chadwick did her best to settle into normal life on the Diamond V. As she watched the others with curiosity as they went about their daily duties, she wondered if they realized how easy they had life here on this beautiful ranch. There was no worry about where the next meal would come from, no concern about whether a storm would flood their village.

Her sister Dianne had turned out to be quite a resourceful woman. Ardith liked her very much. Dianne didn't hold the past against Ardith and had welcomed her with open arms. In fact, her sister's generous, loving care had helped Ardith to feel safe again — no easy feat, to be sure.

The past had a way of picking at Ardith like buzzards to carnage. When memories came to her she crushed them back down, pushing them as deep into the recesses of her mind as was humanly possible. She wanted no part of her past.

Yet she would always bear a reminder in Winona. She could scarcely escape the wretched memories of her baby's birth. The surprise of attack, the hideous war cries of the Sioux and Cheyenne. Her labor had hit hard early on, her water breaking almost at the onset of her pains.

The Sioux broke camp with the warriors heading off to fight and the women and children seeing to the packing. Ardith was easily forgotten by her captors as they focused on staying alive. She quickly gathered supplies and crept away, moving up river to hide and await the birth of her child. She had fallen on the slippery bank at one point, hitting her head against a rock. For a moment she'd thought she might lose consciousness, but the pain seemed to keep her awake. Pain from her head wound — pain from the new life fighting to be born. Born too early.

While Custer's men died not a quarter mile from where Ardith hid, Winona came into the world in a fury. With the noise of Indian war cries, gunfire, and men and horses dying, no one had even heard the small mewling sounds of the newborn. She was a fighter, this tiny ruddy-skinned child. And although Ardith had been prepared to smother her rather than be forced to raise the child of her rapist, Winona stirred something deep inside. Ardith fell in love with the baby upon first sight. The bond between mother and child reached beyond the circumstances of the baby's creation and birth.

Ardith thought she had no more tears. The years of sorrow, and then of torment, had dried her eyes forever — at least she had thought this to be true. Yet the day she had given birth to Winona, Ardith had cried like never before. She had cried for the life of her baby — for the life she herself had lost with her family. She had cried for the future and the past. And now, just thinking about that day brought her close to tears again.

But while Winona's birth was at least a good memory overall, other things haunted her. Visions . . . nightmares that were her reality at the hands of Walks in the Dark.

With Winona sleeping peacefully on Ardith's back, she walked the land around the house and corrals and tried to convince herself that the horrors of the past were really behind her. She was now dressed in her sister's clothes — white clothes. They felt almost foreign. Her hair had been pinned up carefully by Dianne, and that, too, seemed out of place.

Strange enough, the hardest thing was getting used to the food. The tastes and textures were so different from what she'd been used to with the Pawnee and Sioux. It was a time of adjustment, with unexpected surprises at every turn.

She felt as if she'd been reborn — given a new start. She'd been bathed and cared for, dressed and fed, as if these things could somehow eliminate the past and all its sufferings. If only that were true.

Ardith knew she could force most of her memories to the far corners of her mind. She had become masterful at forgetting. Yet sometimes she could still feel Walks in the Dark's hands upon her — still feel his breath on her skin. He was everything horrific and terrible, caring nothing for her fears or needs. There was no forcing that memory away.

Ardith felt bile rise in her throat as her chest became tight. The man was an evil force that she was powerless to fight.

"Hello."

Ardith startled and spun around to find herself face-to-face with one of the ranch hands. She backed up a pace, uncertain as to what he would do. The soldiers had wanted to kill her — they said she'd be better off dead. Would this man feel the same?

"My name is Levi. Levi Sperry. Do you remember me from the wagon train?"

His voice was soft and gentle, and his smile seemed sincere. Still, Ardith had no idea who the man was or what he might do to her. She bit at her lower lip, desperate to figure out what to say or do.

"I didn't mean to startle you. Please forgive me."

She nodded but still found no words. Levi backed up a step and shoved his hands into his pants pockets. The action made Ardith relax a bit. She could tell that he wanted to make himself seem less threatening.

"I'm Dianne's sister."

"Yes, I know. I heard about the miracle."

"The miracle?"

"You. Zane finding you. I remember when you were a little girl. I went searching for you when you were lost. Your family was so devastated — we all were."

Ardith refused to let her mind go back to those times. Memories weren't her friends, and pondering the past only caused her pain. Like that first night with Dianne, bad memories would surface along with the good. She couldn't seem to put them into any kind of proper order, so it seemed best not to remember at all.

Levi pointed to her cradleboard. "Your

baby is real pretty. Like you."

Ardith looked at the ground. His words embarrassed her. She stood there in silence for several moments until finally Levi spoke again.

"Well, I just wanted to welcome you back. I won't keep you."

She heard him turn and walk away. Only then did she glance up. He still had his hands in his pockets, and for some reason that amused her. She smiled — maybe for the first time in a long while.

"I cannot believe this!" Portia cried as she read a letter from her father. "He says the army will be on a campaign to capture Sitting Bull and his men and may not return for months. What am I supposed to do in the meantime?"

Dianne and Koko exchanged glances. They were mending clothes while Portia sat idle and considered her letter for the fourth time.

Dianne knew what the young widow wanted: reassurance. She wanted Dianne to promise that Portia could stay as long as she wanted. But Dianne was hesitant to give that kind of promise. At her best, Portia was a whining nuisance most days, and Dianne would frankly be glad to see her go. Especially now that Ardith was here. Dianne much preferred spending her time with her sister and niece.

"I hate this territory. There's simply nothing of beauty or benefit. I miss going to the opera and theater. I long for a wonderful dinner on beautiful china plates, with crystal goblets and fine linens on the table."

"Things like that wouldn't last long out here," Koko commented softly.

"Exactly." Portia got up and began to pace. "This barbaric place has nothing of refinement. Why even this house," she waved her arms, "pales in comparison to the homes back East."

"Portia," Dianne said firmly, "my uncle planned this house and built a good portion of it with his own two hands. If you think it less than refined, try staying in one of the small cabins on the property. That's how the rest of us lived in the early years. Maybe it would give you a better appreciation for what you have here."

Portia stopped in her tracks, her stunned expression revealing horror at the thought. "I could never live like that." She shuddered, then began pacing again. "Some women are meant for more common living — but not me."

"Then perhaps you should go back East

— or at least to Denver or Kansas City — and await word from your father," Dianne replied. She finished repairing a rip in her husband's shirt, then snipped the thread. With that done, she looked at Portia sternly. "If you remain here with us, you'll have to start putting forth effort to help. Winter will soon be upon us and everyone will be needed to ready the ranch."

The woman turned and said nothing for a moment. Her rosy lips were pursed as if she were about to blow a kiss. There was an exotic beauty to Portia Langford; her black hair and dark eyes were intriguing, set against alabaster skin. There was no doubt she was probably the most beautiful woman in the room, but her personality failed to complement her appearance.

"I've never had to work at household duties," she finally admitted. "My mother desired a better life for me, so she wouldn't let me lift a finger. Then I married and had maids and servants. What you're asking is too much."

Dianne shrugged. "Then you'd best gather your things and head back to Bozeman. I don't say this to be mean, but frankly, you've become a burden. You're extra work. Koko and I have had to care for your clothes and clean your room. We cook for you and do your dishes. I simply don't need the additional responsibility."

"But I don't know how to do any chores. I know nothing about that mending you're working at. I know nothing about cooking and cleaning."

"Those skills are easily taught," Koko said. "You appear to be a smart woman. I've no doubt you can learn."

Portia shook her head. "I'm sure that you're mistaken. Being an Indian, you probably don't realize the needs of a refined woman."

Dianne got to her feet and put aside the shirt. "Portia, you will refrain from insulting my family. Being Indian or not has little to do with what we're speaking of. This is a working ranch. We can't dress in silks and fine fashions as you do. We need sturdy, serviceable clothing. You have your choice. Either I'll have one of the boys hitch up a wagon and take you back to Bozeman tomorrow, or we begin your lessons today." Dianne stood her ground despite the resentment reflected in Portia's eyes.

"You say it's my choice, but I really have no alternative. I can't go to Bozeman. I haven't enough money to stay for an undetermined time." She pouted and looked away as though trying to figure out another way out. Finally she sighed. "What will I have to do?"

"Well, the first thing is to go change your clothes. You can hardly work in that," Dianne declared. Just being around the richness of Portia's heavily embroidered silk dress made Dianne nervous. The creation must have cost a fortune, and while there was a good deal of fraying at the hem, Dianne wanted no part in causing further damage to the gown.

"And what would you suggest I wear?" Portia asked smugly.

"Koko and I have managed to put together a few things for you." Dianne smiled. "You may not like this arrangement, and for that I'm sorry. If you were a guest staying only a few days, it would never be an issue. But you must understand that there is a great deal of preparation for winter, and everyone is needed to work. Once that's done and most of the men lead the herd to winter pasture, we'll have it a little bit easier. But even then we need to help one another so that no one person bears more of a load than the other."

Portia seemed to consider the words for a moment. "Very well. If that's the way it has to be in order to receive hospitality — then so be it. I must say life in the West is nothing like the more civilized East."

"No, I'm sure that's true," Dianne replied. "But then again, in the East you needn't fear Indian attack, or a bear wandering into camp, or facing starvation because you failed to prepare for the long isolated winter. Out here we have no need of pampered ladies and their finery. We need strong women who aren't afraid to get their hands dirty. Believe me, your boredom will pass soon enough."

Portia looked hard at Dianne and with that gaze, Dianne knew that she'd made an enemy of the widow. There was a hard glint in her eyes that suggested in other circumstances Dianne would not have come out of this confrontation unscathed. It was hard to know which enemy to fear more — the ones from outside the ranch or the one from within.

"If I had my way about it," Portia muttered as she pulled off her gown, "I'd leave this place and never return. How I hate this isolated land." She threw the gown on the floor, then stared after it. Realizing that no one would come and care for it, Portia reached down and retrieved it.

She smoothed out the dress, turning it right side out again. She draped it over the back of a chair, then stared at her wardrobe, searching for the "appropriate garment" Dianne claimed to have supplied.

"I can't believe I'm reduced to this, and all because of R. E. Langford and his greed." She hated even thinking of her father-in-law. The man always managed to irritate her, even though he was miles away in Baltimore.

"I was never good enough for you, was I?" she asked, reaching for a plain dress of dark blue serge. "I was never good enough for your social circles — your high and mighty friends and their uppity ways."

She yanked the gown from the wardrobe. "Never mind that I was moving in better circles in New York and London — circles that you would never be welcomed in. Never mind that I was the toast of Paris and that we never went without invitation to the finest homes and the best parties."

She attacked the dress, pulling it over her head as though it were a noose. "How dare you leave me like this! Destitute — facing financial ruin."

She hated R. E. Langford. Hated him almost as much as she'd hated his sniveling coward of a son.

They moved toward winter with Portia doing as little as she could get away with as far as helping around the house. The ranch hands finished the fall roundup, and before the first snows fell in the valley, they moved out with the herd.

Dianne always dreaded the time when the men moved the cattle to winter pasture. The ranch took on such an abandoned feel. The rumors of Indian attack had calmed somewhat, but there was always concern.

Cole went with the men to see the herd secured, then returned two days before a heavy snow buried the roads and made passage impossible. Dianne was glad for his safety and the fact that he would be with her through the winter instead of out on the range guarding the cattle.

December brought more snow and a feeling of isolation that weighed heavy on Dianne's heart. She worried about her sister and whether Ardith would adjust to her new life. Portia often made snide comments for which Dianne had to take her to task. It seemed the widow felt Ardith would have been better off dead. No doubt many felt that way, but not Dianne.

The New Year was celebrated in a somber manner. Luke had taken sick with a cough and runny nose. He seemed constantly to pull at his right ear, and Koko had declared him to have an infection. She treated him with herbs and warm smoke, and before long the baby, who'd turned a year old two days before Christmas, was up and taking full run of the house.

On cold January nights, the family was sometimes rewarded with a spectacular show of northern lights. Koko had shared that her ancestors believed the lights held mystical powers. Some even thought conception would be easier during the light show — as if the lights could somehow create life.

Dianne stood at her window watching the night skies blaze red, then fade to green and white. She never tired of the show, but tonight it made her especially joyful. She'd just come to realize she was expecting another baby, even without the help of the lights.

Cole yawned as he entered their bedroom. "It's cold out there," he said as he closed the door. He went immediately to their fireplace and began putting on enough logs for the night.

Dianne turned from the window. She pulled her wool shawl close and smiled as she watched Cole work.

"Despite the snow, I don't really think we're in for a bad winter." He straightened and noted her face. "What are you grinning about?"

"I have some news," she said, coming to him. "Very good news. Do you want to guess?"

He crossed the room and pulled her into his arms. "They've captured Sitting Bull and his men?" he teased.

"No, silly."

"Portia has decided to leave?"

"I wish that were true," she said, relishing the feel of Cole's embrace.

"Hmm," he murmured as his lips touched against her neck. "I've run out of guesses."

Dianne giggled. "We're going to have another baby."

Cole straightened. "Truly?" His expression was filled with wonder. "Another baby?"

She nodded. "Come late spring or early summer."

He hugged her tightly, then released her. "That's the best news ever. Luke turned out so good, we must be doing something right."

"Children are a gift from the Lord," she said. "I think we should give credit where it's due."

"To be sure," Cole replied, then surprised

Dianne by sweeping her off her feet and into his arms. "To be sure."

CHAPTER 7

July 1877

"He's nothing like Luke," Dianne said as she cuddled her newest baby. Micah, now nearly two months old, was a fussy, needy child.

"Every child is different," Koko told her niece. "I think I can mix a few things together to ease his upset stomach."

"Babies are more trouble than their worth, if you ask me," Portia said absentmindedly. She looked up quickly, as if suddenly realizing she'd spoken the words aloud. "It's just that out here," she hurried to explain, "babies are so easily lost to sickness and the isolation."

"It's true that raising children in the wilderness is more difficult," Koko agreed, "but they are certainly worth the effort. Especially when a woman is in our situation — being a widow."

Portia frowned. "I suppose it might have

been nice to have Ned's child, but the thought of raising a child without a father would be terrifying."

Koko nodded. "It is hard. I would trade most anything to have Bram back with us. The children miss him horribly. There isn't a day that goes by that one or the other doesn't encounter some Papa-sized hole that Bram would have perfectly filled."

Dianne saw tears form in her aunt's eyes, but Portia turned away and walked to the front window to gaze outside for the tenth or eleventh time. "I don't understand why we can't have word from the army. My father should at least have time to write."

Dianne put Micah to her shoulder and began patting his back. No one wanted Portia gone from the Diamond V more than she did. The woman, although she lended a hand at times, was still a constant bother. She would often feign confusion on how to do some task or work some piece of equipment, all the while knowing that it would be easier for someone else to step in and handle the situation rather than take time to teach Portia all over again. "Sometimes those things don't work out — especially given all the conflicts."

"Well, with the governor calling for volunteers to help capture the Indians, you'd think they could at least give some of the army men a short time away with their families."

Dianne shook her head at the thought. "Those men enlist with the knowledge that they must see their duties through to completion."

Portia turned, her expression icy cold. "Don't lecture me about the responsibilities or duties of soldiers. I've lived with this nonsense all of my life."

Dianne could feel her resentment. The look on the widow's face made her feel uneasy. "I wasn't trying to lecture. My own brother is out there risking his life for our safety. He knows the price that has to be paid — your father knows it as well. They've both chosen to pay that price."

"Well, they should have asked their family if they were willing to pay it as well."

Dianne knew there would be no reasoning with the woman. While Portia would lovingly talk about her mother and of her desire to make things right with her father in one breath, she would verbally condemn her parents in the next. There was a dangerous and mean-spirited underlying current that was the very essence of Portia Langford. Trenton knew it to be true as well. He'd warned Dianne many times that the woman was not to be trusted.

Micah began to cry more earnestly. He kept drawing his legs up to his stomach, and Dianne knew his discomfort was acute.

"Let me take him," Koko said softly. "I miss taking care of babies. I'll see if I can rock him to sleep."

"Thank you," Dianne said. Her own exhaustion after being up with the baby through the night was wearing her nerves thin.

"Susannah can play with Luke. Why don't you go and take a little nap? I'll see to everything here."

Dianne couldn't quite stifle her yawn. "I think that sounds wise. Especially if Master Micah is planning another difficult night for me."

"I'm going for a ride," Portia said, obviously bored with both women and their talk of children.

"Stay close," Dianne warned. "No one knows where the Sioux and Cheyenne are hiding these days. Rumors are running wild that there are Indians as close as Ennis. We need to be wise."

"I can take care of myself," Portia declared, stomping from the room as though Dianne had insulted her.

"For someone who can take care of herself," Koko commented, "she certainly relies on the help of others often enough."

Dianne smiled. "I can't figure her. There's a presence about her at times that seems so lost — so troubled. For all her attentiveness to Ben's sermons on Sunday mornings and her continued comments about mending fences with her father, I just don't think that woman has any real idea what it is to live as an example of Christ's love."

"I think she's playing a role — nothing more," Koko said, shaking her head. "I think she's memorized her lines and has come to believe them as truth, rather than the script she's made for herself."

"I think you're probably right," Dianne said, yawning once again.

"Go," Koko urged. "I will care for the boys. You go rest."

Settled comfortably in her bed, Dianne tried to heed her aunt's suggestion, but her mind wouldn't put aside her continued concerns about what was happening in the valleys beyond her home. Dianne worried about Zane, and she prayed continually that God would protect him from harm. But she also worried about her family and the ranch. They were isolated — completely removed from neighbors and help. If hostile Indians did attack, there would be very little they could do.

"Are you sleeping?" Ardith whispered as she opened the door a crack.

Dianne rolled over and sat up. "No. I wish I were, but my heart is troubled."

"May I sit with you for a little while?"

Dianne smiled. Her sister rarely sought out anyone's company, and Dianne didn't want to do anything to discourage this approach. "You know that I love your company. Of course you may join me."

"You may not feel that way after we talk."

"Is something wrong?" Dianne asked, scooting up to rest against her headboard while Ardith took a seat in the rocking chair.

"I suppose I'm worried about the rumors of attack. One of the ranch hands mentioned there's a possibility of attack from the west."

Dianne shrugged. "Someone is always reporting something. I never know what to believe."

Ardith looked to the floor. "I can't go back into that life."

"No one would let that happen."

"You don't know how they can be. Walks in the Dark would force me back into the tribe simply to spite me. He'd know death would be too pleasing an option — just as it would have been when we were together."

Dianne tried not to react to her sister's words, but it was hard. She felt Ardith was trying to tell her something — something Dianne didn't want to hear.

"If they come — if there is no hope of winning the fight . . ." Ardith's words trailed off.

"It won't be that way. You'll see," Dianne moved to her sister's side and knelt on the floor.

Ardith looked into Dianne's face, her expression pained, terrified. In that moment Dianne was taken back in time to those first few days after Ardith had come to live with them.

"I won't go back. Do you understand?"

Dianne understood only too well, but she couldn't bring herself to speak of it. "Ardith, you have a good life here. You're safe. Nothing is going to happen to you or Winona. You'll see."

"I don't feel safe. I don't know if I'll ever feel safe again. I try to put the past behind me . . . but . . . well, it's hard."

"I can't begin to know what you have endured, but I do know that I will fight to the death to protect you and Winona. I know Cole feels the same way. And, if I can be so bold, I believe Levi would beat us all to the task. He cares about you."

"He shouldn't. I can't care about him."

"Why not?" Dianne asked, getting to her feet. "He's a good man."

"Yes, much too good for the likes of me. After what's happened to me, no man of worth would ever want me for more than . . . well . . . it wouldn't be for any decent reason."

"That's not true, Ardith. Things are different out here. Montana Territory is still untamed. People do have their prejudices and fears, but they also know better than to let those things push aside their chance at happiness."

"I doubt anyone could ever find happiness with me. I can't find it within myself — how could I possibly benefit anyone else?"

Dianne gently touched her sister's cheek. "Ardith, God will heal your wounds. But it will come about in His way and His time. You mustn't give up hope, nor give up on life. There's still a chance for you to be truly happy. I think Levi would go a long way to help you find that joy."

Ardith got to her feet. "I can't think like that. Right now, I just want to know that if the Sioux attack and try to take me from here that you'll keep it from happening."

"I won't let them take you," Dianne said,

feeling the need to assure her sister.

Ardith fixed her dark-eyed gaze on Dianne. "Even if you have to kill me to keep it from happening?"

Dianne gasped, drawing her hand to her mouth. She couldn't believe what Ardith had asked.

"You must promise me, Dianne. If they come and take me — take Winona — you'll put a bullet in us before letting them drag us off. I don't want to live like that — I won't live like that again."

"Ardith, I could never —"

"Then give me a gun. A revolver. I'll keep it with me and do the deed myself if the time comes and requires it of me. I won't let the Sioux take us. You'd do well to make provisions for yourself and your own children. They won't be kind — they won't be civil. If you think you've suffered in the past, forget it. I've made my bed in hell, as David spoke of in the psalms." She turned to go, then stopped and looked back at Dianne. "The only thing is, God didn't find me there as David suggested. Even God couldn't look upon that heinous affair."

"Where's Cole?" Gus asked as he came storming through the kitchen.

"I figured he was out there working with

113

some of the colts," Dianne replied as she put the second apple pie onto the sill to cool. "Why, is something wrong?"

"There's news out of Virginia City. I think we need to hold a ranch meeting."

Dianne felt a chill go up her spine. "Is it the Indians?"

Gus nodded stoically. "It don't sound good."

Twenty minutes later the entire family and most of the ranch hands had crammed into the formal dining room. Gus and Cole stood at the head of the table, while Trenton lingered near the door.

"Quiet down. We need to talk this out," Cole announced to the men.

Dianne looked around at the serious expressions — the worried looks. She dreaded hearing what Gus and Cole might have to share.

As the room went silent, Cole began. "Gus just got back from Virginia City. Apparently there've been some new problems to the west. The Nez Perce are on the warpath. They've left their reservation and are headed this direction."

"Where did this information come from?" Dianne asked.

"The sheriff. He had a wire," Gus explained. "Apparently the Indians have been tracked headin' this way. The army hopes to intercept them, but —"

"But we all know better than to place our hopes in the army," Portia said snidely. "I can't believe this nonsense. Did no one learn anything after the battle at Little Big Horn?"

"Portia, you must remain calm," Dianne said, catching a glance at Ardith's terrified expression. "Let's hear the men out and learn what is happening."

"Like that will keep us from being killed in our sleep."

"Portia!" Dianne snapped, her anger evident. "Be quiet."

Portia glared at Dianne, looking for all the world as though she might make this a matter of physical violence. Instead, she drew a deep breath and said nothing more.

Dianne looked to her husband and Gus. She longed to know the details, the truth of what they knew, but wondered if they would simplify this for fear of worrying the women.

"Apparently there's still plenty of time and distance between us and them," Gus said, picking up the conversation. "They believe the hostiles will make their way across the Lolo Pass and head into Montana. The army plans to intercept them."

"It's a good distance from here," Cole

threw in. He met Dianne's gaze and she could almost read his thoughts. He was worried — he was afraid. She'd not seen him like this before.

"However," Gus continued, "the army is worried that this may be a sign to other tribes. If word gets around to other hostiles and they know the army'll be engaged over on the Lolo Trail, other Indians may take this as an opportunity to attack in areas not protected. Plus, there's still Sioux and Cheyenne out there who ain't been caught."

Dianne avoided looking at Ardith. Her sister's words still haunted her, and Dianne had no doubt the young woman would do exactly as she'd threatened if they were under attack.

"What do we need to do?" Dianne asked softly.

"We're going to meet with some of the other area ranchers," Cole announced. "We'll form a plan of protection putting outriders on the perimeters of our properties — determining a series of places where we can meet on the trail and let each other know that things are all right."

"What else is to be done?" Levi asked.

"Every man will have a revolver on him at all times. Extra ammunition as well. Each man also needs to have a rifle."

"What about the women?" Portia asked indignantly. "I can shoot as well as any man here."

"We'll place loaded rifles and shotguns around the house," Cole answered, "ammunition too. I don't like doing this, but it seems necessary."

Dianne felt a sinking desperation fall over her. It seemed she was caught up in quicksand and couldn't fight her way to the top for air. The constriction was almost too much to bear. How could she just sit by? How could she watch and wait to see if hostile Indians would descend upon her family?

"Isn't there something else we can do?" Dianne asked.

"You need to be layin' in supplies here in the main house," Gus said. "Water too. We need to be able to dig in and wait out anything that comes our way."

"Wouldn't it be better to send the women and children away?" Portia asked.

"Where would you suggest we send them?" Cole replied. "Hostiles have been reported in every area that surrounds this valley."

Dianne frankly wanted to throttle the woman for even bringing up the idea of leaving. "You're always free to go," Dianne finally said. "I'll give you the money and a horse."

Portia paled considerably and looked down at the table. *Perhaps she'll finally be silent,* Dianne thought.

"I think we need to work together in order to be safe and sound," Faith said, putting her hand on Dianne's arm. "We'll be stronger if we stand as one instead of picking at each other."

"Well said," Cole agreed. "We've always known the elements could destroy us. A single blizzard could leave us destitute — a flood could ravage all we have. This is no different. We're still making a stand against that which would destroy us."

"We've gotta stand together," Gus said. "It won't work any other way. Everyone here has a part to play in keepin' others and themselves safe. Ain't no time for doin' things halfway."

"I want the women and children to stay indoors," Cole said firmly. "Malachi, I want you and Faith to move up here with the children. No sense waiting until the last minute. If danger comes, it'll come quickly. You can stay in one of the rooms in our wing. Levi, we can use another man at the house. I'd like you to move in here as well. We'll figure out where to put you later, but

118

for now —"

"Negroes living here — with us?" Portia questioned indignantly.

"I've had a lot of folks living here — with us," Dianne said angrily. "At least the Montgomerys are good friends." This seemed to silence Portia momentarily, but Dianne knew it probably wouldn't be the last outburst they would have from her.

"What about Ben and Charity?" Dianne questioned. "They should come too."

Cole frowned at the interruption. "I've already planned for them as well. Ben and Charity will move into Luke's room and he can come back into our room."

Dianne's mind whirled at the thought of all that her uncle had worked so hard to build being at the hands of someone who would seek to destroy it. "Can't we hire more men — post a guard around the immediate yard — the barns and corrals?"

"Yes, what about men standing guard outside?" Koko asked.

"Yes," Portia agreed.

Cole shifted, looking uncomfortable. "Gus, Trenton, and I discussed this and have provisions for seeing to a perimeter around the immediate grounds. I have this under control, so hear me out." The words were addressed to the group, but Dianne knew they were mainly intended for her. She hadn't meant to question Cole and embarrass him in front of everyone else.

"The house will be crowded, the fit tight at times. But again, we must work together. Ben and Levi will be here at the house most of the time. Malachi will be no farther than the barns. We'll move some of his equipment up so he can continue with his work. This ranch still has to be maintained — it won't stop just because of the Indians.

"Faith, you'll need to continue preparing meals for the boys, as usual, only you'll do it from here."

"Did it before, don't see any reason why it won't work that way again," Faith declared, trying to sound cheerful.

"Charity, I'd be much obliged if you and Ardith would work out an arrangement for a nursery. Faith needs to be able to work on the meals, and Koko and Dianne need to be free to shoot and defend the place if it comes to that. I'd like the children set up in the far back room. Susannah and Jamie can help you."

"I'm a man. I shouldn't be with the children," protested ten-year-old Jamie.

"You are a man, although a very young one," Cole replied. "I'm counting on you as one of my house guards. You'll be the nursery guard. It'll be your job to watch for danger and keep the women and babies safe."

Jamie seemed to like the sound of this, as he squared his shoulders and his expression calmed to one of serious contemplation. Apparently Cole had reached through the boy's pride.

"What am I supposed to do?" It was Portia again.

"I'd like you to help Faith in the kitchen. She's going to have the job of feeding all of us and will need the help."

"You can't be serious. You want me to work with . . . with her?" Portia was obviously disgusted by the idea. "I won't work with Negroes. It's bad enough to have them in the house — living under the same roof."

Dianne opened her mouth to reply, but Cole threw her a look that silenced her. "Portia," he said, turning to face her, "you forget your place."

"And your manners," Dianne muttered just loud enough to be heard.

"These are desperate times. We must work together as stated earlier. You will cooperate with my directions or you will need to leave and go elsewhere. Do you understand?" Cole asked.

"So if I don't do things your way, I'll be

thrown out? That hardly seems the Christian thing to do," Portia said, her words dripping sarcasm.

"Neither is it Christian to condemn a person for the color of her skin," Cole said frankly. "We need every man and woman here to see us through this crisis. Either you stand with us — or you stand against us. If you're against us, you're no better than the enemy we're fighting against. I won't have the enemy inside my own home — do you understand me?"

Portia surprised Dianne by turning all teary. "I'm so sorry. It's just terrifying me. I can't think straight."

"It's understandable, but you need to stand firm," Cole said. "We all need to stand firm. There's no telling what might happen tomorrow, but if we hold on together, we'll stand a better chance of dealing with it . . . whatever *it* may be."

The meeting left Portia feeling more than a little bit angry. She returned to her room, slammed the door shut, and tried to figure out what course to take next. She longed for a bottle of whiskey, something to drown her sorrows and frustrations in.

"They've all gone mad," she murmured. She was a prisoner in a strange sort of asylum, and everyone was insane except for her.

"I'll make them all pay for this one day. Just see if I don't."

For a moment she considered Dianne's offer of money and a horse. Perhaps she could ride the horse to Virginia City, then sell the beast and have enough money for a stage to Corrine and then the train to Denver. Denver had been a nice town with decent prospects.

"But if the Indians truly are coming this way, the stage might not even be leaving Virginia City . . . or coming there."

She walked to the window and stared out on the corrals below. "I'm trapped. Trapped and helpless to remove myself." Portia rested her forehead on the pane. "There has to be another answer. There has to be another way."

CHAPTER 8

August was upon them, and the daytime heat left the men and animals parched and weary. Life in the mountains of the Montana Territory was an exercise in adaptability. The days could be blistering hot, while the nights could send you to huddle in your blankets.

Zane felt that kind of chill even now. His men felt it too. They were wrapped up in blankets trying desperately to sleep and prepare themselves for the encounter with the Nez Perce. Zane wasn't sure if it was the discomfort of the cold or the events to come that caused such mass insomnia.

The Indians had been making constant progress toward the east since thwarting the army's efforts to keep them contained in Idaho. They'd moved steadily through the Bitterroot Valley and were now camped in the Big Hole Meadows. The soldiers had worried that perhaps the band would double back into Idaho, leading them on a wild chase that would perhaps end in a trap. But scouts returned with word that the Nez Perce had indeed crossed the Continental Divide and were headed east.

Zane didn't like the sound of that. Straight east would lead the Indians into the area of his sister's ranch. There was no time to warn her or the others that resided along the way. It made him all the more desperate for the army to continue to close the lead on the tribe and take them under control.

Now as they waited restlessly for dawn to make their move on the Nez Perce camp, Zane couldn't help but relive so many other attacks. The anticipation of what was to come was both exhilarating and sickening. He knew there was within this tribe a group of men responsible for murdering white settlers. He knew too that these men — if not the entire group of Nez Perce — would not come back willingly to the reservation and a white man's court.

"Lieutenant Chadwick," a voice whispered, "rally your men." It was Zane's captain.

"Yes, sir." Zane sat up stiffly. The night cold had put an ache in his joints.

"Leave everything that is nonessential to combat," the captain further instructed.

"Leave the blanket rolls, overcoats, extra clothes. Leave it all. We'll be back soon enough for it."

Zane roused his troops and instructed them. "If we can take them by surprise, then maybe no one needs to get hurt."

"You mean no one on our side, right, Lieutenant?" one of his men asked with humor in his tone. Zane said nothing.

They all went on foot, with exception to Colonel Gibbon and Adjutant Woodruff. Moving down Trail Creek, they turned to follow the low foothills. Zane quickly caught sight of the Indian fires. They'd found the camp — just as they had known they would.

Halting before reaching the watery slough that separated them from the camp, the soldiers waited in silence until exactly four o'clock — at least that was the best reading Zane could make of his pocket watch. The skirmish line then headed out through a swampy area of cold water that reached waist deep for some men. Beyond this, willow brush caused the men to break the line. A dangerous situation, Zane noted, but there was nothing to be done about it.

He heard his heart pounding in his ears as the troops advanced. Zane had hoped they would strive to negotiate with Chief

Joseph and the other chiefs, but the army was bent on complete control. No compromise. No parley.

Without warning, four shots rang out. And then the destruction was certain. Guns fired from up ahead. Zane's men advanced at a more rapid pace, stopping just short of the camp. Crouching, they waited momentarily as one of the other companies moved in ahead of them.

"Fire into the tepees, low and steady boys. We'll catch 'em while they sleep," someone called out.

Zane stood and motioned to his men. He'd barely taken a step forward, however, when he felt a rock hit his head. At least it felt like a rock. But as his vision blurred and white searing pain poured down over his face, Zane knew he'd been shot. In another second, he took two bullets in the leg before blackness overcame him.

For all of their precautions around the ranch, no one was more surprised than Cole when Koko's brother, Takes Many Horses, made his way into the house unannounced and unseen.

At the sight of the Blackfoot warrior, Faith cried out and dropped the pan she'd been greasing. "Oh, you gave me a start," she exclaimed. "I didn't recognize you for a moment."

Dianne was snapping beans at the table and had nearly jumped from her chair when Faith hollered out. "We weren't expecting you," she said in greeting. The tremor in her voice, however, left no doubt that she had been just as shaken as Faith.

Takes Many Horses frowned. "I'm sorry for scaring you. I'm on my way north."

"I thought you were already up North," Dianne said, putting her work aside. "Are you hungry?"

Faith retrieved her pan as Portia rushed into the room with a revolver. She pointed it directly at Takes Many Horses. "I'll kill the heathen — get out of my way, Dianne!"

Dianne put herself between Portia and Takes Many Horses. "You will do no such thing. This is Koko's brother."

Portia's expression hardened. "It doesn't matter. He's Indian."

"Put the gun down, Portia," Cole said as he came into the kitchen behind Takes Many Horses. He appeared completely unmoved by the scene. "Go about your business, Portia."

The woman seemed particularly annoyed to be dismissed. Dianne couldn't help but be proud of the way Cole took charge of the situation. She moved to stand between her husband and Koko's brother. "I'm sure you have plenty of mending to do since Faith doesn't need your help here," Dianne announced.

Portia finally turned to leave. "Doesn't seem we have very good protection if an Indian can walk right into our kitchen," she muttered as she exited the room.

Dianne hadn't had time to consider that fact. She looked to Cole and shook her head. "We don't have very good protection, do we?"

"I saw your riders," Takes Many Horses said before Cole could reply. "Is something wrong?"

"The Nez Perce are warring, and of course Sitting Bull and his people have yet to be captured. Rumor has it that there isn't a tribe in all of the territory that doesn't plan to kill us in our sleep," Cole answered. "We had hoped to set up a perimeter of guards to keep an eye out for attack."

"If attack comes from an entire nation you'll probably have plenty of warning," Takes Many Horses said with a grin. "If it's just a few men like me, you'll be hard-pressed to catch them."

"And a few men like you could burn us to the ground and leave us all for dead," Dianne said without thinking.

"I didn't know you thought so poorly of me," the Blackfoot replied with a sly smile.

"You know what I meant," Dianne replied. "You have stealth and years of experience in sneaking around places. Most Indians train in the same manner."

"Well, I won't be here long. I need to push on. The army is after me — heading this way."

"Is it Zane's regiment?" Dianne asked hopefully.

"I don't know. They've been after me for two weeks now. I'm considered hostile, you know." He smiled in his lopsided manner.

"Why are you here?" Cole asked.

"I need supplies, and I wanted to see Koko."

"I'll put some things together," Faith said, hurrying to the pantry.

"Koko's in the back. I'll show you the way," Dianne said. She caught Cole's expression and could tell he wasn't pleased to have this latest guest. She wondered if he worried about how it would look — especially when the army showed up. "You're in luck. She's alone. My sister is elsewhere, so you won't disturb her."

"I don't understand," Takes Many Horses said.

Dianne shook her head. "There isn't time for you to understand at this point. I'll explain later."

There wasn't much time to consider such worries, however. Takes Many Horses' visit was brief — no more than an hour. Koko longed for him to stay, as did Jamie, who absolutely admired his uncle. All the while, Dianne prayed Ardith would stay where she was helping Charity braid rugs. She feared that seeing Takes Many Horses would set the poor girl into nightmarish fits.

"I have to leave. The army will be here within a day — maybe two."

"I wish I could go with you," Jamie said, pouting.

"You need to stay and take care of your mother and sister," Takes Many Horses admonished. "They'll need you to be strong in the days to come."

They all walked outside to bid Takes Many Horses good-bye. He seemed reluctant to leave, but Dianne knew he would disappear as quickly as he'd come. He didn't want to bring trouble upon the ranch, and no doubt he already felt guilty for even coming.

"If one of the horses disappears from the far corral," Cole said in a hushed voice, "I won't worry about it. Especially the black — he's especially fast."

131

Takes Many Horses met his eyes and nodded. Dianne could only pray that all of her men had gotten word that this man was friendly and not the scout of some war party.

"Thank you for your help," Takes Many Horses said to the group, but his gaze was fixed on Dianne. "I needed to see my family, but I'm sorry if I've put you all at risk with the army."

"We'll be fine. Just get on out of here before they show up," Cole said sternly.

A day and a half later, the army showed up as Takes Many Horses had predicted. Dianne was relieved that it was not yet seven o'clock in the morning. Portia wouldn't be up yet to comment to them about Takes Many Horses' arrival.

"Hello," Dianne said, meeting the small group of mounted cavalry. She held a rifle in front of her and tried to appear completely calm. Cole and some of the men hurried to the house as the captain began questioning Dianne.

"We're on the trail of a renegade band of Blackfoot."

"I've seen no band of renegade Blackfoot," Dianne answered honestly.

"We tracked at least one man to this ranch."

"One man?" Cole asked. "The army has time to chase after a single man?"

By this time Koko and her children, along with Ardith and Winona, had come to the porch to join Dianne.

"This woman is a squaw and a renegade," the captain announced, pointing to Koko. "She and her children must come with us. One of my men will return her to the reservation."

"I beg your pardon," Dianne said, casting a glance at Koko. The woman looked positively thunderstruck, while Jamie seemed prepared to do battle. Dianne threw him a cautioning gaze before turning back to the captain. "This is my aunt. You won't take her anywhere."

Winona toddled from where Ardith had placed her on the porch. She'd only learned to walk on her first birthday, but already she was getting into everything. The captain motioned to a corporal at his left. "Take that child. She's a hostile."

Koko stepped between Winona and the approaching soldier. She said nothing, but the look she gave the man stopped him in his tracks.

"Captain?" the man asked, looking to his leader.

"If you won't willingly give up, we'll take

133

you by force," the man asserted, his eyes narrowing.

Ardith pushed forward. "Where were you when the Sioux took me hostage?" she screamed. "Where were you and all of your men when I was taken against my will?" Her voice grew louder. "You would take innocent women and children from their homes — force them to reservations, but you couldn't save one white woman from attack?"

The captain looked from Ardith to Dianne and then back again to Ardith. "Ma'am, I've no idea what your concern in this matter might be, but I'd advise you to stay out of my corporal's way."

"That's my daughter you've sent your man to take," Ardith hissed. She went to stand beside Koko. "This is my aunt. She's half white. My daughter is half white. You can't force them to live on a reservation."

"The law says otherwise. Besides, I have no way of knowing that your story is true."

"I don't care what you know to be true." Ardith put her hands on her hips and glared at the man. "I don't care what happens to the other Indians you and your men round up. I'll happily see them all on reservations where they can't hurt anybody. But this is my family and you'll have to kill me before you can take them."

Dianne stepped forward. "Me too." Cole did likewise, putting his arm around Dianne.

The captain's jaw clenched. He seemed to weigh the situation momentarily. "Corporal, back to your horse." He waited until the young man had followed orders before fixing his gaze on Cole. "Have you encountered any renegade Blackfoot?"

Cole shook his head. "We have not."

"I'll leave this matter for now," the captain said in a low menacing tone, "but we will be back. All Indians are to be on reservations and there will be no exceptions. If we weren't headed west, I'd force this issue now."

"This woman and her children live as white," Cole protested. "There's no reason to force any issue."

"They can live as grizzly bears," the man retorted. "Doesn't make them one. I have my orders. Our orders are to seek out and capture any renegade hostiles who have left the reservation or have refused to move onto their assigned land. Over in the Big Hole Valley, Colonel Gibbon and his men have encountered warring Nez Perce. Gibbon was defeated and those Indians are headed this way. We caught the trail of renegade

Blackfoot, and I figure from the direction they're moving that they'll probably join up with the Nez Perce and work together. If that happens, you'll be guilty of my men's blood and the blood of your neighbors."

"Hardly that, Captain. I fully support you and your men. I'm glad for your protection. But this woman and her children are not the enemy. They've lived here peaceably for many years. In fact, this woman was married to the owner of the ranch."

The captain shook his head. "There is no such thing as a legal marriage to a squaw. You should know that as well as anybody. I'll see these renegades back on the reservation as soon as my campaign in the west is complete." He gave Dianne a smirk and added, "Or I'll see them dead."

Dianne's mind was already reeling from the news about Colonel Gibbon. Zane was with that regiment — what if he were dead? *Oh, God, please protect him.*

The captain moved his men out, leaving Dianne chilled to the bone by the confrontation. "I can't believe anyone could be so cruel. Cole, do you suppose he will come back?"

"A man like that is generally driven to see things done in his own way. I think he'll probably return."

"What will we do to protect Koko and the children?" Dianne asked. She looked past Cole to where Jamie and Susannah huddled against the wall. The fear in their eyes said more than words ever could.

"I don't know. I suppose going to the authorities won't help much. They are the authorities," Cole grumbled.

"But we can't simply stand by and wait to see what happens. We need to have help. We need to protect them."

"Dianne, I completely agree. I'm just not sure what we can do about it. Let me think on it," Cole said, clearly irritated.

Dianne looked to her aunt and sister. "I won't let them hurt you. Not either of you."

"Times are getting harder." Koko shook her head. "I have a feeling they will get much worse before things calm again. People are afraid. I don't hate the army for what they are doing, but I fear it won't bring about the changes they hope for. People will die. Soldiers as well as Indians."

Ardith turned and put her hand on Koko's shoulder. "Thank you for what you did. I know I've been unkind to you, but even so you risked your life for Winona."

Koko smiled. "You've been through much. I didn't blame you for the way you feel. I might have done the same thing in your place. I love you, just as I love Winona. I would never see harm come to either one of you."

Ardith nodded. "Thank you."

"What are we gonna do, boss?" Gus asked from behind Dianne.

Cole and Dianne exchanged a look. Dianne wished she could read answers in her husband's eyes, but in her heart she knew he had no better idea of how to rectify the situation than she did.

"Yeah, what are we gonna do?" Levi asked. "I think we're all missing the important issue here. Takes Many Horses had no trouble getting to the house — to the women and children. Then the army talks about tracking a band of renegade Blackfoot — that means there's a great many more warriors out there who might not treat us very well."

"Yes, that is a concern," Cole agreed. "But one man working alone has an easier time of staying undetected. If the Indians attack, they won't come one man at a time. We'll wait a few days and see what the news is on the Nez Perce. If they're captured or head away from the area, I'll go to Butte and seek help for Koko and the children."

"And if they head straight for us?" Levi asked.

Cole pulled his hat down and stepped from the porch. "Then we'll fight."

Dianne shook her head, trying desperately to dislodge the recurring image of her nightmare. Women and children dead — soldiers too. Cole, Luke, and baby Micah. It was as if they were fighting against the wind — against an unseen force that was bent on destroying them.

CHAPTER 9

October 1877

Everyone seemed to hold his breath while waiting for word about the Nez Perce and their warring activities. Dianne hated the long hot days without word from her brother. Zane had always written regularly — at least when time permitted and there was someplace to post a letter. But she hadn't heard anything from him since earlier in the year. It seemed that after Little Big Horn, Zane had written less and less, almost as if he could no longer bear to share the news. And perhaps he was right to withhold the images, Dianne thought. She often remembered Zane's vivid description of the massacre that had taken place on the Marias River back in 1870. Sometimes she wished she'd never eavesdropped on his conversation with their uncle; then other times she was glad she had. Knowing the horrors that Zane had been forced to face gave her a greater understanding and sympathy for her brother. It also made her wish he'd give up soldiering and return home to the Diamond V.

Word trickled in little by little that the Nez Perce had eventually been stopped near the Canadian border in the eastern reaches of the Montana Territory. Some had escaped to the north, but for the most part the remaining collection of women, children, and the elderly were taken under control by the army after Chief Joseph surrendered.

Dianne breathed a sigh of relief, as did most of the valley. There had been a time when it looked as though the Nez Perce would travel through their land, heading up the Madison Valley and across the Bozeman Pass as they went east to be with their friends the Crow. But instead, they had gone south to the area of the Yellowstone national lands and east. Knowing Morgan, Zane's twin, was in that region, Dianne couldn't help but worry about him as well. Morgan was terrible about keeping in touch, and Dianne was lucky to hear from him once a year. When the Nez Perce had moved through the area without incident, Dianne thanked God for His mercy and continued to pray for everyone's safety.

Then the newspapers poured forth with

141

information about the capture. There had been several skirmishes along the way, with both Indians and soldiers being killed before the final siege and surrender near the Canadian border. With winter coming, Dianne was glad the Nez Perce had been caught. She felt a bit of sorrow for the loss they would suffer in being sent to reservations, but at the same time she only longed for safety for her brother and family.

"I don't suppose they'll simply allow the Indians to return to their reservation without punishment," Faith said as she finished washing the last of the dinner dishes.

"No, I suppose not," Dianne said softly.

She looked at the clock. It was nearly two in the afternoon. Cole should have been home by now. He and some of the ranch hands had taken a herd of cattle over to Fort Ellis the week earlier, but he had promised to return by the morning of the twelfth. That was today. Dianne had begged Cole to let her travel with him to Fort Ellis on the chance that there might be word about Zane. But Cole had been firm that her place was at home with the children, and while Dianne agreed, she was also angry that he would deny her this simple request.

"Don't imagine he'll get here any quicker with you watching the clock," Faith said in her jovial manner.

"I just don't understand why he isn't here yet."

"Worrying won't change that fact. You have to have faith that the Good Lord is watching over him. We've known a good time of peace, and I have to believe that everything will come around right."

Things had relaxed a bit around the ranch, and for that Dianne was grateful. Micah seemed to have outgrown his colicky stomach, and the other children remained healthy. Blessings to be sure.

Portia continued to be a headache, but with the assurance that the men would soon return to Fort Ellis and Fort Shaw now that the Nez Perce were captured, Dianne prayed that Portia's father would come quickly to claim her. In fact, Cole had hoped to learn how soon the soldiers would be back so that he could bring the news to Portia and perhaps even arrange for her return to Bozeman. Dianne knew he was as anxious as anyone to see Portia removed from the ranch.

"I think I'll ride out and see if I can spot them coming in," Dianne said, pulling her apron off.

"Cole won't think much of that," Faith said firmly. She turned and faced Dianne with a stern expression. "You have to let that man be in charge. If you go disobeying him and ride out away from the house, he's not going to be happy about it."

"Don't lecture me," Dianne snapped. "The threat of attack is over — at least for the time. It can't be that dangerous to ride to the top of the ridge. Why, everyone can see me from there."

"But it's not what he asked you to do," Faith replied, seeming unmoved by Dianne's curtness.

"I'm tired of doing things his way," Dianne admitted. "Uncle Bram trusted me to know how to see things through. He gave me the ranch, knowing that I was capable. But Cole treats me like I'm some sort of frail ninny who can't do anything but watch over her children."

"That's a mighty awesome responsibility," Faith commented.

Dianne knew Faith's three children — Mercy, Daniel, and little Lucy — were her absolute joy. Faith adored each one as the most precious of gifts.

"It *is* an awesome responsibility, and I love Luke and Micah with all of my heart," Dianne began, "but I also love my brothers, the ranch, my friends. I want to be useful, and I don't want to be treated like a child."

"So maybe you shouldn't be stomping your foot and throwing fits like a child," Faith said with a grin.

Dianne crossed her arms. She knew Faith was right, but she had no desire to cool her heels pacing the kitchen. For a moment she said nothing. "Oh bother." She plopped down on a chair, arms still folded.

"Don't fret. He'll be here before you know it," Faith said, coming to where Dianne sat. She gently touched Dianne's shoulder. "It'll be all right. You'll see."

"He doesn't understand me," Dianne said softly. Things between her and Cole could be so good at times. They'd been married now for six years. Shouldn't their relationship start to get easier? "Sometimes being a wife is so hard."

Faith laughed. "Don't fret over the fact that he doesn't understand you. Why, I don't think Malachi has a clear idea of what I'm all about."

"But Cole doesn't even seem to realize how he hurts me."

"Hurts you?"

Dianne shook her head. "He doesn't physically hurt me, but he wounds me in my heart. He doesn't seek my opinions on how to run the ranch. He doesn't ask me about things the way he used to."

"He's a man, Dianne. He needs to run this place on his own two feet or his men will never respect him."

"That's what he's always saying to me. He thinks I interfere with his authority."

"And do you?"

Dianne sighed. "There are just times when I know better how a thing ought to be done. I've been at this a lot longer than he has."

"But he needs to learn and to make his own mistakes. He'll do just fine. Give him a chance."

"But he never gives me a chance," Dianne protested. "Faith, I may be his wife, but that doesn't mean I've lost the ability to think or reason. Uncle Bram taught me a great deal. I'm as good at ranching as some of the men in this valley. I certainly know as much about this ranch as anyone else. I simply want Cole to consider my feelings and thoughts when he makes decisions. That's all I'm asking."

Faith shook her head. "Seems to me that's asking a lot."

Ten minutes later, Cole walked through the back door. He was covered with dust and the expression on his face suggested trouble. Dianne jumped up and ran to him. "What kept you?"

Cole pulled her into his arms and held

her close.

"We've been worried," she said against his ear.

Cole held her for several moments, then kissed her forehead. "I was delayed at the fort. Didn't think it would take this long. I'm sorry for worrying you."

"What was the problem?" she asked, pulling away.

"There was information regarding the wounded from the Battle of the Big Hole," he said seriously. "Zane was hurt, but he's going to be all right."

"What!" Dianne shook her head. "How? When? Was he at the fort? Oh, I knew I should have gone."

"Calm down. He wasn't there. He was apparently wounded during the battle in August," Cole replied. "He was pretty sick for a while. They took him to the hospital at Deer Lodge and the surgeons were able to patch him back together."

"Where is he now? I want to see him. We need to bring him here."

"Hold on," he said, reaching out to still her. "That's why I was delayed. I wanted to locate him and do exactly that."

"Well?" Dianne could only think of her brother lingering near death without so much as a friend or family member to hold his hand. It didn't matter that he was supposedly better. She needed to see it for herself.

"He's leaving the army. His enlistment is up in November, but they've decided to give him an early medical discharge."

"Well that sounds like a sensible thing," Faith said, coming to stand beside Dianne. "See there? Everything will be just fine."

"I want him here. I want him here before the snows bury us in this valley," Dianne insisted. "Where is he now? How can we get to him?"

"He's in Butte. I thought I might head up that way and get him," Cole said. "If you'd calm down for a minute, I'd give you the details."

"I am calm!" Dianne nearly yelled, knowing even as she did that nothing could be further from the truth.

Faith actually laughed. "Yes, sir. She's calm all right. She's about as calm as a Missouri twister."

Cole grinned, his gaze never leaving Dianne. His response only irritated her more.

"Cole, this is serious. We need to go to him."

"I will go to him."

"I'll go too."

He shook his head. "No. You need to stay

here. Micah is nursing and Luke needs you as well."

"We can take them with us," Dianne said, nearly hysterical at the thought that Cole would deny her this request.

"No, Dianne. The weather is too unpredictable. I'll go to Butte and find Zane, and then I'll check with that judge we heard about — the one who can make it safe for Koko and the children to stay here. We should be home before the snow gets too heavy."

Dianne knew it was a losing battle, but her anger was mounting at Cole's refusal. "I want to go. I'm a good rider. We'll leave the children here. Ardith can wet-nurse Micah."

"Goodness, just listen to yourself," Faith declared. "You aren't even talking sensible."

"I could have figured you'd take his side," Dianne said, pulling away from both of them. "You may need help, Cole — he may be too hurt to travel on a horse. Have you even thought of that?"

"I have," Cole said seriously. "If that's the case, I'll hire a man in Butte. There are probably a great many cowboys who have no work for the winter. I'm sure I can get help if I need it." He stepped toward her. "Please hear me out. I'm not doing this to cause you pain or make you mad. This is the better way. You aren't thinking clearly because of your love and concern for Zane. That's understandable, but he would never forgive himself if something happened to you. You know that's true."

Dianne drew a deep breath and let it out. Her resignation could be heard in that sigh. "Is that your final word?"

"It is. I want you to stay here where you'll be safe."

"Have it your way," she said, knowing that the wall she was erecting between them was one that would be difficult to tear down. She walked away without bothering to look back. The anger in her heart — anger toward Cole — was something new and overpowering. They'd had their arguments before, endured their moments of temper, but never had she been so furious with him. Never had she wanted to so completely defy him and refuse to follow his direction.

I should just sneak out and make my own way to Butte. Leave before he even realizes what has happened.

She wasn't sure where such defiance had come from. Maybe it was the tension and the worry about Zane's well-being. Maybe it was the fear that had built during Cole's delayed return. Whatever it was, it wasn't pleasant at all. It weighed her down like a heavy horse blanket.

Dianne was still angry after putting the boys to bed. Micah had sensed her rage while nursing. It made them both uncomfortable, but no matter how Dianne tried to relax and release her tension, she couldn't seem to manage. Micah finally fell into a restful sleep, but the experience left Dianne feeling a deep sense of guilt.

Luke slept peacefully in the corner of the room, but Dianne had not been her usual self with the boy and he'd fussed and cried until she'd snapped at him to be quiet. It was a stranger who cared for her children that night. Dianne couldn't begin to deal with the range of emotions within her.

It wasn't only that Cole had refused her the trip; it was everything. Everything that had come to haunt her over the last year. The love she'd once felt for the land was tainted with fear and worry. The peace she'd known in her heart was as distant as the place where God seemed to be hiding from her.

When the door opened and Cole walked in, Dianne forced her gaze to the floor. She rocked in silence as he began to undress and readied himself for bed. They'd not spoken since their disagreement. Dianne had refused to come to supper, something

151

she now regretted, and Cole hadn't come in search of her.

"I was hoping you might be cooled down by now, but I see you're still angry," he said softly.

Dianne looked up and watched him as he folded his shirt over the back of a chair. "I'm more hurt than angry."

"Hurt?" He seemed genuinely puzzled by this.

"Yes, hurt. You don't care about my feelings. You've become bossy and critical, demanding and dictatorial. You used to care about how I felt — about what I wanted. Now it's all about having things your way."

Cole looked at her as if she'd announced that the ranch had been sold. "Is that what you really think?"

"What else should I think? It seems lately you haven't really tried to understand my needs. You just tell me what to do and where to go. I didn't think our life together would be like this."

"My only objective these last few months was to keep you safe. Surely you can see that."

Dianne got up from the chair and paced to the window. "I would have liked it better had you discussed things with me."

"I'm your husband. It's my duty to take

care of you — provide for you. Yet it seems that every time I try to take that job seriously, you rear up like an unbroken colt."

Dianne hated the truth in his words. She knew he was right, but there was no way she could admit it. "If you loved me — if you really cared about my feelings — you would let me go with you to Butte."

"Is that what it's going to take to put things right? Give you your way?" he asked without emotion.

Dianne knew she'd drawn a line. Looking up to meet her husband's sober expression, she said, "It's not about having my way. It's about your caring more for my feelings than having the final say."

"And that's what you believe of me? That I've said no just to boss you around — put you in your place?"

She'd taken the argument too far to back down now. Even though she knew it wasn't the truth, Dianne couldn't help but nod.

Cole stared at her for several moments. Dianne thought she perceived disappointment in his eyes, but her heart was hardened and pride wouldn't let her soften it.

"All right," he finally said. "You can go with me to Butte."

The victory was hollow. Dianne opened her mouth to thank him, but Cole raised his hand. "Don't say anything more. I don't think I could bear it."

He picked up his shirt and headed for the door. "We'll leave at dawn."

Trenton wasn't happy that his sister was heading to Butte with Cole, but the tension between the two was enough to keep him silent. He didn't know what was wrong between the couple, but it grieved him. Dianne and Cole were like the opposite sides of a coin, and he couldn't imagine one being much good without the other. In fact, he'd often been encouraged to hope that there might one day be true love for him, in watching his sister with Cole. But just as such thoughts filled his head, Trenton's heart reminded him that his past would probably forestall any chance of marriage and family. He would have to content himself with his sister's family — in being a good uncle.

With that in mind, he promised to care for the ranch and look out for the women and children, even as Dianne had instructed Ardith on Micah and Luke's care. Such reasonability seemed a far cry from his lawless days.

I wonder what ol' Jerry would think of me now, Trenton considered as thoughts of the outlaw gang came to mind. He pushed the images aside. They were gone — a thing of the past. They couldn't hurt him now. . . . Well, at least he hoped they couldn't.

Cole and Dianne weren't gone even three days when Trenton's relative peace was disrupted by Portia Langford. Somehow he'd known she would be his greatest source of frustration.

"I want to go to Bozeman," she announced.

"No." Trenton continued looking at the week-old paper in front of him, hoping the annoying woman would disappear.

"You can't tell me no. I have a right to go to Bozeman. Cole said my father is returning there this week. I want to be there."

Trenton put the paper down and stared up into the haughty exotic face. There was no denying that Portia Langford was a beauty. Fortunately for Trenton, he knew her beauty ran no deeper than her skin. "No one has time to ride you over to Bozeman. If you want to take a horse and make your own way, be my guest." He lifted the paper again and tried to ignore her.

"You really ought to treat me with more respect."

"I really ought to ask my sister to send you packing."

155

"For a man with a troubled past — one that no one knows much about," Portia said sarcastically, "I wouldn't be inclined to make enemies."

Trenton felt a chill run up his spine. He lowered the paper once again and put it aside. "What are you talking about?"

Portia simpered, her brows rising ever so slightly. "My, my. Now we plan to be civilized."

"I'm not planning to be anything at all — especially civilized. Not when it comes to you."

"I suppose one couldn't expect good manners from a bank robber."

Trenton jumped to his feet and crossed the room to where Portia stood. "I don't know what you're talking about, but I'd advise you to be cautious."

"Oh, don't play games with me, Mr. Chadwick. I had you investigated long ago. I know all about your past. About the gambling and the banks — the Wilson gang you ran with. I know that and much, much more."

Trenton held his anger in check. He kept his gaze fixed on her, knowing he was making her uncomfortable in his silence. How she'd managed to learn so much about his past was a mystery. She said she'd had him investigated, but how much did she really know? And did she have any proof that could bring his past crashing down around his future?

"I don't think you'll be troubling me," Portia said, her voice not sounding quite as sure as it had only moments earlier.

"And I don't think you'll be troubling me," Trenton said in a menacing tone. "Not if you don't want to have to keep looking over your shoulder at every turn." There wasn't much to back his threat up with except for the determination to keep his family from knowing the truth. "You've overplayed your hand, Mrs. Langford. You can't possibly think that I'd let you share this kind of nonsense with my family."

She paled. It was ever so slight, but Trenton knew he'd made his point. There was no time for further discussion, however. A knock at the front door left them both realizing they'd been too engrossed to even hear a rider approach.

Trenton went to the door and opened it. Portia was right behind him.

"Where's Selby?" the man demanded.

Trenton was taken aback at the anger in his tone. "I beg your pardon?"

"Cole Selby. Where is he?"

Trenton studied the stocky man for a moment. "He's not here right now. Maybe I can help you. I'm Dianne Selby's brother. I'm overseeing the ranch in their absence."

"Are you also overseeing the thievery of cattle by your boys?"

"It's Mr. Chester Lawrence, isn't it?" Portia asked as she pressed closer. "I believe we've met, but it's been a long, long while."

Lawrence nodded. "I remember meeting you, ma'am. My complaint ain't with you."

"Mr. Lawrence, I have no idea who you are or what your trouble is all about," Trenton said, standing his ground.

"My trouble is that Diamond V hands are stealing my cattle. You may think it fine to round up cattle that don't belong to you, but I won't stand for it."

"If any of your cattle have managed to get in with our herd, you're welcome to cut them out. We'll be moving to winter pasture before long, and it'll be easy enough to recognize your brand."

"I'm sure you've already rebranded them," the man replied sarcastically. "I'm telling you, I'll see you all hanged as cattle thieves if I don't get my stock back today. I'm heading into Bozeman, and I'll come back with a posse if need be."

Portia put her hand on Mr. Lawrence's arm. "I'm so pleased you remember me."

She batted her lashes and smiled coyly — just like she used to do with Ned. "You're heading to Bozeman, did you say?"

Trenton's blood boiled. He wasn't sure who he was madder at — Portia for reminding him of the past or Lawrence for his lies.

Chester immediately became captivated with the woman, giving Trenton time to think. Portia continued her flirtatious actions, leisurely touching Chester's forearm and then his chest.

"I thought you were about the most handsome man I'd ever laid eyes on when we met in town. I do hope you'll consider setting aside your argument with the Selbys — at least long enough for us to get better acquainted. I'm just dying for a little ride over to Bozeman, and no one here has time to take me. My dear papa is due back at the fort, and I do so long to see him. Perhaps you would consider taking me?"

"Well, I might be able to help you out," Lawrence said, his tone considerably softened. He turned to face Trenton, though his voice lost a bit of its angry edge. "This isn't over. Your boys had better watch themselves."

"Did it ever occur to you that maybe Indians or no-accounts are running off with your herd? The Diamond V has plenty of its own cattle. We don't need yours," Trenton answered with certainty.

"You can manage this later," Portia said in an almost whisper as she leaned closer to Lawrence. "He'll still be here next week." She smiled, seducing the man with her eyes. Trenton had seen it all before. "Now . . . about getting me to Bozeman."

"I'll . . . I'll be back," Lawrence said, stumbling over his words. It was clear he had been completely drawn in by Portia's spell.

For the moment, Trenton couldn't have cared less about the couple. Let them go for their ride — let them do whatever they would do. What he wouldn't stand for were threats. Not from Portia. And certainly not from some no-account rancher.

"Who was that?" Levi asked as he came up behind Trenton.

"Chester Lawrence. One of the area ranchers. Says we're stealing his cattle."

Levi shook his head. "Takes all kinds, I guess."

Trenton closed the door. "I guess so. Portia's trying to talk him into taking her to Bozeman. I hope she succeeds."

"It wouldn't hurt my feelings none either," Levi agreed. "She keeps tryin' to stir up trouble among the boys. Always flirting and causing them to argue amongst themselves. I know she has no interest in any of them, but I think she enjoys the fight that comes after she gets them all mad at each other."

"That's her way. She's like nothing I've ever seen. She stood here cozying up to Mr. Lawrence, and she only met him once. She wanted to get to Bozeman, however, so she didn't care what it took. That's what bothers me most about the woman. She'll do anything to get her own way." Thoughts of her threats still rang in his ears.

"Oh, by the way, Billy Joe and Gabe are back from Virginia City. They've brought this mail." Levi handed a stack of letters to Trenton. "I've got to get back out there and help with the supplies." Levi exited out the front door, leaving it open just long enough for Trenton to spy Portia still clinging to Mr. Lawrence. She appeared to be talking fast and furious.

Trenton shuffled through the letters in his hands. Most were addressed to Dianne, but one, surprisingly enough, was addressed to him. It appeared to be from R. E. Langford, Ned's father.

Amazed at this, Trenton quickly put the other letters aside and opened the missive. Scanning the two-page letter, Trenton felt uneasiness wash over him.

" 'I have reason to believe,' " Trenton read aloud very slowly, " 'that Ned's wife played a hand in his death. Dare I say the word murder?' "

Trenton looked up, his teeth clenched in anger. "I knew it. I knew she was up to no good."

He continued reading. " 'I would be very grateful if you could help to gather evidence that might see Portia convicted. I will pay you well. . . .' "

The rest of the letter was immaterial. Trenton burned at the thought that his fears for Ned had been well founded. If Ned's own father believed Portia responsible . . . Trenton intended to see her pay for her deeds.

"I just knew you'd understand," Portia told Chester. "These Selbys are so used to being in charge that they don't have much concern for the needs of other people."

"Why is Selby gone?"

Portia was already bored with the conversation, but she sensed this man could very well be the answer to all of her problems. "He and Dianne have gone to bring back her brother. The man was a soldier and was injured in a recent Indian battle."

"How long will he be gone?"

"That I can't say," Portia answered honestly. "I suppose it will depend on the weather and Indians."

"Look, how about I promise to take you to Bozeman by the end of the week? I need to tend to some matters that won't wait."

Portia grinned as she turned to go back into the house.

Chester returned a smile that was sly and confident.

CHAPTER 10

Butte was rapidly becoming an impressive town. Already the potential for growth was being realized daily in the form of new mining interests and businesses. Dianne had no idea there was such prosperity to be had in Montana. It was by far and away the biggest city she'd been to in some time.

"We're supposed to meet the judge in ten minutes," Cole said matter-of-factly. He put his pocket watch away and turned to pick up his hat.

Dianne grimaced at his cold tone. He'd barely spoken to her the entire trip. "I'm ready," she said, adjusting her hat of plum and black jets. It nicely matched her traveling suit. "And Zane will join us for supper, right?" She tried hard to sound light-hearted and carefree. She hoped to draw Cole out of his stupor without resorting to an out-and-out apology.

"That's what his note said."

"I wish he'd stayed here to meet us instead of gallivanting off with some stranger."

"Guess he wasn't as worried about seeing you as you were about seeing him." Cole stared at her with a stoic expression.

"That's hardly fair. Zane didn't know I'd be here." Dianne picked up her bag, trying hard to ignore her frustration. "I suppose I'll see him soon enough."

They headed to their appointment with Judge Adams. The man had been recommended to Cole in Virginia City as someone who might be able to influence officials and see Koko and the children left to the sanctity of their home. Dianne could only pray that the man would be willing to help; after all, prevailing thoughts were not kind when it came to the Indians.

After a short walk, they arrived at exactly eleven o'clock and were ushered into a plush office where a balding man of some girth sat behind a massive mahogany desk.

A tall, thin man announced their arrival, and Cole stepped forward and said, "Judge Adams, I'm Cole Selby, and this is my wife."

The man struggled to his feet and extended his short pudgy hand. "Glad to meet you, Selby. What can I do for you?"

Dianne wasn't used to being ignored, nor of having business brought so quickly to the forefront. Nevertheless, she took a seat when Cole motioned her to do so. No sense making a scene when this man might very well be able to help them.

"We have a delicate situation," Cole began, his voice firm and authoritative. "I have a ranch in the Madison Valley south of old Gallatin City." Dianne bristled at the way he left her out of the conversation but held her tongue. She fixed her attention to the rows of books lined in a stately manner on fine oak shelves behind the judge. It was a wonder that anyone could ever read so many books.

The judge nodded, catching Dianne's attention. "I see. Take a seat and explain the circumstance that has brought you here." Both men sat and Judge Adams waved to the man who'd shown them into the office. "Take care of those papers, Simmons. I'll speak with you later."

The man backed out from the office and closed the doors. The judge motioned to Cole. "Please continue."

"The ranch was inherited by my wife upon her uncle's death. Her uncle's wife and children were not able to inherit, due to their being part Blackfoot, so he made my wife a partner in the ranch before his death."

"Wise choice. So what seems to be the problem? Is someone questioning the validity of this transfer?"

Cole shook his head. "Not at all. The problem is the Indian wife and children. The army showed up a few months past while on route elsewhere. They were insistent on relocating the woman and her children to a reservation."

"I'm not sure I understand the problem."

"The problem," Dianne interrupted, unable to remain silent, "is that the ranch is every bit as much their home as it is mine. No one should be allowed to force my aunt and cousins from this home."

Both Cole and Judge Adams looked at her momentarily, then the judge returned his gaze to Cole. "Is it your desire to have this woman and her children remain on the ranch?"

"It is," Cole said, meeting the man's gaze. "They are good people. We made my wife's uncle a promise to see to their care. I'm concerned that the army will return and insist on taking them. There is also the complication of another child, the result of a torture imposed on my sister-in-law. I wouldn't wish to see her removed either."

"The matter isn't an easy one. The government simply has no interest in extending kindnesses to the Indians. Little Big Horn was just a year ago, and right in our own backyard we faced the Nez Perce as they defeated our soldiers at Big Hole. No sir, it's a difficult time to see any consideration given to these people."

"But she's done nothing wrong. She's half white, her children are three-quarters," Dianne protested. "My niece is half Sioux, half white, but it certainly wasn't her choice to be so. My sister was attacked and the baby resulted. She loves the child, even though she hates the baby's father. Surely you wouldn't see a baby torn from the mother who loves her?"

"Ma'am, I am unconcerned with the maternal bonds of your sister." He gave a slight roll of his gaze to the ceiling, then refocused on Cole with a sigh. "Women are such emotional creatures. I had no thought to deal with one today."

"I had no idea that she would accompany me, or I would have let you know," Cole said, as if he were just as exasperated.

"I do apologize for my outburst," Dianne said, realizing that her opinion was of no import to the judge. She worried that he might turn them away, however, in his disgust of her actions. With that in mind, she knew she must be still and allow Cole to speak on Koko's behalf. She folded her gloved hands and determined in her heart to remain silent, no matter the outcome.

The judge leaned toward Cole. "Tell me about your ranch, sir."

The men continued their discussion as if completely forgetting the important issue at hand. Dianne couldn't focus on their trivial chat about herd sizes and growing communities. The events of the day, set against her fight with Cole, were slowly wearing her down. Perhaps she'd been spoiled by her uncle's free hand. Bram had believed her capable of most anything, and perhaps because of their isolation he hadn't concerned himself with her actions. Her own father had always given her a great deal of freedom, but then she had been younger — much younger.

The world doesn't seem as lenient, Dianne reasoned as she tried to sort through her thoughts. Portia often talked of life in the East and how prim and proper women conducted themselves. Dianne had generally commented on how here in the West women were expected to be as hardy and helpful as their mates, but perhaps civilization was coming to the West. And perhaps with it, women would be relegated to having no say over the matters that concerned them.

"I do wish I could offer you something more substantial," the judge said, getting to his feet.

Cole rose as well. "I understand. Fear is a powerful motivator." He extended his hand to Dianne. She looked at him for a moment, then allowed him to help her up.

"Mrs. Selby, I do hope you will enjoy safety in your journey home," the judge said graciously.

Dianne smiled. "Thank you."

They were just stepping into the foyer when an impressive man of short stature entered from outside. "Simmons," he commanded, "I need to see Conrad." He glanced up, rubbing his bushy goatee. "I do apologize," he said, looking directly at Dianne and then Cole. "I had no thought that Judge Adams would be otherwise entertained."

"Take no concern of it, Mr. Clark," Adams announced as he joined them. "These are the Selbys from the Madison Valley. Mr. and Mrs. Selby, this is William Clark — the most important man in Butte."

Clark smiled. "Some would protest that remark, but I'm not one of them."

Dianne was amazed at the man's comment, but even more taken by his eyes. They were cold and penetrating.

"And what brings you to our town, Mr. Selby?" Clark questioned.

Cole had no chance to answer. "They came on a matter of Indian affairs, if you would," Judge Adams declared. "Seems the wife has an aunt who is a half-breed. The soldiers want to move her and her children to a reservation. I was just explaining that it's difficult to muster much sympathy these days for any Indian."

"Very true. But then again, most anything can be had for a price," Clark replied, his tone calculating.

Dianne met his gaze and quickly turned away. She felt a sense of discomfort that left her wishing they'd never met Mr. Clark. Cole took hold of her arm and steered her around the forthright little man.

"Thank you for seeing us, Judge Adams. Good day, Mr. Clark."

Outside the judge's office Dianne shook her head. "He made me very uncomfortable."

"William Clark is known for that," Cole said matter-of-factly.

"I didn't realize you knew anything about him."

Cole looked over, his expression serious.

171

"There's a lot you don't realize."

Half an hour later Dianne sat across from Cole at a nearby restaurant. She sipped creamed coffee and wondered what was to be done next. The future was very questionable, and a certain amount of fear pushed through her hard facade, leaving her feeling shaken and doubtful. The last thing she wanted was for Cole to be her enemy, yet wounded pride seemed a hard obstacle to overcome.

Cole's earlier statement had given her cause to reevaluate her attitude. He was right. There was a lot she didn't know — a great deal that she didn't give Cole credit for. It was difficult at best to know how to resolve matters between them, especially when she'd proven just how little trust she had in her husband.

"I'm sorry we couldn't get help for Koko," Cole said.

Dianne looked up. "Me too." She put down her cup and squared her shoulders. "I'm sorry."

Cole leaned back in his chair. "What are you saying?"

She swallowed the lump in her throat. "I don't want you to be the enemy. There are enough enemies around us to last a lifetime."

"Agreed."

"I was wrong to force my way on this trip. I was wrong to question you and to hold it against you when you didn't give in." Dianne leaned forward. "I feel like so much has changed in my life. I feel like just yesterday people honestly admired my ability to think, to offer sound counsel. People came to me, and it made me feel important."

"You are important," he said softly.

"But I don't feel important. You run the ranch without ever talking to me about what's happening. Uncle Bram used to bring me in on every discussion of importance."

"But that was before you were a wife and mother."

"I realize that, but I didn't stop having a brain just because I got married and became a mother."

Cole grinned. "No one said you did."

Dianne shook her head. "You don't understand what I'm trying to say. Today in the judge's office, I felt like I was less than the dirt on his rugs. He didn't care one whit what I had to say. He acted as though I was nothing more than an annoyance."

"I suppose there are many men in the world who feel that way about women," he admitted, "but I'm not one of them."

"But you make me feel like you are."

"I thought I was easing your burden," he said, reaching out to touch her hand. "I didn't want you to have to work as hard as you had in the past. I want to spoil and pamper you. I'd like to give you a life of comfort."

It was Dianne's turn to smile. "But that isn't realistic in this country — neither is it what I really want. I like working at your side. I like feeling needed. I love mothering your children, but I also like being your wife."

"Then don't try to take my job from me."

Dianne frowned. "What do you mean?"

"I'm the protector and provider for the family now. Not you. You struggled and suffered and kept the ranch and your family together, but now it's my responsibility. We can't both take on the same duties." He paused and looked her in the eye. "Don't you trust me to do a good job?"

Dianne realized the truth in what he was saying. Faith had talked to her about the very same thing. Was it a matter of trust? She'd thought at first that perhaps it was, but now she wasn't so certain. *No,* she thought, *it's pride — pure and simple.* "I trust you."

"Then can we find a way to make things right between us?"

"I want to, Cole. More than you'll ever know. But please don't leave me out. I can't bear it. My brother knows more about what's happening on the Diamond V than I do. I don't want things to be that way. I need to know what's happening. I care about that ranch more than anyone could possibly understand. I gave my uncle a promise, and I have to see it through."

"I understand . . . maybe for the first time," Cole admitted. "We'll start over and do things different."

Dianne looked deeply into his eyes. "Thank you. I do love you. I hated myself for hurting you."

He shook his head. "Don't. Marriage is hard work. We both have to give and take. I wasn't so considerate with the giving part, at least not in the way you needed me to be. I'll try to be more understanding, because I love you too."

That evening Zane joined them at the same restaurant where Cole and Dianne had made their peace. He looked awful in Dianne's estimation. He was much thinner than the last time she'd seen him, and he walked with a cane and a noticeable limp.

175

"Oh, Zane, I thought I might never see you again!" Dianne said as she rushed to embrace him.

"I didn't know you were coming," Zane said as he held Dianne briefly.

"I sort of imposed myself upon this trip," Dianne said, pulling back. She grinned. "I'm sure that's hard to believe."

The corners of Zane's lips turned upward. "Yeah, I can't imagine you being pushy." He turned to greet Cole. "It's good to see you. Thanks for coming, but it may be for naught."

"What are you talking about?" Dianne questioned.

"Let's get some dinner, and I'll explain. I've asked someone to join us. I hope you don't mind. He'll be here shortly."

Dianne tried hard not to show her disappointment. "Who?"

"The man's name is Marcus Daly."

"I've heard of him," Cole said. "He's earned himself quite a name in mining. I've read that he's a master at assessing veins. He's made some great choices of properties. The Emma Mine in Utah put him on the map for silver."

Zane nodded enthusiastically, while Dianne stood back in dumbfounded silence. When had Cole had time to learn all of this?

176

"Daly's found silver here as well. He has property on the Rainbow lode, and it's brought in no small amount of silver over the last year," Zane told them.

"Especially the Alice mine," Cole added.

"Yes, that little beauty has proved itself quite sufficiently."

"I had no idea either of you were so interested in mining," Dianne said, finally finding her tongue.

They were seated at a table in clear view of the door before Zane continued. "I wasn't sure what I wanted to do with myself once I left the army."

"But . . . now you do?" Dianne asked hesitantly.

"Yes."

She couldn't imagine anyone choosing to mine holes in the ground over spending their days in the open mountain valleys. "You want to mine for silver?"

Zane shook his head. "No. Not at all. I've decided to start a freight business, and I was kind of hoping you and Cole might help me with some financial backing. I'd like to start big. Maybe bigger than I should, but the work is here."

"What kind of work?" Cole asked.

"Hauling ore. Without a railroad, the only way to get it to Utah, where Daly's investors are located, is by wagon."

Dianne couldn't help but think of the risk. "Wouldn't it be dangerous?"

Zane held his cup up as a waiter offered coffee. "No more so than anything else. Everything has an element of danger to it. Most of the route is on the old Corrine-Virginia City Road — the one Morgan and I used to freight. I know that road like the back of my hand and can learn the rest of the route as I go."

"But surely the railroad will come to Butte," Cole said thoughtfully. "I seem to remember a line that was started this direction back in '71."

"Yes, but the Panic of 1873 shut it down and the supporters have had no luck getting it started again. Even the territorial government seems unconcerned with pushing it forward."

"No doubt because the railroad is headed for Butte instead of Helena," Cole said with great amusement.

"Probably so. Oh, there's Marcus. Let me introduce you." Zane got to his feet and limped to the entry. He spoke for a moment with the stocky man before heading back to the table.

Dianne couldn't help but wonder if Marcus Daly were anything like William Clark, but as they approached, she could see he was nothing like the other man. Smiling broadly, Daly extended his hand and greeted them heartily.

"I'm pleased to be meetin' ya. Zane's told me a good deal about ya."

Dianne was surprised by his Irish lilt. He seemed to be such a simple, unpretentious man. Burly and beefy, yet charmingly open, Marcus Daly made Dianne feel welcome.

"Mrs. Selby, yar quite a handsome woman. Yar a lucky man, Mr. Selby," he announced as he took a chair.

"Please call me Cole."

Daly shook Cole's hand. "I'll be doin' that."

"I've been explaining about my desire to start a freighting business," Zane said as he sat down again. "My brother-in-law is already impressed with your exploits. He's read much about you."

"Bah!" Daly said, shaking his head. "Probably lies." He grinned. "The only thing they ever seem to get right is that I'm Irish."

They all laughed at this and settled into a comfortable conversation after ordering their supper. Dianne began to see how important the new business venture was to Zane as he continued to talk about the situation in Butte. She knew she'd lost him again — and just when she thought he might come home for a time.

Of course, the ranch has never really been his home, she remembered. *He was never as content there as I. Uncle Bram knew this too.* It was the reason Bram had never considered leaving the ranch to either Zane or Morgan. Dianne determined within her heart not to begrudge her brother his happiness. She loved having her family close but knew it would never please her to have them miserable just to make her happy.

By the time supper concluded, Cole was eager to see Zane started in his new business, as was Dianne. It still hurt to realize he would remain far away, but Dianne was certain it was the right thing for Zane.

"If you can spare your brother, we have some unfinished business," Daly announced as they walked outside.

"I'll see you in the morning," Zane said, turning to Dianne. "You won't leave first thing will you?"

She looked to Cole and smiled. "I suppose you'd need to consult Cole on that issue."

Cole smiled. "We'll stick around a day or two. Dianne needs to have time with you, and I'd like to hear about your fight with the Nez Perce."

Zane frowned. "It's not worth talking about. I'm just glad to be done with all of that." He kissed Dianne on the cheek. "I'll see you at breakfast."

Dianne watched him limp away, his cane clicking in step with Marcus Daly. Dianne couldn't help but wonder at the wounds Zane had suffered. She hardly knew anything about what had happened to him and only now realized that the subject had not come up over dinner.

Cole put his arm around Dianne and pulled her close. He bent to whisper against her ear, "Well, it's just you and me."

Dianne shivered with excitement at the tone of his voice. She looked up at him. "It's the first time we've been alone since before Luke was born."

"I was just thinking that. Thinking, too, about those nights on the trail that we wasted."

She grinned. "I'm all for making up lost time."

He laughed out loud. "My, but you're a brazen little thing." He picked up the pace, pulling her along. "I'm glad I married a gal who knows her mind. Yes, ma'am. Mighty glad."

CHAPTER 11

Ardith watched Winona toddle around the open meadow with Rusty, one of the ranch dogs. Rusty was at her side every step of the way, playing the role of the baby's protector.

Winona could probably do with a protector, Ardith mused. The child seemed positively fearless with her dark-eyed gaze exploring every hole, rock, and blade of dying grass. It was hard to believe that the baby she had so despised during pregnancy had become a lifeline to Ardith in the aftermath of her life with the Sioux. Ardith had always feared that every time she gazed upon Winona, all of the bad memories and experiences would come back to haunt her, but it hadn't happened.

It had been over a year since the soldiers, and subsequently Zane, had found them at Little Big Horn. Over a year since Walks in the Dark had been able to hurt her physically. He still managed at times to hurt her emotionally, but the damage was less and less as time went by. Ardith was learning quickly how to push aside those memories. Dianne had talked to her about a verse in the Bible that spoke of taking thoughts captive.

Just as he took me captive, I will take captive those memories, Ardith determined. *He cannot hurt me anymore.*

She kept telling herself that, but it was hard to accept it as fact. After all, she had no idea where Walks in the Dark had taken himself. He might have followed her here, although reasoning told her it wasn't true. She would never have been worth that much to him. He'd only traded for her because she'd offended him by rejecting his advances. His forced marriage was only a means to inflict his anger and hostilities upon her.

"Mama . . . Mama," Winona called.

Ardith smiled. The sixteen-month-old had only recently started talking. Ardith had actually worried that something was severely wrong with her daughter, but then without warning Winona began babbling. She now said *mama, doggy,* and *horsey,* although that came out sounding more like "sorsey." There were a variety of other less understandable words, but Ardith knew it wouldn't be long before Winona would make herself clear.

"She sure likes playing outside," Levi said as he came up from behind.

Ardith jumped up. He'd startled her and she knew the fear was evident in her expression. She tried quickly to relax her face, but Levi was already apologizing.

"I'm sorry. I figured you might have heard me coming."

"No. I was deep in thought."

He smiled. "Good thoughts, I hope."

"Thoughts of Winona are always good," Ardith said. She pulled her heavy knit shawl closer. The weather had been warm of late, but one never knew when the bitter north winds would strike. This time, however, it wasn't the cold that made her seek the wrap's warmth.

She was nervous under Levi's scrutiny. The man was handsome, there was no denying that, but his interest in her over the last year had made Ardith only too aware of what could never be.

"She's such a strong and healthy girl," Levi said, turning his gaze away from Ardith. "Pretty, too, just like her mama."

Winona came running toward them, and to Ardith's surprise, she threw herself at

Levi's legs. Rusty wasn't far behind and began barking out greetings as he joined the trio. Levi laughed and lifted the child into the air. Winona giggled with glee as he tossed her high and caught her again.

Ardith tried not to let her discomfort overcome her. She worried that too much acceptance of Levi's interactions with Winona might give Levi the wrong impression.

Levi held Winona in his arms and brushed back the blue-black hair from her face. "Are you having fun?"

"No!" Winona said enthusiastically.

That was her newest word and seemed to work interchangeably for acceptance or rejection of whatever came her way.

"No?" Levi asked, tickling her side. "Don't you mean yes?"

"No!"

Ardith couldn't help but smile. "That's her new all-purpose word."

He looked at her and grinned in that mischievous way that made her heart skip a beat. "Kind of like when everything was a doggy?"

Ardith felt her cheeks grow warm. "Yes," she managed to say, but she found additional words were impossible.

"It's going to turn cold," Levi said, placing Winona on the ground. She immediately took off running, Rusty faithfully at her side.

"We're moving the cattle to winter pastures day after tomorrow. I'll be staying out all winter with Gabe and a couple of the other boys."

Ardith nodded, not having any idea how to respond. She knew she'd miss him, but she also knew she couldn't tell him that. She focused on her hands, hoping to steady her nerves.

"I'll miss seeing you and Winona," Levi said softly. "I know you probably don't feel the same, but I've really enjoyed our few talks."

Ardith knew she had to be firm and put an end to this. "Levi, you mustn't care about me," she said matter-of-factly. She looked up and met his dark brown eyes and gentle expression. Another woman — a less worldly woman — might easily lose herself in those eyes . . . those dark lashes . . . that sweet smile.

"Why can't I care about you?"

"It isn't fitting, and you know it."

Levi turned to fully face her. "I don't know anything of the kind. Are you interested in someone else?"

"No!" Ardith declared. She looked to where Winona was playing and tried to think of how best to explain herself. The truth seemed so evident, but apparently Levi didn't understand. Maybe he didn't realize the details of the past. They seemed out in the open for everyone as far as Ardith was concerned, but perhaps Levi, in his simplistic way, didn't comprehend.

"Ardith, won't you please talk to me and tell me why I can't care for you and Winona?"

She licked her dry lips. "Levi, the past — my past — isn't very good. I'm not . . . well . . . I'm not acceptable to a great many people."

"Then those people are crazy."

"No they aren't. Don't you see?" She shook her head and started to walk away, but Levi reached out and took hold of her arm. She looked up, fighting to hold back tears. "You have to understand the truth, Levi. Winona is my daughter — not by choice, but by force. I was forced into a marriage that I never wanted nor accepted."

"An Indian marriage. So what? It doesn't mean a thing."

Ardith shook her head. "I'm not pure. I'm not worth your bother. I wouldn't be accepted or wanted for any decent thing by other white men, and their reasoning is the way the rest of the world sees it too."

"I don't see it that way. Besides, no one

has to know what happened to you."

"They'll see Winona and know. She's my daughter, and I won't deny her."

"I'd never ask you to," he said indignantly. "Besides, there are bound to be other people who feel the same way."

"I seriously doubt it," she said, looking back to the ground. "When my brother found me . . . well, the soldiers were so ugly. They thought I was Sioux and wanted me dead because of what the Indians had done to their friends. When they found out I was white, they all said I would be better off dead. I thought Zane was going to have to fight every last one of them."

"I'd fight for you too."

"Just being friends with me has probably already caused that very thing."

"No, it hasn't. Folks here are truly glad to have you back. They don't think you'd be better off dead. You know, I was with Dianne quite a bit after you were lost. She blamed herself for not being quick enough to catch up with you. She felt so guilty. . . . I cared a great deal about her then, the same as she cares a great deal about you."

"My family may be able to forgive the past — forgive Winona her heritage — but others won't be that kind. Remember the soldiers who came here last summer? They wanted to take Winona." She started walking to where Winona and Rusty were playing. Levi followed her step for step.

"You can't run away from this. I want to be your friend. I'd like to be more than your friend. I'm leaving for the winter, and I'd like to know you'll still be here come spring — that you'll not give your heart to someone else."

"I won't be giving my heart to anyone," Ardith stated without emotion. She lifted Winona into her arms and turned back to Levi. "I can't let anyone bear the burden of loving Winona and me."

"You don't get to have any say over that, Ardith. You can't be keepin' a person from loving someone."

"Yes I can. I must." She began walking back toward the corrals, praying that Levi wouldn't follow her.

"I don't care!" he yelled after her.

Ardith hurried back to where he stood. "Don't be so loud — everyone will hear you."

He grinned. "I don't care who else hears me so long as you hear what I have to say."

Winona reached out for Levi, but Ardith pulled her away. "I don't need to hear you to know that what you want is impossible. My past makes it impossible."

"I don't care about your past, Miss Chadwick," he said, pulling her into his arms. Winona wriggled between them, but still he held them tight. "The past wasn't your choice, but the future is." With that he stunned Ardith by kissing her long and passionately.

When he let her go, Levi stared at her for a moment, his expression serious. "Maybe that will give you something to think about over the long lonely winter." He walked away, leaving Ardith to watch after him. It was all she could do to keep from running after him.

When did I lose my heart to him? When did I let him break through the wall that I'd put around my heart? She couldn't begin to reason away what had just happened, and for once the tidy stoic life she'd made for herself was crumbling, as if on sinking sand.

"Papa!" Winona declared.

Ardith looked at her daughter in disbelief. Now was certainly no time to learn that word. No doubt Winona had picked it up from Dianne's children.

"Hush, baby," Ardith said, pulling her daughter close. "Levi's not your papa. He can't be your papa."

Morgan Chadwick stood up and surveyed

190

the area around him. Below him a large waterfall swirled and plunged into the heart of a valley too beautiful to imagine. Tall pines lined the canyon walls, seemingly growing right out of the granite itself. This area, called Mount Lookout to some and Prospect Point to others, was fast becoming a favorite for visitors. Ever since President Grant set this land aside for a national park in 1872, Morgan had watched people flock to this view. There was even talk of establishing a viewing platform, but he hoped they wouldn't disturb the natural beauty by placing human touches on the scenery. It was magnificent in its purity and perfection, and he loved it like he loved no other land.

All of his life Morgan had felt called to explore unknown territories. He'd read with great interest the exploits of Lewis and Clark as they'd traveled the Missouri River to explore the Louisiana Purchase. With every book or paper he could lay his hands on, Morgan had known an exhilarating thrill of discovery. He'd even taken up reading accounts of John Jacob Astor's Pacific Fur Company and the founding of Astoria, along with accounts from other explorers like Nathaniel Wyeth and Joseph Walker. In fact, Morgan still wanted to go west to California and see the giant sequoias that

Walker spoke of on his journey in 1833.

He'd once tried to talk his twin brother, Zane, into setting up their own exploration company. "We could work for the government," he told his brother with great enthusiasm. "We could go into the unknown territory and create maps and lead parties for those who wanted to study the terrain."

But Zane had shown no interest. He had agreed with his brother that going west sounded like a great plan, but not to work for the government or anyone else. But when they'd finally come west on the wagon train from Missouri, Zane had ended up with the government after all.

Funny, Morgan mused, *Zane never seemed like the soldier type. I can't imagine his taking orders from anyone and living with such strict regulations. I could never live like that.*

But Morgan was glad for the army nevertheless. The Indian conflicts had brought trouble to the Yellowstone area. Only a few months earlier, in August, the Nez Perce had stormed through, taking hostages and killing and wounding many of the visitors who'd come to see the park.

Morgan had been with his partners, Jackson DeShazer and Marley Turnquist, in a southern section of the park. They'd been finishing up a summer of mapping when word came that there was Indian trouble in the area.

The Nez Perce hadn't stayed long, and by the time the men had returned to lend their aid and arms, the Indians had moved on to the east. Naturally, most of the visitors had been greatly discouraged and horrified at what had happened. After all, they'd seen some of their companions slain and their camps and supplies stolen. These were troubled times, Morgan reasoned, but problems were bound to come and go. People couldn't expect to come to such an isolated, exotic location and not face some kind of hardship. Why, he'd endured blizzards and earthquakes, Indians and tourists. There was always some challenge to be met.

Morgan sighed. He hated to leave the grandeur of this place, but he'd promised Jackson he'd be back to camp by nightfall. They were to make a decision by the end of the week as to where they would winter. Already snow had fallen on the mountains and the temperature had dropped. It wouldn't be long before the entire area was covered in a thick blanket of white, and by that time Marley hoped to have his crew settled elsewhere.

"But where?" Morgan wondered aloud.

Heading back down to his camp and

horse, Morgan was reminded of the distance in time and miles from his family. He'd been a poor correspondent. Time just had a way of slipping by without his notice. He would completely forget the days of the week, and if it weren't for keeping meticulous records, he might not even realize the months.

But just as quickly as family came to mind and Morgan determined in his heart to write, a whiff of pine or the scent of grizzly drew him back into the hypnotic spell of Yellowstone and he again forgot his obligations. It was as if the wilderness took possession of him. He couldn't explain it — he didn't even try. This was home, and no other place felt the same.

"Dianne will forgive me," he murmured as he finished loading the last of his supplies on his horse. "She forgave Trenton for all those years without word." Thinking of his older brother made Morgan feel a slight tug to head home. Maybe he would. Maybe he'd winter on the ranch. Maybe he'd suggest they all winter on the ranch. After all, Dianne would probably welcome all three of them with open arms if it meant seeing him again.

"I'll mention it to Marley," Morgan announced. His horse whinnied, as if confirming the plan. He mounted and patted the horse's neck before taking one last look at the beautiful scene. He sighed. "I suppose we must head back."

Morgan returned to a camp in the middle of chaos. Jackson was sitting outside the large tent they all shared. Muttering in between taking draws on his pipe, the normally easygoing redhead was not a happy man.

"Well, Jackson, I'm back as I promised."

Jackson glanced up at Morgan and shielded his eyes. "You'll probably want to turn that old nag right around and head back."

Morgan dismounted and laughed. "What in the world would make you say . . ." His words trailed off at the sound of a woman's voice coming from the tent.

"No!" she yelled. "You're the one who doesn't understand."

"Tourist?" Morgan asked Jackson.

"Hardly. Might be a whole sight easier if it were."

The woman blew out of the tent like a west wind ahead of a thunderstorm. She was a striking little thing with blond curls bouncing down her back. Marley Turnquist followed, raising his hands to the skies as if for divine intervention.

"You're as stubborn as the day is long!" he called after the woman.

Morgan stood still, mesmerized by the young woman. She was decked out in some kind of riding outfit and straw bonnet, but it was the determination and fire in her expression that held him spellbound.

"Maybe it's my Swedish blood," she said sarcastically as she turned back to face Marley. "For years you allowed me to follow you around on your trips. You didn't worry about what people thought then."

"You were a child then," the older man declared. Marley Turnquist was only forty-five, but he seemed to age before Morgan's eyes as he dealt with the angry young woman.

"You're twenty years old," Marley continued.

"I'll be twenty-one in January," the woman protested. "I'm old enough to decide what I want out of life, and this is it. I hate living in Chicago with Mother. And Anna has been impossible since she married Stanley Newcomer. Now all she and Mother want to do is see me married off to one of Anna's old beaus."

"It wouldn't hurt you to marry and settle down!"

"I'd rather eat a live grizzly bear with a

spoon!" Now she was really mad.

But then, too, so was Marley. Morgan watched as the man went nose to nose with the girl. "If you aren't careful, I'll see to it that you get your chance."

They stood in silence for a moment. Both were panting and oblivious to anyone else. Jackson looked up, his expression forlorn.

"They keep doing this," he said, pulling the pipe from his mouth. "Been at it now for about two hours." He looked like a man wishing for a means of escape.

"Who is she?"

Jackson never had a chance to reply.

"Angelina Turnquist," Marley said, waggling his finger at her, "you're going back."

"I'm staying here," she retorted, pressing forward enough that Marley had to lean back. "I worked too hard to get here, and if need be, I'll find someone else to camp with." She stormed back into the tent at this and Marley followed after, muttering a stream of obscenities such as Morgan had never heard.

Jackson got to his feet and pulled the pipe from his mouth. "Old trapper brought her here about noon. At first Marley was kind of tickled to see her, but then the fighting started and it ain't stopped."

"So that's his daughter. She's a pretty

little thing."

"Pretty? Did you see that dress she's wearing — if it can be called that. I ain't never seen a getup like it. I think she's wearin' trousers under that long coat."

Morgan grinned and shrugged. "Still, a fellow could lose his heart pretty easily to someone like her."

"I don't recommend losin' anything to that wild cat. She'll eat you for breakfast and spit you out by noon. No, sir. I wouldn't lose anything around her."

CHAPTER 12

"Marley, I think it's the best choice we have. After all, you said yourself that it looks like winter is going to close in here in the next couple of weeks," Morgan told his partner. "My sister has plenty of room. She's not going to care about a few more folks. We can winter there and have it easy for once. We can even set out and do some mapping in that area if we want to."

Marley nodded. "You're right. It's about the only sane choice. I've got no way to get Angelina back to her mother at this point. Not unless I want to ride down to catch the train, and that's a good two, maybe three weeks of hard travel."

Morgan was glad that Angelina was nowhere around to protest the decision being made without her. She was off bathing in one of the icy streams while poor Jackson stood guard in the distance. Morgan pitied anything or anyone who tried to harass Miss

Turnquist. The woman was an absolute storm waiting to unleash its fury. He grinned as he thought of her, however. She had a spirit that pleased Morgan through and through. It was probably why he'd fallen for her upon first sight. Now if he could spend the winter cooped up with her at the Diamond V, he might be able to convince Angelina to feel the same way.

"We can head out right away. We've got good weather so far," Morgan reminded. "We can put a good ten miles under our belts if we hurry."

Marley sighed. "Yup. Guess that's what we'll do. Sure hope you're right about your sister. My wife would never take to uninvited visitors wandering in."

"Dianne loves uninvited visitors. You just wait and see."

Dianne couldn't have been happier at the prospect of having Morgan home all winter. Zane's decision to remain in Butte had been such a disappointment, but this clearly made up for it.

Now that the Indian troubles had diminished somewhat and folks had begun to relax again, everyone at the ranch had gone back to his own quarters. The only remaining houseguest was Portia Langford, and even she was slated to leave after Christmas. Sam Brady, Portia's father, had written to say he would come and take her back to the fort two days before Christmas. Dianne planned to encourage Sam to stick around until after the holidays so the old soldier could have time to rest and enjoy family life away from the fort. Dianne didn't know if he'd go along with the idea, but she certainly hoped he would.

Portia pulled on stockings and secured them with a garter. Her thoughts were on her future. Her father was coming soon to take her back to Bozeman, only now she wasn't so sure she wanted to go. Living with the Selbys was convenient for her plans, and Mr. Lawrence had proven quite helpful.

She slipped her feet into delicate brocade shoes and grimaced. These were the last truly nice shoes she had. She thought of the trunks of beautiful clothes she'd left in Baltimore. If only old Mr. Langford hadn't been so difficult. His letters questioning Ned's death and demanding to have her relive Ned's suicide were most maddening.

"Stupid man," she muttered to herself.

Ned had been much too controlled by his father. She hadn't seen this early enough, unfortunately. Life in Baltimore had been a series of confrontations, but not between Ned and old Mr. Langford. Rather they had been between Portia and Ned's father.

He had constantly accused her of being a seeker of fortune. Portia had pointed out to him on more than one occasion that she was situated quite nicely in regard to financial need, but Langford never seemed convinced. By the time she found out he'd hired a man to investigate her and her bank account, Portia knew she was going to have to do something about her husband.

"Weaklings. All of them. Stupid and weak, just like all of the men in my life."

Trenton Chadwick came to mind. Now there was a useful man. Unfortunately, he hated her. Still, he was the kind of man Portia could at least admire. He hadn't cowered at her threats, but had countered with his own. For now, she would let him be. In fact, it might be fun to see what would develop.

Of course, there was that silly little Turnquist woman to deal with. She certainly had decided quickly enough to attach herself to the eldest Chadwick son. But it was of no concern. Portia knew that if she decided to take Trenton for her own, it would only be a matter of time until she had him. No one ever told her no — at least not for long.

But Chester Lawrence was proving to be beneficial, and in him, Portia saw a comrade-in-arms. He hated the Selbys, and so did she.

"I'm sure we can be mutually helpful to each other," she said as she took one last look in the mirror. She smiled in approval. "Very helpful indeed."

The weeks went by in pleasurable planning for Christmas. Dianne watched with a hopeful eye at the way Morgan had taken to the young Miss Turnquist. It was evident that he had strong feelings for the pretty blonde, but it didn't appear Angelina felt the same way. In fact, if Dianne didn't know better, she'd think that Angelina was far more interested in Trenton.

"I sure hope we aren't putting you out, ma'am," Marley Turnquist said as Dianne came into the kitchen with a stack of table linens.

"Not at all, Mr. Turnquist. As you can see, we have plenty of room and we very much enjoy the company. It can get very lonely out here at times."

"I can well understand that," the man said as he turned back to the stove where he had been about to pour himself a cup of coffee. "I lived a good part of my life in the big

203

city, however, and it can be very lonely there as well. There were times, in fact, when I was the most lonely of all sitting right in a room full of people."

Dianne placed the linens on the table. "Nevertheless, we're glad you could spend Christmas and the winter with us. It affords me a chance to see Morgan, and since he went away to partner with you and Mr. De-Shazer, I haven't had that opportunity."

"We do keep busy," Marley said, turning with his cup.

"Well, you just make yourself at home," Dianne assured. "I'm especially enjoying the company of your daughter. It's always nice to hear the news from back East and know what fashions are being created. We get newspapers here and an occasional periodical, but it's been more fun to spend hours over cakes and tea discussing such affairs, pretending we're completely up to date."

"I believe Angelina is enjoying herself as well. She's always been an unconventional child. I hold myself to blame for that. I wanted a son, and when my firstborn was a girl child, I was disappointed but held to the dream of a boy. Then Angelina came along and the doc said there'd be no more babies. I figured I could make a son out of a girl just as well as a boy." Marley grinned. "Guess I made a wild cat instead."

Dianne laughed. "She has a zest for life that will keep her strong out here. You have to have that passion — that enthusiasm — or the country will devour you whole."

"Angelina wouldn't stand for it."

Dianne picked up her linens. "No, I don't imagine she would."

Sam Brady showed up a few days before Christmas as promised. Portia made a show of being ever so happy to see the man. In truth, she'd grown weary of even bothering to wait for him. The respite on the ranch had given her a time of freedom, however. She wasn't forced to spend money — money she didn't have, thanks to Ned's stingy father. She didn't have to work all that hard, although she knew far more was expected of her than she delivered.

Frankly, Portia had a very acceptable situation with the Selbys, though she didn't like them — not a single one. The children were irritating. Dianne was too demanding, and Cole had proven unaffected by her flirtatiousness. The rest of the household was equally bad. Portia abhorred the Negro family, and the Blackfoot squaw and her children were no better. It had been a great relief when they'd all gone back to their appropriate homes.

"You hiding in here?" her father asked as he approached her in the front sitting room. She'd chosen this room because it was generally cooler — almost chilly. Others would gather in the main room with its large blazing fire, but not her. Not unless she had to.

"Oh, Father. You know better. I simply enjoy this room. It's very restful."

Sam Brady looked around and nodded. "I suppose it is."

"You're welcome to join me."

Her father rubbed his chin for a moment, then pulled up one of the horsehair chairs. "I figured I might. With the others occupied in decorating the Christmas tree, I thought I might get to the bottom of what's going on with you."

Portia put aside her book and feigned a look of surprise. "Whatever do you mean?"

"Why are you here?"

His question took her aback. She'd been so confident of her performance. She'd done nothing to give herself away — to suggest to him or anyone else that her motives were less than pure.

"I told you I wanted to make amends. Goodness, do you honestly believe I'd sequester myself away out here in the Montana Territory if I weren't sincere?"

Sam shook his head. "Frankly, Portia, I've seen you endure a great many torturous things in order to have what you want. I seem to remember you eating nothing but the tiniest bowls of vegetables for months on end in order to have your waist measure the size you desired for your wedding."

"Oh, Father," she giggled. "How you do go on. Any girl would do that. It's a matter of wanting to look pretty for their husband. Mother understood."

"Yes, your mother always understood you better than I did." His serious tone set Portia's teeth on edge. He had always taken this tone when he meted out discipline or correction. She hated it.

"Perhaps that's because mother was around and you weren't," she said, trying a different tactic. She forced tears to come to her eyes — a technique she'd learned early in life. "Other children had a father under the same roof. Other children were blessed to grow up seeing their fathers on a daily basis."

"Perhaps other children's fathers didn't have to fight wars or defend liberties to keep folks safe."

Portia wanted to reply with a snide comment but held her tongue. "Oh, you have no idea how hard it was to be without you. Mother suffered terribly. So did I. We were often frightened and so very alone."

"That's why I wanted you to move to the fort with me when I took that post in Kansas. Instead, you up and declared that you'd fallen passionately in love with William Travers, and scarcely before you turn seventeen, I'm walking you down the aisle to be his bride."

"Well, I had lost my heart to the only man who was there to share my love with," she said softly. "I only married William because he showed me the affection I so desperately needed from you." She dabbed at her eyes and got to her feet. "This conversation is making me very sad. I hope you'll excuse me."

She had to leave. It was almost more than she could bear. If she had to sit there for another minute and look into her father's stoic face, she would scream. The man had no idea of the scars he'd inflicted on her heart.

"But he will," she muttered as she headed to the sanctuary of her room. "He will."

Trenton saw Portia exit the parlor and head upstairs. He knew she'd been talking to her father, as he'd seen Sam go into the room only minutes before. Sam seemed like the balanced and thoughtful sort of man that Trenton could trust, and because of R. E. Langford's letter, Trenton intended to enlist Sam's help. *If he'll hear me out.*

"I hope I'm not intruding," Trenton said as he came into the room. He noted that Sam looked to be very deep in thought.

"No. Not really."

"I wonder if we might talk. Maybe on the porch, where we will have more privacy. Of course, it's cold out there," he added with a smile.

"Cold doesn't bother me, son. I've slept outside in worse than this. I'm sure your brother must have told you about times when it was thirty and forty below zero and we had nothing more than a tent to protect us from the elements." Sam got to his feet. "I believe my coat is on the back porch."

"Mine too," Trenton said.

They made their way outside, where Sam immediately packed a pipe. "Do you smoke?" he asked, offering Trenton the pipe.

"No, it's one practice I never took up."

Sam shrugged and lit the bowl. "I find it a comfort at times. I suppose it's a habit that helps me in times like this."

Trenton frowned. "What do you mean?"

"Portia. I'm certain she's lying to me, but I can't for the life of me figure her game. Never could."

This was an unexpected blessing as far as Trenton was concerned. Perhaps if he allowed Sam to talk about his concerns, Trenton could bring up the Langford letter without feeling like a complete cad.

"Why do you say that?" Trenton asked softly.

"Portia has spent her entire life caring only for one person: herself. She loved her mother, but even that relationship was strained by Portia's inner demons." Sam shook his head. "That girl has never been entirely satisfied with life. Nothing ever seemed to line up exactly the way she wanted it to, so she started forcing pieces into place. If friends offended her, she got rid of them."

"How would she do that?"

Sam shrugged. "In whatever manner she felt served her purpose. She once had this friend — probably the closest thing to a friend she'd ever had, at any rate. The girl was lovely and sweet, and several of the local boys were taken with her. One in particular thought himself ready to court her, but by this time Portia had decided she wanted the boy for herself. She arranged to put the other girl in a bad situation so that she had to marry another man to save her reputation. Keep in mind the girl was barely sixteen and Portia only fifteen." He shook his head. "It was ugly, and the girl died a very unhappy young woman."

Trenton perked at the mention of death. "How did she die?"

"Childbirth. She died without being able to pass the child, and the doctor had been detained elsewhere. I honestly thought Portia might be contrite at her passing — might be moved enough to change her way of demanding things and forcing them to happen."

"But she didn't?"

"No. In fact, she kept manipulating lives and people until she'd convinced a wealthy young man to marry her and leave for Europe, where the threat of service to the war couldn't touch him. Portia seemed happy with the arrangement. William Travers was a man of some social standing, and when they went abroad, they did so in style."

"What happened to her husband?" Trenton asked, driven to know the truth of Portia's past.

"He died. Strangely enough he was run down by a freighter. It was barely dawn in

London and William had passed out cold in the middle of the street. The driver didn't see him until it was too late, and the wheels crushed his skull. I never would have expected such an ending for Travers."

"Why not?" Trenton asked, feeling disappointed that the death hadn't been more mysterious.

"He wasn't a drinker when he was here in America. In fact, the man was something of a staunch teetotaler. He completely supported the temperance movement. In fact, his father or grandfather was one of the original founders of the British Association for the Promotion of Temperance. When the family came to America, they furthered the cause. The family was quite firm on the issue of liquor. I guess Portia must have driven him to drink. I can't imagine spending four years with her, day in and day out, and not coming to the same conclusion."

Trenton grinned but turned his face upward, as if star-gazing, in the hopes that Sam wouldn't see his reaction. "She does weary a fellow," he said, hoping Sam wouldn't find it offensive.

"She especially seems to hold you a grudge," Sam said, surprising Trenton. "I'd watch out for her if I were you."

Trenton turned and stared at the man.

212

The light from the house windows reflecting off the snowy ground gave Trenton a decent view of Sam's face. The man was serious. "Why do you say that, Sam?"

"People have a way of suddenly dying when they're around my daughter. Travers, then McGuire."

"He was her second husband? The Scotsman?"

"Yes. He was quite a bit older, but healthy as a horse. At least that was the way I always heard it told. The man was a landowner — raised sheep and such. He didn't strike me as the kind of fellow who would fall over dead from pneumonia. But that's what Portia told me. I just don't believe her."

Trenton realized his moment had come. "Sam, I need to ask you something — and I need you to keep it in the utmost confidence. Given what you've already told me here, I have to believe you share some of my same concerns."

"What concerns?"

Trenton drew a deep breath. "I had a letter from Ned Langford's father."

"Go on."

"The man believes Portia had something to do with the death of his son. He's asked me to gather information to try and prove it."

Sam was silent for several minutes. He sucked on the pipe and blew a ring of smoke toward the starry sky.

Finally he withdrew the pipe and said, "I've no doubt she killed him. I've no doubt she killed them all."

"But why, Sam? Why would she kill any of them? They were wealthy. They had the ability to give her anything she wanted. Ned had trouble with the Panic of '73, but his family's fortune wasn't hurt that much. He was still a rich man."

"Portia cannot abide being controlled. My guess is that in each case, something happened to cause her husbands to tell her no. It's just that simple. She probably figured that if they were to die, she'd inherit their wealth and be able to control her own purse strings. That's my guess. Portia's never abided anyone who got in her way — not even me. It's one of the reasons I was glad to marry her off."

"What are you saying?" Trenton asked, studying the man intently.

Sam met his gaze. "I'm saying that I felt certain Portia was out to kill me as well. Matter of fact, I'm still convinced that's her plan."

Trenton had been cold prior to this, but at Sam's declaration a chill like none he'd ever experienced — not even when awaiting his execution for a murder he didn't commit — coursed down his spine, nearly paralyzing him. "Sam, are you sure?"

"She's got no other reason to be here, Trenton — and certainly no other reason to wait out an entire year and then some. She's up to something. It's either you or me — or maybe both. I don't know what she holds against you, but it's clearly there."

"She holds the truth against me," Trenton replied flatly. "I've known her to be an actress playing a part since the first day she pretended to faint, hoping Ned Langford would catch her. Instead, I got the job. I knew from the get-go that she wasn't any more unconscious than I was. I tried a couple of times to confront her, and I definitely tried to change Ned's mind about marrying her. Portia hated me for that. I almost convinced Ned to at least wait a spell, but Portia managed to spin a bigger web than I could knock down."

"Then it could be either one of us. I plan to take her back to Bozeman the day after Christmas. That might afford you some protection, but I'd still be cautious. Portia makes enemies for life. She never forgets a grudge and always finds a way to make a person pay for whatever wrong she's perceived. If she doesn't try to even things up now, she'll try later."

"But what about you, Sam?"

The man shrugged and put the pipe to his mouth. "My life pretty much ceased for me the day my Mary died. Portia can't hurt me anymore."

Trenton found that Sam's words weighed heavy on his heart. Portia was a danger — perhaps more than he'd realized. The thing that worried him most about this black widow spider of a woman was that he'd inadvertently brought her home to his family. She was a threat to every living creature — every person Trenton loved more than life.

"You wanted to see me?" Cole said, pulling on his heavy coat as he came into the barn.

Trenton had sent for Cole, knowing now was the time to confess his past. "I need to tell you some things. Some things about me and what I did before coming here."

Cole frowned, his brows knitting together. "You know that doesn't matter."

"I know you and Dianne can probably forgive me, but there's a new danger from my past, and I can't risk not letting you know about it before it threatens everyone I love."

216

CHAPTER 13

April 1880

Dianne sat atop a feisty four-year-old buckskin named Daisy and surveyed the ranch from her favorite hilltop perch. Dolly, the mother of Daisy, had to be put down the year before after a bad fall. A bear had spooked Dolly, causing her to lose her footing on a rocky stretch. At least that was the best they could figure when they found the mare. The loss of her good friend had left Dianne depressed for days.

Daisy was a fine animal with all of Dolly's sweetness and a fiery spirit that came from a sire named Lightning and, of course, her youth. But for all her wonderful characteristics, Daisy wasn't Dolly, and the death left Dianne feeling rather misplaced.

There had been a great many changes in the years since Dianne had come to the Diamond V. One of the newest was the small community that had come together only about five miles away. They called it Madison, and already it showed signs of being a solid little town.

To Chester Lawrence's credit, the town had been his idea. His drive helped to establish a trading post of sorts, and the rest began to fall into place. Soon there was a post office — although it was located in the corner of the general store — and a bank, and most recently a church and school were added, both run by Ben and Charity.

Charity had even sent word that Dr. Bufford had set up a small office in his new home there. It wasn't much, she'd said, but it was a regular doctor's office nevertheless. The thought made Dianne smile, for Dr. Bufford had vowed never again to hang his shingle, but now there he was. Montana had a way of changing a person's mind — she knew that firsthand.

"We're getting civilized for sure, aren't we, Daisy?"

Even the ranch was changing. They had expanded many times over, improving and enlarging the herd, developing new techniques and advances. The horses were some of the finest bred anywhere, and the army always needed new mounts. This business, which had started out completely as an afterthought — almost a hobby, really — was making them some very solid money.

Added to this, Cole had invested in some of the mining interests in Butte, and those were paying off handsomely. They were wealthy. At least as much as she imagined anyone to ever be. There was never any issue of food or clothing. Everyone's needs were fully met. To her, that was real wealth.

Dianne spotted a couple of wagons being loaded with goods from Malachi's blacksmith shop. He and Faith were moving their family to Madison, and while Dianne knew it was only five miles away, she was devastated at the loss of yet another friend. First Charity had gone, and now Faith. They were her mentors — her mother figures — and now they were gone or would be soon.

"It's silly, I know," she told Daisy, "they aren't that far. A good five-mile ride would do us both good. But it isn't the same. I used to be able to just walk across the yard and there they both were. Close and easily placed for my convenience." She chuckled. "How selfish I've become."

She was actually very happy for Faith. Malachi would own his own business now. He would be an important man in the community with more work than he'd possibly be able to keep up with. Already Faith was encouraging him to hire on a couple of assistants. Faith would no longer cook for the men of the Diamond V, and that would make it necessary to hire a new cook. Dianne knew Cole was already tending to that situation, so she tried not to concern herself with it.

Ever since their misunderstanding in Butte, Dianne had felt a deep desire to trust her husband and to let him make the decisions for the ranch. Cole, to his credit, however, was better about coming to her for advice. He often talked to her about the details of choices that presented themselves. He also listened to her comments and thoughts, and this made Dianne feel more loved and cared about than almost anything else.

Life was good. She had a wonderful life with her husband and children. God had given them three healthy boys, with John Ephraim Selby being born only a year earlier. She'd been hoping for a daughter, but another son was no problem. He was named for his two grandfathers, although Cole's father had always gone by his middle name rather than by John. Baby John was a good-natured child — nothing like Micah, whose colicky stomach had made him miserable for months after birth. John had even taken his first steps last month. Her family was growing fast.

Dianne couldn't imagine a better life, despite the problems and complications. Despite good friends moving away. God had given her much — her cup truly was running over.

Returning to the house, Dianne was surprised to find that Koko's brother had once again managed to make an appearance. He didn't look as haggard or half starved as he had on the last visit. When she rode up to the barn, Takes Many Horses was in a deep discussion with his nephew. They looked up and waved as she approached.

"This is indeed a surprise," she said, sliding off Daisy.

"This isn't that little mare we threatened to take away from you so many years ago when you earned your name, Stands Tall Woman," Takes Many Horses said as he took hold of the reins.

"No, this is Dolly's offspring, Daisy. Dolly had to be put down last year after she fell," Dianne said, giving the mare a pat on the neck. "But she's the spitting image of Dolly with her buckskin coat and black mane and tail. She's a little more temperamental, but in time I think she'll be very dependable."

"I'll put her up for you," Jamie said, taking the reins from his uncle. "Maybe Uncle will tell you what we've been talking about and you can help me." The boy looked to Dianne hopefully.

"It all depends on what you've been discussing," Dianne said with a grin. "I know how you can be. Nevertheless, thank you for tending Daisy."

Jamie grinned in return, his dark brown eyes fairly glowing. He looked so much like Bram that it sometimes caught Dianne off guard.

With the boy gone, Dianne turned to Takes Many Horses. It wouldn't be long before he reached his fortieth year. Maybe another two years at the most, Dianne thought. He was a handsome man with definite Indian features, tempered by his white heritage.

"I've been to the reservation," he said softly. "It's a horrible life."

"I've heard stories. I'd hoped they weren't true."

"Probably even worse than you've heard."

Dianne shook her head. "The government promised so many things. Food, clothing, shelter. I don't understand why these things aren't being delivered."

"They come," Takes Many Horses said,

his eyes darkening in anger. "They come in the form of maggoty meat and diseased blankets and clothes. The Blackfoot have suffered from small pox, measles, mumps, and half a dozen other ailments. There are no animals to hunt — at least not like there were before. The men go off the reservation to bring in meat and then find themselves in trouble for their actions. The meat that comes from the government is never any good. I think they trade the good stuff to the white settlers and take their spoiled meat for the Indians."

Dianne couldn't imagine that being true but left well enough alone. "What of you? How is it that you are here?"

"I sneak on the reservation and sneak back off," Takes Many Horses said with a shrug. "I've never registered. It's as if they don't even know I exist. But I know they remember me — I know they're still looking for me and my friends."

"At least things have calmed down. Your friends won't revolt, will they? Will there be more killings and uprisings?"

"My people are tired and sick. They are half starved. How would they fight?"

Dianne heard the bitterness in his voice. "What can we do to help?"

He shook his head. "Nothing."

"There has to be something. We could buy blankets that aren't diseased. We could buy shoes and coats, send food. I could talk to Cole; perhaps we could send cattle to help them with their beef herds. You did say at one time that they were trying their hand at ranching."

"It would be taken from them. You don't know how this works. The government agents would claim some part of their agreement broken and steal away the animals as payment. There's nothing you can do to fix this or make it right."

"I thought I heard your voice, George," Koko said as she came from the back of the house. "I was just planting part of the garden." She hugged him close and kissed him on the cheek. "It's been so long. I've missed you, my brother."

Dianne was amazed at the lack of emotion between the siblings. They seemed to take their lengthy separations in stride, whereas Dianne felt desperate at times to see her brothers.

"I've missed you too. That's why I'm here. Sometimes it's just worth the risk to see my family and loved ones. I spoke with Jamie. He's very restless. He's asked me to take him with me when I go."

"He's nearly thirteen," Koko said stiffly.

"Nearly thirteen and has no father to raise him and teach him to be a man. You could take that job — if you would only choose to stay here and do so."

Takes Many Horses shook his head. "Ranch life is not for me."

"Neither is reservation life," Dianne threw out.

"True, because both are nothing more than prisons of different makings. I wasn't created to live within boundaries. Why, I even see some of the farmers and ranchers putting up fencing. This isn't the way of my people."

"The way of your people — of our ancestors — is gone," Koko declared. "You will be gone, too, unless you learn to bend your will. Jamie needs you here. You could do much with the boy."

"What would I teach him? The unfairness of white laws that refuse him the right to inherit his father's ranch? Would I teach him how the Indians are savages, no better than animals to be caged? But because we're part white and can cut our hair and dress appropriately, we might be able to fool folks into believing we are as good as they are?"

"We are just as good," Koko replied.

"Yes, you are," Dianne agreed. "You know you're welcome here. Koko is absolutely right. Jamie needs you. Cole can't keep up with him. He has his own three boys to look after."

Takes Many Horses smiled. "Three boys, eh? I would have given you ten sons by now."

Dianne blushed and looked away. The man always had a way of saying something that would get the subject off of him and onto someone else.

"I'm only asking help with one son," Koko said seriously. "Your own nephew. Flesh and blood. How can you stand before any of our people and tell them that you denied your own family's need?"

At this he was taken aback, his discomfort evident. "Jamie wasn't allowed to take over his father's land. He's not allowed to take over the land of his mother's people either. In both cases the white government has seen to that. What would you suggest I teach him? Bitterness? Rage? Because, sister, those are the things I know best." His face contorted as he continued.

"I am an outlaw. I am hunted and will one day be found and killed. My blood will fall on my own hands. My will and decisions will have brought me to that place. Do you want that for Jamie as well? Should I teach him the same things?"

"Of course not," Koko whispered. His words had clearly upset her.

"Our people are dying, Koko. They are dying from starvation and exposure. They have nothing. They are given nothing. I can't hope for you to understand the bleakness of it — or the horror that those people are facing. You are lucky to have been taken as wife to Bram. He was a good man. I loved him as a brother. You have good men here even now. Men who do not turn away from this place because a *squaw* and her children live here." He spoke the word squaw with such hatred that Dianne actually cringed.

"I am glad you will never have to face the reservation," Takes Many Horses said, shaking his head. "Because it is nothing but a place to await death."

"Mama, I want to go with Uncle," Jamie said as he joined them again. "I'm a man now and I want to travel the land and learn the ways of the Blackfoot."

"You are white," Koko said frankly. "While I cherish my mother's people and have even taught you children much about the Blackfoot, I will not have you dishonor your father by choosing their ways over his."

"I don't like the way our Blackfoot people are treated," Jamie declared. "You've also told me stories about those things. Maybe I can help."

"Yes, maybe you can," Takes Many Horses said firmly. "But not by running around the countryside with a renegade. You could stay here, study and become a lawyer or an advocate for the Real People."

Jamie frowned. "I don't like school. Reading is hard, and I hate arithmetic. I'd rather come with you."

"You are not being given a choice," Koko said in a commanding voice. "Now go inside and do your schoolwork. I will be in shortly to check your figures."

"But I want —"

"You dishonor your mother," Takes Many Horses interrupted. "Go."

Jamie looked as though he might say more, but with one look at his uncle's stern countenance, he fled without a word.

Dianne pulled off her leather gloves and slapped them against her leg. "You're welcome to stay as long as you like. I have guest rooms free, as well as a couple of the old cabins. Supper will be at six."

"I'll stay for a few days. Maybe in that time I can convince Jamie of the powerful things he can do as a white man helping the Blackfoot."

Koko smiled. "Thank you. I would be glad for that help. Just don't fill his head with all

228

sorts of stories about your days of glory and bravery. There will be time enough for those things when he's old enough to know his place in this world."

She walked away, leaving Takes Many Horses and Dianne alone once again. "Come on inside," Dianne urged.

As they walked to the house in silence, Dianne couldn't help but wonder where Takes Many Horses had been and what all he'd seen and done. The things he mentioned about the reservation were enough to keep her from seeking details, but she couldn't help but be concerned for his welfare. Maybe they would yet convince him that his place was on the Diamond V.

"This house seems to grow all the time," he said as they entered.

"We did add some more rooms to the back," Dianne admitted. "My sister Ardith . . ." Her words trailed off. "Oh, dear. She doesn't know about your being here. She knows about you, but seeing you might well send her into a fit of terror."

Takes Many Horses looked at her oddly. "Why?"

"She was brought to us after the Sioux battle at Little Big Horn. She's the sister who fell in the river on my family's trip out here. We thought she drowned, but the

229

Pawnee found her. They had her a time, then the Sioux raided the village and took her hostage. She was treated poorly and eventually given over to a warrior. She hated the man and he was very unkind. She has a little daughter from him."

"I understand," Takes Many Horses responded. "Show me where you would like me to stay. I'll wait there until you have time to talk to her. Then you can come for me."

Dianne nodded. "That would be best."

They moved toward the stairs, but charcoal drawings on the wall caught the man's attention. "Are these your children?"

"Yes. A wonderful young man by the name of Charlie Russell came through these parts earlier. He had a marvelous talent for drawing and did these two pictures for me. It was his way of paying for our hospitality."

Takes Many Horses studied the drawings for several minutes. "They are very fine."

"Yes. I was impressed with his work."

"No, I mean your boys. They are better sons than I could have given you."

Dianne felt her cheeks grow hot. "I . . . uh . . . you know that kind of talk makes me uncomfortable." She started up the stairs.

He chuckled and followed after her. "I didn't think anything could make Stands

Tall Woman uncomfortable — especially the truth."

Dianne paused and looked back at the man who made no secret of his love for her. "The truth often makes me very uncomfortable," she admitted. "But I do prefer it to lies. Even so, some things are better left unsaid."

He met her gaze, and for a moment the passion in his expression was almost more than she could bear. How could he care so deeply for her when he knew she belonged to another?

He sighed. "I'm sorry. You're right. Some things should be left unsaid."

There was a deep regret in his tone that put a sorrowful damper on Dianne's otherwise jubilant heart. She wanted to say something to encourage him not to despair over something that never had been. But even as she thought of what she might say, she knew her previous advice was best — leave it unsaid. With no other word, she once again began to climb the stairs.

Portia Langford slowly did up the buttons of her blouse, all the while watching Chester Lawrence finish pulling on his boots. He straightened and put on his jacket.

"I like the way these range shacks afford

231

us a little afternoon privacy," she said coyly. "I just wish they were a little more hospitable."

Chester laughed. "They weren't created for hospitality, but rather shelter. Although I don't suppose they offer much of that either."

"I'm glad my father agreed to settle in Madison now that he's finished with the army." She came to where Chester stood and walked her fingers up his rock-hard chest. For an older man, he was remarkably well muscled.

Chester looked at her for a moment. "You're enough to exhaust a man, but I'm sure I'll bear it well enough. Have you gotten me any new information?"

Portia shrugged. "Not much to tell. The Diamond V added over a hundred new calves this spring. The army is buying at least that much in steers, but the real news seems to be the horses. Apparently they are breeding something called steeldust horses. At least that's what my father called them. He and Trenton Chadwick get together nearly every week." She looked at Chester for a moment, then added, "Have you heard of these steeldust horses?"

"Incredible stock. Those beauties have the durability of the Spanish barb and the speed of the Thoroughbred."

Portia rolled her eyes at the excitement in Chester's voice. It seemed pure insanity for a man to get that worked up over a horse. She turned and walked back to the rough-hewn bed and sat down. Pulling on her stocking, Portia decided the time had come to let Chester in on a little of the Selby-Chadwick family history.

"I know you fancy the idea of pushing the Selbys out of this territory. I heard something interesting while staying with them. Something I think you might be able to work to your advantage."

"What is it?"

Portia looked over her shoulder even as she affixed her stockings. "What benefit will it have for me?"

"If the information is as valuable as you suggest, I'll give you whatever price you name. I intend to take this valley over for my own. Selby's in my way. If you have a means by which I can eliminate the man and his family, I'll give you whatever you ask."

Portia grinned and finished securing her second stocking. "The ranch originally belonged to Bram Vandyke, Mrs. Selby's uncle. The man was married to an Indian squaw, and he knew she could never inherit

233

the land." Portia got up and pulled on her skirt, talking all the time. "Apparently, Vandyke learned that the only way he could keep the ranch in the family was to bring Dianne in on the deed and make her a partner. Her brother Trenton was not in the area at the time and her other brothers had no interest in ranching."

"I fail to see how this is to my benefit," Chester said, giving her a frown.

Portia shook her head. "What if the papers making her a partner were not legal? What if they were never properly filed or properly designed? What if, in fact, there are no records of them existing at all?"

"Do you have reason to believe this is true?"

"I have reason to believe that you have enough money to make it true," she said with a sly grin.

Chester looked at her dumbfounded for a moment, then began to smile. "I think you just might be right. Maybe it's time for me to do a little digging at the courthouse in Virginia City."

"Maybe so," Portia said, already thinking of what she would demand of him when he made his dream a reality.

CHAPTER 14

Trenton was in no mood to deal with Angelina Turnquist, but the woman was persistent. She was pretty too. Pretty and smart and not afraid of anything. He couldn't help but admire her, but his past didn't allow for falling in love. For reasons he didn't understand, Portia Langford had kept silent about the details of his life before coming to the Diamond V. He was constantly waiting for the moment when someone would show up to confront him about the deeds he'd done, but so far, nothing had happened. No doubt she was waiting until the most advantageous moment before she pounced to destroy him. Just as she had no doubt done with her now dead husbands.

"Are you busy?" Angelina asked as she came into the study.

"Yes." Trenton looked up from the ledgers. "I'm recording information for Cole. What do you need?" He tried not to sound affected by the way she looked. He'd thought her the most handsome woman in the world when he'd first met her nearly three years earlier.

"I thought we might talk. My father plans to leave here tomorrow. He's anxious to get some of his findings back to his investors in the East. He insists I go with him, but I thought perhaps you would help me change his mind."

Trenton shook his head. "Change his mind about going east?"

"No . . ." she said, moving closer to the desk, "change it about taking me."

Trenton leaned back in the chair and said nothing for a moment. He simply studied Angelina's face — the delicate arch of her blond brows, the upturned nose and full lips. She was dressed in a serviceable blue gown with some black braided trim. She almost looked prim and proper, but he knew better. The woman was anything but that.

"You should go see your family. How long has it been since you've seen your mother and sister?"

Angelina frowned. "I don't want to be with them. I want to be with you."

Her boldness left Trenton speechless. He knew he looked as shocked as he felt but did nothing to hide his reaction.

"I know. You don't think we have anything in common. You think I'm too young to know my own mind. You think me better suited to Morgan."

"I'm mighty glad *you* know what I'm thinking, because I'm feeling rather stumped right now, myself," Trenton finally said.

Angelina stomped her foot and put her hands on her hips. "You know exactly what I mean. I've had feelings for you since we first met. I know you feel the same way. I can tell."

"What if I do? What of it?" he questioned. "Your father wants to go back East, and you have family there. Your place is at his side."

"My place could be at your side."

Trenton got to his feet. Walking slowly around the desk, he stopped directly in front of Angelina and took hold of her by the upper arms. She closed her eyes and offered him her lips, as if fully expecting him to kiss her. For a moment, he was sorely tempted.

He swallowed hard. "Open your eyes, Angelina."

She did so, a puzzled look spreading across her face. "What's wrong?"

"This is wrong. We're wrong."

"No. We're very right. Don't you see?"

Trenton sighed. "You know nothing about my past. You only know me as Morgan's brother. I haven't always led a respectable life. I've done things I'm very ashamed of, and I've been wrongly blamed for even worse. You don't want to end up with someone like me."

"But that's all in the past, right?"

"What of it?"

She smiled. "The Lord forgets your past and remembers it no more. The Bible says that. God can forgive you of your wrongdoings and wipe it all clean."

"God very well may, but I doubt the law will feel the same way."

Angelina shook her head. "Trenton, don't send me away. I love you."

He stepped back as if she'd slapped him. "You don't know what you're saying. You hardly even know me."

"I know you well enough. We spent that entire winter together back in '77 and '78. Then every year since we've come here for at least a short visit. I've gotten to know you better each time, and I've grown to care for you deeply. If we were to marry, I could stay here permanently and not have to return to Chicago with my father."

"So now you're proposing to me?" Trenton shook his head and walked back behind the desk. He felt the need to keep some sort of barrier between them.

"You won't do it, so I figured I might as well. Is it such a bad suggestion? Am I such a poor catch?"

He looked at her as if she'd spoken Greek. "How could you even say such a thing? I think any man would be very fortunate to have you as his wife."

"Any man but you, is that it?"

Trenton sat down hard on the leather chair. "Angelina, you need to go. This isn't a conversation we should be having."

"I think it's a good conversation for us to be having. I think you feel the same way I do."

Trenton couldn't deny the truth in her statement. He did care for her, and if he were a different man, he might very well have taken her up on her proposal of marriage. Trenton picked up his pen and dipped it in the ink. "Leave, Angelina. Go with your father and forget about me. I can't be the man you want me to be."

He focused on the ledger, hoping she would take this as his final word. He didn't want to hurt her and prayed she wouldn't start crying. That would surely be his undoing.

"If that's the way you want it," Angelina

239

said, moving to the door, "then so be it. For now."

Once she was gone, Trenton put down the pen, realizing that his hand was trembling. He rubbed his eyes and drew a deep breath. Blowing it out in the silence of the room, he forced himself not to go after her. This was the better way.

A knock on the door, however, made him certain she'd returned. Getting up, he fought his feelings. How could he let her into his life with Portia knowing the details of his past? The woman would stop at nothing to hurt him — and in turn, Angelina — for whatever wrongs she perceived him to have done her.

Trenton opened the door, hoping to have the strength to send Angelina on her way once and for all. Instead, he found Sam Brady standing on the other side.

"Your sister told me I'd find you here," the older man said, smiling.

Trenton tried to hide his surprise. "Come in," Trenton said, pushing back the door. "I thought you were someone else."

"Portia insisted we come for a visit. She also declared an interest in buying a new horse. I figured we'd take care of business and pleasure in one trip."

Trenton went back to the desk. "I was taking care of some entries for Cole, but I can certainly be interrupted from that. Would you like me to get us some coffee?"

"No," Sam said, glancing over his back. He turned and closed the door. "I thought we might discuss your progress in gathering information."

Trenton shook his head. "I haven't found anything worthwhile. However, the last letter I had from Mr. Langford gave me numerous details regarding Ned's death. Apparently the man shot himself while lying in bed. Mr. Langford believes Portia killed Ned while he slept. After all, what man dresses for bed, gets in and pulls up the covers, and then puts a gun to his head while his wife is sleeping soundly beside him?"

Sam rubbed his chin. "Sounds suspect, all right."

Trenton pulled the latest letter from a side drawer where he kept it with the others. He opened it and read, " 'Portia was the only one in the room at the time, and she claims to have been sleeping. The gunshot awoke the household, and Portia began to scream down the house. We ran to their room and found Ned had expired. Blood was pooling in the bed around Ned, yet Portia was surprisingly untouched. There wasn't so much as a droplet of blood on her white robe and gown.' "

Trenton stopped and looked up. "How could she have been in bed beside him when he shot himself and not have at least some small amount of blood on her person?"

Sam sat down in the chair opposite Trenton. "I've no doubt she shot him. The question is, how do we prove it?"

"Langford says if you can just get her back to Baltimore, he has convinced the police to arrest her. He even hired a specialist in this kind of thing. The man has studied the entire matter — even the body, as I understand it."

"After all these years?" Sam asked in disbelief.

"Apparently. Here, let me read what he says." Trenton shuffled the pages and scanned for the part he wanted to share. " 'We believe the information put together by Mr. Grissom is sub . . . substantial,' " Trenton stammered over the word. His reading still wasn't all that great. " 'Evidence shows that from the angle of the bullet and the wound at the point of entry, Ned could not have been the one to fire the gun.' "

Trenton put the letter down. "He feels certain they can see Portia pay for what she's done."

"If that's the case, then I'll have to see to it that she returns to Baltimore."

"Langford suggests that he can have his lawyer send a letter to her. The details would intimate that Mr. Langford has agreed to allow her a sizeable portion of money from Ned's estate. Apparently he's been able to put some kind of a lien on it all these years. He said he would have the letter drawn up if we would do what we could to get her there."

"I think if Portia believes a small fortune awaits her, she'll have no trouble agreeing to return to Baltimore," Sam said, his shoulders suddenly slumping. "I can't believe we're having this conversation. My daughter is a murderer. A cold-blooded killer. How can this be?"

Trenton shook his head. "I don't know. I know desperation led me to do things I didn't want to do. Bad things. But for someone to have a life of ease, with good things and people who truly care about them, and then to turn around and murder them . . . well, it docsn't make sense to me either."

"Send him the letter," Sam said sadly. "Tell him that I'll see she gets there by the quickest means."

Trenton folded the letter and met Sam's

sorrowful gaze. "At least it will stop her from killing again."

"Let's pray that's true."

Outside the office, Portia burned in rage. She'd heard most every word uttered by the two men inside. She'd feigned a headache, and Dianne had graciously shown her to one of the guest bedrooms. Then as soon as she could, Portia made her way down the back stairs and to the room she'd seen her father enter.

Sneaking back to the sanctuary of the guest room, Portia clenched her teeth so hard her jaw burned. She closed the door and leaned against it, her fists balled, her body rigid.

"How dare they plot against me? I've been more than merciful in keeping Mr. Chadwick's past a secret, but no more. Tomorrow I go to the sheriff and tell them everything. Then I'll deal with my father."

Portia remained restless throughout the day, and by the time her father was prepared to return to Madison, she forced herself to pretend nothing was amiss. Focused on making plans, Portia said very little on the ride home.

She had to admit there were many reasons for hiding out in Montana. Langford's threat of proving that she murdered his son was right at the top of her list. *I should never have shot him,* she told herself. *I should have poisoned him like the others, then worked out the details of his situation afterward.*

Portia knew from experience that poisoning was very difficult to prove. Especially when using some of the poisons she had tried. William had been such a simpleton with his dedication to temperance and other foolish notions. Worst of all, he was a boorish man. His manners were abhorrent and he often embarrassed her. Poisoning him, then dousing him with whiskey, had been easy enough. The trouble came in finding a man desperate enough to take her money, ask no questions, and run a freight wagon over the dead body of her husband.

Angus had been an even bigger challenge. The man had a keen intellect and was very intuitive, making Portia believe him capable of reading her mind. Angus had decided it was time for Portia to give him a family. The man had been positively inhuman in his desires. She shuddered now even thinking about it. The poison she'd given him caused respiratory distress. The lungs filled with fluid and were unable to process the matter. The doctor, as hoped, was positive it was pneumonia; the Scottish ninny had no idea there would be any other cause.

Now, however, Ned Langford rose from the grave like a specter to haunt her. *Well, I won't let him destroy me.*

Seeing that the turnoff to the Lawrence ranch was approaching, Portia made a decision. "Father, I'd like to visit with Cynthia Lawrence. I promised her I'd come by as soon as time permitted. Why don't you head on home, and I'll join you a little later."

Sam eyed her suspiciously. She hated him for that. He had always looked at her as if trying to size up what mischief she was up to. Other fathers doted on their little girls, but not Sam Brady. No, Sergeant Brady thought the worst of his child and now intended to see it proven.

"I don't like your riding out unescorted," her father finally said. "It hardly seems appropriate."

"There are a great many things in this life that seem inappropriate," Portia said, trying hard to keep the bitterness from her voice. "I'll see you at supper."

She reined the horse hard to the left and kicked her heels into the gelding's side. With any luck at all, she thought as the horse sped down the road to the Walking Horseshoe Ranch, she and Chester would figure out a way to put an end to Trenton and her father before another day could pass.

"Stop worrying," Lawrence told Portia as she paced. "I can have the deed done by tomorrow afternoon. I'll send them each a message from the other one. What kind of thing would bring them together without questioning whether the note was authentic?"

Portia smiled. "I have the perfect message."

"Sam Brady wants me to meet him near the old buffalo jump," Trenton said, looking over the slip of paper. The boy who'd brought it had already headed back to town, otherwise Trenton might have asked for more information. It seemed strange that Sam would already want to discuss this matter, when he knew full well Trenton needed to get a letter to Langford first. "I can't imagine why he wants to venture out all that way."

Dianne shrugged. "It's hard to say. Maybe he's looking into land up that way and wants your opinion."

Trenton knew better.

The ride was uneventful, but Trenton tired of waiting for Sam to appear. He had almost given up when the older man finally appeared, coming up the old Indian path Trenton had ridden an hour earlier. Riding down to meet him, Trenton felt an uneasy sensation wash over him. Something about this just wasn't right.

"You sent for me?" Trenton asked as their horses came together.

"No. You sent for me. I got your note about two hours ago."

Trenton shook his head. "I didn't send for you, Sam. I think we've been had."

Just then a rifle shot rang out. The sound cracked loud in the silence of the open range, then seemed to ricochet off the rocky hillside. Sam clutched his neck and stared with wide empty eyes before falling from his horse.

As Trenton threw himself from his mount's back, a bullet cut into his arm and then another into his chest. The wind went out of him and he hit the ground hard. His last thoughts were that Portia had somehow managed to rid herself of both her father and himself, all with one clever little trick.

Portia burst into tears when the sheriff came, accompanied by Chester Lawrence, to their house to tell her that her father had been found dead with a bullet through his neck. He asked her if she knew of any enemies that her father might have made and immediately she answered.

"Trenton Chadwick. He held my father a grudge. He even threatened him the last time we were at the ranch."

The sheriff looked to Chester Lawrence. "Chadwick is dead. They must have ambushed each other." He looked at the floor. "I'm sorry, Mrs. Langford."

"Oh, this is perfectly awful," Portia sobbed. Her mind raced with a hundred thoughts. She wanted — needed — to know the details of how the men had been killed. "What happened?"

"Your father took a bullet in the neck. Chadwick must have waited for him in the rocks, then shot him. When he came down, apparently your father wasn't dead yet and he got off a couple of rounds."

"Where is my father now?" she asked, dabbing at her eyes with the handkerchief.

"At Doc Bufford's. He said he'd ready the body for burial."

"And what of Mr. Chadwick?"

"I had one of my boys take his body back to the Diamond V. Figured they'd want to deal with him."

"I'm sure my dear friend Dianne will be positively devastated. It's just too horrible to even speak of," she murmured and burst into tears anew.

"I'm sorry for your loss, ma'am," the sheriff said, tipping his hat as he backed out the front door.

With the sheriff waiting outside, Portia looked up to find Lawrence watching her closely. "Thank you," she whispered.

"You can thank me later," Lawrence said in a low gravelly voice.

Portia smiled. "You know I will."

CHAPTER 15

The events of the previous forty-eight hours left Dianne numb. Zane's arrival coincided with a visit from the sheriff, who wanted to know if anyone on the Diamond V knew why Trenton had gone gunning after Sam Brady.

Angelina was inconsolable as she pined for Trenton. Her father had delayed their trip back to Chicago at the news of Trenton's death. He wanted only to comfort his child, but there was no comfort to be had. Zane and Morgan appeared completely devastated by the news and could only shake their heads when questioned by the sheriff as to Trenton's motives.

"I don't know how much you know about your brother's past," Sheriff Ferris Tibbot was saying, "but he was pretty notorious in the Midwest. His outlaw activities were enough to see him hanged many times over."

"That's not true!" Angelina Turnquist protested. She got to her feet and stood directly in front of the sheriff. "Trenton Chadwick was a good man. He would never willingly harm anyone."

Her father came up to take hold of her. "Come, Angelina. The man is just trying to do his business."

"These are lies contrived to make Trenton sound bad, but I know he was a good man."

Angelina took her seat and began crying anew. The sound of her mournful sorrow was almost Dianne's undoing. The woman was clearly in love with Trenton and she wasn't about to see his memory smeared. Dianne had been shocked by many of the details given them from the sheriff. She had known Trenton desired revenge for their father's death — revenge against the Union, whom he blamed. But she couldn't believe him capable of murder or the multiple bank robberies that Trenton was being blamed for.

"We realize there's very little to be done at this point," Tibbot continued. "Obviously Chadwick mortally wounded Mr. Brady and then Mr. Brady returned fire on your brother. Mrs. Langford was simply hoping to better understand your brother's reasoning."

Dianne had finally had enough. She knew it wasn't her place to dismiss the sheriff, but she was tired of hearing the details and being asked over and over again why her brother would commit murder. A rage was burning in her heart. A rage that demanded revenge.

"Sheriff, I'm certain there must be other tasks that await you. We are in mourning and need to arrange my brother's funeral. I would ask that you respect that and take your leave."

Cole said nothing, standing protectively at the back of Dianne's chair. She was glad he didn't try to calm her or question her.

"Ma'am, I am sorry for your loss," Sheriff Tibbot said, getting to his feet.

Dianne was sure of one thing — the man was not at all sorry. She couldn't help but wonder exactly what part he might have played in the ambush of her brother and Sam Brady. Tibbot had been appointed by Chester Lawrence, and she had no doubt that he was nicely paid to look the other way when it suited Lawrence.

Dianne steadied her nerves and stood. For a moment she looked down at the floor, unwilling to meet the sheriff's gaze. She was so afraid of betraying her emotions — of giving him more information than he needed.

"Thank you for coming," Dianne said softly. She measured each word with great care. "I know that my brother wasn't a murderer. I would appreciate it if you would attempt to learn the truth of this situation rather than accept the word of those who hated him."

"Ma'am, I'm not exactly sure what you're saying."

Dianne seethed and her head snapped up. "I'm saying that you should seek the truth in this matter. My brother and Sam Brady were good friends. Sam sought Trenton out at his last visit here. He didn't try to avoid Trenton, as Portia has suggested. I think it might do you well to go back and dig for the truth from Mrs. Langford."

Tibbot shook his head. "The woman cries all the time. Can't get a word out of her that isn't muffled and slurred by her cryin'. She can't help me at this point."

"And neither can we," Cole said, coming up beside Dianne. "This entire matter is grieving my wife, and I don't like seeing her like this."

The sheriff looked as though he might say something in protest, but instead he picked up his hat and headed for the door. Dianne refused to budge. She wasn't about to follow the man out and be questioned further.

Angelina sobbed quietly against her father's chest. Dianne couldn't help but be moved by the girl's sorrow. "Why don't you take her to the cabin," Dianne suggested to Turnquist. She'd given them one of the small cabins for privacy's sake when they'd first shown up four weeks earlier. Now, given the circumstances, she was glad for this choice.

Marley agreed and pulled Angelina to her feet. "Come, daughter."

Dianne watched them walk from the room, heading to the back of the house, where they would exit through the kitchen. Without another word to her brothers, Dianne gathered her skirts and climbed the stairs. She walked the long corridor from the guest rooms, past her bedroom and that of the boys. Morgan and Zane followed, knowing she was going to the room where Trenton had been taken.

In silence they opened the door and walked into the darkened room. Koko looked up from where she'd been tending Trenton. Zane closed the door behind them, and Dianne drew a deep breath.

"The sheriff shared a great many details about your past," she said to Trenton.

"I'm sorry," he replied. "I should have told you myself."

"How are his wounds?" Dianne asked, still not sure she could accept that Trenton was guilty of so much.

"If the sheriff's men hadn't bound him up in that blanket and tied him across the back of the horse, he probably would have bled to death — or at least stopped breathing," Koko said. "I think the jostling probably saved his life, while the tight ropes kept him from losing too much blood."

Dianne nodded. "What are we to do?"

"I'm going to leave, of course," Trenton replied. "I'm dead. Remember?"

"Where will you go?" Morgan asked, sitting on the bed beside his brother.

Trenton winced and then shrugged. "I'll go to Seattle or maybe up into Canada. I'm not afraid to lose myself in the wilderness."

"Angelina is devastated," Dianne suddenly declared. "I think we should let her know that you're all right."

"No!" Trenton's reply was firm. "I don't want anyone else to know. Just you here, and Cole. That's enough. I need to start over, and Trenton Chadwick needs to remain dead and buried. I can't do that with Angelina knowing the truth."

"But she's hurting," Dianne protested.

"It's unfair to make her suffer."

"Better she suffer now, thinking me dead, than suffer later, living a life on the run."

"It isn't fair," Dianne said, taking hold of Trenton's hand. "I lost you once before, and now I must lose you again." She felt a tightness constrict her chest. At least he was alive, she told herself. He would live and be healthy and safe by taking on a new identity.

Zane cleared his throat. "I'll go with you to Seattle. I have business there. I'll load you in my wagon to get you out of here. We'll have a better chance of keeping you hidden if we do it that way."

"I'll stay here and deal with Angelina," Morgan said, eyeing his older brother seriously. "I know she's in love with you, but I'm in love with her. If I can, I'll see that she is comforted in that love."

"I'm glad," Trenton remarked. "I know you're a better man than I'll ever be. Take good care of her."

"I will."

"You'll have to change your name," Dianne said, trying to think of the details.

"I've already thought of that. I'll go by my middle name — Nicolaas. And I'll use our great-grandfather's last name — Mercer. I'll be Nicolaas Mercer from Omaha, Nebraska. I lived there a time and can describe it as well as any place."

"So you've already got this all planned out," Dianne said softly.

Trenton met her gaze — his expression taking on a look of deep compassion. "I know this is hard on you, and I don't think I've ever regretted anything as much as I do having to walk away from the life I so love. But if I stay, they'll hang me for Sam's death and Portia will go on murdering at will. You and the twins have to figure a way to stop her. You have to get her back to Ned's father and the law in Baltimore."

"We'll do what we can," Dianne said, knowing it wouldn't be easy.

"How soon do you think I can travel?" Trenton questioned, looking to his aunt.

"I'd say in another three, maybe four days. You don't want to rush the healing. Since you're going by wagon instead of horseback, you'll probably be able to leave a little sooner — but only if Zane can keep you well cushioned."

"I'll see to it," Zane replied.

Dianne sighed. She was so glad to have Trenton alive. She wasn't about to question God on what had happened or to cry out to Him about the unfairness of this horrible situation. She could only remember seeing the sheriff's man throw Trenton's blanket-wrapped body to the ground and declare him dead after a shootout with Sam Brady. Dianne could still feel the way the news had settled over her like deep waters, stealing her breath, crushing in from every side.

At least he's alive, she told herself. *He's alive and will leave this place to start a new life.* Then the thought of Portia Langford came to mind. The woman had to pay for what she'd done. Dianne didn't know if Portia had fired the shots, but either way, Dianne would see her pay.

Morgan found Angelina sitting in the rocking chair on the front porch. She looked so pale and thin. She'd stopped the constant crying, but she still wasn't eating much. Her father had already planned for them to leave for Chicago. They were all to meet up again in July at Yellowstone Park. There they would learn what new funding Marley had managed to take on from the universities back East. Maybe then Morgan would have time to build a new relationship with Angelina.

"Would you care to walk with me?" Morgan asked as he approached her.

"No. I'm not in the mood for company."

"I know. You've told me that more than once. I don't want to impose myself on you;

259

I just thought maybe you'd like a bit of a change of scenery. You don't have to talk if you don't want to."

Angelina looked up and for a moment Morgan was certain she'd say no, but then she surprised him and got to her feet.

"All right. But I don't want to talk."

He tried to assist her down the porch steps, but she refused to take hold of his arm. Instead, she wrapped her shawl more tightly around her and walked toward the back fields.

Morgan kept pace at her side. The guilt of not sharing Trenton's survival weighed heavy on his heart. He wanted nothing more than to spend his life with this woman, but how could he even think such thoughts knowing how she felt about Trenton?

"I can't believe he's gone," she said softly.

Morgan wasn't even sure she'd really spoken, but as she continued and the words poured out of her like flood waters over a dam, he settled in to listen.

"I know I was an annoyance to him," Angelina continued. "I'm much too outspoken — too bold. Every time I tried to talk to him alone, he took on that caged animal look. I suppose given his past, he didn't think I could forgive him."

"Not many women would," Morgan said

hesitantly. He didn't want to do anything to cause her to stop talking.

"If they were in love with him, they would forgive and forget anything," she replied. "He was a good man. He gave generously from the heart. I watched him work with some of the men — the younger new men who had no idea what they were doing. He was so patient and kind. For all his gruffness and outlawing past, Trenton Chadwick was a gentle man."

"He did trust the Lord," Morgan said, knowing his own history in that area left much to be desired. "He once told me it was only by trusting in Jesus' power to forgive that he could get through the day. I didn't know what he meant then — I had no idea of his past. But it sure gave him peace of mind."

Angelina grew silent for several minutes, and Morgan worried he'd said too much. "If Trenton thought it important to trust Jesus, then I suppose I must learn more about Him myself. I've never had much interest in religion, but I could sure use some peace of mind."

Morgan had to admit he could too. His stomach churned at the thought of Angelina pining after a man who was still alive — but who wanted her to believe him dead.

It caused Morgan's thoughts to be all twisted and tangled together. On one hand he wanted to give Angelina the truth — after all, she could hardly go running after Trenton. He was set on disappearing from the world. On the other hand, Morgan knew enough about Angelina Turnquist to know that something that simple would never keep her from going after the man she loved.

Shoving his hands deep into his pockets, Morgan swallowed down the guilt and tried instead to think of how he could convince Angelina to love him. There had to be a way.

Portia paced the small space of the home she'd shared with her father. It was worrisome to know that Ned's father knew where she was. It was even more troubling to know that he'd been suspicious all along of Ned's death and that he'd gone to great lengths to try to prove her guilt.

Anger at her father and Trenton had caused her to act quickly to see them eliminated, but perhaps she had moved too quickly. There had been no satisfaction in their deaths. Relief, yes, but no real sense of accomplishment. There was still the matter of Langford and his hired investigator.

"I don't know what the next step should be," she muttered. "I can hardly stay here and risk Langford sending someone after me."

Then a thought came to her. If Langford thought she was dead, he'd have no reason to pursue the matter any further. But how would she convince him of this?

Portia stopped in midstep. "I can write him a letter. Only I'll write it as if I were Dianne Selby. I'll tell him of my brother's death — how he killed Sam Brady and . . . his daughter, Portia."

She grinned. It was priceless, really. If Langford thought her dead he wouldn't send anyone to accuse her or bring her back to Baltimore. He also would never suspect or be on the lookout for her coming back to settle the score.

"Stupid man. Thinks he can stop me — thinks he can blame me for the death of his equally stupid son. Well, he can just think again."

CHAPTER 16

"But I'm absolutely convinced that Portia is behind the shootings," Dianne declared to Charity Hammond.

Charity poured tea for both herself and Dianne. "But you have no proof."

"I have the concerns of Ned Langford's father." She pulled a letter from her pocket. "Mr. Langford had been corresponding with Trenton regarding the supposed suicide death of his son. He believed Portia to have caused Ned's death and wanted Trenton's help in proving she was guilty. After the death of Portia's father and Trenton's . . . departure," she said, lowering her voice, "I wrote Mr. Langford to let him know what had happened. I didn't tell him about Trenton. I figured there is always a risk of the letter being intercepted."

"I wish there were something I could do to offer you comfort," Charity said as she stirred cream into her tea.

Dianne was surprised by her friend's words. "I don't want comfort; I want to see that woman behind bars. If she's committed the murders of several men, she deserves to hang."

"Your anger is understandable, but you can hardly take up your brother's cause by chasing after Portia Langford. You have three little boys who need you. You have a husband who needs you as well. Cole would never approve of your getting involved in something this dangerous."

Dianne frowned. "Someone has to do something. Portia will get away with this otherwise. I know she's the one who planned the deaths of Trenton and Sam, whether she actually pulled the trigger or not." Dianne got to her feet, nearly knocking over the tea tray. "What if it were your brother? What would you do?"

Charity put her spoon down. "I suppose I would feel just as passionate about it as you do. However, I would hope to have a friend — a very good friend — who would work to talk me out of doing anything foolish."

Dianne heard the concern in Charity's words and sunk back into the chair. "I feel so hopeless. If I don't do something, Sam will have died in vain." She whispered the words on the chance they might be overheard. The small house was close to the main street of Madison, and there was no telling who might wander by. She had told the Hammonds the truth about Trenton. It had been necessary, since Ben was the one to perform the ceremony at the mock funeral. Charity could be trusted, Dianne knew, but she also knew that Charity would offer good counsel and wisdom. Which was why Dianne had come to her.

"What have you heard of Portia? I've not seen her since the funeral over a month ago."

Charity shrugged. "She hardly seems to be in mourning, if that's what you're asking. She parades around this town like she owns it. She hasn't been in church since her father's passing, but of course you know that."

Dianne nodded. She'd not missed a single service since Ben had declared the church open for public worship. Most of the community had joined the little log church — some out of true desire to fellowship with other Christians, some out of boredom. Then there were those whom Dianne believed only came in order to keep track of other folks. Like Portia and the Lawrences.

"Let's not worry about Portia and what she's doing. I'd rather not spend my time in gossip, and I know you feel the same."

Picking up her tea, Dianne sighed. "I just don't know what I should do."

"Of course you do," Charity said with a gentle smile. "You need to pray. God is the one who has the right to seek revenge. He will see things made right, even if you never figure a way to bring it about. Maybe even in spite of your trying to bring it about."

"I feel helpless. I mean —" she looked to the window and then back again to Charity — "if you'd have seen him."

"I'm sure it was absolutely horrible."

"I thought he was . . . well . . . you know."

"But he wasn't. That's what you have to remember. God was merciful to you and your family. Poor Sam was all alone in the world — perhaps the quickness of his death was mercy as well."

"But murder isn't a mercy," Dianne protested.

"No, I'm not suggesting that it is," Charity said before taking a long sip of her tea. She put down the cup and looked thoughtful for a moment.

"I liked Sam Brady a great deal, but the man was lonely and longed for the day he would leave this world. He loved his wife very much, and losing her was hard on him. Then this trouble with Portia surely must have weighed on his mind."

"I can't imagine how I would feel if Luke or one of the others grew up to be a murderer," Dianne said, shaking her head. "It would break my heart."

"And no doubt it broke Sam's heart as well. I wish I could say that everything will work out, but sometimes evil is allowed to flourish. I do know that eventually every evil deed will be answered for. God will not be mocked."

"But sometimes that reckoning doesn't come in our lifetime, is that it?"

"All in God's time, child."

Dianne drew a deep breath and let it out slowly. "I feel so angry inside. I don't know how to let this rest in His timing."

"You must pray and take every thought captive. It's never easy to stand against a strong wind and not fall . . . or at least exhaust yourself in the battle. When those thoughts come to you — thoughts of revenge and anger — you must take them captive. Refuse to let them have power over you."

"That won't be easy."

Charity lifted the pot to pour herself another cup of tea. "No, it's never easy. But doing the right thing is often difficult."

Dianne knew it to be true. She dropped

her chin and stared at the letter she'd let fall to the table. R. E. Langford asked her to help pick up where Trenton had left off. Dianne had no idea how she could do that without arousing Portia's suspicions. Worse yet, she had no idea how to do it without arousing Cole's concerns or his disapproval.

Leaving Charity's house nearly an hour later, Dianne was determined to get her shopping done and find Levi and Cole. They'd come to town to have some work completed by Malachi and would surely be done with it by now.

Dianne couldn't help but ponder Charity's words. They were nearly the same suggestions Faith had given her. She hadn't planned on telling Faith the truth about Trenton, but it had just spilled out in their conversation. Faith was relieved to know that Dianne's brother was safe and alive, but she chided Dianne to refrain from mounting a campaign to catch Portia Langford as the responsible party.

"No doubt she had to have help to manage something like that," Faith had told her. "You'd better be careful about who you cross paths with. Those Lawrence boys are meaner than a hound with a sore tooth. Their papa is worse still, and he seems

269

pretty cozy with Portia."

Dianne had never met the Lawrence boys, nor did she have any desire to meet them. It was bad enough that Cole was confronted on nearly a weekly basis by Chester Lawrence. He always wanted to accuse the Diamond V of one offense or another. Lately it was some inordinate protest about the number of twin calves born to Diamond V cows.

"Mrs. Selby, I see you're looking well," Cynthia Lawrence remarked snidely.

Dianne looked up, amazed to find the woman standing directly in her way. How ironic that she had just been thinking about the Lawrences when she nearly ran into one.

"Hello, Mrs. Lawrence." Dianne fought to keep her voice even.

"I saw your husband over at the smithy's. No doubt he's spending money earned off of Walking Horseshoe cattle."

"I beg your pardon?"

Cynthia Lawrence sneered. "You'll get no pardon from me. You're robbing us blind."

"I have no idea what you're talking about," Dianne said, trying hard not to lose her temper. From the rumors she'd heard, she had some thought as to what Mrs. Lawrence was getting at, but she wanted to hear the woman declare it for herself.

"Your ranch hands are stealing our calves after the mama cows are killed or run off. We were lucky to see a new calf in one out of five cows."

"I'm sorry to hear that, but I hardly see how that condemns my men of stealing."

"Your cows produced an unusually high number of twins this year — at least that's what I've heard your husband say."

Dianne could see where the conversation was headed. "Yes. We had a large number of twins, but in each case the calves and mama cows were clearly matched up. There were no strays out there."

"I find that impossible to believe."

Dianne shrugged. "I hardly find that to be my responsibility. I cannot force you to believe the truth."

Just then two young women joined Cynthia. Dianne knew the girls only from afar. They were Mara and Elsa Lawrence, the only daughters of Cynthia and Chester. Elsa was the spitting image of her mother, temper and all, while Mara was much less objectionable.

"Why are you talking to her?" Elsa asked disapprovingly.

Cynthia waggled her finger. "Don't take that tone with me, missy. I've enough to deal with right here. I do not need my own flesh and blood questioning me."

Elsa put her hands on her hips. "You're stealing our cattle," she accused Dianne, "and we intend to get the law to do something about you."

Dianne noted the fiery glint in the young girl's eyes. She was no more than fourteen, but already she carried a chip on her shoulder. No doubt it had been placed there by her father and mother, who seemed determined to bad-mouth the Selbys at every point.

"As I told your mother, we are not stealing your cattle. We have no need to do so; we're already very prosperous. Why would a few head of scrawny English beef interest us when we have hearty Texas and Scottish stock?"

"Our herd is just as strong and solid as yours!" Elsa protested.

"The girl is right," Cynthia replied angrily. "There's nothing but good reliable stock in our herd."

"Which is why you have so many calves and mama cows dying in the winter," Dianne said, unable to keep the sarcasm from her voice. "Your cattle are apparently unable to adapt. Perhaps you should head south to a warmer climate."

"We're here to stay — you might as well

know that," Cynthia said, taking a step toward Dianne. "We intend to see you put off of your land before Christmas. We have the law on our side."

Dianne couldn't imagine what the woman was talking about. How could they possibly bring this into any kind of legal forum? The Selbys had done nothing illegal. It certainly wasn't against the law to have bred better cattle.

Mara stepped in at this point. "Mama, it's not good for you to get all worked up." She looked to Dianne apologetically. "Remember what the doctor said."

Dianne had no idea what kind of ailment Mrs. Lawrence might be suffering, and frankly she couldn't be bothered at that moment, for much to her dismay, Portia Langford was headed straight for them.

"I'm afraid we'll have to save this conversation for another day," Dianne said, gathering her skirts. "I'm already late to rejoin my husband."

"We'll have this conversation, all right," Cynthia shouted after Dianne. "My Chester is taking matters to the law and his new Cattleman's Association. You won't get away with this."

Dianne wanted to turn around and comment but knew better than to open her mouth. If she stopped to say anything, it would only invite comment from Portia, and that was something Dianne wanted no part of. If Portia were to start in on the sad loss of her father and her belief that Trenton was the one responsible, Dianne knew she'd be unable to keep silent.

Things were no better at Malachi's blacksmith shop, however. Dianne entered to find Cole standing nose to nose with a man who could only be described as a younger and meaner looking version of Chester Lawrence. The man spoke a string of obscenities that left Dianne wide-eyed.

"You've taken our calves for the last time, Selby."

"We have no need of your calves. Like I told your father, feel free to come by and inspect the calves. You'll clearly see they have absolutely nothing in common with your herd."

The man narrowed his eyes. "Bad things have a way of happenin' to cattle thieves in these parts. I heard tell of a man dragged behind a horse for five miles for stealing. Wouldn't hurt my feelings at all if the same was to happen to you."

"Cole, yo horse be ready," Malachi said, coming to stand beside the two men. Dianne breathed a sigh of relief. Malachi had arms like tree trunks and fists the size of hams. If there was to be a fight, Dianne knew whose side Malachi would take.

"Get outta my way," the younger man growled, pushing at Malachi. The big man wasn't even moved. "I said, get outta my way." His right hand went to the handle of his gun.

"Do you plan to shoot the man in cold blood, Jerrod?"

Dianne turned to see Chester Lawrence stride into the room. She didn't know whether to be relieved or further concerned.

"We'll let the law handle this matter," Lawrence said, coming alongside Dianne. "Mrs. Selby," he said, touching his hat. "Come on, boy. We've got work to do."

Jerrod reluctantly relaxed his grip on the revolver and stormed out of the shop. Chester looked hard at Cole. "We've turned this over to the law, just so you know. I've helped form a new Cattleman's Association to deal with situations such as this. Smaller ranches don't appreciate folks stealing away their stock."

"If you're trying to say something," Cole said in a tone that caused the hairs on the back of Dianne's neck to prickle, "then just come right out and say it."

"I intend to see you charged with cattle

rustling to start with," Lawrence said matter-of-factly. "And I intend to see you run out of this valley before winter."

He stomped out of the shop in much the same fashion as his son. Dianne looked to Cole in confusion. "His wife said something similar. She suggested we had taken their calves after killing or running off the mamas."

"Lawrence knows nothing about ranching in Montana. His experiences have been back East. As I hear it, his English-born grandparents moved to America and began raising cattle in Massachusetts. His parents tried their hand and then Chester heard about the big land grants being given out here for desert land."

"The Lawrence property can hardly be called desert. Surely he didn't qualify for the Desert Land Act."

"I'm not completely certain," Cole said, his gaze still fixed to the door where Lawrence and his son had exited. "But if there was a way to cheat the government out of good grazing ground, I'm sure Lawrence figured it out."

Dianne nodded. The entire family was trouble, she really had no doubt of that. Though Mara had seemed very decent and had actually played peacemaker between

Dianne and Cynthia. Maybe there was hope for at least one member of the Lawrence family.

CHAPTER 17

Months later the Selbys were still waiting for the Lawrence threats to manifest themselves. It was like being under siege — watching and waiting for the attack to come. They couldn't see the enemy, but he was out there, just the same.

"What do you suppose they mean to do? They've been threatening us for months — and all because spring roundup didn't go their way. Now we're heading into another fall and they still are making threats but doing nothing. What does it mean?" Dianne asked Cole as they sat with Koko in the main sitting room, enjoying the evening. The boys were all asleep and it seemed the perfect time to get a grasp on the situation regarding Chester Lawrence and his family.

A tray of hot coffee and tea sat nearby. Getting to his feet, Cole crossed to the refreshments and picked up a cup. He looked thoughtful as he poured a cup of coffee. "I have no idea what Lawrence is up to. I've heard some troubling rumors but thought to ignore them. Guess I can't ignore them now."

"What rumors?" Koko asked. She had sent her own children upstairs to ready for bed.

"There's talk that Lawrence has been threatening area ranchers. Especially the smaller operations. He wants everyone to join his Cattleman's Association, and apparently some men, like Whitson Farley and G. W. Vandercamp, have refused."

"Because of our stand against it?"

"Probably. I know Whit talked long and hard to me a couple months back, and when I pointed out that everyone of power in these parts was benefiting in some manner from Lawrence, I think he realized for himself how dangerous the situation could be. He told me he didn't plan to join anything headed up by that man."

"And Lawrence has threatened him?"

Cole nodded and took a long drink. Dianne could tell by his tone that he was worried. He'd been testy and difficult for several months — especially since the encounter in Madison with Lawrence and his son.

"Do you think —"

Rusty began to bark wildly. Cole jumped

to his feet and reached for the rifle that hung over the door. Dianne followed her husband to the front door, taking up a table lamp as they went.

"Stay here. It might be bears again."

Dianne nodded. Koko stood not two feet behind. The women exchanged a worried glance but said nothing. Dianne stepped to the door and held the lamp up. The sight that greeted her completely stunned her.

"Whitson?" Cole questioned, putting the rifle aside in order to help the man.

Dianne could see that Whitson Farley was in bad shape. He sat on his horse looking as though he'd been beaten, his face bloodied and swollen. Instead of dismounting the horse, he swayed and fell toward Cole.

"Get a bed ready," Cole declared, hoisting the man over his shoulder.

Dianne hurried to do as Cole had instructed. "The bedroom at the top of the stairs would be best."

"I'll get my medicine bag and some hot water," Koko said, moving off toward the kitchen.

Dianne rushed up the stairs with Cole coming fast behind her. She barely had time to pull down the covers when Cole deposited Whitson Farley on the bed.

Dianne gasped. It was much worse here

in the light of the room. The man was barely recognizable. Teeth were missing and his eyes were nearly swollen shut. His clothing was in shreds, as if he'd been dragged behind his horse.

"Whit, who did this to you?"

The man could barely move his swollen lips. ". . . ar . . . ance."

Cole shook his head and looked to Dianne. Dianne shrugged.

Cole knelt beside the bed. "Whit. What happened? Where's Maggie?"

Dianne hadn't even thought of Whit's wife. She placed the lamp on the bedside table and quickly lit another lamp to give better light.

". . . ar . . . ance boys." The man gasped for breath. The wheezing sound convinced Dianne he was suffering from damage to his lungs. She remembered a similar sound when one of the cowboys had punctured a lung.

"The Lawrence boys?" Cole asked.

Dianne froze in midstep. The words made sense now that Cole had voiced them.

Whit nodded, his head barely moving.

"Was Chester with them?"

Whit drew a ragged breath. "No."

"Did they come to the ranch?" Cole asked.

"Yes."

"What did they do to you?"

"Dragged . . . behind —" he paused and winced "— a horse." He broke off again. "Beat . . . with . . . shovel."

Dianne gasped.

"Is Maggie hurt?" Cole asked.

"Dead."

Dianne gripped the footboard of the bed. A wave of dizziness washed over her. Koko came into the room and moved to the opposite side of the bed from where Cole knelt.

"Maggie is dead?" Cole asked in disbelief.

Whit nodded, his eyes closing.

"Whit, did the Lawrence boys kill Maggie?"

Whit again nodded.

Cole looked to Dianne. "I'll get some of the boys and head over to the ranch. I'll send Levi for Doc Bufford and for the Hammonds — just in case."

Dianne thought she might faint as Koko cleared away the strips of Whit's shirt. The man's chest was bleeding profusely. In all her days of dressing wounds and patching up damaged cowboys, she'd never seen anything this bad.

"What if the Lawrences are still there?" Dianne whispered.

"They won't be there," Cole said, getting

to his feet. "They'd have never let Whit leave. They probably figured him to be dead — like Maggie."

Dianne looked back at the bed. "Why would they do this?"

Whit tried to open his mouth to speak, but no words came from the misshapen jaw. "They probably came to scare them — get them to leave. Things obviously got out of control." Cole's stoic expression left Dianne trembling inside. How could he go out there — out into the danger of the night? How could she let him leave? What if the Lawrences were waiting out there for him? What if it was all a trap?

"Please don't go," she said, rushing to Cole's side. "They might want to kill you too."

"I'll have plenty of men with me. I'll leave some here as well. Keep things locked up. Stay inside. Only let the doctor or the Hammonds in."

Dianne knew there was no sense in arguing. Cole had clearly made up his mind.

"Dianne, please come help me," Koko requested.

Dianne looked into Cole's eyes. She longed to kiss him, to hold him close, but the anger she heard in his voice kept her from doing that. He had every opportunity to touch her, but instead his hands were balled into fists at his sides. Dianne stepped back. "Please be careful."

Cole nodded and left without another word. Dianne went to the door and watched him rush down the stairs. She heard the door open and close and felt the overwhelming urge to run after him.

"You have to stay here and wait," Koko said softly. "I'll need your help with Whit."

Dianne knew she was right but felt so very helpless. "What if they're waiting out there? What if this is just a trick to get Cole out there alone?"

"Cole has already said he wouldn't go alone. Now come help me."

The authoritative command of Koko's voice nudged Dianne from her stunned contemplation. "What do you want me to do?"

They did all that they could for Whit, but he died nearly an hour after showing up at the Diamond V. Dianne watched Koko pull the sheet up to cover the poor man's butchered face and broke into tears for the first time that night.

"How can they both be dead? I saw them at church just last week. We were talking about having a harvest party next month."

Koko washed blood from her hands and arms. "It would seem the Lawrences have decided to take this into their own hands rather than wait for the law."

"Do you suppose they plan to come after us next?"

Koko dried her hands. "We're not alone, as the Farleys were. The Lawrences know we have a good many men."

Dianne heard voices coming from downstairs. She opened the bedroom door and rushed to the top of the stairs to see what was going on. To her surprise, Levi was pointing the doctor to the stairs at the same time he was holding the sheriff back.

Dianne met Bufford midway. "He's gone," she said softly.

Dr. Bufford's sympathetic expression was nearly her undoing. "I'm sorry. I'll go ahead and look in on him if you don't mind."

"That would be fine. Koko's with him." Bufford nodded and continued up the stairs while Dianne met the questioning stares of the men below.

"What are you going to do about this?" Dianne asked the sheriff.

Tibbot seemed surprised. "I'm here, aren't I? I came to arrest Farley for the death of his wife. They had quite a fight tonight."

Dianne laughed cynically. "Maggie and Whit had no fight. The Lawrence boys killed her and then beat Whit half to death. He died just a few minutes ago."

"That's a pity," Tibbot said. "I would have enjoyed hanging him."

"You're not hearing me. Whit told us everything." Dianne moved toward the man, but Levi intercepted her.

"Any word from Cole?" he asked, taking hold of her arm.

She looked into his dark eyes and shook her head. "No. I'm worried the Lawrences will kill him too."

"Now, Mrs. Selby, I can tell you with great certainty that the Lawrences had nothing to do with this murder."

Dianne met the man's gaze. "Whit told us the Lawrence boys killed Maggie. You're free to go see his body and then explain to me how he got that way if not for the Lawrence boys doing him in as well. I can't see Maggie being able to beat him that badly. He was no doubt dragged behind the back of one of the Lawrences' horses."

"He's mistaken. It couldn't be the Lawrence boys."

"And why not? Because Chester Lawrence pays you on the side to say it wasn't them?"

Tibbot clenched his jaw as he scowled.

"Are you accusing me of lying?"

"I'm not accusing you of anything. I'm telling you that a dying man told us exactly what happened and you're doing nothing about it."

"It wasn't the Lawrence boys. They were with me all day, and then we were all at the Walking Horseshoe tonight. It wasn't them." He spoke the words with great contempt.

Dianne stiffened, realizing the Lawrences were going to get away with murder. "How did you know about Maggie's murder if you were at the Lawrence ranch all evening?"

Tibbot narrowed his eyes. "I was headed out there because of another matter. I got there just as your husband was arriving with his men."

"Cole was all right?"

"Looked to be fine. We talked about what had transpired. He said Whit was here and was hurt. We found Maggie dead, and I had no reason to believe that anyone but Whit was responsible."

"Well, if this man was responsible," Dr. Bufford said as he descended the stairs, "then someone tore into him after the deed. The man is barely in one piece. It's a wonder he was able to ride from his ranch to the Diamond V."

"Well, that ain't my concern."

The sound of a wagon approaching sent the group out onto the porch, where they could see that it was Ben and Charity. Diane had never been so happy to see anyone in her life. There was a comfort just in having them here.

"We came as quickly as we could," Ben said, helping Charity from the wagon.

"How's Whit?" Charity asked.

Dianne shook her head. "He's gone. Maggie too. The sheriff intends to do nothing about it." They all looked to the sheriff.

Tibbot grew uneasy. "You have no proof that the Lawrence boys were involved. I was with them, and I'll testify to that fact if you try to prove otherwise." He turned in a huff, marching to where he'd tied off his horse. "If I were you," he declared after mounting, "I'd stay out of it. You're gonna have your own problems as soon as a judge rules on the validity of your claim to the Diamond V. I'd be prepared to move if I were you."

Dianne felt as if she'd been slapped. "What are you talking about?"

Tibbot laughed harshly. "You'll hear about it soon enough. You should have known better than to lie about inheriting the ranch from your uncle. Fact is, the man died without a will."

"He didn't need a will to leave me this

ranch," Dianne replied angrily. "He had my name added to the deed."

"Well, that's not what we've found. There was only one deed and one name. Bram Vandyke. Fact is, even that deed is questionable. We're waiting to hear what the judge thinks on that, and then we'll be back to deal with you properly." He reined the horse hard to the left and headed out, leaving the collection of people to stare dumbly after him.

CHAPTER 18

Ardith sat with Charity while Dianne explained what had transpired that evening to Cole. Ardith marveled at her sister's strength. She'd always admired that about Dianne. Even when they'd been children, Ardith had felt the need to play the tomboy in order to show that she, too, was not afraid of life. But she'd been terrified of so much.

"Can they take the ranch away from us?"

Ardith heard the worry in her sister's voice. They all looked to Cole for answers. He shook his head. "We've got friends in the government. They go all the way up to the territorial governor. Don't worry. No one is going to steal this ranch from us."

Ardith wanted to take comfort in his words, but she knew there was too much that could go wrong. Life had a way of taking bad turns. It was one of the reasons she couldn't say yes to Levi's proposals — no matter how much Winona saw him as a father figure. No matter how much they both needed him.

"So has our Levi convinced you yet to marry him?" Charity asked as Dianne and Cole continued to discuss their plan. "For as long as he's known you he's been in love with you."

Ardith stiffened. "He should forget such notions."

Charity frowned. "Don't you like him? Isn't he good enough?" She sounded genuinely hurt.

Ardith shook her head vigorously. "It's not like that. I'm not good enough for *him*."

"Nonsense!" Charity said, a bit too loud. Cole and Dianne turned to see what was going on, then quickly resumed their discussion. Lowering her voice, Charity continued. "Why would you ever say such a thing? Levi adores you and Winona. He would make a good husband and father."

"Yes, but I wouldn't make a good wife. He deserves better."

Charity laughed. "Child, there is absolutely nothing better than marriage to the woman you love. Levi is positively wasting away for want of your love. Why are you denying him — and yourself? I know you love him."

Ardith couldn't believe the older woman

would pose such questions. The events of Ardith's past were so fresh and raw in her own mind that she couldn't believe they weren't equally obvious to everyone else.

"I do love him," she admitted, finding it strange that she should be so open with Charity Hammond. "But I can't marry him."

"Pshaw. Do you have a better idea?"

Ardith decided to speak despite the worried conversation taking place between her sister and Cole. "I love him, but I want him to have good things in life. I want him to marry a woman who hasn't been . . . used . . . like me."

Charity reached over and took hold of Ardith's hand. "You know full well after what happened here earlier — what's happening here now — that life out here is hard. It robs children of their youth and women of their hope. There's more than one way to lose your innocence in this territory."

"But I worry that if I marry him, he'll one day come to resent me for the past — resent Winona. I know that Dianne will never feel that way. She'll let me stay here forever; she's already told me as much."

"Dear child, Levi will never come to resent you. The poor boy has his own past, and for a long time he bore it in shame. Orphaned, with no people, he felt completely worthless. No one could vouch for him, and back East you know what that means. You can't get a decent job without someone standing up for you. Ben and I have loved Levi like he was one of our own — but now it's time for you to take over."

"I'm afraid."

Charity grinned. "We're all afraid of something, but a person doesn't ever need to be afraid of love."

"You're a useless excuse for a son," Chester Lawrence declared. His third born, Joshua, stood across from him.

Chester pushed aside the papers he'd been working on and motioned the boy to take a seat. "You've always got your nose in some fool book. I need ranch hands, not scholars."

"I'm no good at ranch work, Father. You know that."

"Don't sass me, boy. I won't tolerate it. I need you to help your brothers."

"Begging your pardon, sir, they don't want my help."

"They don't want your whining and nonsense. Get out there and help them build those stalls. I don't want to have to tell you again. After you get done with that, you can help them round up those steers we plan to sell."

Joshua nodded, but Chester could see that the boy was not at all compliant in the matter. He was nothing like his brothers, Jerrod and Roy. He was soft and meek. Weak.

"Get out of here and get to work!"

"Yes, sir." Joshua didn't attempt to argue with him, and Chester was glad for that. He was in a fighting mood already, and he didn't need an excuse to explode. The judge had told him that the Selbys were well liked in the valley and that Bram Vandyke had been even more esteemed than they were. It would be hard to pull off the scheme Chester wanted, but in time — maybe in a few years — the judge thought it might be possible.

"I don't want to wait years," Chester said, slamming his fist on his desk. He got up and grabbed his gun belt. Buckling it on, he strode to the front door.

"I suppose you're going to her again," Cynthia Lawrence said from the staircase.

Chester turned as he took up his hat. "What I do is my business, woman. You'd do best to remember that."

"What I remember is that my money helped get you here. I don't intend to be the laughingstock of this valley while you go behind my back with her."

"Well, maybe I should just bring her home with me. You want to set her up in a room?"

Cynthia scowled and approached Chester. "Maybe you should build a brothel to go along with that silly town you've put together."

He slapped her hard across the face but was surprised by her return blow. He grabbed her wrist and twisted her arm back and to the side. "Don't you ever lay a hand on me again, woman. Do you hear?"

She fought to get away from him, but Chester only tightened his grip. "I'm waiting for an answer."

"I hear you," Cynthia said, nearly falling backward as Chester released her.

"Good. Now I intend to hear nothing more about it. Don't wait supper for me."

Portia paced the small confines of the range shack and waited for Chester to finish dressing. "I can't stand it. Having nothing more of you than these occasional afternoons is so hard to bear. I want you to marry me."

Chester fairly growled. "Aren't you forgetting one minor detail? I'm already married."

"But that could change," Portia said smoothly. She didn't know why he was in such a foul mood, but even their time together had not helped to restore his spirits. "I mean . . . it could change very soon."

Chester stopped pulling up his suspenders and looked at Portia. His eyes narrowed. "What are you saying?"

Portia shrugged and cocked her head to one side. "Things happen. People get sick and people die. Something could happen to Cynthia."

Chester relaxed his gaze and nodded. "She hasn't been feeling well. I guess you're right."

Portia came to where he stood. "I thought she looked in poor health."

"Life out here has never agreed with her. She's come to the place where she's seeing Doc Bufford on a weekly basis."

"That's sad," Portia said, tracing her fingers along Chester's whiskered jaw. "You're such a vibrant man. I'm sure having a sickly wife makes it difficult — even lonely."

Chester took hold of her wrist. His grip was tight, almost painful, but Portia said nothing. The man was powerful — powerful enough to give her what she needed. And with any luck, he'd have the Diamond V by Christmas, tripling his wealth. "I don't know what's going on in that little head of yours, but if you're suggesting that something could happen — something to hurry along Cynthia's passing — well . . . don't count on me."

Portia's countenance fell. She'd hoped Chester would feel the same way she did. She'd hoped that her enticements and occasional meetings for an afternoon of stolen pleasure would give him reason to want Cynthia dead and gone.

"I can't stand people who are all talk. If you intend to take care of the matter, then do it. Don't talk about it. If she's gone, I'll marry you."

Portia nearly gasped. He was so matter-of-fact about the issue that he'd taken her off guard. When he released her, Portia could only stare after him as he went about continuing to dress. He didn't care if she killed his wife. He just didn't want to know about it or be a part of it. And that was fine by Portia. She always hated having to involve others in her plans.

"You going to keep moping?" Morgan asked Angelina as they rode the valley in search of horses. Angelina's father wanted Morgan to pick them up a string of horses from the Diamond V. They needed to be swift and strong, as Marley wanted to make a fast trip to Utah, where supplies were awaiting them at the Corrine depot. They needed to make the trip and be back to the Diamond V before the heavy snows fell in the mountain passes.

"I asked if you were going to keep moping."

"I heard you."

Morgan turned and shrugged. "Well, you didn't say anything, and for all that your father has taught me, mind reading isn't on the list of accomplishments."

She frowned. "How can you act like this? Your brother is dead. Tragically gunned down. How can you pretend that nothing is wrong?"

Morgan swallowed hard. He couldn't bear lying to Angelina. He wanted to marry her — he loved her more than he'd ever loved anyone or anything. Including his freedom.

"Trenton wouldn't want us to grieve. He was a man who enjoyed life."

Angelina looked away quickly and Morgan was certain she was crying again. For several minutes neither of them said anything.

Morgan hated that he couldn't be honest with her about Trenton. He wanted to tell her the truth at least a dozen times a day, and if it weren't for the possibility of the killer finding out that Trenton was alive, he might have broken the silence.

But I can't tell her. Not without first talking to Dianne. I promised I wouldn't say anything, and it's got to stay that way.

"When I wake up in the morning, he's the first one I think of," Angelina finally said, her voice barely a whisper. "Then as I pass through the day, I can't help but remember things about him. Little silly things." She dabbed at her eyes with her gloved hand. "Then when I find the end of the day has come, I feel worse than ever. I think of how we sometimes played a game of chess or checkers. I can almost hear Trenton talking about breaking one horse or another. I'm so grateful for the time we shared — the winter we spent on the Diamond V — but it wasn't enough."

"I guess it never is." *Just like my love for you isn't enough to wipe out Trenton's memory.* Morgan shook his head. *But how could she love me when I'd lie to her about something like this? I thought maybe with Trenton gone she'd realize it was really me she loved, but instead she only misses him more and more. How can I keep lying about it?*

"I never meant for you to get hurt, Morgan," she said softly.

That only made it worse. Morgan turned

his horse. "I think we should check over there." He urged the horse to a trot, not bothering to look back. He knew Angelina would follow — sooner or later.

That evening after completing their selection of stock, Morgan and Angelina joined the family at the dinner table. He was surprised to hear his sister chiding Angelina for her sadness. It wasn't like Dianne to be so hardhearted.

"Life is difficult at best in these parts. You need to recognize that — maybe even return to Chicago, where the world is more civilized."

"I can't bear Chicago. My mother would only attempt to marry me off to yet another suitor."

"Maybe that would be for the best," Dianne replied.

Morgan toyed with the silver fork. His sister set a nice table — almost as fancy as the hotels they'd stayed in once when they'd gone to Denver.

Angelina got to her feet, bringing every gaze to settle on her. "I don't know how you can all just sit here feeling right as rain. Trenton is gone, and while that may be easy enough for you to overcome, I find it a tiny bit difficult." Her sarcasm was not lost on anyone.

"No one is pretending that having Trenton gone is easy," Cole said. "He was better at breaking horses than anyone I've ever known — myself included. He was also one of the best people to sit and talk to. I could bring him an idea and he was always good at listening and figuring out if it might work."

"I miss him too," Ardith said softly. "I would love for him to watch Winona grow up."

"We all miss him," Dianne said, looking most uncomfortable. "But he's gone, and the last thing he would want would be for any of us to give up living. We must go on — if for no other reason than to honor his life."

Angelina lowered her head. "I go on living, but not because I want to." She left the room without waiting for a response, and Morgan knew he had to get Dianne's permission to tell Angelina the truth.

"Dianne, I want to talk to you — now."

His sister looked up. "We're still eating."

"It's important or I wouldn't take you away."

Dianne looked to Cole and then back to Morgan. "Can't it wait?"

"No. Please."

"Go ahead," Cole said, nudging her to-

301

ward the door. "I'll see to the boys."

"I'll help him," Ardith offered.

Morgan took Dianne by the arm. "Come on."

They walked outside, the darkness wrapping itself around them like a shawl. There was no moon and very little light. Morgan was almost glad. He didn't want to have to look Dianne in the eye and lose his nerve. She was always so sensible, so capable. He had always found it difficult to exist in her shadow. He knew she'd never understand that, but even their trip west had proven her abilities more so than his own. She was strong in so many ways where he failed. But of course, that conversation needed to wait until another day. Right now he really needed to get her to understand the importance of coming clean with Angelina.

"We have to tell Angelina the truth."

"No. It would only jeopardize Trenton."

"She's half sick with grief. It's not getting any better. Every day I have to live with the fact that she's bearing such sorrow — sorrow enough to put her in the ground."

"She won't kill herself — she's much too strong for that."

"Listen to yourself." Morgan took hold of her shoulders. "Angelina is a good woman. She won't cause Trenton any trouble, but she very well may die from a broken heart. Could you live with yourself if that happened? I know I couldn't."

"Morgan, don't go on so. Angelina is strong — you'll see. She'll be fine."

"Dianne, I've tried hard not to go against you, no matter the decision or choice. You've always seemed to know the right thing to do, and I've respected you for that. But I won't do this anymore. Either you go with me to tell her the truth — or I'm going to her alone."

He felt his sister's shoulders slump. "But it might cause all kinds of problems. Have you thought of that? Because I have."

"I've thought of the possibility — no, the probability that she'll want to find him."

"And what if she does? How will you adjust to losing her, loving her as you do?"

Morgan dropped his hold. Her words stung him and for a moment he wanted only to walk away and forget the conversation. But instead, he stood his ground. "You can't lose what you never had."

Dianne could not persuade Morgan to let the matter drop, and after a brief discussion with Cole, they agreed that it would be best to explain the situation to Angelina. Dianne worried at what the young woman's reaction might be. There would be no simple way to tell her the news, and she would be incensed at their deception.

When Morgan appeared with Angelina, Dianne wanted to call the whole thing off. She worried that even one more person knowing the truth might very well mean Portia Langford would learn it as well.

"Morgan said you had something to tell me?" Angelina questioned.

"Yes, please sit here beside me," Dianne said, pointing to the opposite end of the settee. "I hardly know where to begin."

Morgan took the chair opposite them, and Dianne could see in his eyes that there was a mixture of regret and relief. She felt so sorry for him. He'd loved Angelina from first glance. But for equally as long, Angelina had loved Trenton and had made no pretense of anything else.

"Sometimes things aren't as they seem, and we make them that way in order to keep something worse from happening," Dianne began. "I made the decision to do something in order to keep something worse from happening."

Angelina shook her head. "What are you talking about?"

Dianne bit at her lower lip, uncertain as to how she should proceed.

"Trenton isn't dead," Morgan blurted.

Angelina turned ashen and looked to Morgan and then Dianne. "What?" She was barely able to croak out the word.

"What my brother is trying to say is that because of the attempt on Trenton's life, and with reason to believe that further attempts would come, we let most everyone believe the attack had been successful. As you know, Trenton's injuries were so extreme the men who found him didn't realize he was alive. But he healed quickly and we got him to safety."

Angelina jumped to her feet. "How could you keep this from me? You know that I love him. You know that I only desired to marry him!"

Dianne nodded. "I know how you feel about my brother, but isn't it better knowing that he's alive? He isn't dead, as you've believed. Let it comfort you, and then go forward with your life."

"Not without him. I want to go to him." Angelina turned and paced the room. Each time she turned, her burgundy gown swirled out behind her in a dramatic flare. "Where is he?"

"I can't tell you where he is. I'm not completely sure myself. It's for his safety that we made this arrangement."

"I won't just stay here and do nothing. I want to be with him."

"But he doesn't want you to be with him," Dianne said.

Angelina stopped in midstep. "What are you saying?"

"I wanted to tell you the truth from the very beginning. I thought he'd want you to know that he was alive, but Trenton wouldn't let me." She saw Angelina's expression fall. "Listen to me. It had nothing to do with you and everything to do with Trenton. He did some things before he came to Montana that he's deeply ashamed of — things that have left him on the wrong side of the law."

Angelina shook her head. "I don't want to live without him," she cried emotionally. "I know what the sheriff said, but I don't care what he did in the past — I only want his future. What's done is done, but I know that together we could have a beautiful life."

Dianne knew the woman was sincere, and a part of her felt confident that Trenton would be blessed to have Angelina in his life. But another part of her worried, wondering what kind of life it would be for Angelina.

"You wouldn't be able to use his real name or live your life without constantly looking over your shoulder. You would never be able to live your life fully."

"I can't live it this way either," Angelina said. She threw herself at Dianne's knee. "Please. Please don't do this to me. Don't give me back hope and then keep me from him. You've no idea how hard I've prayed that something like this might be the truth. You've no idea how hard it's been. You've known that he was alive and you could console your heart with the fact that you might one day see him again — but I didn't have that. Now I do, and you want to take it away from me."

"I only want his safety. I only want him to be able to live to be an old, old man," Dianne said, knowing she was losing the battle.

"And I want to grow old with him."

Dianne shook her head. "Who would take you? It's a long way, and a woman certainly cannot travel alone."

"I'll take her," Morgan said without hesitation.

Both women turned to look at him. The woman Morgan loved wanted only his brother. He wouldn't recover this loss easily.

"If that's the way you want it," Dianne said, finally relenting.

Morgan smiled sadly. "It's what she wants that matters most."

"Can we talk?" Levi questioned as Ardith stirred the wash water.

Winona was playing with Rusty and seemed content to leave Ardith and Levi to themselves. Ardith sighed and looked up to meet Levi's gentle expression.

"What about?"

Levi leaned against the porch post. "About us."

Ardith stopped stirring and went to retrieve more wood for the fire. Levi hurried to help her. "I know you think there's no chance for us, but you're wrong. We love each other. I know you love me. I can tell by the way you look at me — by the things you say."

Ardith straightened abruptly. "I've never told you that I love you," she declared.

Levi grinned. "You've never told me you didn't either."

Unnerved, Ardith quickly bent down to pick up the split logs. How could she continue to fight her emotions? How could she fight both herself and this man?

"I want to marry you," Levi said, helping her stoke the wash fire.

Ardith said nothing. How could she? She

wanted to marry him just as fervently as he wanted to marry her. *So why don't I just accept his proposal? Why can't I shake loose of the past and accept that God has given me something better?* Why was it so easy to believe that God would mete out punishment, but not be as confident that He would give blessings?

"Ardith, I know you're afraid. I know that other man was cruel to you — hurt you. But I promise not to be like him. I promise to wait until you're ready. I promise to treat you special and to always take your feelings into consideration."

Tears trickled down Ardith's cheeks and she turned away from Levi, pretending to prepare more clothes for the wash. No one had ever made her feel this way — so loved, so cared for. And it wasn't only her. He loved Winona dearly. He played with her every evening after supper. There wasn't a day that went by that Levi didn't do something special with the child. In a sense, he'd courted Ardith through Winona.

He took hold of her arms and very gently turned Ardith to face him. "I won't say the past doesn't matter, because it's obviously hurt you greatly. But I want you to know that what we can have together will be so much better than what happened in the past. I love you, and I love Winona. Please marry me."

CHAPTER 19

September held the lingering memories of a pleasant summer. Amidst the warmth was the hint of a chill — especially at night. The days were growing shorter, but everything was still lovely in tones of green and gold. The year had been a prosperous one for the Diamond V. The hay harvest had been exceptional, and the Selbys had been able to secure a nice winter supply for the horses and milk cows. The livestock had grown fat over the summer, the general health and well-being of the family was good, and even the vegetable gardens had yielded an abundant crop. There was much to celebrate.

But perhaps the best part of this Indian summer was that Ardith had finally agreed to marry Levi. Dianne was more pleased than she could say. For so long Levi had pined over Dianne, but when Ardith had come to live with them, everything had changed. Levi clearly loved her and Winona, and everyone was delighted to see the couple join in marriage.

"I have an announcement," Cole said in his booming baritone. The wedding supper had barely begun, but already the merriment was evident.

Ardith and Levi paused in their conversations with Charity and Ben and looked to Cole in anticipation of his declaration.

"I know there has been much discussion about where the newlyweds would live, but Dianne and I have kind of taken matters into our own hands. The ladies have been busy all week." Dianne shared conspiratorial glances with Koko, Charity, and even Faith. The women smiled. Even one-year-old John laughed and clapped as he sat on Dianne's lap.

Cole continued with a grin. "We gentlemen have been busy as well. We've been making some furniture and doing some fixing up and adding on to the far back cabin. Dianne and I would like to give this to Levi and Ardith as a wedding gift. It's a way for all of us to help you start out your marriage on the right foot."

"I don't know what to say," Ardith said, her hand wiping away newly fallen tears.

Dianne took special pride in her sister's appearance. She had made the wedding

312

dress for Ardith, spending many hours talking about the future while sewing stitches. The dress was nothing fancy, but rather very practical. The powder blue wool complemented Ardith's dark hair and eyes. The gown would serve her well for years to come, but for now it would be Ardith's Sunday dress. Ardith was positively radiant.

"Thank you for all you've done for us," Levi said, pushing back his hat. "I didn't expect to have such an easy way."

"Well, we aren't exactly making your way easy. There is one tiny string attached," Dianne announced. She looked to Cole first and then to Gus. The man was aging fast and it was time for his retirement. He would live out the rest of his days on the Diamond V — at least as long as the ranch belonged to them.

"What kind of string?" Levi asked, looking to Ardith. When Ardith shrugged and shook her head, he looked back to Dianne and grinned. "What are you up to?"

"Gus has decided to finally take our advice and hand over the reins of foreman to another," Dianne announced. "It hasn't been an easy decision, but we feel that Gus deserves to relax and enjoy life a little. He served Uncle Bram with honor and dependability, and we are blessed to call him family."

Gus blushed several shades of red but said nothing. Cole picked up where Dianne had left off. "We would like to offer Levi the position."

Levi's grin widened. "I'd be happy to take the job, but only if Gus will postpone his complete retirement and oversee me in the position. He's trained me since my first day here at the Diamond V, and I have nothing but the utmost respect for him."

"If Miz Dianne and Cole don't mind, I'd be right happy to take you up on that offer. Ain't right for a man to sit around and do nothing."

Dianne nodded, appreciating the gracious way Levi had allowed Gus to feel important. She could see Gus's chest swell with pride as what could have been a difficult moment for him was eased over in love.

"So if we're all agreed," Cole said, pulling Dianne close, "I propose a toast to the happy couple, their new family, their new home, and Levi's new position on the ranch."

"Hear! Hear!" everyone cried in unison and lifted their glasses of punch.

There were other toasts and other gifts, but Dianne knew that Ardith would have been equally as happy if the entire matter were over with Ben's pronouncement of them as man and wife. Ardith was still uncomfortable with large crowds of people, and since some of the local families from the surrounding areas had come, the gathering was quite large.

"Come on Luke, Micah," Dianne said, standing and swinging John to her hip. "Let's take a walk by the river and see if there are any summer flowers left."

"If there are, can we pick 'em?" Luke asked.

"Pick 'em," Micah parroted.

Dianne smiled. "Of course. We'll pick them and take them to Aunt Ardith and Uncle Levi's new cabin." This seemed to satisfy her boys nicely.

Dianne enjoyed the stroll and knew that these quiet moments with her boys were more valuable to her than all of the cattle and horses in the world. The boys were the spitting image of their father, although there were times when she saw a bit of Chadwick in them as well. Cole couldn't be prouder. The boys were his joy, pure and simple. He loved showing them how to ride and care for the animals, and he never tired of playing with them when time permitted. *Life is good,* she thought. *So much better than I could have ever imagined.*

Still, there were moments of sadness. Fear of what might happen with the ranch loomed in the back of her mind. Then, too, thoughts of the Lawrence family awakened horrible memories of what had happened to Maggie and Whitson, and Trenton and Sam.

The party lacked the complete joy that might have been had the others been in attendance. Dianne still found it hard to believe they were gone. People came and went on a daily basis in this part of the country, but a few hardy ones never left. They planted deep roots and survived in spite of the storms. Whit and Maggie would never have gone on their own accord. They were buried on Diamond V property — side by side, companions in death as they had been in life. Trenton might as well have been dead — he could never come back. At least not as Trenton Chadwick.

"You look a little sad," Ardith said, surprising Dianne.

"Oh, you startled me. I'm afraid I was deep in thought." Dianne cradled John, glancing down to see that his eyelids were drooping. She hugged him closer and looked up to her sister. "Are you happy?"

"I never thought I would be again, but I am. Before, when I first came here, I was just relieved to be rid of the nightmare that had been my life. When I saw how secluded the ranch was, I thought this was a good place to hide from the world. But I guess the world came looking for me." She smiled and took hold of Dianne's hand.

"I'm grateful for the way you've taken care of me and Winona. I thought so often of my family when the Indians held me. Through the good and the bad, I always imagined how it would be to someday find you all again. I used to lie awake at night and think of seeing Mama and what she would say. I'd think about how everyone would look — whether you and Betsy would be married."

Dianne thought of the painful days after Ardith's disappearance. "Oh, Ardith, it was so hard losing you. I resent the lost years. I try to understand why God allowed such a thing, but I just can't. Charity says we can't know the mind of God — that His thoughts aren't our thoughts, His ways aren't our ways. She says hard times are times of learning — times when we have to trust in faith that God is still watching and caring for us as tenderly and completely as when times were good."

"I'm trying to hold fast to that belief as well," Ardith responded. "I talked to God a lot when I was held captive. He gave me great peace, but at the same time He infuriated me. Does that make sense?"

"Perfect sense. You could be speaking my mind right now."

Ardith cocked her head to one side. "How so?"

"Trenton. I have great peace regarding God's mercy and deliverance." She glanced around, worried that someone might overhear. John came to life in her arms and struggled to get down and join his brothers, who were playing about fifteen feet away.

Seeing no one else, Dianne continued. "At the same time I'm infuriated that He would allow such tragedies and heartache. I don't understand why Trenton should have had to suffer so much."

Ardith chuckled, surprising Dianne. "Trenton told me it was his past catching up with him. He said it was a miracle such a thing hadn't happened a long, long time ago. He seemed almost relieved to let Trenton Chadwick die."

Dianne knew it was true; Trenton had told her as much. He wanted a new start. A new life without having to drag around the baggage he'd acquired as a young man. Was that an even greater mercy in God's plan? To everyone but family, Trenton Chadwick was dead and buried, along with his past. No one cared about Nicolaas Mercer. Still, was it wrong for Trenton to live a lie? Even if it saved his life?

"God will make even this rough place smooth," Ardith said, sounding very wise to Dianne.

"There are a great many rough places in this territory. So many that maybe even God won't have time to smooth them all."

Ardith shrugged. "If God doesn't take care of them, maybe we don't need to worry about them. He won't be mocked. You've told me that enough times yourself. He will avenge His own — in His time. Isn't that what you and Charity are always saying? If it's true for me and what I went through, then it must be true for Trenton as well."

"I know you're right," Dianne said with a smile. "Besides, it's your wedding day, and I don't want to continue with such talk. We're supposed to be celebrating, and that's exactly what I intend to do!"

"Look, Mama, we found some flowers for Aunt Ardith," Luke declared.

Dianne laughed. "See, even the boys know this is a time for joy and happiness . . . and flowers."

"And love," Ardith added. "Thank you for loving me in spite of the past. And thank you for loving Winona."

"How could I not?" Dianne watched as the other boys joined them, their hands full of wild flowers. "Love makes it all better. It heals old wounds and overlooks mistakes." The boys held up their offerings to Ardith.

She smiled and reached down to take the flowers. "These are beautiful. Thank you for picking them."

Luke wiped his dirty hands on his shirt. "Papa said snow will come soon. They would die if we didn't pick 'em."

"And if you didn't pick them, I wouldn't have a chance to enjoy them. I know Winona and Levi will like them too."

Ardith looked back to Dianne. "I hope someday I'll have boys as wonderful as yours."

"You will. I just know it," Dianne said softly. "I just know it."

"I'm glad you could share tea with me today," Portia said in a sugary sweet voice. She smiled at Cynthia Lawrence and her two daughters. "Here in the West, we women must stick together. Otherwise we might perish for want of female friendship."

Portia placed a silver tea tray on a highly polished tea cart. The furnishings were both gifts from Chester, but Cynthia Lawrence would never know that. Portia picked up the teapot and began to pour. "I sometimes just pine away for a chance to talk new fashions and such with another woman."

"Not much time out here for fashions — new or otherwise," Cynthia replied snidely. "You aren't a rancher's wife, so maybe it comes a little easier for you."

Portia forced back a sarcastic reply and instead replied, "You are right. My life here in town is much simpler. Why, the time I spent at the Diamond V proved that to me if nothing else did. Of course, Dianne Chadwick never had to work as hard as I'm sure you and the girls work." She offered Cynthia a cup of tea and then poured cups for Mara and Elsa.

"Mrs. Chadwick doesn't have to work hard?" Elsa questioned. "Why would that be?"

Portia waved her off and lied, "Oh, goodness, the woman has many servants. She doesn't have to lift a finger. Why, just last summer they brought in a full-time cook for the house, as well as another for the ranch hands. She has maids too. Money is nothing to them. They spend it like there was a never-ending fount of the stuff in their backyard."

"Well, it won't be that way for long," Cynthia said, glancing at Mara. "They'll soon be off their land, and we'll be the new owners."

Mara looked away, obviously uncomfortable with the conversation. Portia had never cared for either of Chester's daughters and planned to see them both married off as soon as possible, but she disliked Mara even more than Elsa. Elsa was a hothead like her father, and she wore his personality traits like a well-fitted glove. Mara, however, was soft. She was sweet and gentle spirited. She and her brother Joshua were both that way, and Portia knew it grieved Chester. The boy positively had no future as a ruthless cattleman.

They drank the tea and ate the little cakes Portia had prepared. The conversation ran dry long before the delicate china cups did, however, and if it weren't for the argumentative nature of Elsa, Portia might have died from boredom.

"Can't we please walk around town while you two visit?" Elsa whined after getting nowhere in her request that they finish the tea and head home.

"Yes, Mama," Mara agreed, "can we please walk around a bit? Maybe do some shopping?"

Cynthia narrowed her eyes. "I suppose it

would be fitting to have you look into some new dress material, but don't be frivolous. Have the storekeeper put it on your father's account, and don't be gone more than ten minutes."

The girls immediately got to their feet. "Thank you for the tea, Mrs. Langford," Mara said, moving to stand behind her mother's chair. "I very much enjoyed myself."

"You're quite welcome, Mara." Portia turned to Elsa and added, "As are you, Elsa."

Elsa frowned and joined her sister. "The tea could have been hotter."

Portia stiffened. "I'll try to remember that next time."

The girls went to the door and opened it. "Mama," Elsa said, motioning for her mother, "I need to tell you something."

Cynthia Lawrence seemed to sense the importance and rather than argue with her daughter, made her way to where Elsa stood. Portia took the opportunity afforded her by the turned backs of her enemies to slip a poisonous, but tasteless, concoction into Cynthia's teacup. Pouring the woman a bit more tea, Portia smiled as Cynthia finally rejoined her and the girls exited the small house.

"They were worried about getting their father a birthday present," Cynthia said, raising the cup to her lips. "Sometimes they can be sentimental." She took a long drink and replaced the cup on the saucer.

Portia knew the poison would act fairly quickly and hoped to end her tea party so that the woman might collapse elsewhere. "I truly hate to be rude and put an end to our time together," Portia said, frowning, "but I suddenly have a terrible headache. I wonder if we might do this again another day — soon?"

Cynthia shook her head. "I doubt it seriously. I only came here today to give you a piece of advice."

Portia feigned surprised. "Advice? Whatever about?"

"My husband."

"I'm sure I don't understand."

Cynthia got to her feet. "And I'm equally sure that you do. Keep away from Chester. He's married to me, and I don't intend to see that change."

"Why, Cynthia Lawrence, I have no idea what you are saying. Are you accusing me of something?"

"I don't have time for accusations. Count this as an honest-to-goodness warning."

Portia got to her feet and followed Cynthia to the door. "I'm sure you are mistaken in your thoughts. I have no interest in married men."

Cynthia held Portia's gaze. Her eyes looked like hard pieces of flint. "I don't play games, Mrs. Langford. If you won't heed my words, you'll regret it."

Portia smiled. "Now, now. We neither one want anything to regret." She watched as Cynthia grimaced. No doubt the stomach cramps were already beginning. "I, for one, have a philosophy of living life without regrets."

"Nevertheless, stay away from Chester."

Portia clenched her teeth together and met Cynthia's harsh stare. "I hope we'll share tea again soon," Portia finally managed to say.

"Good day, Mrs. Langford."

"Good bye, Mrs. Lawrence."

Word came several days later to Dianne that Mrs. Lawrence had suddenly passed away. Charity sat opposite her in the sitting room sharing the only information she had on the matter.

"Ben performed a small ceremony. It was just the family. He said no one seemed overly sad or concerned, with exception to Mara. She appeared quite devastated."

"Cynthia wasn't all that old, was she? I thought someone said she wasn't even yet fifty. Is that right?" Dianne questioned. Already she was wondering what Portia Langford might have had to do with the event.

"I think so, but while she wasn't old, she had been sickly. She'd twice asked me for remedies that might help with stomach disorders. I prayed with her both times, but she didn't seem overly impressed with God's abilities."

"How sad for her to die so young and quickly like that," Dianne said, still pondering the events, hoping she might somehow come up with some unknown clue. Trenton had been very vocal about Portia's interest and flirtatious nature where Chester Lawrence was concerned. If Portia wanted Chester for her own, she'd no doubt have few qualms about eliminating the only person in her way — Chester's wife.

"This sounds so odd," Dianne said, shaking her head. "I know this country is hard on folks, but I have a strange feeling the hardships of the land had little to do with Cynthia's death."

"What are you suggesting?" Charity asked.

"I'm not sure," Dianne replied. "I have some thoughts on the matter, but I can't speak of them now. I just pray that we can figure out the truth before anyone else mysteriously dies."

With snow threatening, Morgan and Angelina finally arrived at a small secluded cabin in the Washington Territory. Morgan could see that Angelina could barely contain herself. It had been difficult to find their way, and without the help of more than one grizzled backwoodsman, they might not have ever found Nicolaas Mercer.

Morgan slid down from his mount and held the reins for Angelina while she dismounted. From the look of it, someone was at home. The light shining in the cabin window was clear evidence of that.

"Do you think he's here?" Angelina whispered.

A cold wind blew down through the tall pines and Morgan shivered. He'd resigned himself to the inevitability of this moment, but for all his good intentions, he was still heartbroken to be handing the woman he loved over to another man. Even if that man was his brother.

"Somebody's here, and from the way folks have talked, I don't think he lives with anyone else."

Angelina followed Morgan as he went to

tie the horses off. "It feels like snow."

Morgan knew she was trying to keep their conversation casual and light. Just as they had for all the months they'd been searching for Trenton. Most women would have worried about their reputation — about traveling alone with a man she wasn't married to. But Angelina seemed only concerned about finding Trenton.

Realizing it was probably their last chance to speak, Morgan turned to her. "Look, you know how I feel about you — how I've felt since I first laid eyes on you."

Morgan could barely make out her features from the light in the cabin window, but he could see her nod. He pulled his glove from his hand and touched her cheek. He knew it meant nothing to her, but he had to do it.

"I've only done this because I love you. I love you enough to give you to Trenton, knowing that he's the only one who will make you happy. But I want you to know, if he doesn't want you, if he says no to your staying, I'm still here."

Angelina reached up and touched Morgan's face in return. The action sent heat radiating throughout his body, stirring his emotions in a way he'd just as soon avoid.

"You're a good man, Morgan. I never

wanted to hurt you. You must know that."

"I do."

"I'm sorry this has caused you such pain. Please know that I will always care about you." She dropped her hand and drew a deep breath. "No matter what happens, thank you for bringing me here."

Morgan quickly released her and nodded. "Come on. Let's see if he's here."

Trenton opened the door after Morgan's knock. It was harder to say who was more surprised. Morgan at the sight of this be-whiskered mountain man or Trenton at the sight of his brother and Angelina.

"What are you doing here?" Trenton asked in a low voice.

Angelina stepped forward and put herself between Morgan and Trenton. "Nicolaas Mercer, I'm here to marry you. Now, it's freezing out here, so please let us come in and warm up."

Trenton stepped back and Angelina walked into the cabin without further comment. Morgan couldn't help but grin at the look on his brother's face.

"We had to tell her," Morgan finally said. "She was hardly able to go on without you. I'll think you fifteen kinds of fool if you turn her away. And I'll probably have to throw a few punches into that woolly face if you dare give me a hard time for bringing her here."

Angelina turned, dropping the hood of her cloak. She fairly glowed from the joy of finally seeing her beloved. Morgan winced and looked away.

"Who said I'd ever consider turning her away?"

"Good," Morgan said. "Just so long as we understand each other."

Trenton put his arm around his brother's shoulder. Morgan looked up to see the compassion in his brother's eyes. "I think we both understand. . . . Thank you."

CHAPTER 20

January 1881

"I think you all know why I've called this meeting," Cole announced as many of the local ranchers gathered to take a seat in his sitting room. He'd relegated the women to the second floor and asked them to remain there for the evening. Cole had long seen the necessity of rallying those ranchers he knew who would make a stand against Chester Lawrence and his boys, but the events of the last few months had made it absolutely urgent.

"Lawrence is gaining control of this valley through his money and hired hands. He has the mayor, sheriff, and many others sewn up tight, so getting things accomplished through legal means is going to be difficult at best. Many of you have complained of missing livestock, water problems, and threats, so it's clear we can't just leave this situation without resolution."

"If the law won't help, then what are we supposed to do?" G. W. Vandercamp asked. His ranch was about fifteen miles north-northeast of the Diamond V. "I've had Chester Lawrence on my doorstep more times than I care to admit. He's been pressing for me to sell out to him. Frankly, he and his boys are scaring my womenfolk."

"The Lawrences may be annoying," another man from a small sheep ranch to the south spoke out, "but I doubt they're all that dangerous." Some murmurs of agreement arose.

Cole knew the time to tell them the truth had come. "I don't know exactly what each of you have heard about the deaths of Whitson and Maggie Farley, but I think the time has come to set things straight. Whit didn't kill Maggie or the other way around. Whit showed up on my doorstep beaten half to death. On his deathbed he told me the Lawrence boys had come calling. They dragged Whit behind a horse until he was nearly dead, then beat him with a shovel."

The men began to talk amongst themselves. To Cole it looked as though they were seeking permission from one another to believe such a tale. "I found the shovel with blood and hair caked on it."

"But how can you be sure it was the

Lawrence boys?" another rancher questioned.

Cole tightened his grip on the piece of paper he'd brought with him to the meeting. "Whit told me it was. Why would a dying man have any reason to lie about his killers?"

"Maybe he held them a grudge," someone suggested.

"If anyone had the right to hold someone a grudge, Whit did. I haven't told this to anyone else — only the few men who accompanied me that night to Whit's know the truth — but Maggie Farley was raped before she was killed. Men who would do such a thing need to be stopped. Those men are still out there. I think we have good reason to worry about our women and children's safety."

"No one is going to believe the Lawrences had anything to do with Whit's and Maggie's death," G.W. said, shaking his head. "No, sir. Chester's lawman won't be locking up his boys."

"Probably not," Cole replied. "Which is why we need to figure out what to do. Lawrence is threatening to steal my ranch through legal means. He killed Whit for his land. How soon before he comes after the rest of you? Right now he's just nagging you from day to day about selling. What happens when he loses his patience and decides to take matters into his own hands and hurry the process along?"

"Was she really raped?" an older man asked. "Only an animal would do such a thing."

Cole nodded. "That's exactly the way I see it. Those who were responsible for Whit's and Maggie's death were no better than animals."

"Well, up in these parts we trap and kill vicious animals," Slim Smith, a short, wiry man, announced. He owned a small spread about three miles south of Madison.

"We can hardly be killing men — that would make us no better than them," Cole said, trying to maintain control of the meeting. "What we need to do is get them out of here and off to a bigger city, where Chester can't corrupt the law."

"With enough money you can corrupt most anything," G.W. said sadly.

Cole looked hard at his friend. "Could they corrupt you, G.W.?"

The man straightened a bit. "No. No, they couldn't. No matter how much money they offered."

Cole smiled. "I have a feeling most of the men in this room feel the same way."

All of the men nodded and agreed with Cole's statement, commenting to one another and raising the level of conversation to a confused pitch.

"Men, hear me out!" Cole shouted above the growing din. The men fell silent and looked up. "We have very few options. What we need to do now is figure out which ones will accomplish the most and work the best for us."

"I think we'd better start any serious consideration with prayer," Ben Hammond interjected.

Cole looked to the older man. "We're going to need it."

As the temperature dropped into the teens and then below zero, Dianne despaired of it ever being truly warm again. She worried about the boys and tried to keep a hot fire going in their bedroom stove. John still shared his parents' room, where the fireplace was always lit to keep the room ready for his naps. He was nearing age two but was small for his age, and Dianne fretted that he might suffer more than the others.

Even now as she tucked him in for the night, wrapping a warm beaver pelt cover around him, Dianne worried. Sometimes the winters were mild, but other years they were harsh and cold. Sometimes the snows came and sometimes they didn't, but it was always a battle to keep children alive. Neighbors had lost babies to one sickness or another. Faith had nearly lost little Lucy, her youngest, to scarlet fever. Death was all around them — especially in winter.

"Is he asleep?" Cole asked as he entered their bedroom for the night.

"Yes. He woke up fussing, and I rocked him a bit and put him back to bed. He probably just had a bad dream," Dianne said, hoping and praying that John wasn't coming down sick. "How did your second meeting go? Did you come up with any ideas of how to stop the Lawrences from taking over the valley?"

"No, not really. However, a couple of the men pointed out that nothing more has happened. Guess even the Lawrences have hunkered down because of the cold."

Dianne looked at her husband in disbelief. "So you're all going to do nothing because it's cold?"

Cole frowned. "I didn't say that."

"Well, it sounds as though the men think everything has gone back to normal. It will never be normal around here as long as killers roam as free men."

"Dianne, I wasn't suggesting that we

336

forget about doing something. I was merely pointing out what was said."

"I know, but I also know that Maggie and Whit need to be avenged. For that matter, so do Sam and Trenton. The Lawrence boys may well have been the ones Portia got to do her dirty work."

"But you don't know that," Cole said as he sat down wearily.

"I know that Mr. Langford believes Portia killed his son. I know that Trenton was helping to gather that information and that Portia probably found out about it. She probably decided to take matters into her own hands."

" 'Probablies' don't hold much weight in court."

Dianne put her hands on her hips. "Someone has to do something. It's not right that all this time has gone by and still no one is paying for the death of Sam or the near death of Trenton. Most are happy to believe that Trenton and Sam killed each other."

"Dianne, I can't help that. We can't press that issue. . . . Portia is throwin' in with the Lawrences — at least that's what it looks like. Ben said she's out at the Walking Horseshoe Ranch most every time he goes out there to call. If Lawrence is behind Whit and Maggie —"

"If? You said *if?* You know Lawrence was behind their deaths. He wanted their land, and surprisingly enough, he now has it." She knew her tone had grown bitter, but Dianne couldn't help herself.

"My brother had to leave the comfort of his home," she said, lowering her voice to a whisper. "He's out there — only God knows for sure where. He might be half dead from cold or starving. I have no way of knowing."

"You had no way of knowing for all those years he was outlawing either. He's a grown man who is capable of caring for himself and Angelina — provided he lets her stay."

"But he deserves our attention to seeing this matter resolved."

"So this is really about Trenton and getting revenge for him?"

"It's about all of them," Dianne said angrily. "You obviously don't seem to care."

"I formed the men up, didn't I?" His eyes narrowed. "Do you know how hard it was to bring those men here — to suggest we do something to take the law into our own hands? I sat in a similar meeting nearly twenty years ago, and the outcome wasn't so good, if you'll recall. Vigilante justice may be widely accepted in the West, but I'd much rather see guilty men tried in court than hanged by their neighbors."

Dianne remembered the story Cole had told her of his one and only ride with vigilantes. A woman he loved was killed accidentally by Cole's father. It had separated the men for years and left a painful scar on Cole's heart.

"All I want is justice," Dianne said, trying not to see the hurt in her husband's eyes.

"You just want Portia Langford dead."

"Well, given the fact that she's been responsible for so many other people's deaths, what's wrong with that?" Dianne asked stubbornly. She could no longer deny her hatred for Portia, and yes, she did want the woman to hang. The thought momentarily startled Dianne. *When did I become so coldhearted?*

"You think that if Portia is found guilty and executed or imprisoned, then Trenton could come back to the ranch, is that it?"

"Well, why not?"

"Because Chester Lawrence no doubt knows all the details of Trenton's past, as would his lackeys. Trenton can't come back here — not now, not ever — don't you see? Not unless you plan to go down the line and kill everyone with whom Portia shared the truth about your brother."

Dianne felt tears come to her eyes. She knew Cole was right, but it hurt so much to be unable to have Trenton here where he belonged. Portia Langford had ruined everything.

Cole crossed the room and drew Dianne into his arms. "I know this is hard. I miss him too. I feel like I lost my best friend."

"It isn't fair. She's here and he's gone. It's not right."

"But we can't interfere and break the law to see things changed."

"I know," Dianne said, sniffing back tears. "But I wish we could."

"No you don't. You haven't got a law-breaking bone in your body. You would never hurt anyone — not even Portia."

"Don't be so sure," Dianne replied. "There's a lot of bitterness in my heart toward her."

"Bitterness will only spread and take over like those weeds in the garden you always fuss about. If bitterness takes over your heart and kills everything lovely, where will that leave me and the boys?"

Dianne closed her eyes. "I love you and the boys. It's Portia I hate."

"You can't hate her and keep your love for us untainted. It isn't possible. I know. I hated my pa for what he'd done to Carrie. That hate ate away at me until I couldn't love anyone — I almost lost out on loving you because of it."

"I don't know how to do anything but hate her. It's so easy in light of all the problems she's been involved with."

"You need to take it back to God," Cole said, smoothing back Dianne's hair. He kissed her forehead. "You need to let Him love you and show you how even this will be dealt with in His time. He won't be mocked, Dianne. He won't see His children forsaken. God will deal with Portia and Chester — maybe not in the way we'd like to see it happen, but He will resolve this."

Dianne straightened the cushions on the settee and stood back to make sure everything was in place for an afternoon of sewing. She'd invited Charity and Faith to join her at the ranch along with Koko and Ardith. They hoped they might get a regular sewing circle started.

"Look, Luke," Winona called from the frosted windowpane where she stood on a chair. "I can make a picture." She dug her finger into the icy glaze and drew her version of a cat. "See, a kitty. Mama says we're going to have a bunch of new kitties in a few weeks."

"Yeah, well, we're going to have new calves in the spring," Luke said proudly.

"And Papa says I can go help at roundup, but you can't 'cause you're a girl."

Dianne forced back a laugh. "Now, Luke, don't be unkind. Winona has made a very nice picture. Why don't you go to the other window and draw some calves?"

"Can I help?" Micah asked. At three and half, he was his brother's shadow.

Luke shrugged. "I guess so. You can draw all the legs. There's going to be a whole bunch of them, though."

Micah nodded, his expression serious as the weight of his task settled upon him. "I can do it."

Dianne laughed as the boys went to work. Winona, not to be out done, began making more kittens.

The sound of a wagon approaching caused Dianne to note the hour. It was nearly eleven. They were right on time. She untied her apron and placed it across the back of a chair. Then, smoothing down her gown as she walked, Dianne went to the front door.

She opened the door just as Levi showed up to help Charity from the wagon. "It's sure cold today, isn't it, Levi?" Charity said, hugging him close. "Goodness, but that wife of yours must be feeding you well. You look to have put on at least ten pounds."

"She's a good cook to be sure." He

reached up to help Faith from the wagon, then after she was safely on the ground, Levi helped Mercy and Lucy as well.

"I'll take care of the horses. You get inside," Levi ordered.

"Oh, but those girls have grown!" Dianne exclaimed as the party hurried to the house.

"Well, Mercy will be ten next April," Faith declared. "I still can't believe that."

"I can't believe it either," Dianne said as she closed the door once everyone was inside. "It also means I've been married ten years." She marveled at the way time had flown. "It can't really be ten years, can it?" She met Faith's amused expression and had to laugh. "I suppose most women are better at keeping track," Dianne said, shaking her head, "but I've truly lost track of time."

"I'm fwour," Lucy said, holding up her hand to reveal four fingers.

Dianne laughed. "Yes, I know you are. I was at your birthday party, remember?"

Lucy nodded. "You gave me a dolly with a red dress."

Dianne couldn't believe the child had remembered. "Yes, that's right. I did. Do you still play with her?"

Lucy shook her head, her black braid bouncing. "She gots a broken leg."

Dianne looked to Faith, who hurried to

explain how a cloth doll could have a broken leg. "I'm afraid our dog, Bart, decided to take a bite out of Miss Dolly. We need to repair her. She's amongst my sewing projects for today."

"Well, then, we'd best get to it, hadn't we?"

Charity turned to Ardith and embraced her. "How's our girl? Are you keeping Levi happy?"

"Oh, your cheeks are so cold — come in by the fire," Ardith said, pulling Charity along. "And yes, we're both very happy."

They gathered in the smaller sitting room, where the heat could be more contained and hence, more effective. Dianne took her seat and pulled out a basket of sewing projects.

"So what's the news from Madison? Did the new dressmaker come in from Denver?"

"She arrived just before that first heavy snow last week," Charity announced. "It was the day after Portia married Chester Lawrence."

"They finally married? What kept them so long? Cynthia's been dead at least what — four, five months?" Dianne asked sarcastically.

"Well, at least they aren't living in sin," Charity declared. "I much prefer to see folks

344

legally wed. Ben performed the ceremony. Said it wasn't much, but they seemed happy. The children didn't seem too pleased, however. I don't reckon they cotton to the idea of a stepmother who's so much younger than their father."

"Maybe they just don't like Portia," Dianne replied. She tried to focus on her sewing, but the old anger was creeping into her heart.

"Well, that aside, the deed is done. Her little house was rented to the dressmaker. That's why I thought of it in the first place," Charity said, beginning to stitch on a quilt square.

"Those Lawrences are certainly a mean bunch," Faith said as she settled Mercy and Lucy with a piece of embroidery to work on. "Malachi had a run-in with the oldest — Jerrod. That boy has a hot temper, and he isn't afraid to lash out at anybody who offends him."

"How did Malachi offend him?" Ardith asked.

Faith shrugged. "Jerrod had brought in a string of horses to be shod. Malachi did the job and then Jerrod started ranting about how the shoes were poorly made — how Malachi's work was shoddy. He told him he wouldn't pay, so Malachi started taking the shoes back off. Jerrod really lost his temper then. He began throwing whatever he could lay his hands on and finally Malachi told him to either pay and get out or leave until he could remove all the shoes."

"What did he do?" Dianne asked, hoping there hadn't been a fight over the matter.

"Jerrod backed down. He paid and left. He was heard muttering obscenities all the way out of town."

Charity shook her head. "That family is obviously suffering. The good Lord needs a better place in their hearts."

"The Lord doesn't need a better place," Dianne replied snidely. "He needs to be introduced there first."

"Well, let's not gossip," Charity said, offering Dianne a warm smile. "I'd much rather hear about your boys. How are they doing?"

Dianne realized it was probably for the best that they put aside discussion of Portia and the Lawrences. "John is cutting teeth again. Micah is Luke's constant shadow, and Luke follows poor Jamie around like some puppy who has found his long lost master."

Charity laughed. "I can just see it."

"Jamie is not very kind about Luke's adoration, I'm afraid." Koko picked up a piece of tanned hide and added, "He often shuns the boy in favor of work. Something I didn't think I'd ever see."

The ladies laughed and Dianne had to admit it made her feel much better to share the humor of their lives instead of their sorrows.

"What other pleasant news can we share?" Faith asked as she began to work on Miss Dolly.

Ardith cleared her throat and let her sewing rest on her lap. "I have some news." Everyone looked up. She smiled and held up a tiny white flannel baby gown. "Levi and I are going to have a child."

Dianne lowered her gaze to the shirt she'd been working on for Luke. Ardith had confided the news to her several days ago. The expected baby seemed to give Ardith a zest for life that even Levi and Winona had failed to bring.

Charity was thrilled. "Oh, I had hoped for this. I didn't want it to be too soon, but then for me, it couldn't be soon enough. I feel like I'm going to be a grandma all over again."

"Yes, you will be grandmother to our baby. Levi and I have already determined that."

"I'm so happy for you, Ardith," Faith said.

"But you know what this means, ladies. We must put away our other sewing and make things for this baby."

"That's right," Koko agreed. "You'll need lots of things."

"When is the baby going to come?" Charity asked.

Ardith blushed. "As near as I can tell, August."

Charity clapped her hands together. "Good. A nice summer baby. Those are best around these parts. It'll have a good chance to put on some fat before winter."

"You make the baby sound like one of the calves," Dianne said, laughing.

"Well, maybe so, but in these parts, it's best to go into winter with a little extra weight, rather than too little."

"I agree with Faith," Dianne said, tying off the seam she'd just sewn. "I think we need to make plans to get together at least once a month to make clothes for Ardith's baby."

"And maybe some other ladies will eventually join us," Charity added. "I know few want to travel out in this cold, but maybe come spring."

"Come spring we'll be rounding up the herd and branding calves. You know how busy things get," Dianne replied. "We'll be lucky if we have time for a short spell of sitting, much less an afternoon of sewing."

"Maybe we should all plan to help with roundup," Ardith suggested. "We could go out and cook and share company. The children would enjoy it too."

Dianne nodded, feeling a stir of excitement. "I haven't been to a roundup in a long time. It might be just the thing. Cole already planned to take Luke, so maybe he won't mind the entire family coming along."

"Malachi will be there. Cole already asked him to come and see to anything that was needed. I don't think he'd mind if we joined him," Faith said, grinning. "Not if he knows it's for a good cause."

"I'll talk to Ben, and if he agrees to the idea, I'll get the word out at church and let the other ranchers' wives know," Charity declared. "That way, maybe we'll get some of the other ladies to join us."

For Dianne the plan was a mixed blessing. She worried that Portia would show up with Lawrence's daughters, even though Cole and Levi had pastured their cattle as far away from the Walking Horseshoe as possible.

Still, I shouldn't borrow trouble, she chided herself. *Mama always said trouble would come looking for you all by itself — without invitation. Seems she was right. But she didn't tell me trouble's name was Portia Langford Lawrence.*

CHAPTER 21

Portia's life as Chester Lawrence's wife was not at all what she had anticipated. First there were the early morning risings that Chester insisted on. He wasn't about to have his wife linger in bed when the day was underway. Portia argued that there was a housekeeper and a cook to see to the family's needs and she needn't lose sleep over such matters. But Chester would have no part of it.

Added to this was trouble in the form of Chester's two older boys, Jerrod and Roy. None of the Lawrence children liked her, but Jerrod and Roy were downright dangerous. It was nothing for them to pass Portia in the hall and shove her out of the way. One morning before she went for a ride, Portia even found her cinch strap cut just enough that if she'd gone into a gallop it would have torn completely in two. There was no way to prove that Jerrod and Roy had done it, but she was confident they were responsible.

The third son, Joshua, was a little better. He was the only gentle spirit among the brothers. He had a poet's heart, Portia thought. He read a great deal and loved to discuss intellectual matters. He was kind to Portia, but his demeanor was an irritation.

Then there were Mara and Elsa. Neither girl wanted anything to do with Portia, and that was fine by her. Mara was at least civil, but Elsa was belligerent and hostile. Elsa constantly badgered Portia about stealing her father and being the death of her mother. Of course Portia knew the girl didn't know the truth. No one did. Cynthia Lawrence's death had been chalked off to intestinal troubles. The doctor even suspected a blocked bowel.

The only truly nice thing was that the Walking Horseshoe was a lovely ranch. The house wasn't nearly as grand as the Diamond V, but Portia could be patient knowing they'd soon take over the Selbys' house and lands. The thought positively exhilarated her, and as she rode out across the valley on this pleasant April day and headed up into the hills, Portia felt confident that all of her plans were finally coming together.

"There has to be a way to deal with his

children," she muttered.

She'd suggested to Chester that the boys were all too old to be living at home — that they should perhaps file for land of their own and create an even bigger empire. But that was when Chester explained that they had done just that. The Lawrence sons had land that adjoined the Walking Horseshoe. They were even working to prove up the claim and meet the homesteading requirements.

The very idea of those animals being around for much longer, however, kept Portia from truly enjoying her accomplishments. The girls she could get married off. There were enough cowboys and other eligible young men in the territory to marry them each several times over. Women were scarce in these parts. Portia had received at least a dozen proposals a month since coming back to Montana after Ned's death.

Ned.

The very thought of him irritated her. She couldn't help but stew over Trenton Chadwick and R. E. Langford's plans to get her back to Maryland. The feeling of betrayal left her heart more firmly encased in ice than it had been before. How could a father make such plans against his own flesh and blood?

Portia reined back the horse and paused as she spotted Jerrod and Roy approaching from the west. She contemplated making a dash back to the ranch, but then decided she wasn't about to live her life in fear. There was no sense to that.

She waited them out, not even bothering to ride down to meet them. Jerrod spit chaw and halted his sorrel stallion not but a foot away. Roy did likewise with his black. The gelding seemed unnerved by the sorrel, however, and kept dancing back and forth between Jerrod's mount and Portia's.

"What do you want?" Portia asked, casually draping her gloved hands atop the horn.

"What I want is you out of our lives," Jerrod grumbled. "I've never had much use for you, and I have even less now."

"You may have blinded our father," Roy declared, "but we see you for what you are."

Portia feigned indifference. "And what would that be?" she asked, as though bored with the conversation.

"You're after him for his money," Roy replied, "but you're too late. My father's will leaves his property and money to his children. Not wives. Even our mother didn't stand to inherit."

Portia tried not to appear surprised by the news. Instead she looked hard at Roy. "Do you think your father hasn't discussed all of his financial arrangements with me? Do you suppose I'm stupid enough to marry any man without knowing the truth of his business? Do yourselves a favor. You're both old enough to make a life for yourself elsewhere. Why don't you each find a wife and make your own home. It's hardly your father's place to take care of you and wipe your snotty noses for the rest of his life."

"You're nothin' but an uppity female with big notions," Jerrod said, the anger in his tone clear. He narrowed his eyes and leaned forward. "You'd better heed our warning, lady. We don't want you here. We don't want you stealin' from us. Why not do yourself a favor and have this sham of a marriage annulled?"

Portia arched a brow and smiled sardonically. "And what makes you believe, for even one moment, that my marriage is a sham? I'm making your father a very happy man, but I can make you two just as unhappy."

"You ain't got the guts to make us anything. You watch yourself. One of these days you'll ride out here and meet with an accident," Roy said, turning his horse. "Come on, Jerrod. I've had about as much of her as I can stand."

Jerrod opened his mouth and then closed

it again, as if he'd forgotten what he was about to say. Instead he pointed his gloved finger at her, then wheeled the stallion around and headed off down the hillside.

"Abominable little monsters," Portia spewed. She knew from past experience that matters like these had to be dealt with early on. Jerrod and Roy had been harassing her for months. Now was the time to teach them a lesson.

"You watch yourself. One of these days you'll ride out here and meet with an accident." Roy's words echoed in her mind.

"Of course," Portia murmured, smiling. "I just might."

She would have to stage things carefully. If she fell with too much force, she might really hurt herself. If she didn't fall with enough momentum, she wouldn't do the appropriate damage.

Pressing her horse into a run, she skirted through pines and rocky outcroppings. She knew the perfect place to set her plan in motion. She'd nearly taken a tumble there two days earlier.

Portia rounded several stubby cottonwoods and a tall pine. As she maneuvered around the last of the trees and headed up a small embankment, she yanked back hard on the reins, stunning the horse and causing him to rear. As he did, she slid off its back and tumbled end over end. She landed hard, much harder than she'd intended.

Unable to slow her downward momentum, Portia smacked up against a boulder, hitting the side of her face and her right shoulder. For a moment, she saw stars and worried that she'd done more damage than she'd intended.

The horse was well trained and stood fast not ten feet up the small hillside. Portia knew he'd stay there forever if she didn't send him off. Getting to her feet and wincing at the pain of a bruised hip and skinned knees, Portia staggered up the hill to where the horse waited patiently, munching fresh grass.

She took out one of her hat pins and mercilessly plunged it into the horse's flank. The animal protested loudly before taking off as if the devil himself were giving chase. Portia smiled and replaced the pin before assessing her clothes.

They were dirty from the fall, but with exception to a small tear, they were undamaged. Portia began to rip at her blouse, hoping to make matters look much worse than they were.

"When the horse returns without me, someone will come to rescue me. And when they do, I'm sure they will be surprised to hear all about how Jerrod and Roy tried to beat me before stealing my horse and leaving me behind — injured."

She smiled at the simplicity of her plan and began walking back to the ranch. "I'll teach those fools to make threats against me."

But after walking for nearly an hour, Portia felt like she was the fool. Her face and shoulder were throbbing and her body ached from the long and difficult walk. Not only that, but her pride was smarting from the fact that no one had even missed her.

After another fifteen minutes had passed, Portia was beginning to get angry. It was then that she spotted a rider. She waved her hands feverishly. The rider apparently caught sight of her and headed his mount in her direction. By the time he'd come within a hundred yards, Portia could see it was Joshua Lawrence.

He drew his mount up inches from Portia. "What happened?" he asked, concern in his voice.

"I . . . I . . . oh, it was terrible," she said, gasping for breath. She pressed her hand against the gelding as if to support herself.

Joshua jumped down from the horse and caught her just as she pretended to faint dead away. She didn't open her eyes again until they were entering the front door of the house.

"What happened?" Chester growled as Joshua came through the foyer.

"I don't know. I found her walking across the pasture all torn up like this," Joshua replied.

Portia rallied enough to catch sight of her husband and his daughters. "Oh, I'm so glad it's you. You won't let them hurt me again, will you?" she whimpered.

"Who did this?" Chester demanded, taking Portia from his son.

"Jerrod . . . Roy." She barely breathed the names. "They told me I wasn't good enough for you. They beat me and stole my horse. They said . . ." She fell silent and pretended to succumb to her pain for a moment. "Oh . . . oh . . . I'm just so afraid." She studied her husband's stunned expression and knew he would need a moment to fully comprehend the situation.

Reaching up, Portia grasped Chester's shirt. "They said you didn't care what happened to me. They said they were going to force me to leave."

"I can't believe this," Chester said, looking from Portia to Joshua. "Were you with them?"

"No, Father. I was out checking that north pasture like you asked and found her wandering around."

"Did you see your brothers?"

Joshua shook his head. Elsa chimed in, "They rode out early this morning. They couldn't have hurt her."

Portia knew it would be difficult to convince Elsa, but she felt confident that Chester would be drawn in by his drive to control and protect what was his. "I only pray," she whispered, "that they didn't cause me to lose the baby."

"Baby?" the girls questioned in unison.

Chester turned his gaze to her. "You're going to have a baby?"

Portia nodded and laid her head upon his shoulder. "At least I hope so. Jerrod was terribly hard on me, and Roy was no better. They both hit me several times in the stomach. They said it wouldn't show as bad there as here." She lifted her hand to her face.

"I'll kill 'em," Chester said, turning to his daughters. "Go pull down the blankets on our bed so I can make her comfortable. Joshua, you ride for the doctor."

Portia let herself go limp in her husband's arms. She smiled, knowing that no one could see her as she buried her face against

Chester's shirt.

Let that be a lesson to you, boys. The idea to pretend she was pregnant had only come to her shortly before reaching the house. She knew her monthly time was due and if it came as usual, she'd tell everyone she had miscarried. And if it didn't come, she'd praise God above that the baby had come through the attack unharmed. It was a perfect situation; there was no way to lose.

As Chester placed her in bed, Portia moaned softly for effect. It was all too simple.

"Mara, go get Mrs. Fisher. Have her come help you and Elsa get these dirty clothes off of Portia. Have her bring hot water and bandages."

"Yes, Father," Mara said, not presenting the tiniest protest.

Elsa, on the other hand, stared down in open hostility at Portia. "Why can't we just wait and let the doctor do those things? She doesn't look to be dying."

"Young lady, you heard me," Chester replied in a stern manner. "I'm going to expect my commands to be heeded or there will be a reckoning. Do you understand me?" Elsa nodded solemnly. "It's bad enough I have to deal with your brothers in this matter. I don't want any sass from you girls.

"Portia, I'll take care of this situation — don't you worry." He stomped from the room like an angry, injured bear.

"This is all your own fault," Elsa muttered. "If you hadn't come here, Jerrod and Roy wouldn't have gotten mad."

Portia thought to threaten the girl, then decided a little drama would cause more reaction. She grabbed at her stomach and gasped for air. "Oh, the baby. I think I'm losing the baby."

Elsa paled and stepped away from the bed. "I don't know what to do. You need a doctor." She ran from the room calling for Mara.

Portia nearly laughed out loud. Maybe this would be a good way to control Elsa as well. She could always threaten to tell the girl's father that she hadn't helped at all. Mara wouldn't be a problem, but Elsa bore some consideration. Either way, Portia felt confident she'd just won this little game.

Ardith strained against the pain that wracked her body. Heartbroken to be miscarrying Levi's child, she fought the contractions and cried to God to make the nightmare end.

Koko helped her raise her head and presented a cup of steaming tea. "Drink this; it will help with the pain."

"Why can't you give me something to keep me from losing the baby?" Ardith cried, refusing the drink.

Dianne reached over and took hold of her sister's hand. "I'm so sorry this is happening, Ardith, but I'll be here for you. I won't let you bear this alone."

"Nor will I," Koko added.

Ardith shook her head from side to side. "I wanted this baby so much. How can I be losing him? Why would God do this to me?"

"I don't know why this is happening," Dianne answered, "but I know God grieves for you. He loves you and He won't leave you without comfort."

The words seemed hollow even in Dianne's ears. Her sister's grief was so raw and fresh. She'd seen this same kind of sorrow in Faith. All those years ago when Faith had first come to the Diamond V, she had been overwhelmed in her sadness. Faith would know how to reach Ardith.

Dianne let go of Ardith's hand. "I'll be right back. Do what Koko says now and drink the tea. It will help."

She hurried from the room and found Levi pacing in the hall. "Is she . . . will she . . ." He didn't seem capable of finishing the sentence.

"She's going to be fine, Levi. But of course it's hard for her. She wanted this baby so much."

"She won't die?" His dark brown eyes glinted with unshed tears.

"No. At least I see no reason to believe she will." She smiled and patted his shoulder. "Now I want to find someone to ride to Madison and bring back Faith. She's gone through this before and I haven't. She'll be able to comfort Ardith in a way that no one else can. Can you get one of the boys to go?"

"I'll go myself. I'm going crazy just waiting around here. If you're sure she won't die while I'm gone —"

"She won't die," Dianne interjected. "Now please hurry. Tell Faith everything so she'll be prepared. Tell her why I sent you — she'll understand."

"All right. Should I take the wagon?"

"That would be best," Dianne replied, knowing it would be good for him to keep busy. "Now hurry and fetch Faith."

By the time Faith arrived, the worst was over. Faith trudged up the main staircase, remembering too well what it felt like to lose a baby. Her heart was overwhelmed with sorrow for the young mother. *Oh, Lord,* she prayed, *give me wisdom to speak the right words. Let Ardith and Levi be comforted.*

On her trip out to the ranch, Faith had talked in a gentle, almost motherly manner, explaining to Levi what he might expect in the weeks to come. She explained the loss would be deep for both of them and that they should cling to each other for strength.

"Some folks, like me, take it out on their husbands. I hurt Malachi something fierce. I didn't mean to," she'd told Levi.

"Will she hate me?" Levi had asked sadly.

Faith shook her head, remembering her own pain. "No," she said softly. "She'll hate herself."

The words still rang in Faith's ears as she reached for the bedroom door.

Dianne met Faith at the door and glanced back over her shoulder at Ardith. "Thank you for coming. I knew you were probably the only one who could help her right now."

Faith nodded. "The Lord will help her. I'll simply be His handmaiden."

Dianne was surprised to see Morgan riding slowly toward the house. It was early, and because the boys were still sleeping, Dianne decided to walk out and meet him. She'd often wondered if he'd found Trenton or if Angelina had changed her mind. She knew Morgan was heartbroken to be losing the woman he loved, but she also knew he was completely unselfish in the matter.

"I'm so glad to see you. How are you?" she said when they were no more than ten feet apart.

Morgan stopped the horse and dismounted. "I'm all right."

"Tell me everything."

He drew a deep breath. "We found him. He's well. Has a cabin up in the mountains and does some logging for a living. He took the money you sent and said he was much obliged and to send his love. Said he'd pay you back one day."

"And Angelina?"

"He took her too. They married right after Christmas. I was Trenton's best man."

Dianne felt the pain in his words. "I admire you more than words can say. I know it means nothing, but I want you to know that anyway."

"Just don't tell me how someone else will come along and mend my heart. How eventually I'll feel better and forget all about this time in my life. How what I felt for her wasn't really love."

Dianne fought back tears and shook her

head. "I won't. I promise."

"Thank you."

CHAPTER 22

"I'm sorry," Dr. Bufford said as he completed his examination of Portia. "You're bleeding."

Portia pretended to cry softly into her pillow. "Oh, how can I ever bear this?"

"You're still young enough to have other babies. You can't be far along. This should probably pass in short order. If you have any problems, just send for me."

Portia nodded, by now managing to sound as though she were sobbing. She couldn't believe how well things were going. Everyone was completely convinced of her condition. "Will you . . . could you . . . tell Chester? I can't bear to break his heart this way."

Dr. Bufford closed his bag. "Of course. I am sorry, Mrs. Lawrence."

He studied her for a moment, making Portia feel very uncomfortable. She turned away and pretended to cry even harder, hoping he wouldn't ask her any questions.

Perhaps he realizes I wasn't really pregnant, she thought, fearful that he might reveal her deception.

"Again, I'm sorry for your loss."

He left the room and Portia smiled in relief. "Oh, I can hardly wait for the results." She'd heard the cook tell Elsa ten minutes ago that the boys were back. No doubt the little minx had gone to warn her brothers, but it would take more than a warning to get them out of this mess.

She strained to hear what was happening downstairs but didn't hear anything. Going to the window, Portia watched as Dr. Bufford drove away in his buggy. Perhaps Chester would come to her and offer his comfort and condolences. She hurried back to the bed just in case.

"Whatever possessed you to hurt her?" Chester bellowed. His voice came easily through the floorboards.

Portia couldn't refrain from grinning. Chester had bought it — he'd bought the entire story. The beating. The baby. He'd believed her.

"We didn't do anything!" Jerrod yelled back.

"She's lyin'!" Roy added.

"She's lying all right," Chester hollered back. "She's lying in bed upstairs losing my baby. She's black and blue and says you were the ones responsible. You've been giving her nothing but grief since I married her."

"Well, that much is true. I hate her. She's come in here like some sort of royalty — takin' over our mother's place." Portia couldn't tell if it was Roy or Jerrod who'd made that announcement. No doubt they both felt that way.

"She's my wife!"

Portia felt the overwhelming sensation of satisfaction. Her face hurt something terrible, but it was worth it. Surely Chester would kick the boys out of the house now. The door to her bedroom opened, so Portia immediately clutched her stomach and moaned.

Elsa came into the room with a tray. Portia could see the pot of tea and shook her head. "I don't want anything."

"The doctor told Cook to fix this up for you. It's got medicine in it and you have to drink it," the girl replied. "It's to help you since you're losing the baby."

Portia had no idea what herbal remedy they might have concocted, but the last thing she wanted to do was find herself drugged. "Nothing can help."

Elsa placed the tray on the stand beside

Portia's bed and scowled. "I'm glad the baby died. I just wish you would have died too."

Portia momentarily forgot about the role she was to be playing. She eyed Elsa sternly. "You'd better be careful of what you wish for, little girl. Bad things seem to have a way of happening around here."

"Yeah, ever since you came into our lives," Elsa countered, apparently unafraid.

Portia shook her head and remembered she was supposed to be in great pain. She clutched at her stomach and pretended to wait for the pain to pass before speaking. "I knew this young girl once," Portia began very slowly. "She was . . . oh . . . probably your age. She fell in the river and drowned. It was so very sad. No one was around to know when or where it happened. One day she simply disappeared and then her body washed ashore." Portia watched as Elsa's eyes widened. She knew the girl understood the threat, but Portia wanted to drive the point home.

"My own dear friend died when she was probably not much older than your sister, Mara. She had argued with me about a boy we both liked. I guess she was just too upset to know how dangerous an open window could be. She fell out of her upstairs bedroom window and broke her neck." Portia narrowed her eyes. "Bad things happen — especially to bad people."

Elsa backed up to the door. Her face had paled noticeably. With a shaky voice she tried her best to sound defiant. "Then you'll probably be seeing a lot more bad things come your way." With that the girl fled as though her skirt were on fire.

Portia would have laughed out loud had the open door not afforded her the sound of Chester threatening his sons.

"If anything like this ever happens again — if she so much as tells me that you looked at her wrong — I'll kill you both. Understand?"

"But, Pa —" Roy protested.

"I don't want excuses or denials. I want you and your brother to pack up your things and bed down in the bunkhouse. I won't have animals in the house, and anyone who'd beat a woman like you did Portia deserves to lose the comfort you've grown so accustomed to."

"You didn't think it was a problem when we taught Maggie Farley a lesson."

"I'm not married to Maggie Farley," Chester raged. "She was no-account trash. Portia's my wife and you'll treat her with respect."

Portia smiled and settled back in great satisfaction. With Elsa afraid of what might happen and Jerrod and Roy dealing with their enraged father, Portia felt that she had once again gained the upper hand. *Let them all fight amongst themselves,* she thought. *Let them be divided . . . because surely they are much easier to destroy than when they are united.*

"Are you suggesting that Chester Lawrence stole our calves?" Dianne asked. Cole had only returned from roundup the day before. It had been hard to remain at home after planning for months to be with everyone at roundup, but Ardith's miscarriage had made it necessary to put the venture aside. Now Cole had returned and informed her that the number of live calf births was way down and that a number of cattle had gone missing all together.

"I'm just saying it's a possibility," Cole replied, waving Koko off when she offered him a third cup of coffee. The children were finishing their breakfast and chattering amongst themselves. "There are a lot of cows without calves, and no sign of dead animals. Well . . . there were a few, but not enough to account for the missing stock."

"Then what else could it be?" Dianne asked. "You said yourself that some of the men had seen the Lawrence boys skulking around."

"That doesn't make them thieves. They could have been in the same area for another reason."

Dianne's anger grew. "I can't believe you are making excuses for them."

"I can't believe you're so willing to judge them without proof."

"Are you mad at Papa?" Luke asked his mother matter-of-factly.

Dianne was ashamed of the way she'd behaved. Every time Portia or the Lawrences came up, she always ended up angry. "Mama is just mad at the situation, Luke. I'm mad because of all the missing calves."

She tried to further calm her temper before continuing. "What do you plan to do about it?"

Cole shrugged. "Not a lot I can do short of going to the Walking Horseshoe and accusing the man of stealing my stock. You know how he's set with the law. The sheriff won't do anything about it, and Lawrence will have the satisfaction of throwing the entire matter in our face."

Dianne held a fragile hold on her rage. "So you'll let him get away with it?"

Cole frowned. "I hardly said that, Dianne."

"Well, if I were allowed to own and run my father's ranch," Jamie Vandyke piped up, "I'd go to the Lawrences and demand my property."

Dianne looked from the boy to her husband and waited for some response. Cole toyed with his silverware for a moment, then looked at the young man. "Do you suppose they'd keep such animals in plain view for everyone to find? And even if I found his herd with all my calves, how would you suggest I go about proving the matter? They weren't branded, and I can hardly bring every mama cow who's missing a calf with me."

"But if he has a large number of calves — say, a lot of twins," Dianne began.

"You mean like we had last year?" Cole asked with an almost sarcastic tone.

Dianne couldn't argue with that. The Lawrences had made it clear that they thought the Selbys had stolen their calves. "It just seems ironic that the thing they accused us of last spring is the very thing we're facing now."

Jamie slapped the table with the palms of his hands. "This isn't fair. My father worked hard to build this ranch. Are we going to do nothing?"

"That's my question," Dianne said, looking once again to Cole.

"What would you have them do, son?" Koko asked Jamie.

He appeared to consider his mother's words for a moment, reminding Dianne of her uncle. Jamie's dark hair and eyes were the only real indicators of his Indian heritage. He clearly looked more white than Blackfoot. Dianne thought it a pity he couldn't have inherited the ranch for his own. Maybe her entire life would be different if Bram had married a white woman instead of a half-breed Blackfoot.

"I would sneak around and find the animals. I would see if they were the same breeds as the other Lawrence cattle or if they were Diamond V cattle."

"That's a possibility," Cole replied. "However, if Lawrence has stolen our calves, he'll have them well guarded or already removed to some other location altogether."

Dianne knew her husband was probably right. Lawrence was no fool — he and his boys had planned and accomplished too much.

Cole got up from the table. "We definitely need to pray on it."

"Prayers are for weaklings," Jamie protested, getting to his feet also. "I'm not a weakling. I'm a Vandyke and we are strong."

"Yes, you are strong," Cole affirmed, "but you can never be so strong as to not need the Lord."

"God doesn't care about Indians."

Dianne was taken aback by Jamie's words. "Why would you say that?"

Jamie turned a fiery expression on her. "How can I not? Look at what has happened to my mother . . . to my uncle . . . to Susannah and me. Look what has happened to the Blackfoot people — to all the Indian nations. If that's God's way of showing His care, then I hope He forgets about me."

"Jamie, you can't mean that. Your father was a man of God. He cared deeply for God's purpose and direction in his life," Dianne replied.

"My father trusted God and now he's dead. Why should I trust God?"

Koko shook her head. "I did not know you felt this way, Jamie. You have never spoken to me about this before."

Jamie softened. "I'm sorry, but I knew it would make you sad. I thought you were sad enough from losing Father."

"I am sometimes sad from your father's death — even after all these years. I will never love another man in the way I loved your father. He was a good man and he loved us. Which is why I am most grateful that he looked out for us by giving the ranch to Dianne. We would be on the reservation now if not for her and Cole."

"I'd rather be on the reservation. At least there I'd be a man — a Blackfoot, proud and sure. Here I'm nothing. I'm not white and I'm not Blackfoot."

"You are wrong, son. The Blackfoot would not accept you. They would see you as white. My brother was only accepted because he lived from time to time among our mother's people. They accepted him because he proved himself to think like they did. You do not think as a Blackfoot."

"But I could!"

"Jamie, you're more white than Indian. You cannot deny that heritage," Dianne protested. "You would dishonor your father to deny your white ancestry."

Jamie lowered his gaze to the floor. He stood in silence for a moment. "My father was ashamed of his ancestry too, or he'd have never come west. You told me that he left his people and came west because he was unhappy with them."

"True, but he didn't deny who he was, and you mustn't deny it either," Dianne replied.

"But you're asking me to deny that I'm Blackfoot." His anger was evident.

"No one is asking you to deny it," Cole interjected. "We just don't want you to deny your white heritage either."

"I don't have to deny it," Jamie spat, "the world denies it for me." With that he stormed from the room.

Koko got to her feet to go after him, but Cole shook his head. "Let me go talk to him. I'm the one he resents. I'm the one he needs to vent this out on."

Cole followed after Jamie, leaving Koko and Dianne alone with the children. "I hope he can reason with Jamie."

Dianne shook her head. "I had no idea he was so angry."

Koko turned to eleven-year-old Susannah. "Why don't you take the boys to wash up. Then we can get started with our lessons." The young girl did as she was asked, helping Micah from his chair as Luke slid down from his.

Luke paused and looked up at Dianne. "Is Jamie an Indian?"

Dianne looked to Koko. The expression in the older woman's eyes was a mix of frustration, fear, and sadness.

Dianne looked back to her son and smiled. "Jamie is a Vandyke. His father was my uncle. His mother is Koko, but you already know that."

Luke nodded. "Why is Jamie mad?"

Koko spoke up. "He's mad because he misses his papa."

Luke seemed to understand this concept. "I would be mad if my papa went away. Will Jamie's papa come back?"

Dianne shook her head and smoothed back her son's sandy colored hair. "No. Jamie's papa lives in heaven now with God."

Susannah grew impatient. "Come on, Luke Selby." She always called the boys by their first and last name when particularly irritated with them.

Dianne fought to keep from smiling as Koko reprimanded her daughter. "You mustn't be so intolerant with Luke. He's just worried about your brother."

"Oh, don't worry about Jamie. He says our uncle is coming to take him away. I'll be glad when he goes, 'cause he's always pulling my hair."

Koko's eyes narrowed. "What are you talking about?"

"I wasn't supposed to tell you," Susannah said, looking to the ground.

"Well, you'd best tell me now."

The girl looked up at Dianne. "He said you stole our ranch and he was going to get

Takes Many Horses to help him get it back, but first he would have to go away and learn to live like the Blackfoot so he'd be strong."

"I cannot believe this," Koko said, shaking her head. "And right under my nose. I can only imagine how long the boy has been planning this little adventure."

"Don't be angry at him," Dianne said softly. "He's growing up — faster than any of us realized. He's hurt and naturally so — the only thing his father could leave behind for him can't be his. Maybe he'll tell the whole story to Cole."

"If not, he'll share it with me tonight," Koko said, her tone firm.

"Did you steal the ranch?" Luke asked Dianne, his eyes wide with wonder.

"No, your mother did no such thing," Koko declared before Dianne could answer. "She saved the ranch. She saved it for all of us."

Luke smiled and wrapped his arms around his mother's skirt. "I knew you wouldn't do something wrong."

Dianne picked him up into her arms, realizing as she did it she wouldn't be able to lift the five-year-old much longer. "Luke, we all make mistakes — do wrong things. I'm not perfect; no one on earth is. But your papa's right. We need to pray and ask God

381

to help us in everything we do. But we especially need to pray that He'll guide us so that we make the right choices and decisions."

"I'll pray," Luke agreed. "I'll pray twice, 'cause Jamie said he won't pray. So I'll pray for him."

Dianne smiled and tousled her son's hair. "I think that would be wonderful."

"I do too," Koko said. "I think even Jamie would be proud to know that you care about him so much."

"He's my family," Luke said soberly. "And Papa says we always stand by family — no matter what."

Dianne met her aunt's gaze. "No matter what."

Morgan readied his horse for the trip to the northern glacier regions. He'd heard marvelous accounts of the glorious countryside in the northwestern parts of the territory. It seemed like a good place to make a new start.

"You sure picked a pretty day to head out," Ardith said as she came up behind Morgan in the barn.

"Looks like it'll stay nice. Hopefully I'll have an easy way of it." He turned. "How are you feeling?"

"I'm fine, and you?"

Morgan gave her a sad smile. "I'm as fine as you are."

Ardith grinned and looked to the ground. "Then you have my pity."

"We're a pair, eh?"

"Guess misery really does love company."

Morgan reached out and squeezed her arm. "I promise to get better, if you do."

Ardith looked up. "I want to get better. I want to be happy again."

"I do too."

"Sometimes it's hard to figure out why these things happen," she said softly. "It sure doesn't make sense. Doesn't seem like the kind of thing a loving God would allow. But just when I think I have God all figured out, I come to realize how little I know."

Morgan nodded. "I've never thought I had God figured out — never was really sure where to actually find God. But maybe that's where I need to head next. Maybe that's what I really need to explore."

"It's gotten me through a lot of painful moments," Ardith said with a smile. "Even now. I know without Him, I'd lose my mind and probably my life."

"Then I'm grateful He's given you strength, because I'd hate to lose you a second time."

"You will be careful, won't you?"

Morgan took up the horse's reins and led him from the stall. "I'll do my best."

"I'll pray for you."

He met her eyes and knew the sincerity of her heart. "You do that, little sister. You pray hard, and maybe things will actually come around right."

CHAPTER 23

July 1881

Dianne listened to the music of the fiddle and guitars. An impromptu band had been formed to play as the community danced in celebration of the Fourth of July. She easily recognized the "Virginia Reel," and since many citizens in these parts were former Confederates, the crowd seemed quite pleased with the selection.

Madison had grown to a town of fifty-some people, but when the surrounding ranchers and their families and crews joined in, the place swelled to at least two hundred. The shops had been open earlier in the day to accommodate shoppers who might have driven in from twenty miles away. Now as the supper tables were set with a bevy of food choices, all brought to share freely by each of the families, people were splitting their time between food and dance.

The entire party might have been more

pleasurable for Dianne had Portia not been so intricately involved. Chester Lawrence garnered more respect and attention than did the mayor or sheriff. It was clear that everyone knew who really ran the town.

Dianne shook her head as she watched Portia Lawrence flaunt her position to the other ranchers' wives. Portia seemed out of place no matter how hard she attempted to fit in. Even her gown was all wrong for the celebration. Most of the women wore simple calico or gingham dresses. A few wore dresses with more braiding or lace, but none were as fancy as Portia's. Dressed in burgundy silk, Portia fairly glimmered in the fading sunlight.

The gown was stylish, showing off Portia's feminine curves. The sleeves were fitted to the wrist and trimmed in smocking, lace, and ribbons. True to the very latest of *Harper's Bazaar* fashions, she had smocking across the bustle and a gathered cascade of material that fell from the bustle to the floor. This, too, was trimmed in delicate gathers of lace and ribbon.

She smiled and batted her eyelashes, flirting with every man who passed her way. She wore her hair up in a fanciful style of curls and twists and topped this with an elaborate hat of silk ribbons and feathers.

For effect, Portia would, from time to time, turn her head first one way and then the next in order to bounce her curls. She reminded Dianne of a sixteen-year-old rather than a woman pushing forty.

Still, Dianne had to admit she felt dowdy compared to Portia. She looked down at her own new gown of dusty rose. The high neckline was trimmed in black cording and the bodice was pleated, but otherwise the creation was simple. Dianne had made the dress herself, knowing exactly what would be useful in the future. Had she ever had a gown just for fun? A frivolous dress with frippery like the one Portia wore?

What good would it do? I can hardly work a ranch and keep a horse while wearing silk. She crossed her arms and tried not to feel jealous. It was silly to be jealous of a woman like Portia — a murderess.

"You look awfully deep in thought," Cole said as he came up beside her.

Dianne turned to smile. All day she'd wanted to share some news with Cole and now seemed like a good time. "I am deep in thought. I have something to tell you."

"Tell me while we dance." Cole took her by the arm and pulled her to the street, where other couples were enjoying a waltz. It wasn't anything like the refined ballrooms back East; of this, Dianne was certain.

Cole whirled her into the crowd of people, and Dianne waited to share her news until they'd caught the pace of the music.

"So what did you want to tell me?"

Dianne smiled and met her husband's curious eyes expression. "We're going to have another baby."

Cole's eyes widened. "Truly?"

She nodded, enjoying his delight. "Truly."

Cole pulled her closer and kissed her soundly. "How long have you known?" he asked as they stumbled the steps.

"I've only been sure for about the last day or so. Do you suppose we might have a daughter this time?" she asked, cocking her head to one side. "Aren't three boys enough for now?"

Cole threw back his head and laughed heartily. "You may certainly have a daughter now if that's what you desire. Don't you like my boys?"

"I like our boys plenty. I just think it would be nice to have a little girl."

"I wouldn't mind the idea. Are you feeling all right?"

"Physically, I feel fine. I'm worried about the problems we're dealing with on the ranch —"

"That's not for you to worry over. You just

stay healthy and keep things running smoothly at the house. I'll deal with the ranch and the Lawrences and any problems they might try to bring our way."

Dianne felt a sense of comfort in Cole's confidence, while at the same time she wanted to be consulted in the matter of the ranch deed and the legal problems Lawrence was trying to stir up. She wanted to help make the choices and decisions related to something as important as the possibility of losing the ranch.

"Isn't that Zane?" Cole asked as he maneuvered Dianne to better see. "It's either him or Morgan."

Dianne followed his gaze. "It's Zane, all right. I wonder if something is wrong. I certainly wasn't expecting to see him anytime soon. His business keeps him too busy for pleasure visits."

They left the dancers and moved through the crowd to where Zane stood. Dianne hugged her brother tightly and then pulled back to ask, "What are you doing here?"

Zane smiled. "Hello to you too."

Dianne drew him away from the crowd. Once she and Cole were alone with Zane, she pursued answers. "Is something wrong?"

"Does something need to be wrong just because I show up for a Fourth of July celebration?"

Dianne shook her head. "I suppose not, but you have to admit it is a surprise. Did something go wrong with the freight business?"

"You mean other than the railroad breathing down my neck?" Zane replied. "Right now I have a lot of long-haul business, but when the rails connect to Utah, I'm going to lose out in a mighty way."

"I've read that they plan to be done with the railroad sometime this year," Cole threw out. "What are your plans then?"

Zane shrugged. "I'll keep working. Local businesses will still need someone to haul for them. If that doesn't work, I'll get out of Butte and go elsewhere. Madison's growing; maybe I could earn a living freighting here."

"That's always possible, but if you work here, you'll no doubt be as controlled by Chester Lawrence as the other store owners are."

"Well, I'm just glad I got you paid back," he said. "If the business fails, I won't worry about being in debt. I'm free and clear, and I'm doing all right for myself. I'm sure the Lord will keep an eye on me." He glanced up the street and then behind him before adding, "I had a letter from Angelina."

Dianne could hardly believe her ears. "Why didn't you say so earlier? What did she say?"

Zane smiled. "They're both doing well. Tre . . . Nicolaas works in a logging camp and Angelina has been cooking and sewing for some of the men. They sound happy."

"What a relief," Dianne said with a sigh. She looked to Cole, who was smiling. "I suppose you're going to tell me that you knew this would be the result all along."

"I didn't know what the outcome would be," Cole replied, "but I had faith that God would make it all good. I'm just blessed to hear that they're happy."

They walked back toward the party and Zane asked, "Where are the boys?"

"They're back at the ranch. We figured they were a little young to be out late," Cole answered. "Ardith and Levi stayed behind with Koko. They're supposed to be having their own celebration tonight."

"Not that Jamie feels like celebrating American independence. He feels completely torn between worlds," Dianne said. "He loves his mother and father, but he also loves the excitement of the world he sees through his uncle, Takes Many Horses."

"Surely he knows the life of an Indian can hold no future for him."

Dianne nodded at her brother's comment. "But he continues to feel torn."

"Poor boy," Zane said. "It's hard enough just being that age and trying to figure out what you want out of life and how you plan to make your living."

Dianne saw Chester and Portia approaching. They could scarcely avoid them without making an obvious choice to move away. "I wonder what they want."

Cole looked up and shrugged. "Hard to tell. I guess we'll have to hear them out and then we'll know."

"Evening, Selby," Chester Lawrence said as they neared and stopped. "Mrs. Selby." He tipped his hat with a nod.

"Mr. Lawrence." Dianne's greeting lacked emotion. She narrowed her eyes and stared at Portia but said nothing.

"It's been a good party," Cole said, his voice low and certain.

"Chester planned it all out," Portia said, smiling. "He always knows exactly what to do."

Cole looked around at the town. "Seems he does."

"I heard you had trouble this winter," Chester said, changing the subject completely.

Cole turned back with a blank expression.

Dianne seethed and was befuddled as her husband responded, "Why, no. Not that I know of."

Chester looked to Portia, his expression changing from confident to confused. "Well, someone told me you were low on calves. Same as we were the year before."

Cole shrugged. "We've been really blessed. I can't complain. Don't know why anyone would be spreadin' gossip like that."

Dianne held her tongue and tried not to betray her feelings. She couldn't understand why Cole wasn't confronting Chester with the truth.

"Well . . . I . . . I guess," Chester stammered, looking from Portia to Dianne and back to Cole, "I was misinformed. I'd heard there were problems."

"Nothing beyond the usual things. Fact is, we've enjoyed a very productive spring and summer. Not only that, but Dianne just told me that we're going to have another baby."

Portia paled at this, surprising Dianne. "We should go," she said to Chester. "Don't we have other people to meet?"

"Ah . . . yes." Chester said, still appearing baffled. He took hold of Portia's arm. "Why don't you go ahead? I'll join you in a moment."

"I don't want to greet people alone," Portia said from between clenched teeth.

"I said I'll join you in a moment." Chester's self-assured nature returned and it was clear he'd brook no nonsense. Portia must have sensed this as well. She finally nodded and moved away from the Selbys — an unattractive pout on her face.

"I had hoped to speak with you alone, Selby," Chester began.

"Anything you have to say to me can be said in front of my wife and her brother. As long as you mind your language."

Chester frowned. "You know that I've challenged your claim to the Diamond V ranch."

"Yes, we know that." Cole's words were slow, monotone.

"There's no deed registered with your wife's name added on," he continued. "I think for everyone's sake, it would benefit you to drop this game now. Sell to me rather than allow the government to take it, and I'll make you a fair offer."

Cole appeared to be considering the man's words. "I know that the paper work was legally filed. Now, if someone is working to illegally file things, I can't help that. Truth is, I don't need to rely on the courthouse for my proof."

Now Lawrence seemed completely perplexed. His face contorted as if he were trying to decide on an expression. "This isn't going to end in your favor. Just remember: I wanted to make you an offer that would have been fair and beneficial to both of us."

"I'll remember," Cole replied evenly.

Lawrence started to leave, then turned. The anger in his eyes was evident. "There are worse things than losing a few head of cattle. You may have the world fooled, but you aren't fooling me." With that he stormed off down the boardwalk.

"What's wrong with you?" Dianne questioned softly. She smiled as several couples walked past them. "Why did you let him say those things and not confront him for having a hand in the losses we suffered?"

"Because until this moment, I wasn't convinced that Chester had done anything wrong," Cole replied, meeting her accusing tone.

"What?"

"I gave the men strict orders, on penalty of being fired, to say nothing about our herd and the losses. I confided in no one with exception to Ben and Malachi, and I instructed them both to say nothing and to have their wives say nothing. After all, I knew you would talk to both Charity and Faith."

Dianne looked to her brother. "Do you understand what he's saying?"

"Sounds to me like there should have been no reason for Chester Lawrence to know about a shortage of calves or any losses."

"Exactly," Cole replied. "But he does know. Which means there's only one way he could know."

"Because he took them," Dianne said as the realization sunk in.

"Right."

Cole thought about the situation long after the Lawrences had hurried away. Leaving Dianne in Zane's company, Cole decided it might benefit him to slip in among the other cowboys and see what he could learn. He'd already instructed his own boys to keep their ears open.

Moving toward the heavily laden tables of food, Cole caught sight of a movement down one of the side streets. Although it was dusky and the lanterns had been lit, Cole recognized one of his wranglers being confronted by Jerrod and Roy Lawrence.

He started heading down the street just as Roy took a swing. Billy Joe easily ducked and maneuvered his slender frame around the heavier man. "You guys are thieves and killers, but you don't scare me."

"I'll do more than scare you," Roy snarled, this time delivering a punch to Billy Joe's face.

The younger man swayed but stood his ground and to Cole's surprise fired off a blow with his right and then his left fist. Jerrod spewed a string of obscenities and comments that made Cole grateful that no womenfolk were close by.

"What's going on here?"

The fight stopped and everyone turned to Cole. Jerrod stepped forward and growled, "This isn't your concern. Get outta here unless you want the same."

"You happen to be roughing up my wrangler. That makes it my business." Cole stepped closer to Billy Joe. "Why don't you head back to the party."

"I can handle this, boss."

"I'm sure you can, but I need you ready to break that stallion tomorrow, and I don't want you doing it with scraped knuckles."

Billy Joe grinned. "Yeah, that would be kind of painful, eh."

"You ain't goin' nowhere. You called me a liar, and I don't take that from no one," Roy said, approaching Billy Joe.

Cole moved to put himself between the two, but to his surprise, Jerrod pulled a gun and closed the distance. Pointing it directly at Cole's chest, he shook his head. "You Selbys have a way of irritatin' folks. My brother has a reason to deal with this scum. You ain't gonna interfere."

Cole leaned forward. "We aren't going to fight you. There's no reason." He turned to motion Billy Joe back to the street party. This time the man moved off quickly. Jerrod cocked the hammer of his revolver.

"Well, big man, we'll see how well you handle yourself with a bullet in your chest."

Roy laughed as though Jerrod had told some great joke. "I only wish Pa was here to enjoy this moment. If you don't need my help, I'm goin' after that rat."

"Go," Jerrod replied. "I have all the help I need."

Roy disappeared down the street after Billy Joe while Cole held Jerrod's gaze. "You know you could never get away with something like this. You might have gotten away with killing Whit and Maggie, but something like this is going to be hard to run from."

"You'd like to believe that, but truth is, you know my pa has this territory wrapped around his little finger. He has the law on his side and men fear him."

"It seems you fellows are missing the party," Ben Hammond said as he seemed to appear out of nowhere.

Jerrod narrowed his eyes. "Stay out of this, preacher."

"God would much rather you be at peace with each other. The Good Book says, 'Blessed are the peacemakers.' Now, why don't you put down the gun and make amends."

Jerrod turned back to Cole and pushed the muzzle of his gun against him. "Preacher, this matter don't concern you. Take your Bible and go. This man has insulted me and mine, and I intend to see that he pays."

Cole could feel the hard metal against him. He felt afraid for the first time since the confrontation had begun. But then at the sound of another hammer being cocked, Jerrod's expression changed to one of surprise.

"I said, 'blessed are the peacemakers' — Colt revolvers or otherwise," Ben said without the slightest hint of concern.

"You're a preacher. How can you pull a gun on me?" Jerrod questioned, a trembling in his voice.

"We use whatever tools we need to spread the Good News," Ben said, pressing his gun against Jerrod's head.

"This don't seem like good news to me," Jerrod said, slowly lowering his gun.

Ben pulled back as Cole sidestepped to stand beside him. "The good news tonight is that you live to see another day. Maybe you can reflect a bit on how foolish it is to threaten the lives of honest citizens. Maybe you can even think of how the Lord sent me to intercede and save your neck from a hangman's rope."

"Nobody woulda hanged me. I'm a Lawrence. We own this valley."

Cole shook his head. "So you intend to go bullying your way around, is that it? Never mind the law or what anyone else wants."

Jerrod laughed. "We *are* the law, mister, in case you haven't figured that out."

"Why don't you go on back to your people," Ben suggested in a tone that sounded more like a command.

Jerrod eyed him for a moment. "You'll pay for this, preacher. I don't appreciate being interfered with."

Cole and Ben watched as Jerrod shoved his pistol into his holster and headed in the direction Roy had gone. Cole took a deep breath and let it out in one loud whoosh. "I have to admit, I was a little nervous. I'm glad you came along."

Ben smiled. "Just looking out for my flock."

Cole shook his head, knowing the matter was far from over. "You're probably going to have your hands full in the days to come — and you can't be everywhere."

"No, but God can."

"He's gonna be busy then. The Lawrences are going to be riled up after tonight."

Ben patted Cole's back. "Then let's go back to the party and enjoy the night. We'll let tomorrow worry after itself." As they started back toward Main Street, Ben added, "I think it might be wise for you and Dianne to spend the night with us. Going home in the light of day would be much better than trying to fend for yourself in the dark."

"I feel like we're going to be fighting in a lot of darkness in the days to come."

"Good thing we have the light."

CHAPTER 24

"So Sitting Bull has finally been captured?" Levi asked as he noted the headlines on Cole's newspaper.

"Isn't he the one who led the battle that took Custer's life?" Dianne questioned.

"Right on both accounts," Cole said. "It says here he surrendered along with some one hundred and eighty-seven Sioux men, women, and children. They were starving to death in Canada, so they decided even reservation life would be better."

"I can't say that I'm sorry to see it happen. We've lived in the constant threat that he and his Sioux warriors would rise up again," Dianne said. "After all, it's only been five years since the Battle at Little Big Horn."

Zane came into the kitchen from the back porch. "If you're ready to go, Cole, we'd better get a move on."

Cole put the paper down and leaned over

to kiss Dianne on the cheek. "I guess I've got my marching orders."

"How long do you suppose you'll be gone?" she asked, getting up from the kitchen table.

"Hopefully no more than two or three weeks," Cole replied. "Don't send out a search party if it takes longer than that, though, because frankly, I'd like to see this matter settled once and for all regarding the claim on the ranch. I'm hoping Zane's friend Mr. Daly can help us."

"I pray so too." She hugged Cole close, relishing the warmth of his arms around her.

Lifting her face to Cole's, Dianne stretched up to receive his tender kiss. "Don't worry," he said, gently stroking her cheek. "I'll be back before you know it." He kissed her once more, then released her and turned to Zane. "I'm ready."

Dianne watched them leave. "It'll feel like forever before they get back," she told Levi.

"Not if we stay busy, and there's plenty to do. I need to get those horses over to Fort Ellis. They won't be too happy if we're late on our delivery."

"Well, at least that's one thing Chester Lawrence hasn't been able to take from us. He doesn't have much time for raising horses what with his political interests and town planning."

"He wouldn't dare. It's too much work. Cattle can just graze and fatten up — 'course there's more to keeping the ranch running than just that — but horses have to be trained. We've got the best wranglers in these parts and they are loyal through and through. Most of them got their start from Bram, when nobody else would even look at 'em twice. Lawrence won't worry about the horses."

Dianne knew if Lawrence and his boys could take the horse trade from them, he would. Maybe it was because of the extra work involved that they'd steered clear, but maybe it was because the profit that could be generated hadn't occurred to Chester.

"It'll be nice when the railroad comes through," she said. "The line from Utah to Butte should be in this year. Cole read that the line coming in from the east will come close enough to the north of us that we can move cattle and horses all over the country."

Levi pushed back his dark hair. "That'll be nice, but for now we don't have that luxury. Look, are you sure you don't mind sparing Ardith and Winona? I know they'll enjoy the trip, plus Ardith can handle the wagon to bring back supplies. But if you need them here, I'll understand."

"I don't mind at all. I think it will do both of them a world of good. Spoil them for me," Dianne said with a grin.

"I will. Now, the boys have their instructions. You'll have several of them close at hand if you need them for anything. Most will be right up here close to the house working with those green broke colts. I'll be back in a few days."

"Don't worry about us," Dianne said with false bravado. "We'll be fine."

But in the days to come, she felt more and more uneasy. It wasn't just that Cole was gone or that Levi was in Bozeman. Something simply didn't feel right.

"I don't know what's wrong," Dianne told Koko.

"Perhaps it's nothing," her aunt said as she kneaded bread dough.

Dianne looked out the kitchen window. It was almost as if she expected some monster to stare back at her, but instead she saw a beautiful summer sky without so much as a single rain cloud present.

Letting the curtain fall back into place, she sighed. *I suppose I'm just uneasy with so many family members gone.*

"Perhaps you should —"

The women both jumped in surprise as a loud crash on the back porch interrupted

Koko's words. Dianne eyed the rifle that hung over the kitchen door. Koko seemed to understand and moved to the side of the back door to retrieve the weapon. Before she could pull it down, however, another crash came followed by a scuffling sound from behind the closed door.

"It's probably just an animal," Koko said, taking hold of the rifle.

"Probably." But in her heart she knew neither of them believed that. Still, they'd heard no one approach, and with all the men working just beyond the barns, Dianne had a hard time believing anyone could have made their way to the house without being seen.

Koko reached for the knob just as the door burst open and a man stumbled in and fell across the kitchen floor. The women gasped in unison. It was Takes Many Horses.

"George, what are you doing?" Koko questioned, tossing the rifle to Dianne. She quickly knelt down to feel his brow. "He's not feverish."

"I'm not sick," he said, gasping for air. "I'm exhausted and hungry. I've been on the run for weeks. The army is right behind me. I'm sorry," he said, lifting his gaze to Dianne. "I didn't . . . didn't mean to bring . . . them here."

"How far back are they?" Dianne asked, going to the window once again.

"A couple hours maybe. Like I said . . . I'm sorry."

Koko helped her brother to a chair. "I have some tea I can fix you. It will help so that you can eat without getting sick."

The man nodded. "They are trying to kill me. I have to hide. I can't go on like this or they'll capture me."

"Have you done something wrong?" Dianne asked, coming to stand directly in front of him. She was already trying to put together a plan of action.

"No. They simply want me because I'm Indian. There is a great campaign to round up all of the remaining Indians and put them away on the reservations. In case you haven't been keeping up on the affairs of this land, Montana Territory wants to become a state. You can't convince the government in Washington to do that when you have Indians running wild. They had me once, but I escaped. Hit the guard over the head."

Dianne couldn't hide her reaction. She bit her lower lip and tried to force the worried expression from her face.

"Don't worry," Takes Many Horses said.

"I didn't kill him. But I couldn't let him keep me imprisoned. We were halfway to the reservation when I got away. I thought they'd give up, but they won't rest until every last one of us with Indian blood is removed."

Dianne remembered the last time soldiers had come to her house. "Then they'll be after Koko and the children too. I'll have to hide all of you." She looked at Koko, who'd stopped what she was doing and slowly turned.

"Hide us?"

Dianne began to gather up food. "You know they'll try to take you again. We have the new cellar under the storeroom. I'll hide you there and get one of the boys to help me put the heavy chest across the trapdoor. Then I'll pile things around it to make it look as though they've been there forever." She drew a deep breath and met her aunt's grave expression. "I won't let them take you or the children . . . or you," she said, looking to Takes Many Horses.

"Now go get the children quickly. Tell them what you must. I'll tell Luke and Micah you had to go away."

Takes Many Horses got to his feet. His knees buckled but he caught himself on the table. "I can't stay here. I can't do this to

408

my own flesh and blood."

"You have no choice," Dianne declared. "There isn't time for anything else. It was bound to happen sooner or later." She deposited the things she'd been gathering in a wooden bucket. "I need to go speak with the men. I'll get someone in here to help you into the cellar."

"We can make it on our own," Koko said. "Just go and do what you must, and we'll do likewise."

Dianne could hardly bear to leave. She thrust the bucket into her aunt's hands. "Gather whatever you think I missed. Don't forget water." She hurried from the room, afraid that if she remained she might be unable to think clearly.

Dianne felt her heart pounding hard. She was almost dizzy from the worry of what might yet happen. Hurrying to the corrals, she spotted Billy Joe and Gabe and motioned them over.

"We have trouble."

Both men eyed the house, then looked back to Dianne. "What is it?" Billy Joe asked.

"Koko's brother has just arrived. He's half dead from exhaustion and starvation. The army is chasing him, and they're only an hour or two behind. We can't let them find him, because if they do, they'll also find Koko and the children. The army won't let them remain here."

"What do you need us to do?"

"Spread the word about what's happening. Tell the men that they are to say nothing. If cornered or questioned about Koko and the children — if it should be the same men who were here before — tell the men to feign ignorance. I don't want anyone to have to lie, but if pressed, I plan to say they've already been removed to the reservation."

"Where are you going to hide them?" Gabe asked, pulling off his gloves.

"The new cellar. Very few people know about it, but I know you and Billy Joe helped Cole dig it out. I think it's going to be the best place. I only hope they won't suffocate down there."

The men exchanged a look of concern. "If they have to be down there very long," Gabe replied, "it might not be good."

Dianne shuddered. "We'll just have to trust God to multiply the air, like He did the loaves and fishes." She tried not to worry that God might not honor her prayers because they were technically breaking the law. The law was wrong, she thought, but the Bible did say to obey the laws of the land. Dianne was torn as to what she should do. Her loyalty to family, however, was strong.

Lord, I don't want to sin against you, she prayed silently, overwhelmed with hopelessness. *I don't want to lie to the soldiers or put anyone's life in jeopardy, but I can't let them take Koko and the children . . . or Takes Many Horses.*

"I'll tell the boys," Gabe said. "Billy Joe can come up to the house and help you. After I get the word spread here, how about I come get Luke and Micah? I can take them to the river to fish. It will seem like things are just routine that way."

Dianne bit her lower lip and nodded. Luke, especially, would be beside himself with curiosity as to why they were hiding Koko's family in the cellar. "Yes, thank you. John just went down for his nap, so he'll probably sleep right through it all."

"Good. Then we have a plan."

Dianne wished she didn't feel so afraid. "Thank you both. This has to work. It just has to work."

"But I don't want to hide. I want to fight," Jamie declared. "You keep telling me I'm white. That I look white — that I'm more white than Indian, but now you're telling

411

me I have to hide." Koko began to sob, and Susannah clung in terror to her mother's skirt.

Dianne grabbed Jamie by the arm and pulled him from the kitchen into the dining room. "Look, you need to think about someone other than yourself this time. If the soldiers come, they might very well leave you behind, but they won't leave your mother here. Nor will they leave your uncle, whom they've been pursuing for weeks. You have the ability to be a hero in this matter. Your mother and sister need you. Takes Many Horses needs you as well. He can hardly stand, much less defend himself."

Jamie's stiff stance relaxed a bit. "But I could stay here and fight with you."

"But your mother will never go into that cellar without you," Dianne whispered. "Don't you understand that? She won't allow us to protect her if her children are in jeopardy."

Jamie said nothing for a moment, then exhaled heavily. "I'll go. I don't like it, but I'll go."

"Thank you. You are an honorable son. Your father would be so proud right now. You may not think it honorable to hide, but sometimes the Lord asks us to rest and wait upon Him. That's all you're doing now. You aren't a coward."

"No, you are not a coward," Takes Many Horses said from the doorway. "You are going to be my strength, for I surely have none left."

Jamie straightened at this, the proud spirit returning to replace defeat. "I will be your strength, Uncle."

"Good. Then let us hurry, for the time has grown short."

Jamie went to Takes Many Horses and put his arm around him in support. Dianne followed, feeling helpless to make matters right. By the time they got to the storage room, Billy Joe had already managed to get Koko and Susannah down into the cellar.

Takes Many Horses went down the ladder next, with Koko steadying him from beneath and Jamie helping him from above. Dianne could see the fear in Koko's eyes.

"I will keep you safe," Dianne whispered. "*He* will keep you safe."

"We'll be praying," Koko offered in return. "Don't risk your life for ours. I could never forgive myself if you were killed and left the boys without a mother."

"They'll have to go through us to get to her," Billy Joe said sternly.

Jamie hurried down the ladder just as the sound of horses' hooves could be heard rumbling in the distance. There was no more time for words. Dianne caught sight of Takes Many Horses and read the longing in his eyes. Longing to be free instead of captured in a hole in the ground. Longing to say words that had to remain unspoken.

"Help me maneuver this chest over the trapdoor," Dianne instructed Billy Joe. "Then pile all of these things around so it looks like they've been here forever." She grabbed armfuls of blankets.

The two of them quickly had the trapdoor hidden away. They took the supplies that had been sitting behind the chest and arranged them around it to look natural.

"Come on. We'll have to go greet them. They'll know something's amiss if we don't show up quickly at the sight of an army in our front yard." Billy Joe followed her out. Dianne stopped only long enough to lock the storage room. "They'll no doubt insist on my opening it, but at least it's a small deterrent."

They hurried to the front of the house, where the commander was dismounting when Dianne came through the front door. "Why, hello, Captain," she said in her most cheery greeting. "Welcome to the Diamond V." She didn't recognize him from having been there before, but that was no reassurance that he didn't know about Koko and the children.

"Ma'am," he said, touching his hat. "We are tracking a dangerous man — a Blackfoot runaway. He's been on the run for several weeks, and our scouts have tracked him here."

"I'm afraid your man is mistaken. I've seen nothing of a dangerous Blackfoot."

"I'm sure he wouldn't just present himself to you. We're going to search the premises. I'd advise you to stay inside so as to be safe."

Dianne felt a bit of relief course through her. Maybe they'd have no interest in searching the house. But just as she thought this, the captain motioned one of his men.

"I want you to accompany this woman into the house and then search to make certain he's not inside hiding. Take two men with you."

"Yes, sir," the private replied.

Dianne swallowed hard, but the cottony dryness of her mouth left her feeling gagged. Billy Joe stood faithfully at her side as Gus approached from the barn.

"What's going on here?" he demanded to know.

"We're searching for an Indian. We've tracked him here and we intend to flush him out," the captain replied. "I'll trust you'll direct my men to places they might look — places where an animal such as this could hide."

"You bet," Gus answered. "I don't want any vicious varmints around here. You boys come on along with me. I'll grab my gun and we'll go huntin'."

Dianne would have smiled had the situation not been so grave. The private returned with his two companions and motioned Dianne into the house. "Ma'am, if you'll lead the way, please."

Dianne gathered her skirts and entered her home. She could hear her heart pounding in her ears. Billy Joe followed her, but his presence offered her little comfort. She wished Cole were home but at the same time worried about how he might have handled the matter. His nonaggressive stance against the Lawrences had left her puzzled as to who he was and why he didn't act. She would have demanded Chester and Portia stop their threats and underhanded scheming by now.

"Where does this hall go to?" the private asked.

Dianne turned. "It goes to the back of the house. There are stairs there to the second floor."

"And this way?" He pointed in the direction of the dining room and kitchen.

"There is a small sitting room and then the dining area. The kitchen is to the back of the house, and a small storage room. Then there's an enclosed mud porch that leads outside. Oh, and a narrow hall leads to the back stairs. It goes full circle."

"Let's start that way," the solder said, pushing past Dianne.

The men fanned out and searched behind furniture and under the dining room table. When they came to the kitchen, two of the men went immediately to the back porch, while the private in charge checked the room by himself. Coming to the locked storage room door, he turned to Dianne.

"Where does this go to?"

"It's a storage room. We keep it locked unless we need something from it."

"Open it."

Dianne tried to look baffled. "I'm not sure I have a key. My husband generally keeps those things, and he's gone to Butte."

The private frowned, then without warning kicked the door in. Dianne shrieked and drew her hand to her throat. The soldier went into the storage room and looked around. He lifted the pile of blankets and looked behind a stand of flour sacks. Appearing satisfied, he returned to the kitchen

417

just as two of his comrades came in from the porch.

"There's quite a mess back there," one of the men said, motioning over his shoulder. They all three looked to Dianne.

She smiled. "My boys play there."

"Where are your boys now?"

"Two of them are down at the river fishing with one of my men. The baby is sleeping upstairs."

Satisfied with the answer, the private motioned his men to follow as they made their way to the back stairs. "We'll go up this way and search through the upstairs, then move to the front staircase."

Dianne followed in silence. There was nothing else to be done. She could only breathe a sigh of relief that the man had decided the storage room wasn't worth his trouble.

By midday the soldiers had exhausted their search. The captain was ill-tempered and in no mood for nonsense. He motioned to his tracker and questioned the man at length before approaching Dianne. "He says the tracks lead here. They stop down by the river, and your man who's down there fishing says one of your boats are missing."

Dianne gasped and held her hand against her breast. "Oh, you don't suppose he got

418

this close — truly?" It was her very best acting — playing the damsel in distress.

The man softened his tone. "Don't worry, ma'am, he's not here. He's probably taken your boat and headed off, thinking to throw us off his scent. I'll send men both up- and downstream. We'll catch him — dead or alive." He tipped his hat. "I thank you for your cooperation."

Dianne nodded, wanting nothing more than to scream at the man for his insensitivity.

"Mount up!" the captain called.

The men who weren't already aback their horses hurried into their saddles. One pudgy sergeant pushed his mount forward and leaned down. "So whatever happened to that Injun squaw who lived here with her children? I didn't see nothin' of them."

All eyes turned on Dianne. The moment had come that she had dreaded. "They're gone," she said matter-of-factly. "The army's been through here more than once."

"So they finally got 'em to the reservation, eh?" the man replied, not sounding entirely convinced that she was telling the truth. "Good. We don't need 'em out here breeding with decent white folk."

Dianne stared at the man, trying hard to keep her temper in check. "Yes, we certainly don't want decent folk bothered."

The man held her gaze for several moments, then straightened. He nodded at the captain, who in turn gave the order to move out.

Dianne feared they'd remain close at hand for some time, however. They would be running up and down the river trying their best to find Takes Many Horses. It could be days before they completely left the area.

With Billy Joe's help, Dianne made sure those hiding in the cellar were getting enough air, then went about her business, hoping to know when it was safe to bring her family back up.

By the next afternoon, she sent out riders to see where the army had gotten off to. Unable to wait for news, she saddled Daisy and rode to the top of her hill to look down on the valley. There were no signs of the blue-coated soldiers.

She contemplated whether she'd done right in the eyes of the Lord. She knew full well that she'd done right by her family. In her heart, there was no other recourse.

"Lord, if I have sinned, please forgive me."

A noise behind her caused Dianne to whirl Daisy around as though she were cutting out a calf for branding. To her surprise Mara Lawrence was riding as if the devil himself were after her. Her long dark hair rippled behind her in the wind.

Waving, Dianne called to the girl, "Mara! Mara! What's wrong?"

The girl made her way to Dianne. She looked terrified, and it was obvious she'd been crying. She yanked back on the reins of her dark brown gelding. "I hate that woman! I hate her for what she's done to my family."

"Who?" Dianne questioned.

"Portia. She's ruined everything. I hate her and I hate my father for bringing her to our home. She's cruel and vicious. Always threatening us behind our father's back. She's even mean to Joshua, and he's so kind. He's nothing like Jerrod or Roy. They're mean to the bone. But not Joshua."

"I'm sorry, Mara. But what can I do?" Dianne asked. She wasn't about to reveal her own feelings for Portia.

"I can't beat her at her games," Mara admitted. "She's much too clever. She won't rest until she has managed to send us all away. I know it's an imposition, but I came to see if you could help me."

"Help you? How? You know your family isn't friends with ours. Your father is trying to take our land. I can hardly go and speak to him on your behalf, and there aren't any legal courses. Portia is your father's wife."

"I know," Mara said. "I know all about Father's schemes to run you out of the territory too. I've come to bring help, in return for yours."

"Help?" Dianne questioned.

"Yes." Mara pulled a folded piece of paper from her jacket. "These are papers my father took from the courthouse in Virginia City. They show you as the legal owner of the Diamond V."

CHAPTER 25

Cole returned to the Diamond V in the last week of August. He had no answers for his family and felt a sense of defeat as he came through the front door. He hated to face Dianne empty-handed. She already felt he was failing her where the Lawrence problems were concerned. He couldn't go into detail, however, and explain that he and his men were gathering evidence against Lawrence. First, she wouldn't see it as doing enough. Second, she'd want to help, and he couldn't allow her to risk her life.

Cole sighed. It wasn't like the information was doing them much good. He'd had a chance to present some of his findings to a Butte lawyer in order to seek direction as to what they should do next. But the man felt their evidence was circumstantial at best and hearsay at worst.

Cole's biggest regret was that he couldn't give Dianne a solid answer with regard to the ranch. There just seemed to be nothing to aid their cause.

"I've got the most incredible news," Dianne said as she hurried down the staircase to greet him.

"Well, I don't," Cole admitted.

She smiled. "I have papers from the courthouse in Virginia. They show that Uncle Bram made me part owner before he died."

"Where in the world did you get them?"

"Mara Lawrence."

"You're joking, right?" Cole's disbelief was evident.

"Not at all. She's absolutely reached the end of her patience with Portia, and her father has become abusive and neglectful, taking Portia's side over that of his children. Mara didn't want him to get away with stealing our land. She felt that all of their troubles started when her father began causing us problems."

"She'll pay for that."

"What of you? What happened in Butte?" Dianne asked, hugging him close.

Cole momentarily forgot his frustration and breathed in the lilac scent that permeated Dianne's clothes. He held her, wishing they could be alone, but even now someone approached from behind. He released his wife and turned to find Koko and Takes Many Horses.

"I didn't know you were back," Cole said in greeting. "How are you?"

"He was half dead and being chased by soldiers when he showed up here," Dianne declared. "But we hid him in the cellar, along with Koko and the children. The soldiers searched and moved on. So they're all safe."

"For now," Koko interjected.

"Hopefully forever. They believe Koko and the children had already gone to the reservation, and they didn't seem to understand that Takes Many Horses was related to them and had a reason for coming here. I don't think they'll waste their time coming here again."

Cole tried to take it all in. "The army showed up here?"

"Yes, but Billy Joe and Gabe were wonderful to help me. Everyone was. We used the new cellar and covered the trapdoor with that big chest in the storage room. We do need to replace the door to the storage room, however. One of the soldiers got impatient for me to produce a key," Dianne said, her voice more animated than he'd heard in months.

"We'll have to speak more about this," he

said, looking directly at Takes Many Horses.

"So what is this about papers?" Koko asked.

Cole looked to Dianne and she smiled. "We didn't want to worry you," Dianne began. "The Lawrences have been trying for some time now to discredit my claim to the ranch. They said there was only proof that Uncle Bram had owned the land, not that he had ever added my name to the deed. In fact, no one could even find a deed."

"Why didn't you ask me?" Koko questioned. "I have the deed."

Cole and Dianne stared at her with open mouths. Koko couldn't help but laugh. "See where secrets get you? You shouldn't have worried about my feelings or fears! Bram gave me the deed long ago. I just forgot about it and it never seemed important."

"Well, it is," Cole said. "We need to get my name on that paper and put everything in order before they decide that causing Dianne some permanent harm will be the way to leave the land ownership in question. By law it should come to me, but let's not take chances."

"I agree," Koko said. "I think we're coming into an age where corruption will reign supreme. I'll give you the deed tonight, but please promise me you won't keep things from me. I'm not fragile."

"No, my sister has a gentle strength," Takes Many Horses said softly.

"Why don't you boys have a rest out on the porch? Koko and I will whip up some lunch and bring it to you."

"That sounds good," Cole said. He was still unable to imagine all that had taken place in his absence.

"You look worn," Takes Many Horses said as they took their seats.

"I am. I guess the mental exhaustion alone has taken its toll. I felt so defeated in returning home without good news to share, and here God had provided in my absence."

"He has a way of doing that. I knew coming here was a dangerous risk, but I had nowhere else to go. The army was breathing down my neck, and I knew I couldn't go on. I prayed that God wouldn't punish you and yours for my sins, and when the army moved on without locating me, I felt He had forgiven me and heard my prayers."

"What will you do now?"

Takes Many Horses grew thoughtful. "Koko wants me to stay and live as a white. She makes a good argument." He looked to Cole, as if trying to ascertain his feelings on the matter.

"You are always welcome here. I know Dianne feels that way. I know Bram felt that way too."

"Has it been hard living in the shadow of a great man?"

For a moment the question caught Cole off guard. Was he referencing himself or Bram Vandyke? "I suppose," Cole began slowly, "that there are times when I wish I could start over and make a ranch of my own instead of picking up where someone else left off."

Takes Many Horses nodded in understanding. "A man needs land of his own — a place to call his own. He needs to know that he has accomplished something of value."

"Yes. I'm not sure I can say that here."

"I think you can. You could have deserted my sister and her children. You could have been the kind of man who didn't care about the promise between Dianne and Bram. You are a godly man — probably the most godly man I've ever known. Sometimes you shame me because you've been here for Koko when I've been selfishly seeking my own way."

"You had to do what seemed important to you," Cole said softly.

"I've wasted my life."

"No, not really. You still have a good portion of your life to live."

"But how shall I live?" Takes Many Horses stood and leaned on the porch rail as he looked out across the ranch yard. "When we were in hiding, my sister asked me if this was what I wanted for Jamie. Hiding — running — fighting to survive. It was then that I realized how wrong I'd been. I wanted to be a great leader, but instead, I failed my people."

Cole studied the man for a moment. He was still dressed in Blackfoot fashion, with leather leggings and a long cloth shirt. His long hair gleamed blue-black in the noon sun. Cole drew a deep breath and let it out slowly. "Jamie's at a very impressionable age. It's not too late to influence him for good."

Takes Many Horses turned. "How can I do that now?"

"You can put the past behind you and look forward to a different future. You can live by your white heritage now. As you've said before and know to be true, the time of the Blackfoot — of any Indian — is passing by quickly."

"And you honestly think this will impress my nephew? My settling down to be a rancher? After hearing my stories of wild buffalo hunts and trekking across the untouched mountains for weeks on end, you honestly expect him to be excited by my living as white?"

"I don't think it much matters how excited he gets about your life. I think what counts is that he sees that you changed your heart in order to better others. That's a powerful lesson to teach someone. Putting yourself aside for the sake of your loved ones."

Takes Many Horses met Cole's eyes. "You believe this. . . . I can see your heart in this matter."

"Only because I had to make the same choices. I had to make things right with my parents by putting my desires aside in order to help them. I found that in doing so, however, my desires changed. I still wanted to marry Dianne, but I knew that I was worthy of becoming her husband. Before, I was far too selfish."

The silence fell between them for several minutes as Takes Many Horses appeared to wrestle with his emotions. Finally he spoke. "I'll consider this more in prayer. I know what you're saying rings of the truth."

Dianne was delighted when Cole asked if she'd like to accompany him on a short ride to enjoy the afternoon. A fresh breeze was blowing across the valley and the temperatures had cooled quite pleasurably. Soon the leaves would begin to change colors and autumn would be upon them with frosty mornings and chilly days.

"How are you feeling?" Cole asked.

"I feel fine. No morning sickness or any problems."

"I'm glad. I worried about you while I was gone."

"With exception to the army intrusion, we've been operating well. God has truly been looking out for us all along. The cellar wasn't big enough to fit anyone else, so it was a blessing that Ardith had taken Winona and accompanied Levi to Bozeman. We didn't have to worry about finding a place for them to hide."

"That was a blessing."

"I've tried to be cheerful for Koko's sake, but I keep thinking about the fact that Portia knows very well that she's here. If she should figure out that this will cause us grief, I know she'll do what she can to spread the news."

"Maybe she'll forget. The Lord could cause her to do just that. We have to have faith that God is protecting His own." They rode down through a stand of trees as the wind picked up. The aspen leaves quaked as they passed alongside.

Dianne decided now was as good a time as any to bring up the subject of Mara Lawrence. "I wanted to talk to you about Chester Lawrence's daughter."

Cole looked at her in surprise. "Why?"

"Because she's been helpful to us, at great risk to herself."

"We didn't ask her to risk her standing with her father and betray him. I don't approve of what she did, in spite of the way it helped us."

Dianne frowned. "God provided for us through Mara."

"The provision was always with us in Koko. We just pridefully thought we'd take care of matters on our own."

"It was to save her feelings, Cole. We weren't being prideful."

He stopped his horse and shook his head. "We were wrong not to talk to her about it. After all, she's the true owner."

Dianne tried not to let his comments anger her. "Mara needs help. I'd like to invite her to come here to live."

"I don't know how old she is, but my guess is that she's plenty under the legal age. There's no possible chance of Chester allowing her to come here, so we can't very well impose that on him."

"But she's unhappy," Dianne protested. "Besides, this would be the perfect solution."

"To what? Getting back at Chester for stealing our calves? He steals a few calves and steers, so you want to steal his daughter?"

Dianne detested that Cole could so easily see her desire for revenge in having Mara come to the ranch. She couldn't deny that this was part of her reasoning. She wanted to hurt Chester — hurt him for the death of Whit and Maggie, for Portia and her escapades, and for trying to steal the ranch from right under her nose. When Mara had come to her in such misery, Dianne had immediately begun to plan how she might use the situation to help them all.

"I can see my words have touched on the truth," Cole said softly. "How would you feel if someone tried the same thing with Luke or one of the others?"

Dianne swallowed hard. "I know what you're saying, but something has to be done. Chester Lawrence continues his underhanded schemes, and no one is doing anything to stop him."

"We're trying. We're trying to gather enough proof to have the law intercede, but Chester is smart. Probably too smart. He covers his tracks well, and he has most people bullied or paid off so that no one will give testimony against him."

"I'm tired of doing things by the law," Dianne said frankly. "He's not abiding by the law, so maybe we should meet him where he's at and deal him the same kind of hand."

"Listen to yourself. You, the one who used to be so strong in your faith. You, who helped me find my way back to God. You want to break the law in order to exact revenge on the Lawrences? What happened to revenge belonging to God?"

Dianne grew angry. "You just don't want to deal with it because you're afraid of him. I can see it in your face."

Cole narrowed his eyes. "I'm not afraid of him. I'm afraid of what I'm capable of if I let my anger rule me — like you're doing."

"I'm not —"

He held up his hand. "No more. I want no more of this. I'd like you to go back to the house now. I want to be alone for a while."

Dianne started to say something, then decided against it. She'd not seen Cole this angry with her in the whole time of their marriage. Had she truly overstepped her bounds? As she rode back to the house, she came to the sinking realization that she'd practically called him a coward.

I shouldn't have said that, she told herself. Then she reconsidered. *At least I certainly didn't mean it. But I thought it might stir him to take more aggressive action.*

But where could that more aggressive action take them? Physical violence? Death? Were these prices she was willing to pay? She reined back on Daisy and turned to see Cole disappear over the ridge. She wanted to go after him and apologize but knew he was in no mood to hear her now.

"What have I done?" she murmured.

Portia sat in her window seat and watched dark clouds roll in from the south. Someone had mentioned a dry thunderstorm heading their way — one that had already set small forests on fire near Ennis.

A fire might be the perfect solution, she mused. *A strike of lightning in just the right place could end all of my worries. A fire could spread quickly and destroy the ranches along the way. Particularly the Diamond V.* It seemed like such a simple solution. No one could ever tell whether the fire was intentionally set or just the result of the storm's fury.

"Portia! Portia!"

It was Chester. His frantic search for her

435

could only mean that he'd managed to mislay something important — again.

"I think he's getting too old for me," she muttered as she got to her feet.

"Where are you, woman?"

She opened her bedroom door and went down the hall to the top of the stairs. Chester was already barreling up them, taking the stairs two at a time.

"I'm right here. What's the matter?"

"Do you know where my papers are — the ones I have on the Diamond V?"

Portia had seen the papers several weeks ago but hadn't thought about them since. "No. I don't."

Chester was fairly frothing at the mouth. "They're missing. Missing! I need those papers, and I need them now."

"They have to be here," Portia replied, already bored with the matter. She stifled a yawn. "I'm not feeling very good. I think I'll go lie down."

He grabbed her arm and held her tight, causing pain to travel up to her elbow. When he was like this he reminded her of Angus, her second husband.

"You have to help me find those papers. There's no time for sleeping. This is vital to our plan."

Portia felt her expression harden. "You're

hurting me. Release me at once."

"Shut up, woman. Do you hear me? Those papers are more important than anything else. If they get into the wrong hands, the Selbys will be able to prove their legal right to the Diamond V."

Portia was unwavering in her stand. "I'll walk out that front door and leave you without another word unless you let go of me. No man treats me this way and gets away with it."

"Are you threatening me, Portia?" Chester asked, his eyes narrowing. "Don't forget, I know things about you that you'd rather not be told."

Portia laughed and yanked her arm away from his hold. "You don't know anything about me at all. You only suppose you do. Try to expose me, and it won't bode well for you or your murdering offspring." Chester paled. "Yes, that's right. Jerrod and Roy would look awfully good to me dangling from the end of a rope, but I seriously doubt you'd be very happy about it."

"What are you getting at?"

Portia rubbed her sore arm. "Just this: never think to boss me around or threaten me. I'll do as I will and you'll live with it. Or you won't. The choice is yours."

CHAPTER 26

Days after their harsh words, Dianne approached Cole in order to apologize. She didn't want him to believe she thought him a coward. But at the same time, she needed him to understand why she felt so angry.

It would help if I understood that anger, Dianne thought as she made her way to the barn. Cole and Luke were going to ride out to build a training corral, which was part of a new plan devised by Levi. They were to assemble several training corrals away from the main yard and closer to the bunkhouse. There was to be a new foaling shed and other equipment that would allow for them to double their production of horses for the army.

"Cole?" Dianne questioned as she entered the barn. The warm, musty smell of horses and straw filled her senses.

"We're saddling up," came his curt reply.

Dianne approached. "Luke, why don't you

438

walk your pony outside? I need to talk to Papa for a minute."

"Can I ride him out?" Luke asked, his voice full of excitement.

"You know I don't want you doing that," Cole answered as he secured his horse's cinch. "Too many things to spook your pony — too closed in."

"All right, Papa," Luke answered, sounding dejected.

"But if you'll walk him out and stand there patiently, we'll race down to the corral. How about that?"

Luke's face lit up. "I'll bet I can beat you this time."

"Maybe you can," Cole said, laughing.

Dianne waited until Luke had gone from the barn before she turned her attention on Cole. "I know you're busy, but I tried to talk to you about this before breakfast and you didn't seem to have time."

"What is there to discuss? You think I'm a coward. You think I would risk my family's well-being because I'm afraid to deal with Lawrence."

"I spoke out of anger. I didn't mean what I said," Dianne said, moving closer to where Cole stood. "I'm sorry for what I said."

"You might be sorry for it, but I think down deep inside, you feel that way. You

439

think that I'm keeping peace because I don't have the courage to fight, but nothing could be further from the truth." He turned to look at her, and the hardness of his expression left Dianne feeling uneasy.

"You have no idea," Cole said, turning away to untie his horse, "how hard it is to keep the peace. You can't even imagine how many times I've had to sit down and talk things out with Ben just to keep my rage under control." His words surprised Dianne. She truly didn't have any idea that her husband felt this way.

"I'm trying to trust the Lord to guide me, Dianne, but you seem to want emotion to do the leading." He drew his gelding along with him and paused as he came up even with Dianne. "I'm sorry I've disappointed you in how I've handled this situation, but truth be told, you've disappointed me in how you've handled it."

With that he moved out and left Dianne to stand alone contemplating his words. She felt like a small child, reprimanded for having stolen cookies. There was a time when his words might have made her angry, but this time, all she felt was shame.

Takes Many Horses looked once again at his new clothes. They felt foreign to him after a lifetime of dressing as a Blackfoot. The trousers in particular were uncomfortable — as were the heavy boots. Living as a white man would be no easy task.

He came into the formal dining room and waited for the reaction. Everyone stopped talking and looked up to fix his gaze on the transformation. Takes Many Horses smiled.

"I suppose I owe you all an explanation."

"You've cut your hair!" Koko declared.

He reached up to touch his shortly cropped hair. "Yes. I figured it was necessary."

"But why? You are Blackfoot," Jamie protested. "You look like a white man now."

"Exactly," Takes Many Horses said. "I borrowed clothes from Cole and boots from Levi."

"I think you look quite good," Dianne said as she brought in a tureen of soup.

"You've betrayed the Real People," Jamie said in a barely audible voice.

"I've betrayed no one. I've been reasoning with everything that has happened — with the things that are bound to happen if I continue as I have in the past. It's time for a change. I will live as white and stay here on the ranch to help my sister."

"What good news," Koko said, her eyes brimming with tears. "I'm so proud of you."

"Well, I'm not!" Jamie slammed his napkin onto the table and jumped up from his chair. "You are disgusting to me." He ran from the room before Koko could even respond to his outrage.

Koko started to get up from her chair, but Takes Many Horses waved her off. "I'll go after him. It's time his uncle George dealt with such matters. After all, I'm the one who fed his passion for the ways of our people."

Koko sat back down. "All right. As you wish . . . George."

He left the surprised dinner party and went after his nephew. "George," he murmured to himself. It would be hard to get used to the name. His sister often called him by it, but very few people knew him by it.

It was easy to see that the boy had gone to the barn. The tracks weren't hard to miss, but even more so, George could see that the door was open. Pushing it back even more, he entered and called to the boy.

"Jamie. If you feel I've been dishonorable, the least you can do is be honorable and face me."

"I don't want to face you," the boy declared.

"I know you're disappointed in me, but I

only ask you to talk this out like a man."

Jamie emerged from behind a pile of hay. "I'm here, but I don't know what good it will do."

George sat down on the barn floor and motioned Jamie to do likewise. "White men don't sit on the ground," Jamie said snidely.

"Of course they do. Have you never been to a roundup — never on a cattle drive? When white men camp out in the wilderness, they do so much the way the Blackfoot or Sioux might."

Jamie held his ground, staring down at his uncle. "You were proud of the Blackfoot — now you're ashamed."

"Not at all. I was and always will be proud of my Blackfoot heritage. I will never forget that I am part of that world. But I won't live as they live now."

Jamie frowned. "What do you mean?"

"They live like caged animals, unable to properly hunt or fend for themselves. The reservation doesn't have enough room or game to sustain the people. The United States government tries to help, but often the meat they send is rancid by the time it reaches our people. The government sends blankets that make our people sick with small pox, measles, mumps, and other diseases. Our people suffer greatly."

443

"But at least they do not betray who they are."

"And neither do I. Rather, I don't want to see that life for your mother and sister. Do you?"

Jamie seemed perplexed. "Why would you ask that?"

"Because if I don't change my ways and live as white, they very well might end up living on the reservation. The army won't always be put off. They will eventually come back. Someone will tell of your living here, and you'll be rounded up like the cattle in the spring. You might well survive such a thing because you are a man, but your mother and sister would probably die."

Jamie dropped to the ground to sit opposite his uncle. "Do you truly think this is the only way? Why couldn't we go north with you — north to Canada?"

"That isn't any hope for us. Look at Sitting Bull. His people were dying from starvation in Canada. They were sickly and hungry. Even reservation life sounded better than wasting away in the frozen wilderness."

"But it seems wrong to just give up."

George shrugged. "I don't see it so much as giving up. I see it as closing one book to open another. You read well — I

444

know, because your mother told me. You must finish one book before you open another."

"I can read more than one book at a time," Jamie argued.

"Ah, but not at the same time. You must focus on one only, is that not true?"

"I suppose so."

"I feel it is the same for me. I focused on being a Blackfoot for most of my life. Now I will open a new book and focus on being white."

"Whites will never accept us," Jamie said sadly.

"Perhaps they won't, but we will not provoke them by acting or dressing in ways that frighten them."

"Frighten them?" Jamie asked. "You think they hate us because we frighten them?"

"Fear is a powerful tool," George said, meeting his nephew's intense gaze. "Fear causes people to act in ways they might not otherwise have chosen. Indians have long grieved the white man. Whether because we actually did something to deserve their feelings or not, they have heard stories since first coming to America."

"Both sides have their stories. You told me this was true."

"Yes, but both sides did not win this

battle. Only the whites won."

"So we are supposed to just forget we are Blackfoot? Even though the whites who recognize our heritage won't let us forget?" Jamie questioned.

"We never forget who we are — that we are a part of the Real People," George said softly. "But just as the Real People found it necessary to adapt their habits in order to survive over many centuries, we must adapt in order to live into the next century. In time, the laws will change and the white will no longer fear the Indian."

"Do you really believe that?"

"I have to. To imagine any other outcome is too discouraging. Besides, look what happened with the black men. They were once slaves and now they are free. It's possible that a day will come when Indians will live free as well."

Jamie let out a long sigh. "And is this God's will for our people?"

George shook his head. "I don't know. I only know that God asks me to trust Him with every aspect of my life. I must trust Him with this as well."

"I don't think God cares about the Blackfoot," Jamie said sadly. "I'm not sure He cares about us at all. My father is dead. I cannot own the land he worked. My mother must live in fear. What hope is there for any of us?"

"God is all the hope we need, Jamie. You must not let the way people act drive you away from the love God has for you."

"It doesn't seem God has any love for the Blackfoot."

"I don't believe that. I think that God has His purposes and ways, and I do not always understand them. However, I will go on trusting Him, just as Job did when bad times came. Besides, how do you know there will be bad days to come? You might well go and receive an education, and in doing so find a way to help the Blackfoot. Think of that. You might one day rise up to be a great advocate for our people."

"Do you think so?" Jamie asked, his voice edged with excitement for the first time since they'd come to talk.

"I believe it is possible, because with God all things are possible. Your mother tells me that it says so in the Bible."

Jamie nodded. "I've heard her say that as well. I guess it must be true."

"I do not want you to hate me for my choices. I am doing what I feel is right. It doesn't mean we can't discuss the old days and some of the good times I shared with our ancestors. But it does mean that you and I both need to try harder to make changes here," he said, pointing to his chest, "in our hearts."

Portia listened to Chester as he stormed through the house bellowing and accusing. She rolled her eyes as she heard him contend once again that the papers were his only chance of moving the Selbys from the Madison Valley.

"You think in such narrow perspectives, my dear," Portia murmured aloud.

She pulled on her riding boots, listening to the rumble of thunder overhead. It wouldn't be long now before the storm passed. There had been very little rain, only a sprinkling, in fact, but the lightning had been fierce. She knew it was the very storm she'd been waiting for. She would ride out, and if fires were not already kindled, she would intercede in the matter.

"Jerrod, are you certain you haven't seen those documents?"

"You forced Roy and me from the house, because of *her*," Jerrod yelled back. "How would we have had any chance to get at your papers?"

"Don't take that tone with me, boy."

How irritating they were. How very childish. Chester's tirade had gone on for nearly three days. It was unbelievable. He'd start in with first one person and then another. And always it was the same questions: "Where are my papers regarding the Diamond V?" "Did you see my documents?" "Have you been in my office?"

She was weary of the entire matter, and if it would only benefit her to do so, Portia would have gladly eliminated the conflict. But she was still working out the details of how she might profit from her marriage to Chester Lawrence. She'd most likely have to kill off the boys. They'd be far too inquisitive — too aggressive.

"Too bad we can't have a good old-fashioned round of cholera," she mused.

Looking in the mirror to make certain her hair was in place, Portia paused. She didn't like the way time was aging her. She looked more and more haggard as the days went by. Part of that came from living in the middle of nowhere, and part of it was from living with the Lawrences.

She touched her hand to her cheek. It was almost leathery instead of soft and supple as it had been when she'd lived in the ease and comfort of Baltimore's favored society.

"I've grown old," she breathed with a sigh.

She thought back on all that she'd done — the lives she'd taken — the lives she'd wounded. As a child she'd often been lonely and sad. Most likely because her mother had also been lonely and sad.

"I can't change the past," she told her image. She remembered arranging for her father's death. She'd been certain that when the old man was dead and buried, she would feel the burden lifted from her soul. But it hadn't happened.

So often she'd rid herself of annoyances and interferences, and yet it never took away the deep, painful hole in her heart. She met her own gaze and was almost startled at the emptiness in her eyes.

"Montana is killing me. There's just no way around that. I should probably go east and rest."

She secured her riding hat and turned to look for her gloves. "I could convince Chester that it would be good for all of us. The girls and the boys. And who knows what might happen to them in the big city."

But first she had to take care of the Selbys. They knew too much, or at least they thought they did. She didn't know how much information Trenton had shared with his sister, but sometimes at night Portia's imagination ran wild, and she couldn't sleep for fear of the door being broken down and R. E. Langford taking her in hand.

"They'll all pay. I'll see to that."

She went to her dresser and procured a box of matches. She couldn't be sure how many fires she'd need to set in order to see the Diamond V burned to the ground, and she couldn't take a chance that she might run out before her job was completed.

"No one hurts me and gets away with it. No one."

Roy and Jerrod Lawrence leaned against the bunkhouse, sharing a cigar. Jerrod was livid that his father had relegated them to nothing more than common hands on the ranch.

"She's prob'ly got his stupid papers," Jerrod said, taking a long draw on the cigar.

"Prob'ly. She thinks she's queen of the world, sitting on high, causing problems for everyone."

"She'll pay, Roy. I'll see to that."

Jerrod passed the cigar to his brother just as Portia let the back door slam shut. Both men looked up as she crossed the yard quickly and approached the barn.

"Where's she headed?" Roy asked.

"I dunno, but I think we oughta follow her. Maybe we can give her a little payback for the position she's gotten us into."

"Pa would skin us alive if she came home all banged up."

"Maybe we can buy ourselves a couple of witnesses who'll swear to Pa that we was with them the whole time. Then we can knock some sense into her," Jerrod said, trying to think the matter through.

"Maybe she could have a worse accident than before," Roy suggested. "Maybe one that takes her life."

"Maybe. It's worth considerin'."

The boys maneuvered themselves so they could watch when she exited the barn. It didn't take long. She rode out on the back of her favorite mount and headed off toward the river.

Jerrod smacked Roy against the chest. "Come on. Let's get those witnesses and then follow her."

CHAPTER 27

"I'm pretty good with horses," George said as he watched Cole work with one of the three-year-olds. "I didn't get the name Takes Many Horses for doing nothing."

Cole nodded. "Koko told me you would be a great asset to us in wrangling." His tone was serious, and George couldn't help but wonder what was wrong. For days Cole had seemed very burdened — almost troubled.

Cole took up the halter and approached the skittish white. "Easy, boy. Easy." His voice was low and soft as he tried to sooth the animal.

George continued watching as Cole rubbed the horse ever so gently with the halter and with his hand. The horse seemed to calm.

"He knows you," George commented.

Cole said nothing until after managing to slip the halter over the white's head. "We've been working for a while on this." After he secured the halter, Cole pulled the strap gently to the right. The white followed. Cole walked in circles around the corral while George watched.

"He nearly kicked my head off the first time we worked together," Cole said as he rounded the pen. "Didn't want any part of this."

George leaned against the pole pen. "I can see he is spirited."

"And mean," Cole replied. "Not the kind of thing a coward would want to deal with." His tone sounded bitter.

"What are you talking about?"

Cole continued walking the horse. "Oh, it's just something Dianne said. She thinks I'm a coward because I won't hunt down the Lawrences and deal with them at the end of a gun."

George laughed softly. "My nephew thinks I'm a coward because I won't take on the entire army and force justice for the Black-foot people."

Cole looked up and smiled. "Guess we're in good company."

"Not bad for cowards."

Cole stopped what he was doing and shook his head. "She has no idea how I have to fight myself to keep from doing exactly what she thinks should be done. She doesn't realize that I could probably kill Lawrence's sons for what they did to Whit and Maggie."

"Just like Jamie doesn't realize that I would gladly kill the soldiers if it meant freedom for my people. He thinks that by living as white, I've given up my dreams and hopes that the Blackfoot might one day be allowed to come and go at will."

"I want peace. I know you do too."

George shrugged. "Sometimes I think we're the only ones."

"Mara! What brings you here?" Dianne questioned after opening the front door. Mara Lawrence stood before her, looking frazzled.

"I had to come. There's going to be trouble this afternoon, and I'm hoping you can stop it."

Dianne ushered the girl inside. "Why don't you come have something to drink while you tell me what's going on."

"Thank you. I'm quite parched."

Mara and Dianne made their way into the kitchen. Dianne was grateful that no one else was around. She took down a glass from the cupboard and poured some chilled cider she'd just brought up from the cold cellar.

"My aunt made this from apples. I think you'll find it very pleasant and refreshing," Dianne said as she placed the glass in front of Mara.

Mara took a long drink. "It's wonderful. Thank you." She glanced around. "Is your husband here? There's going to be trouble and you'll need him. Probably need all of your men."

Dianne frowned. "He's down at the corral. I could send for him."

"Would you, please? There's going to be an attack on one of the ranches."

"Whose?"

"The Vandercamps."

Dianne felt her breath catch. G.W. and Hilda had worked hard to stake their claim on the land. G.W. and Cole were good friends and often shared equipment and breeding stock. To imagine their suffering the same fate as Whit and Maggie was almost more than Dianne could bear.

"I'll send for Cole. Wait here."

She hurried into the hall and found Luke coming down the stairs. "Luke. I need you to fetch your papa. He's down at the corral training one of the horses."

"Can I ride there?" Luke asked, excited at the prospect.

"No. He's not that far. Just run," Dianne

said. "Tell him to come to the house quickly. Tell him it's important."

Luke fairly flew out the front door. Dianne wondered if Cole would refuse because of his anger toward her. She hoped he could put aside their differences and realize that this was gravely important.

Returning to the kitchen, Dianne noted that Mara was working feverishly to put her hair back in place. She smiled at the young woman. "You must have ridden very hard."

"Well, I had to," Mara admitted. "When I heard them talking about their plans for the Vandercamps, I knew I had to tell someone. I hope we won't be too late."

"I hope not too."

Mara finished pinning her hair and turned to Dianne. "I have something to ask you. I hope you won't think me too forward."

"What is it?"

"I wondered if I could come and live with you here and work for you. I'd be happy to be your housekeeper or whatever else you needed. I'm almost seventeen, and I'm a good worker. I know how to cook too."

Dianne raised a brow. "I have to admit the thought had already come to mind to invite you to stay with us — but not as a maid. I feel sorry for your having to deal with Portia's nonsense and the other things that are going on. Still, your father would never let you go."

"He might. If I threatened to tell everyone everything I know, he might let me go. Portia just wants me gone — I don't think she much cares where I go. Father doesn't pay me much attention, and frankly, I think he'd be equally glad to be rid of me."

"I can't imagine that being true, but maybe he'd be less inclined to cause us harm if you were here."

Mara shook her head. "No, I'd imagine it to be the opposite. He's got a mean streak a mile wide."

"It would be difficult to cross him. He'd no doubt want some sort of revenge for your interference in his plans."

"That's why I want to come here. I know he'll make me miserable if he figures out what I've done. He's been storming and snorting over those papers I took ever since they disappeared. But on the other hand, Portia is making me more miserable than he ever could."

"Has she threatened you?" Dianne couldn't help but ask.

"She plans to marry me off to some man in Bozeman who plans to move to Texas. She says he's wealthy and has shown interest in me."

Dianne looked out the window to see if she could spot Cole or Luke. There was no one out there, however. "I hope Luke didn't misunderstand. Sometimes he's that way. Only hears what he wants to hear." She turned away from the window and shook her head. "I'm sorry, I really was listening. I don't understand why Portia would want to marry you off."

"I think it's because she wants my father and the ranch all to herself. She got Jerrod and Roy blamed for some accident she had — at least I'm pretty sure she must have had an accident. I don't think the boys are stupid enough to hurt her. But she was all banged up and miscarried a baby."

"A baby? Portia? That seems completely out of character for her."

"She said she and my father were beginning a new life together and this baby was the beginning of an entirely new empire."

"I can't imagine Portia wanting to be a mother. Not for any reason."

"She's dangerous. I can't tell you why, but I know it's true," Mara said sadly. "I think she actually had something to do with my mother's death."

"Truly?"

"Yes. Mother was fine until we went to tea with Portia. After she left the tea,

Mother was sick — very sick. By the time we arrived at the ranch, she was almost delirious. It was no more than an hour before she was dead."

"You think Portia poisoned her?" Dianne asked. She had always been suspicious of Portia's involvement in Cynthia Lawrence's death.

"I think it's very possible. We all drank from the same tea, but that doesn't mean Portia couldn't have given her something after Elsa and I left to go shopping. Mother was with her alone for at least ten minutes."

Dianne couldn't understand where Cole and Luke were. "Stay here, Mara. I'll go see where my husband is. We'll talk more about this — I promise."

Mara's worried expression softened a bit. "Thank you. I know you could believe the worst about me — even think I was here to spy on you, but I'm not. I'm afraid. Afraid of the things my father is doing to the people in this valley, and afraid of what Portia might do to me personally."

Dianne thought of Mara's words all the way out to the corral. Finding no one there, she looked in the barn. The place seemed deserted. Cole's horse was gone, as were the dogs. She thought maybe George would be nearby, but a quick search of the grounds proved fruitless.

Then Dianne caught sight of something in the distance. On the hillside to the west, the trees were blazing with orange flames.

Her heart skipped a beat. Fire! It almost seemed unreal. She turned to race back to the house when Cole came riding out of the forested land to the south. George was riding beside him.

"We need to round up everyone. Get all of the wagons hitched and ready to move out. Take whatever we need — only what's important," Cole declared, giving Dianne no chance to speak.

"What happened?"

"Probably lightning," George said, jumping from the back of his mount.

"It's burning fast and heading directly for us," Cole said. "I've sent the boys out to round up the horses and cattle and move them north."

Dianne then remembered what Mara had told her. "Cole, there's more trouble than just the fire. Mara Lawrence is here. She told me that her father is headed to the Vandercamps' to force G.W. to sign over the ranch. She says he plans to take it by force if necessary."

Cole clenched his jaw so hard that the skin turned white around his lips. Dianne saw the rage in his face as his eyes narrowed. She knew saying anything more was useless and unneeded. It was only then that she realized Luke was nowhere to be found.

"Where's Luke?" she asked the men. "I sent him after you nearly twenty minutes ago. When Mara came."

Cole shook his head, his anger still evident. "I haven't seen him. Look, there's no time for this. Get the children and everyone else alerted. Levi's already out with some of the men on the north pasture. You'll need to help Ardith."

"I'm not going anywhere without Luke," Dianne declared. "He's got to be here!"

"He's probably already gone back to the house," Cole said, his clipped tone revealing his mood.

"I'll help you find him," George said, reaching out to take hold of her arm.

"I'll look for him as I notify everyone. If I don't see you again before you leave, head to Madison. We'll meet at the church."

"Cole," Dianne said, pulling away from George. She went to Cole's side and touched his leg. "Please be careful. . . . I love you."

Cole leaned down. "I love you, and I'm sorry things have been so bad. I promise to make it up to you."

"Me too." She felt tears come to her eyes and didn't know if it were purely the smoke or the building emotion in her heart. "Please find Luke. I'll leave a note tacked to the porch if I find him."

"Good. Otherwise, I'll get him out."

Dianne nodded and let him go. He reined the horse around quickly and headed out across the field.

"Come on," George encouraged. "There's no time to waste."

She turned to George, her heart racing. "He's just a little boy. He won't know what to do."

"You go warn the others. I'll start looking for him. Can you hitch the wagons by yourself?"

"Yes, the horses are in the corral. We can get them. Just find him, please."

Dianne felt hopeless as she raced for the house. Already the skies were turning hazy from the smoke. Hurrying to her sister's cabin, Dianne pounded on the door. "Ardith! Ardith, hurry!"

Ardith came to the door. "What is it?"

Dianne pointed to the west. "Forest fire. It's serious. Cole's gone to warn some of the others. You need to gather what's important and get Winona to the barn. Can you hitch one of the wagons?"

463

"Of course," she said, her eyes widened in fear. "Where's Levi?"

"Up north. He's safe, but I can't find Luke. George is helping to look for him — so is Cole."

"How could he be gone?"

Dianne shook her head. Her thoughts were swirling. "There isn't time to explain. Just hurry. I'll meet you with the others at the barn." She started to leave, then turned back. "You'd better tie the milk cows to the back of the wagons."

"I'll do it," Ardith promised.

Dianne raced for the house. She had no idea how much time they actually had. "Mara! Koko!" She screamed the names as she hurried through the door.

Mara was where she'd left her in the kitchen. "There's a forest fire. We're in danger. You should probably ride home and warn the others. Your place is far enough away that they'll no doubt be fine. I wouldn't expect the fire to cross that much open land."

"No, I want to stay and help. What can I do?"

"My little ones — Micah and John — are upstairs. I need to go up and gather some things. If you can help me, that would be great."

"What's all the commotion?" Koko asked as she came into the room.

"There's a fire heading this way." Her aunt's jaw dropped. "Luke is missing and George is trying to find him. We need to get the children and load up the wagons with whatever things we can't live without. Send Jamie to hitch up the other two wagons. Ardith is already taking care of one."

"All right. I'll gather some food as well. You go to the boys."

Dianne and Mara hiked their skirts and took the stairs two at a time. They burst into the boys' room without so much as a word to each other. Dianne quickly pulled the blanket from Luke's bed, ever mindful that she didn't know where he was.

Micah sat up rubbing his eyes. He was still sleepy from his nap. "What are you doing?" he asked.

"There's a fire, Micah," Dianne began. "We need to take the animals and get to safety. Can you be a big boy and help me?"

"Yes," Micah said matter-of-factly. "Who's she?"

"This is Mara. She's come to help us."

"Is she an angel?"

Mara laughed and lifted the boy into her arms. "No, but I can help just the same."

Dianne gathered some clothes for the boys

and rolled them into Luke's blanket. "Can you take this?" she asked Mara.

"Yes. I'll meet you downstairs," the girl said in an even, sure voice.

Dianne panted for breath as she gathered the still sleeping John. She pulled a stack of blankets from the wardrobe and followed after Mara. She paused at her bedroom door, wondering if she should try to salvage anything there. They would need clothes, she decided, and hurried to grab the larger of two carpetbags. She placed John on the bed and hurried to pull together clothes for both herself and Cole. She stuffed the hodge-podge into the bag, then spun around to see if there was anything else she might take.

Her cedar chest was full of a lifetime of mementos, but there was no time or energy to be wasted on such frippery. Instead, she closed the carpetbag and picked up John and the blankets. Then with her arms full, she strained to get both the empty and the full bag. It was difficult, but not impossible.

Dianne's arms ached as she struggled to the steps. *How much time do we have? How close is the fire?* she wondered. But the more pressing question was, *Where is Luke?*

She tore through the house, leaving the empty bag on the hall floor, and flew to the wagon. She handed over her things to Mara, then ordered the girl to climb up. "Take John and Micah and keep them in the back. We'll pack things around you. I need to make sure Koko has everything she needs."

Dianne left her sons to the care of her enemy's daughter and hurried back to the house. Just as she reached the porch, a crying Susannah came through the front door.

"Are we going to die?" she asked Dianne.

Dianne shook her head. "No. We have plenty of warning. But we do need to hurry. You go get in the wagon with my friend Mara. She's got the boys and she'll be happy for your company."

Susannah bit her lip and nodded. Dianne didn't wait to see if the girl obeyed or not. "Koko! Where are you?"

"I'm here," Koko said calmly. "I have my herbs. Did you get the papers — the deed for the ranch?"

"Oh, I completely forgot. They're in Cole's office. I'll get them now."

Dianne grabbed the empty bag and flew down the hall to Cole's office. She was relieved to find the door unlocked. Inside she gathered the ledgers he always kept and all of the papers that were in his top desk drawer. She tucked the papers inside the ledger, making sure the deed and courthouse registry were on top. She remembered that Cole kept money in a small wooden box on top of one of the bookshelves. Taking a chair, she quickly climbed up to have a look and figure out where the box was hidden. Spying it on a bookcase across the room, Dianne quickly climbed down and dragged the chair to the case. She took the box in hand, then jumped down.

Looking around, she wondered if anything else should be taken, but again thoughts of Luke overcame her concerns for the house.

"I have to find him," she said and tore from the room as if the blaze had reached its walls.

Outside she settled the papers and ledger into her carpetbag. George appeared, but there was no sign of Luke. He shook his head at her unasked question.

"Where is he?" she asked, unable to keep from sobbing. Tears poured down her cheeks. "Luke!" she screamed.

She ran past George to the barn and began to saddle Daisy. "Luke! Are you here?" She called him while she worked, feeling that at least she was doing something toward the goal of finding her boy.

"I've been all through the barns and corrals," George said. "I haven't seen anything of him. I also searched through the bunkhouse and old blacksmith cabin."

"He can't simply disappear," Dianne said, dread washing over her in waves that made her nauseous. "He's just a little boy. He's just . . ." Her words were choked in her throat. She fell against Daisy's side and cried.

George pulled her close and held her tight. Dianne found no comfort in his concern or his promises. "We'll find him. He'll be all right. He's probably just hiding around here. He probably thinks it's a great game."

"I can't . . . lose . . . him." Dianne struggled to speak. She coughed and realized the smoke was thickening. "He won't be able to see. He'll lose his way." She looked up at George. His expression was so tender. "I can't leave him. I can't go without him."

"You must. You must get the others to safety. You must care for your other boys. I'll remain to look for him, but you must go — for them — for the one you carry."

Dianne had momentarily forgotten about her unborn child. There was little she could do. The truth of it settled upon her like some great hulking animal ready to devour her. She would have to leave without Luke.

"Oh, George, don't make me do this. Don't make me leave him."

George put his finger under her chin and lifted her face to his. "You must be strong, Stands Tall Woman. You must be strong for him and for your other children."

"I can't do this. I don't have that kind of strength."

"But God does. God will give you the strength you need. Even in the darkest hours — even in death."

Dianne knew God was her only strength — there was nothing of herself that was of any use. She almost laughed at how ridiculous she was in her pride. Believing she could take on this territory and win. Now it threatened to take the life of her child — of all of them — and once again she was required to stand against the odds.

"You do not have to do this alone," George whispered. "Your husband is capable, and he will find your son. Your family is good; they love you and will be brave if you are brave. I am here for you — as I always have been — as I always will be. You aren't alone."

"Thank you," Dianne breathed as she pulled away from the man who had loved her almost as long as her husband had. "I'll finish saddling Daisy." She wiped at her

470

tears and hurried to finish adjusting the stirrup.

George left quickly, much to her relief. He had always remained honorable, but his love — his desire — was very evident. She sighed and looked back at the empty barn as she led Daisy from the stall. Would there be anything left after the fire swept through?

She looked up at the grand house her uncle had planned and built. Would anything remain?

She mounted Daisy, unable to even think of Luke. If she did, she knew she could never leave — never take her other children to safety — never protect her unborn baby. *This isn't fair, God,* she cried deep within her soul.

"I'm staying with Uncle," Jamie announced.

Koko looked down from the wagon, where she sat ready to take up the reins. "You can't stay."

"I'm old enough to help the men," Jamie declared. "I want to help look for Luke."

Dianne heard the exchange and thought to intercede, but before she could say a word, Koko gave in. "I'm proud of you for your concern and willingness to help." She looked beyond Jamie to where George stood in silence. "You will watch over him, won't you?"

"I will guard him with my life."

Koko drew a deep breath. "Very well." She grabbed the reins and looked to Dianne. "I'm ready."

Dianne knew Koko's heart was breaking from the choice she'd just made. Dianne's own heart was already shattered from the choice she had to see through. "Move out!" she called, riding to the front of the first wagon. "We're to go to Madison — to the church. Cole and the others will meet us there."

CHAPTER 28

Portia watched as the fire spread quickly in the dry undergrowth of the forest. The crackling sound and the thick sooty smoke excited her. It was her moment of triumph. The wind picked up and fanned the flames until they swirled in a wild flurry.

"Sometimes you just have to take matters into your own hands," she mused as she gazed across the valley from beyond the blaze. The winds were pushing the fire away from her, so there was nothing to fear.

Her entire life had been a series of actions taken because someone else refused to take responsibility or to see matters as they truly were. Though it was a nuisance, she'd accepted that this was her lot in life.

"Chester is so dimwitted. If he'd only once thought of how simple this truly was, he would have done it himself. Why bother to play at legal games for months when such a simple resolution was at hand?"

She looked at the sun and then at the fire. Smoke snaked out across the sky, already muting out the light. If she didn't hurry, the fire would block her way home and then she'd be forced to spend the night in the wilderness. She maneuvered her horse down the hill and around the edges of the river. The water level was quite low, indicative of the dry summer they'd endured. It all played perfectly into her plans. No one would suspect anything other than God's wrathful nature at hand. And those holier-than-thou Selbys wouldn't even see it as that. They'd still revere and esteem God as some good and wondrous Father in heaven.

"Wondrous Father — ha!" Portia declared. Her mount snorted nervously. "No father is good or wondrous."

But let the Selbys think what they would. Portia would know the truth, and as despair settled over them, she and Chester would be there to reap the benefits.

Ever mindful of the fire's location, Portia couldn't help but wonder how it would all play out. There was no guarantee that the fire would consume the Diamond V ranch; however, from her viewpoint earlier, it appeared to be likely if the wind would just hold and keep the fire moving in the right direction. She liked to imagine Dianne

Selby in tears, searching through the ashes for some memento of her previous life. It stirred something inside her to think of them all questioning God and wondering why such a thing could happen to them.

"But they probably won't question God," she muttered. "Not the almighty Selbys."

The horse whinnied softly, and Portia realized all at once that she wasn't alone. Jerrod and Roy sat atop their horses not five yards ahead. It was just her luck she'd paid no attention to the road.

"What are you doing here?"

"Watchin' you set fires," Roy said snidely.

Portia refused to be concerned. "I'm helping your father accomplish what he wants. Nothing more."

Jerrod pushed back his hat. "You're prob'ly planning his murder right now — along with the murder of everyone else who can't escape this fire."

"You two are out of your minds. I suppose I'll have to talk to your father about this."

"Lady, when we get finished with you, you ain't gonna be talkin' to nobody."

"Have you forgotten how poorly you fared after the last time you crossed my path?" Portia questioned with some amusement. "I thought the baby was a particularly nice touch. Didn't you?"

"I never did think there was no baby," Jerrod replied angrily. "You lied to our father about that and everything else."

Portia casually crossed her right hand over her left and set both on the horn. She wasn't about to be bullied by these two. "Boys, I think it's time you came to understand something. I've put three husbands in the ground. I'd have very little regret in seeing you two buried."

"And it wouldn't bother us none seeing *you* dead and gone," Jerrod returned. "I don't see that you're carryin' no weapon."

Portia felt a moment of distress for having left her revolver at home. *If only I hadn't been in such a hurry, I might have remembered.* She wasn't about to let Jerrod and Roy see her fear in this realization, however. So she shrugged.

"Do you honestly think I'd travel all this way unprotected? Does that really seem like the kind of thing I'd do?"

She hoped the bluff would give them at least pause to consider their next move. Portia was already eyeing the terrain around her and realized that her best hope would be to climb the side of the mountain, about forty yards to her right. If she hurried, she could be up and over the top before their

476

heavier mounts could make even a quarter of the climb.

"I don't see any way out for you . . . this time," Jerrod said, moving his horse forward a pace and then another.

It was all Portia needed. She dug her heels into her gelding's side and yanked the reins hard to the right. Laying low against the horse's neck, Portia urged the animal up the very primitive path. She could hear Jerrod and Roy yelling behind her. It only served to excite her as she whipped the reins from one side of the horse's neck to the other.

The horse faltered, slipping on the rocky path. Portia kept the horse's head up, saving them more than once from a bad fall. She knew they were going to make it. They were heading very close to the fire, but Portia felt confident of her mount. The gelding had never failed her.

Then without warning the wind shifted, blowing the fire back toward her. They were nearly to the top, and just as Portia had figured, Jerrod and Roy were far below. She slowed the horse's pace a bit, but as smoke and heat rolled over the ridge and the horse caught scent of the danger, Portia had to fight to keep control of the beast.

"Whoa," she called. "Take it slow, boy."

But the gelding would have no part of her comfort. He reared once, then took off, heading back down the side of the mountain. Portia wasn't ready for this antic. She pitched forward and the horse lost his footing.

Portia knew she was falling, but even so she figured she'd be okay. It wasn't until she realized the horse was falling as well that Portia knew the situation was much worse than she'd figured it to be.

"What if we can't find him, Uncle?" Jamie asked as they searched for Luke Selby.

"We will find him. We have to find him," George replied. The last thing he could imagine was facing Dianne without Luke safely in tow. He would rather die than go back to her without the boy.

"But maybe we won't. You said that sometimes God allows difficult things to come into our lives. Like this fire. You said this fire was not necessarily a bad thing."

George ran a hand through his cropped black hair. "The fire will cleanse the land and new growth will come. Sometimes these things are necessary."

"But I heard Uncle Cole say they will dig out fire breaks around the house and barns. I heard him say that unless we can stop the fire's progress, it will burn down everything."

George continued pushing forward in the smoky air. "That's true."

"How can that be God's will for us? Does God not care that my father built this house? That this place is all I have of him?"

George stopped, hearing the sorrow in his nephew's voice. "Jamie, the house is not the only legacy your father left you. He left a huge part of himself here," he said, touching Jamie's chest. "You have learned his ways. Your mother and cousin have shown you examples of your father every day. They have shown you his heart and desires — they've taught you his beliefs."

"My father believed God was good — that He cared about each of us."

"Yes, I can vouch for that. Bram was a good man. When my own father died, he was very good to me. He cared about my feelings and tried to comfort me. He loved your mother, my sister."

"Would he believe God still cared about us even now, with the fire?"

George looked to his nephew. The boy's dark hair and eyes could have been a gift from either parent, but the expression on his face was purely that of his father. "I know in my heart," George said, putting his arm around the boy's shoulders, "that your father would have trusted God's love even now."

"All right then," Jamie said. "If he would trust God, then I must too."

George nodded. "It's the only way."

Portia felt her bones break as the horse crushed down upon her. She was amazed she was still alive after such a horrible fall, and had she not been in desperate pain from the horse's bulk lying partially atop her, she might have thought herself dead.

"She's still alive," Roy said as he and Jerrod made their way to where she lay.

"Well, just look at you," Jerrod said, coming to stand directly in front of Portia's twisted frame.

"Get this animal off of me," Portia demanded, her voice raspy.

"I don't think I can do that," Jerrod said, squatting down. "You see, I figure this is all a part of God's scheme. This way, I don't have to kill you. God killed you for me."

Portia pushed at the horse and felt a sharp, piercing pain rip through her upper body. She had no idea what type of injuries she'd sustained along with her broken bones, but she wasn't about to give up and let Roy and Jerrod leave her for dead.

"They'll blame you, you know," Portia said as she ceased her struggles. "I have a letter to be given to your father should anything happen to me. I spell it out very nicely, letting them all know that you and Roy have been plotting to kill me for some time."

Roy looked shaken. "She's lyin', right?"

"Don't much matter," Jerrod said softly. "She has no purpose to be down here." He glanced up at the fire creeping down the mountainside. "The fire will take her. It'll be easy enough to see that she fell and was trapped by the horse. You and me'll be back on the ranch with those witnesses we paid."

"You can't leave me here," Portia pleaded, feeling truly afraid for the first time. She'd never before found herself so completely trapped. If not for the horse, she would crawl out of here no matter the pain.

Jerrod got to his feet. "Come on, Roy. Fire's headin' this way, and we'd best clear out before our horses make a run for it."

Portia screamed after them — at least she tried to scream. Her lungs hurt from the pressure of the animal, and very little air seemed to come into her — no matter how hard she tried to draw it.

She heard the boys' horses gallop away and felt the dread of surrender wash over her. She'd once dreamed that R. E. Langford was leading her to the gallows. She remembered specifically the churning in her stomach and the hopelessness that left her breathless, almost dizzy. She felt that way now . . . that horrible feeling that the truth of what was about to happen could not be stopped.

Looking up the mountain, she saw the fire pushing ever closer. The smoke burned her eyes and throat. She could feel the heat against her face.

"Your wicked ways will catch up to you one day," she heard her father say.

The voice seemed so real, so clear, that for a moment Portia thought her father's ghost had come back to haunt her — or to gloat upon her condition.

"It's never too late to turn to the Lord," Dianne Selby had once told her. "He will always hear you and forgive you."

Portia laughed. It wracked her body with blinding pain. "God doesn't exist," she muttered, her sight failing her and blackness threatening to steal away her conscious thought. "God is dead, and so am I."

"Do you think they'll ever find her body?" Roy asked Jerrod as they neared the Walking Horseshoe Ranch.

"I don't imagine — at least not for a while. Even if they did find her right away — say the fire shifts and she don't burn to a crisp, it'll be evident that the horse fell. No one can blame us for this one."

"What about the Farleys?"

Jerrod laughed. "Selby already tried to spread that story. No, we're Lawrences. No one is gonna better us — no one is gonna arrest us."

"Pa was pretty mad at us when Portia told him we'd beat her. He might just stop protecting us and turn us in."

"Naw, he won't do that. He might've been mad, but he'll get over it. Especially since she won't be coming back to cause us problems."

Roy laughed. "Just like Trenton Chadwick and Sam Brady, eh?"

"Just like them and all the rest."

"It's not the killin' that bothers me," Roy said as they approached their barn. "It's the idea of being blamed for something I didn't do. I don't want to be accused of killing that witch."

"Don't worry. No one, not even Pa, is gonna care about what happened to her — not when he learns that the Selby ranch has burned to the ground."

CHAPTER 29

To Dianne, the five-mile drive to Madison had never seemed so long. She continued to look back over her shoulder, hoping against hope that she'd find Luke running after her. But always there was nothing but the billowing smoke against the hazy horizon.

Pulling up in front of Ben and Charity's small house, Dianne brought her horse to a stop. "Whoa," she called, pulling back on the reins. She turned to Mara. "We'll take refuge here. If nothing else, we can stay at the church."

"Will they mind that I'm with you?" the girl asked.

Dianne shook her head. "No. They'll be glad you've come."

"But they know what my father and Portia have done to you and what they've done to others in the valley."

"Yes, but they won't blame you for the sins of your father. That isn't right in the eyes of the Lord."

"You really believe there is a God who cares about us?" Mara asked.

"I know there is," Dianne said. But in her heart she was filled with questions. If God really cared, why was Luke lost somewhere back at the ranch? She jumped down from the horse as the front door of the house opened.

"We saw the smoke," Charity said as she and Ben came out of their cabin. "Was it your place?"

"It was the forests to the south of our place. Very close to us," Dianne answered. She reached up to take John from Mara and handed him to Charity. "The pines are going up like dried kindling."

Mara stepped down and reached back up for Micah.

"Miz Charity," Micah said in his boyish innocence. "Luke is in the fire." He sounded impressed with his brother's involvement with the blaze.

"What's this?" Charity asked, looking to Dianne.

"Surely Cole isn't having the boy help fight the fire?" Ben questioned.

Dianne's eyes filled with tears. "No. Luke isn't helping."

Koko and Ardith and their children came

up from the other wagon and took Micah and John in hand. "Come on, boys," Koko said. "We'll go look at Mrs. Hammond's pretty flowers." She led the children away from the wagons and up to the house.

"We cannot find Luke," Dianne said as soon as Micah was out of earshot.

"What happened?"

"I sent him to get Cole when Mara showed up. I sent him to the corral, but apparently Luke misunderstood or became fascinated with the fire. I just don't know. All I do know is that when we went to look for him, he was gone. Cole stayed behind to search for him. So did Koko's brother and Jamie."

"Oh, dear," Charity said, putting her arm around Dianne. "Then we must pray."

Ben bowed his head. "Heavenly Father, you know where the boy is and we're asking that you would allow him to be found safe and unharmed. We ask, too, that you would give Dianne and her family peace of mind as we wait for Luke's safe return, along with the return of the others. In Jesus' name, amen."

"Thank you," Dianne said, feeling some reassurance from the prayer.

"Do you truly believe God heard that? Do you honestly believe He cares?" Mara asked, desperation in her voice.

"As I said earlier, I believe there is a God who cares," Dianne told her. "I believe He hears our prayers and loves us."

"But how can you believe that? So much has gone wrong in your life. My father's actions alone have been so awful."

"Yes, but God has kept us safe from your father."

"Then what about the fire?" Mara asked. "The lightning no doubt set the blaze, but if God cares so much, He could have stopped that."

"Yes, He could have," Charity responded, "but sometimes He allows trials to come into our lives. We are on this earth to learn and grow. We are like gold in the fire, being purified for the perfect use God has for us."

"My father told me that's what people always say when they can't explain or figure out the painful things in their life. He said people who are weak need something like God to hide behind when things get bad."

"I don't hide behind God," Charity replied. "I hide *in* Him. There's a big difference."

Mara's puzzled expression preceded her question. "How is there a difference?"

"Hiding behind God implies that we are somehow trying to use Him to our advantage. That we aren't with Him, but merely using Him. It doesn't show a relationship with God. He wants us to know Him so intimately that we can hide *in* Him — trust *in* Him."

Dianne wondered if Charity's words were given as much for her as for Mara.

"Are you familiar with the Psalms?" Charity asked the girl.

"Something in the Bible, right?"

"They are a collection of Scriptures — a book in the Bible," Charity replied. "The psalmist speaks of trusting in God. Psalm eighteen says, 'I will love thee, O Lord, my strength. The Lord is my rock, and my fortress, and my deliverer; my God, my strength, in whom I will trust; my buckler, and the horn of my salvation, and my high tower.' See all the various ways the psalmist sees the Lord?" Mara nodded, and Charity smiled at Dianne.

"He continues and says, 'I will call upon the Lord, who is worthy to be praised: so shall I be saved from mine enemies. The sorrows of death compassed me, and the floods of ungodly men made me afraid. The sorrows of hell compassed me about: the snares of death prevented me. In my distress I called upon the Lord, and cried unto my God: he heard my voice out of his temple, and my cry came before him, even into his ears.' You see, He hears us, Mara. He truly hears us."

"But what if Luke is never found? Can you trust in Him then?" she asked, turning to Dianne. "Will you still believe He hears you even if Luke is lost forever?"

Dianne met Charity's eyes. She knew the unspoken question reflected there mirrored Mara's spoken heart. *Will I still trust God even if Luke perishes in the fire?*

"I won't lie to you and say that it wouldn't devastate me to lose my son. I can't even think of what life would be like without him. But . . ." She let the word trail as she swallowed. The truth of what she was about to say pierced her heart. "Even if Luke dies, I will still trust God."

Charity's compassionate expression filled Dianne with peace, as did the assurance that there was no doubting in what she had just said.

Ben interceded. "God gave up His Son, Jesus, to die for our sins. He gave Jesus so that we might be reconciled to Him, as our heavenly Father. It was no doubt a difficult choice to make, but He did so for you, Mara, and for all of us. Jesus went willingly to the cross because He looked beyond that moment and that pain, seeing what was ahead."

"And what was it He saw?" Mara asked.

"Eternity — our eternity with Him. Our reconciliation to our Father in heaven."

"But why should God care about me?" Mara's voice was tinged with sadness. "I'm not a good person. My father is an evil person. How could God love me?"

Ben put his arm around Mara's shoulder. "How is it that you came to help Dianne today?"

"I rode to her house to warn her about something bad that was going to happen to another rancher. Then the fire came and . . . well . . . she told me to go on home, but I couldn't. I wanted to help her — to see that the babies were safe from the fire."

"Why?"

"Because they needed help."

"And if you, the daughter of an evil man, would show such a kindness, why do you imagine God would show any less concern for His children?"

Mara shook her head. "It's just so much to believe. I wasn't even raised to believe that there was a God."

"So what would it take to make you believe?"

Mara looked to Dianne. "I would believe if Luke came back safe to us. If Luke comes back unharmed, then I will believe there is a God and that He hears people's prayers."

"You can't put God to a test like that," Dianne said sadly. She wanted more than anything for the Lord to prove himself faithful to Mara — faithful in a way that would bring back her son, safe and alive. But she couldn't deceive the girl. "You can't say you will only trust Him if He first does something miraculous for you. After all, He sent His Son, Jesus, to die for your sins. That was miracle enough."

"I don't care," Mara said, standing her ground. "I will believe if Luke comes back. If he comes back, then I'll know that what you are saying is true and I'll believe God is faithful."

Dianne looked to Charity and Ben with tears running down her cheeks. "And I will believe He is faithful even if Luke doesn't come back safely."

Mara shook her head. "But why? Why trust Him if He isn't going to do what you ask Him to do?"

"God is not a puppet or a child who seeks direction from me," Dianne said softly. "So much has happened in my life, Mara. So many people have perished; others have been born. I've lost good friends and found new ones. I cannot base God's faithfulness on whether I get my own way, but rather I base it on whether He is true to His words in the Bible. I base it on my knowing Him better and better each day." She reached out and took hold of the girl's hands. "God is good, Mara. Even when bad times come — He's still good."

"I'll still wait to see what happens with Luke," the girl said, looking from Dianne to Charity and then Ben. "If He can save Luke, then He can save me."

"Have you seen Portia?" Chester asked as Jerrod and Roy finished mucking out the stalls in the barn.

"Sure," Jerrod said. "Saw her ride out this mornin'. Her horse is still gone."

"It's not like her to be gone so long and not tell me where she's going," Chester said, rubbing his jaw.

"Maybe she had someone to meet up with. Kinda like you two used to meet," Roy said suggestively.

"Shut your mouth. I don't want you talking about her that way."

Jerrod elbowed Roy. "I thought we agreed we'd be nice."

"I guess so."

"What about your sister?" Chester asked. "I haven't seen Mara all day."

"I don't know about her. I ain't seen her

at all," Jerrod declared.

"Well, I looked in the corral and her horse is gone. She must have ridden out. I hope she didn't go all the way into Madison. That girl has been troubled since your mother died. I don't want her going all soft on me and seeking out religion."

"Boss!" cried one of the workers as he came running into the barn. "There's a big fire to the south. I was down at Madison fetchin' that feed like you told me. It's moving pretty fast. Looks like it might burn down the town and head this way."

Chester acted as though he didn't believe the man. He rushed outside and raised a hand to his forehead. The air was hazy, and billowing clouds that rose up from the ground proved the man's words.

"If the wind doesn't shift, it'll blow that fire all the way up here," Chester said, shaking his head. "Cursed lightning."

Jerrod and Roy exchanged a look. Jerrod knew his father would never want to hear the truth of the matter. "What should we do, Pa?"

Chester shook his head. "I don't know. I guess I'd better ride down Madison way and see what's going on."

"You want us to go with you?" Roy and Jerrod asked in unison.

"No, you'd best stay here. Start getting things loaded in the wagon, just in case. Get Joshua's nose out of whatever book he's reading and get him to help."

"What should we load?" Jerrod asked.

Chester shrugged. "I don't know. Get your grandparents' wedding picture and the papers from my safe — and your mother's jewelry. Get Elsa to pack some clothes up, and I suppose she should ready some food and water. Pack whatever you think could be valuable and important to us. The biggest concern will of course be the animals. We have the biggest part of our herd up north a ways. If the fire heads this direction, we'll make for the herd and drive them ahead of us."

"What about Mara . . . and . . . Portia?" Jerrod asked, knowing full well Portia no longer mattered.

Chester shook his head. "I don't know. Maybe I'll run across them in town." He made for the barn after that and Roy and Jerrod exchanged a guarded look.

"Where do you suppose Joshua is?" Roy asked.

Jerrod looked to the man who'd warned them about the fire. "Hitch the wagons and drive them up to the house."

"Yes, sir." The man jumped the fence to

the corral and took up a rope.

"Let's go find Joshua," Jerrod said, starting for the house.

"Lotta good he'll be," Roy grumbled.

They headed into the house and bellowed for anyone who would take notice. "Elsa! Joshua! Where is everybody?"

"What's all the hollering about?" Elsa asked as she came to the top of the stairs.

"There's a fire to the south — may come this way. Pa said to pack clothes for all of us and get some food put together. Cook can help."

Elsa's eyes widened. "A fire? Is it close?"

"Well, it's close enough to get to work," Jerrod said, unsympathetic to her fear.

"I don't know what to pack."

"Just get some clothes together for everybody. Nobody has seen Mara, so you'd best pack for her too."

"What about Portia? She's not been around all day. Should I pack clothes for her?"

"I wouldn't worry about her," Jerrod said. "I doubt she'll be needing much of anything." Elsa frowned but said nothing.

About that time Joshua came meandering in from the study. "What's all the yelling about?"

"There's a fire coming this way," Elsa said

before her brothers could answer.

"Pa said for you to help us load the wagons with anything we need to take. We're s'pose to get all his papers from the safe, along with Mother's jewelry."

"Fire? Here?" Joshua asked, going to the front window.

"No, south of here. Now put up your book," Jerrod said, pointing at the one in Joshua's hand, "and give us some help."

"Where are the others? Where are Pa and Portia? Where's Mara?"

Jerrod shrugged. "Pa's ridden to town to see how close the fire actually is to coming this direction. As for the others, I got no idea. Don't much care either. If they aren't smart enough to get themselves out of harm's way, they deserve whatever happens to them."

"How can you say that?" Joshua questioned, taking a step toward Jerrod. "Mara's our sister, and while I don't like Portia, she is married to our father."

"Mara's no fool. She'll find a way to safety. Portia's on her own. She's dealt this family dirty since marrying Pa. I don't much care what happens to her," Jerrod said matter-of-factly. "Now, go gather up Grandpa Lawrence's wedding picture while we get the papers in the office. If you see anything else that Pa would want, grab it too. You'd know better what that might be than me. I only listen to the old man when I have to. I sure never heard him talk about any affection he held for doodads."

Joshua looked as though he might say something more, then let out a loud breath and left to do as he was told.

"You too. Get to it!" Jerrod bellowed at Elsa. The girl jumped and then ran down the hall.

Jerrod smacked Roy with the back of his hand. "Come on. We'd best get to this. Next thing you know, Portia will have burned us down along with the Selbys."

Joshua stood in the doorway, watching his brothers cross the front room to their father's study. He'd wanted to ask them about their mother's china, but because they were talking, he'd remained silent.

So Portia had set the fire? He couldn't imagine anyone being so careless. Why would she do something so heinous when the summer had been so dry and the threat of fire so much of a concern?

He wanted to ask Jerrod and Roy but knew better than to do so. His older brothers had neither time nor patience for him. If they'd wanted him to know the truth about

Portia's deeds, they would have told him. For some reason, they were keeping this matter to themselves, and for the time being, Joshua thought it best to play ignorant.

Ardith sat quietly on one side of the church. So many people had come to gather for protection here that the place was filling up quickly. Winona sat sleeping, at last, on her lap, her head tucked against Ardith's shoulder. The fire had terrified Winona, and while Ardith had tried to comfort her daughter, she realized her own worries over Levi were threatening to bring her to tears.

If ever she had doubted her love for that man, she could no longer do so. She'd been unable to think of anything else since they'd abandoned the ranch. Ardith knew he was out there somewhere, driving the cattle and horses to safety, but it did little to offer her comfort. It might be days or even weeks, she'd heard someone say, before the fires would be put out and they'd know the extent of the damage.

Ardith saw Dianne helping Charity create some spaces for the families who'd gathered. They'd taken the pews and rearranged them to quarter off sections for those who wanted to create pallets and seek rest. In Charity's house, Ardith knew that Koko and Faith were working to feed the growing numbers. Ardith thought she should go and help, but she felt so weary — so hopeless.

I can't lose hope, she told herself over and over. *I lost hope once, and God restored it.* She thought back to the miscarriage and how tenderly God had nurtured her spirit and body. Surely He wouldn't bring her this far only to desert her now.

Charity approached her, as she always seemed to do when Ardith was at her lowest point. "You look tired. Why don't you go on over to our house and have a rest on our bed?"

"I can't stop wondering about Levi. Aren't you worried?"

"Terrified," she said as she slipped into the pew beside Ardith. "I want him here with us, but I know he has to do his job."

"I know that too. It's just that we need him so much."

"No one knows your needs better than God."

"I realize that. I'm trying to be faithful."

Charity hugged her close. "Oh, child, just remember He is faithful even when we are not. He knows how hard this is for you. He loves you . . . despite your worries, your doubts."

Ardith met the woman's confident gaze.

In so many ways, Charity had become like a mother to her. She opened her mouth to ask how she might help when Ben approached. His expression was grave.

"The fire is heading this way. It looks like it might very well burn Madison to the ground."

CHAPTER 30

"This is a losing battle," Cole announced to George and Jamie. "I can't keep fighting for the ranch and look for Luke at the same time."

"The ranch is a goner," George said stoically. He put his arm around Jamie's shoulders. "That fire is heading here too quickly. The south pasture is already burning."

"I have to find my son," Cole said, the desperation in his soul spilling into his tone of voice. "I can't believe we haven't seen some sign of him."

"We've searched everywhere. Jamie went through the house and looked in all the hiding places they used to play in." George shook his head. "He doesn't seem to be anywhere."

"I've gone over and over what Dianne said. She told him to go down to the corral and get me, but he never came. Or if he did, I was already gone to inspect the fire."

"What route did you take? Is it possible he saw you leave and came after you?"

George's words hit hard. "I suppose it's possible," Cole admitted. "But he would have been on foot. We took his pony out with the remaining horses nearly an hour ago."

"It's worth a look to see," George suggested. "Rethink your path. Which way did you go?"

"I headed to the river. I knew it would be the easiest way to survey the fire. The water is low and the horse had no trouble picking his way along the shore."

"Then let's go." George motioned Jamie to mount up.

"All right. It's worth a try."

"Cole!" Gus called from the bunkhouse as they passed by.

Cole walked the horse to where Gus stood. "Why are you still here? You need to get out. Get whoever else is here and leave immediately. We'll meet up in Madison at the church."

"I was just going to tell you that we were heading out," Gus said, his bandanna drawn up around his face. "You'd better wear those kerchiefs. That smoke ain't healthy to breathe."

Cole knew Gus was right and pulled up his neckerchief to ward off as much smoke as possible. George and Jamie did likewise. "We're heading to the river to retrace my steps. It's possible that Luke followed me down there and just couldn't keep up."

"Are you sure the line of fire won't cut off your route back?" Gus questioned.

"If it does, we'll make our own way. We'll head north and come into town that way. If you see Dianne, don't tell her we talked. She'll only fret if she thinks we haven't found Luke. I need to be the one to tell her if it all goes wrong."

Gus nodded. Cole could only see his eyes, but they were filled with compassion — maybe even a tear or two.

"We're wasting time," Cole said, mounting and urging his horse back to the trail. "I'll meet you in Madison, Gus. Don't try anything heroic."

"I might say the same for you," Gus called after him, "but I know I'd be wastin' my time."

The heat was unbearable as they drew nearer the fire's edge. The flames were licking up the sides of green pine and fir, shooting some seventy feet into the air. The smoke was so thick now that it was nearly impossible to see more than a few feet ahead of the horses.

Coughing, Cole tried not to think of Luke being choked to death on the smoke. He tried not to think of Dianne sitting in Madison with John and Micah, worried and full of sorrow over the loss of her eldest child.

Oh, God, Cole prayed, *comfort her. Comfort her and give her peace. Give her hope. Let her know that you haven't forgotten her . . . or Luke. Help me to find my boy, Father. You spoke of leaving the ninety-nine to find the one. This is no different. I love that one, the same as I love the others. I would give my life for him, and if that's the price, then I accept it gladly. Just save him. Please, save him.*

Joshua Lawrence had no idea why Portia would set a fire during the driest season of the year. And he had no idea why Jerrod and Roy would know about it. They seemed, however, to be quite at peace with what had taken place.

Sometimes Joshua felt like he didn't know his own family. They were all such a mystery, with exception to Mara. She was only a year his junior and sweet-tempered. His seventeen years had not been easy in a family of cutthroats who would just as soon sell each other out if it meant making a profit. But Mara had made it bearable. She often shared his feelings and concerns that their family had more than the average amount of troubles.

He couldn't understand his family. The more he read about ideals — about cultures and their religions, about philosophy and what people perceived as truth — the more Joshua was inclined to believe that his family was either insane or the most ignorant bunch of ninnies this side of the Mississippi.

As he secured the bags that Elsa had packed, Joshua couldn't help but worry about Mara. It wasn't like her to run off. She usually would let him know what she was thinking — doing. She'd even confided in him that she'd taken the paper her father had stolen from the courthouse in Virginia City. She explained that she'd given it back to the Selbys because she couldn't stand to see her father cheat even one more person out of his rightful share.

He had told her she'd done the right thing. And she had. He would believe that as long as he lived, and he would go to the grave keeping her secret.

"Joshua! Come get these bags. They're too heavy. Stop wasting time!" Elsa bellowed like their father.

He left what he was doing and hurried to the porch. "You could have just waited. I would have come to get them."

Elsa dropped the bags and put her hands on her hips. "You would have stood there daydreaming if I hadn't hollered at you. Mother always said you were the dreamer in the family. Well, there's no time for that when the entire countryside is burning down around us. We could all be dead in a matter of hours."

"And if you died — if we all died — don't you wonder what would happen then?" Joshua asked as he picked up the bags.

Elsa frowned. "What a stupid question. When you die, you're dead. That's it."

"Is it?" He'd read enough to convince himself that there was an afterlife. He just wasn't exactly sure which religious belief was the right one. All ways seemed to point to God, or in some cases, gods. He liked the idea of eternal life but didn't know if he preferred ideas that suggested eternity in a heaven where he would spend time worshiping God with the angels or if the idea of reincarnation — coming back to life as something or someone completely different — was more appealing. Surely the idea of starting over and making right one's mistakes during another life had its appealing side.

"I don't know what's wrong with you.

We're in the middle of a fire," Elsa complained. "Papa's not back, and we don't know where Mara is. And you want to talk about what happens after a person dies?"

"Well, like you said, it's possible we'll all be dead soon." Elsa shook her head as if not wanting to hear anymore. Joshua took pity on her. "I just wondered what you thought. That was all."

He picked up the bags and turned to go, but Elsa called after him. "Josh, wait." He stopped and looked over his shoulder to see her run down the porch steps to come even with him. "What do you know about what happens after a person dies?"

Joshua shook his head. "I really don't know. There are lots of beliefs out there."

"What about the ones they talk about in the church at Madison? You know that stuff about Jesus dying for our sins so that we can have eternal life?"

Joshua smiled. "So you were listening, eh?"

Elsa looked close to tears. "I know Papa only wanted to go so he could hear the latest gossip. He doesn't even believe in God, but ever since Mother died, I can't help but wonder about those things. She believed there was a God. I know, because she told me she was taught to pray and believe in

God when she was a little girl."

Joshua had never heard these stories. The girls were the ones who heard most of the tales from their mother. From the time he'd been old enough to sit on a horse, his father had tried to make a rancher out of him. But ranching just wasn't in his blood.

"Mother was no fool. She might have been intimidated by our father and his opinions, but she wasn't stupid. If she believed in God — the Christian God — then I would say it merits some attention."

Elsa nodded, her fear evident in every move, every expression. Joshua put the bags down again and opened his arms to Elsa. It was the first time since she'd been a little girl that he'd even offered such a thing. She quickly embraced him, burying her face against his chest.

"I'm scared, Josh. I'm scared through and through. Please tell me it's going to be all right. Please tell me I'm not going to die before I even get my first kiss — my first beau."

Joshua smiled. "I'll take care of you, Elsa. Don't worry. We'll get through this just fine."

"Promise?"

He felt a confidence that he couldn't explain. Was it because of Elsa's words about their mother's beliefs? Was this the sign he needed to know which direction to go? "I promise," he said softly. "I promise we'll make it through this, and I promise to figure out about what happens after we die. And when I do, you'll be one of the first to know. Deal?"

Elsa lifted her head to reveal her tear-filled eyes. "Deal."

Levi was smoke blind. There was no chance of figuring out which direction he needed to go. He'd come after strays, thinking there was enough time to get ahead of the fire, but the winds were blowing too hard.

Coughing and unable to get a decent breath, he knew there was little hope of making it out alive. His horse stumbled, wheezing and snorting in the poisonous air. He should have stayed with the others. He shouldn't have tried to be heroic.

He fell forward against the horse's neck. The smoke was going to kill him, as sure as anything. He gagged and wheezed, then fell from the back of his mount, hitting hard on the ground below.

Levi tried to get back up, but he couldn't find the strength. His lungs were filled with the hot noxious gases.

Ardith, I love you. I never knew what love

was until I met you. I wish I could tell you that just one more time. I wish . . . I wish . . . I . . . could . . . see you . . . and Winona. I wish . . . our baby would . . . have lived.

He fell flat on his back, fighting to keep from losing consciousness, but it was hopeless. *Oh, God,* he prayed in his final moments, *forgive me my sins and take me to your bosom.*

"Have you seen anything?" Ardith asked Dianne as she joined her outside.

Dianne had been faithfully watching the horizon for the past hour. "No. I know they'll be here. I feel confident of that."

Ardith shook her head. "I think it's bad, Dianne. I think we have to accept that something very bad can happen in this."

Dianne turned to meet her sister's worried expression. "I don't care about the house or anything else. I just want Luke found and the rest to return safely with him. Nothing else is as important as our loved ones."

Ardith said nothing for several moments, then asked, "Where will the men drive the cattle? Can we go there after Cole and Luke come back?"

"I don't know where they've gone. They'll go wherever they can to escape the blaze.

510

We'll have to ask Cole where he instructed them to go."

Dianne put her arm around Ardith. "I'm sure Levi is fine. He's a good rancher, and he knows his way around the valley. He's been here, after all, longer than I have — barely." She smiled. "He used to like to tease me about that. Said it gave him the right to boss me around."

Ardith smiled. "He loved you very much back then."

Dianne felt her cheeks grow hot. "You know about that?"

"He told me. He didn't want there to be any secrets between us. He said he thought he was in love with you as a man should be in order to marry. But after you and Cole were wed, he came to realize it was your strength and fortitude that he loved. He always felt like he had to prove himself — to show that he had strength and was of good character. It was hard for him, but with God's help, he overcame that. I'm proud of him for that."

"I am too," Dianne said, hugging her sister. "I'm proud of you, too, for not being jealous of what never really existed. I always worried that you'd hear about the way he felt and be uncomfortable or worried that I'd do something to come between the two

511

of you."

"No, I know he loves me," Ardith said softly. She turned as Dianne released her. "But what of Koko's brother?"

"Takes Many . . . I mean George?" Dianne questioned. She grew uncomfortable. Ardith would no doubt find it difficult to understand the relationship she and George shared.

"Yes. What of him? He loves you. I think even Cole realizes that."

Dianne looked away. "Yes, Cole knows that. But he also trusts George. You see, when George could have seen to Cole's demise, he chose instead to risk his life to bring Cole back to me. Cole told me he knew from that moment on that there would never be a man whom he could trust with me as much as he could Takes Many Horses."

"It must be hard on George to watch you from afar and know that you are in love with someone else. I know it was hard on Levi, until he found me."

"It is hard to love someone and feel their love is unreturned. I went through times like that with Cole. Ours was such a strange courtship — not truly a courtship at all. I cared for him and he cared for me, but our lives were so entangled with other problems

— with other people. Then he finally declared his love and asked for my hand, and I thought I'd never be happier."

"But something happened?"

"Yes. He felt obligated to go back to Kansas and make amends with his father and mother. It was partially my fault. I knew he could never be the man I needed him to be until he let go of his bitterness and hatred toward his parents. He went to make amends and stayed to help them establish their farm. On his way back to me, his wagon train was attacked and he was taken hostage. Then when he was finally returned to me, we married. We hardly knew each other, but in some ways, I felt I'd known him all of my life."

"You were friends before you courted. Mama always said that was for the best."

"I remember that," she said as the memory came rushing back. She could see her mother kneading bread and instructing them on courtship and other things to come.

Dianne closed her eyes and quoted, " 'A man and woman are better off friends for a good long time before they take marriage interests in each other. That way they have something to build their marriage on other than physical attraction and romantic notions.' "

"Yes," Ardith agreed. "That was it exactly."

"Cole and I have had our rough times. I'm not very good at letting him lead — at trusting him to know the right thing for the ranch. But now, in the middle of all of this, I suddenly realize it really doesn't matter what he knows or doesn't know. He'll make his mistakes and learn from them — or he won't. But he loves me. He loves our children."

"And that's all that really matters," Ardith said softly.

Dianne caught sight of movement in the smoky landscape to the west. She strained her eyes to see if it was yet another neighboring rancher and his family or if Cole and the others were finally coming to safety.

She took several steps forward, then a few more. It was George and Jamie! She ran down the road, hoping and praying. Surely they hadn't come alone! As she neared, the smoke cleared enough to reveal Gus and several of the ranch hands. They all looked filthy and worn out — all wearing matching expressions of discouragement.

She stopped in the middle of the road. The riders parted enough to reveal Cole as he rode toward her. In front of him sat Luke — safe — alive. Barky, Luke's dog, ran beside them.

She burst into tears and ran the rest of the way. She gave no thought to George or Jamie. She didn't even bother to acknowledge Gus or the boys. Instead, she had eyes only for her son and husband.

Cole slid from the horse as she approached. He pulled her into his arms and she fell against him as if all of her strength were suddenly drained.

"Oh, you're safe! You're safe and you found him!"

"Are you all right?" he murmured against her ear.

Dianne nodded and sobbed in a great release of emotion. God had heard her prayers and had been faithful. Now maybe Mara would believe. But whether she did or not, Dianne knew that something was forever changed in her heart that day. She could let Cole lead — she could trust him with the ranch, with the animals, with her uncle's legacy. But she could especially trust him with her heart — because he'd just given it back to her safe and unharmed.

CHAPTER 31

"We found him sitting in the river," Cole said as they gathered in Ben and Charity's house.

"In the river?" Dianne questioned.

"You said if there was a fire to go to the river," Luke stated. Beside him, Barky sat faithfully, head on Luke's lap, big brown eyes gazing upward. Cole had told Dianne how the dog had been right beside Luke the entire time.

"He told me he saw me head out toward the river and followed. He could see the fire in the distant trees and figured we were all heading to the river. He and Barky got there and couldn't find me."

"But I knew Papa would come back," Luke declared.

Mara stood to one side, and Dianne looked up to catch her gaze. The girl had been very quiet ever since Luke had been returned to them.

"Apparently he sat there the entire time," George stated. "Sat there and waited."

"Good boy. You did good," Dianne said, hugging her son close for the tenth time. His damp clothes brought to mind the need to change him. "Let's go see what clothes I brought. You're soaked clear through and need something dry."

"I'm hungry. Can we eat?" Luke questioned. He seemed no more upset by the day's events than if he'd witnessed Barky chasing a rabbit.

"I'll get him a bowl of stew," Charity said. "You go ahead and take him to our bedroom."

Dianne lifted Luke in her arms and carried him away from the crowded room. For a moment she just breathed in the scent of him, cherished the feel of his hair against her cheek.

"I was so worried about you," she told him. "I didn't know where you'd gone."

"That's sure a big fire, isn't it, Mama?"

She sat him down upon a wooden chair. "Yes, it's a very big fire and we might even lose the house."

"Did Papa get all the animals out? Did he get my pony?"

"Yes, the animals have been taken to safety. Now we must wait and see what the fire does — whether it comes to the town."

"If it comes here, where will we go?" Luke asked innocently.

Dianne pulled off his boots. "I don't know. Uncle Zane lives in Butte, and I suppose we could go stay with him until a new house could be built."

"Is Butte far away? Will we see Indians?"

Dianne laughed. "It is far, but I doubt we'd see Indians." Her mind whirled with the possibilities of what their future might hold. She would trust Cole to know where to take them and what to do.

She helped her son get out of his wet clothes and into dry ones as he continued to chatter about the fire. *Oh, thank you, God. Thank you for bringing him back to me. Thank you for watching over him.* Dianne forced back tears of joy. God had been so good to her.

"Is he all right?" Mara asked from the doorway.

"He's fine," she said, motioning her in. "Come see for yourself."

Mara acted rather shy as she inched into the room and leaned back against the wall. "I'm glad he's all right."

Luke looked at her and smiled. "It's a big fire."

"Yes it is," Mara answered, "and we were

very worried about you. We couldn't find you."

"I was just fine," Luke said, sounding very grown up.

Dianne helped her son with his socks. "We'll put your boots by the fire to dry. Hopefully they won't shrink. You be sure and stay in the house. I don't have another pair of shoes for you."

"I'm hungry, Mama," Luke reminded her.

"You go find Miz Charity and she'll set you up with a bowl of stew. There might even be some bread."

Luke hurried out of the room. "Miz Charity! Miz Charity, I'm ready to eat."

Dianne smiled as she spread her son's clothes out over the back of the ladder-back chair where he'd been sitting.

"I guess God heard your prayers," Mara said softly.

Dianne turned. "I'm sure He did. But, Mara, you must understand something. Sometimes things don't work out the way we want them to. I've prayed and asked God's protection for everyone, but no doubt someone will be hurt — even lost — in this fire. The men have been outside of town trying hard to plow furrows of dirt so the fire will have no fuel when it reaches that point. But that doesn't mean no one will get hurt."

"I realize that. I've heard Pastor Ben talk about that before. Father isn't all that supportive of religions and church. He doesn't believe in God, but church has served his purposes at times. So the times I've been here I've listened. My brother Joshua has been reading a lot of books — well, whenever he can get his hands on them. He reads about religions and about what different people believe about God."

"And what did he conclude?" Dianne asked.

"He didn't. He wasn't sure what to think. It seemed to him that every person was equally convinced that his way was the right way."

"I've no doubt that's true. I guess it's a matter of God making himself real to you in His own personal way. I went to Sunday school and church when I was young, but it never seemed all that important to me. My teachers were often mean and harsh, and that was certainly not very appealing to a child."

"When did you decide that the Bible was real and that God really heard your prayers?" Mara asked.

"When I was seventeen my mother was missing — she'd wandered out in a snowstorm. I was heartsick from loss. My youngest sister, Betsy, had been kicked in the head by a mule and had died on our trip out here from Missouri. My sister Ardith had fallen into a river and was swept away. I figured her dead too. And my father, a good and loving man, had been shot in the crossfire of soldiers as they tried to quell southern rebels. I was overwhelmed with grief. My mother was expecting another baby, and I had tried my very best to care for her. I felt I had failed when I came to find her gone."

The memories came flooding back to Dianne as if it'd been yesterday. "I couldn't bear the pain alone. I was so miserable. I finally realized that my heart was raw from the loss — that I was somehow trying to find my comfort among dead men's bones."

"Sometimes I feel so alone," Mara confided. "If it weren't for Joshua and his kindness, I don't know what I would do."

"But why would you come to us if Joshua is at home? Surely you wouldn't want to just leave him behind."

"He plans to leave. He's decided to go back East and see about getting an education. He's very well read, as I mentioned. I think college would be a good thing for him. He talked of having me come with him, but I know I would only slow him down. He'd have to worry about supporting me and seeing that I was cared for."

"So you told him to go ahead without you?"

Mara met her eyes. "Yes. It was the hardest thing I've ever had to say. But all the while I thought of you and your ranch. I know you have no reason to believe in me, but I hope you'll help me."

"I want very much to help you," Dianne said, "but I also want you to know the truth about the Lord. He loves you very much, Mara."

"I'd like to believe that."

"You can — and in time, you will."

The town gathered at the church around ten o'clock that night. The temperature was still quite warm, but no one seemed to think much about it. No one could think past the threat of the fire.

Ben Hammond encouraged everyone to quiet down as he began to speak. "We have been told by our brave men who are plowing that the fire is only about half a mile from the furrows. The plowed ground is only about another mile from town. In a short time we will know whether the firebreak will save the town from destruction or whether we'll need to evacuate."

He cleared his throat. "We have everyone standing by, with wagons ready to leave at a moment's notice. I know you're all worried about the outcome of this fire — about what might await us yet this evening. Truth be told, I'm not going to be able to give you much assurance in such matters. Fires seem to have their own way no matter how much we try to control or tame them."

Dianne saw the nods of her friends and family members. Faith and Malachi had slipped into the church and had come, along with their children, to sit beside Cole and Dianne. Faith reached over and slipped her hand into Dianne's. Dianne looked up and found comfort in Faith's smile.

"If the word comes to evacuate, we'll work together to keep one another from harm. Stewart Blackaby has offered the use of his ranch. His land is twenty miles northwest. We can push that direction and probably find safety. The winds have been prevailing from the west and hence the fire has pushed east. I think his land is probably as good a place as any to keep us out of harm's way."

Dianne glanced to her husband. He held John on one knee and Micah on the other, while Luke sat between him and Dianne. Luke had been particularly loath to part from Barky, but Charity comforted both the boy and the dog by giving Barky a large bone to gnaw on in Luke's absence.

"I know many of you are afraid, but that is why we come together. As a family, we will work together to help and reassure one another. We've all brought certain provisions, and if we put our goods together, we can stretch them out over a longer period of time, with no one going hungry and no one suffering," Ben continued.

"In the book of Acts, the church came together and provided for one another. The Word says in the second chapter of Acts, 'And all that believed were together, and had all things common; and sold their possessions and goods, and parted them to all men, as every man had need.' The early church saw that it was right and good to take care of each other, and that is what we shall do as well."

Without warning, the back door flew open. Chester Lawrence stormed into the church as though he owned the place. "Have any of you seen my daughter or my wife?"

"We were just sharing the Word of God," Ben said firmly. "Please feel free to join us."

"I'm not here to join you. I haven't got time for such nonsense. I want to know if you've seen my wife or daughter."

"I'm here," Mara said, slowly rising to her feet.

"What in the world are you doing here, girl? Your brothers and sister are at home packing in case the fire gets that far while you're here playing church?"

"I'm not playing at anything. I've been helping our neighbors."

Mara was standing in front of Dianne. She glanced back at the Selbys, as if pleading for help. John had begun to cry at the fierce bellowing of Chester Lawrence, so Dianne reached over and took him in her arms. She didn't know how she could help the girl — she'd not even had a chance to speak to Cole about Mara since he'd returned with Luke.

"Get out here, girl. We're going back to the ranch. That fire is sure as sin going to burn this town to the ground."

"I'm not going back to the house," Mara said, making her stand.

Dianne wanted to cheer the girl, but at the same time she knew that the Bible spoke of honoring one's father. She was torn, wondering how she could make this situation right. Then it came to her in a wash of peaceful understanding. This issue wasn't hers to make right.

Chester marched over to Mara. "Are you

going to defy me? Here in front of everyone?"

Mara leaned forward and whispered, "I don't think you want me to explain why I'd rather remain here. I know a great deal about the workings of our ranch — if you get my meaning."

Chester pulled back abruptly, his eyes narrowing. "Are you threatening me?" he asked in a voice that was barely audible.

Mara met his angry stare. "I would never dream of threatening you. I'm merely suggesting we make our own brand of peace. For the sake of many — but especially for the sake of your industry."

Chester threw back his head and laughed. "Well, you stay here in town — go ahead. And how do you suppose you're going to support yourself? Money doesn't just fall out of the sky. There's only a couple of ways a girl like you can earn a living. You going to start a new brothel? Maybe you could work at one of the saloons."

Dianne could take no more. She started to get to her feet, but Cole held her back. He looked at her and shook his head. Dianne seethed. How could he let this man speak in such a manner — and in church of all places?

But before she could say a word, Cole got

to his feet. He placed Micah on the pew, then turned to Mr. Lawrence. "I believe you've said enough. This meeting is intended to unify hearts and minds, but you've done nothing but stir dissension."

"Stay out of this, Selby. You have no right to interfere."

"I have a right. Your daughter has asked for my protection."

Chester's expression contorted. "Protection? From me? She's my child — my flesh and blood. You have no right to offer protection."

Cole stood his ground. "Nevertheless, she has asked for help, and I intend to give it."

Chester turned to the girl. "Is this true? Have you gone to my enemies — against me?"

"They aren't your enemies unless you make them that," Mara said matter-of-factly. "The Selbys are good people. The others here are good people too, but you are too busy trying to destroy everyone else so you can take everything for yourself. You can't even see what good there is."

"Have it your way. Go with Selby, if that's what you like. But don't ever show your face at my door again. When you're in trouble — for whatever reason — don't you come crawling back to me."

Mara nodded with conviction. Her choice had been made in front of a hundred witnesses. Dianne rejoiced in her husband's stand against the ill-tempered Chester Lawrence. She had never been prouder of his actions.

Lawrence turned to go, but he'd not even made it to the door before one of the men who'd been working the plow line entered the church. "The fire," he said, gasping for air. Everyone turned to him, desperate to know the truth of what was happening. "The fire . . . has . . . jumped the break. We're . . . going to have . . . to evacuate."

Joshua Lawrence settled into a rocker on the porch, watching for his father's return. Everything had been made ready, but as the hours passed and there was no word, everyone had grown bored. Jerrod and Roy had decided to head out with the ranch hands and see to the herd. They'd made Joshua promise to wait until their father returned and to see the others to safety. Joshua resented their bossing him around, but at the same time he was almost sorry to see them go. He would have liked to have their strength and ability available should something go wrong.

Elsa had finally gone to bed — at Joshua's

insistence — but he doubted that she was sleeping very well.

Dozing in the chair, Joshua found himself dreaming of strange places — cities that seemed to go on and on forever. He was searching for something — some particular place — but he couldn't find what he was looking for. Sometimes he startled awake, only to fall back asleep, dreaming once again of the same setting.

The dream grew more vivid, almost as if he'd truly stepped into the scene.

"What are you looking for, boy?" a gruff old sailor asked him.

"I can't find my way," Joshua declared. "I need to locate this address." He fumbled with a piece of paper only to realize it was blank. He looked up in confusion, but the old man was gone.

He began pushing down the walkway, sometimes asking passersby for information, only to have them ignore him or shrug. "I can't find my way. I don't know where to go!" he shouted.

When he woke up, Joshua was in a cold sweat and his body trembled in fear. He wondered at the time and yawned. Surely it was close to midnight. Maybe later. He got up and went into the house, glancing at the grandfather clock that stood at the far end of the foyer. It was nearly two in the morning. Where was their father? He should have been back by now.

Joshua went upstairs to his parents' bedroom, knowing that their window would afford him the best view of the fire's progression. He searched the landscape to the south and saw the blaze. It was still far enough away that he had no reason to fear immediate danger. He breathed a sigh of relief. At least they were safe for the time being.

The sound of a single rider approaching caused Joshua to abandon his post and run from the room. He jumped the first five stairs, stepped down one, then jumped another few. He landed not far from the bottom as his father came storming into the house. The man never walked into a place, but rather invaded it.

"Where's Jerrod and Roy?" he asked, not even acknowledging Joshua.

"They've gone north with the herd."

"Where are the others? Did Portia show up?"

Joshua shook his head. "No, and neither did Mara."

"Curse Mara. She's a traitor to this family."

Joshua shook his head. "But why?"

"She was with the Selbys. That's where she's been all this time, and with us sitting here in worry." Chester beat his hat against his leg. "My own flesh and blood."

"Is she going to stay with them?" Joshua questioned, feeling almost a sense of relief for his sister.

"If Selby has his way. He probably fancies her."

Joshua had no desire to hear his father talk in such a manner. "What about the fire?"

"It jumped the fire line the town built. We'll know by morning if it's going to consume us. The wind's been blowing to the east-northeast, so I'm thinking we may escape harm. Can't hurt to be ready just in case."

"We're all packed. I sent Elsa and Cook to bed a few hours ago. I promised them I'd wait up for you and watch the fire. By the way," Joshua asked, wondering what his father might say, "do they know what started the fire?"

"Lightning, most likely. Can't say that anyone knows for sure, but that storm that blew up earlier had a great many lightning strikes."

Joshua nodded. Maybe his father really didn't know about Portia starting the blaze.

Maybe he hadn't been a part of it.

"Where are the others going to go if their ranches and the town is destroyed by the fire?"

His father laughed harshly. "I don't know, and I don't care as long as they keep going away from this place. This is a good stroke of fortune for us. We'll most likely escape the fire, but most everyone else has already seen their places destroyed. If I were a man who believed in God, I'd say He's just blessed me with the desires of my heart." He tossed his hat on the foyer table. "I'm going to bed. That fire isn't going to reach us before dawn if it even comes this way. Get some sleep, and we'll discuss what to do come morning."

Joshua bid his father good-night, then sank to the steps and wondered what to do. A part of him wanted to run to Mara — to ask the Selbys to take him in as they had done his sister. But then there was Elsa to consider. He hated to leave her behind. The feeling from his dream washed over him again and again. *I don't know where to go. . . . I can't find my way.*

CHAPTER 32

The Blackaby ranch resembled a mining town with its makeshift tent village and outdoor camps. After two weeks of living in the smoky haze, rains finally came and put out the fire. Dianne knew most of the folks sharing her fate were probably homeless now — just as she was certain to be. Cole hadn't even evacuated the property until the fire was burning the south pasture. No doubt the ranch house and outbuildings were gone.

"It's already September," Dianne said as she and Cole sat sipping coffee early one morning. "What are we going to do?" The weather had remained warm, so that at least was a blessing for the many families who were forced to live outdoors.

Cole stirred some sugar into his coffee. "I don't know. I've been giving it a lot of thought, however. We're more fortunate than most. You thought to bring my money box, and that will help us a great deal to rebuild. We might be able to get some supplies in here right away. Maybe even help some of the other folks to get supplies as well."

"There's money in the bank at Virginia City," Dianne commented. "I suppose we could use that too."

Cole smiled. "I knew you'd feel the same way."

Dianne met his loving gaze. "We're all in the same fix now. We need to work together or we'll never make it."

"Some are already making plans to leave the territory. Said it was just too hard to earn a living up here. I guess I understand them well enough."

"Are you saying you want to leave Montana?" Dianne asked, her chest tightening at the very thought.

"No, this land speaks to me. God's given me something through this land I never had — confidence. I believe everything will come around to good in this situation. Sure, the fire has been devastating, and, well . . . there's always the chance that we could rebuild only to see it all burn down again. But it feels like the right thing to do. And then there's the prideful side of me," he added with a mischievous grin.

"You, prideful?" she teased.

"I won't let this land defeat me. I belong here. So do you."

"Yes. I belong here. This is the land of my heart."

"Most of the cattle and horses survived, but the pastures are burned and useless, unless we move the livestock farther north," Cole said, shaking his head. "Maybe we should sell off most of the stock. After all, it's better to sell now than see them starve through the winter."

Dianne appreciated that he was discussing the matter with her. "Yes. I think you're wise. The army posts would no doubt take most of the horses and probably a good portion of the beef. If you can wait for the railroad, we could probably move them south to Utah and then east or west."

"But the railroad won't be complete until winter," Cole replied.

"No. It won't be complete to Butte. It's already well into Montana Territory. We could simply drive the cattle to wherever the nearest depot is and load them up."

Cole grinned. "You're a smart one. Guess it pays to talk these things over."

Dianne reached out and touched his face. "I love you more than life. I hate to think what I would have done if you had been lost in the fire. I can't imagine the suffering Ardith is going through — not knowing for sure about Levi."

"Levi is gone. I feel certain of that. His horse was found wandering, and my guess is that he was overcome by smoke or that the fire came back on him. We'll search better once we get back to the ranch. That was the other thing I wanted to talk to you about. Koko and Faith said they'd keep the children if you wanted to ride over to the ranch tomorrow with me and some of the ranch hands. It's going to be quite a ride, so we'll probably have to stay the night."

"I want to go," Dianne admitted. "I need to go. I need to see what's left — if anything."

"It won't be easy."

She smiled. "Nothing up here ever is."

The group was set to ride out the next morning when Ardith showed up, pulling her sorrel mare behind her. "I want to go with you."

Cole seemed to understand. "Sure, Ardith. I wasn't sure you'd want to leave in case . . . well . . . in case Levi showed up here."

"He's not going to show up," she said stoically. "He's dead."

Dianne looked down from her mount.

536

"Ardith, you don't know that."

"Yes, I do. I feel it here," she said, putting her hand to her heart. "If Levi were alive, he would have crawled here on his hands and knees if necessary. I think the sooner we accept his death, the better off we'll all be."

"Do you have your things?" Cole asked. "We'll be gone overnight. Did you arrange for Winona?"

"She's going to stay with Charity."

"Then mount up. We're heading out," Cole announced.

The ride thoroughly discouraged Dianne. She'd had no idea what to expect, but as brown prairie grass changed to blackened stubble and ashen ground, she could only shake her head. The odor of burnt hay, grass, and pine was still heavy on the air. Tall charred sentinels were all that remained of the once lush, forested land. Dianne would have wept if Ardith hadn't been along. How could she cry over the losses of the land when Ardith had lost her husband?

"The ground will be rich and healthy once it starts to grow back," Cole said, as if reading Dianne's mind. "Fire never permanently hurts the land. It actually makes it better. Farmers oftentimes burn off the stubble and old vegetation in their fields to make a healthy start for the new crops."

"It's just hard to see it like this," Dianne commented softly. "So barren — so desolate."

"But it won't stay like this forever. We need to remember that."

Dianne thought of Ardith and glanced over to where her sister rode apart from the others. George and Jamie had come too, along with several ranch hands. They all cut Ardith a wide berth, almost afraid to approach her for fear of reminding her of Levi.

Would Ardith remain like this forever — desolate and barren? It had taken so long for her to love again — to hope again. How could she possibly face yet another sorrow in her life?

How did anyone face the hard times? One step at a time? One moment at a time? Dianne remembered praying through the long days when Cole had disappeared. She knew what it was to wait and wonder. Most people would have believed Cole dead and buried, but she knew in her heart he was alive. Just as Ardith knew in her heart that Levi was dead.

Oh, help her, Father, Dianne prayed. *It's so hard to see her like this — to know what she is feeling and thinking. I want her to know joy and happiness, and instead she's once again facing the most devastating loss. Please help her.*

Dianne glanced out across the blackened cursed land. *Help us all.*

They approached the Diamond V property around four o'clock, coming upon Dianne's favorite hill. Dianne steadied herself for the sight but realized as the valley came into view that nothing could have prepared her for this.

The fire had eaten away at everything — every standing structure. The fences and corrals were in blackened pieces; the barn and various buildings were nothing more than a few pieces of burned framing that had somehow managed to remain in place.

The house — Uncle Bram's house — was a total loss. Dianne felt tears trickle down her cheeks but did nothing to hide them. Rock chimneys remained as sad reminders of what had once been a glorious home.

"Well, we've got our work cut out for us," Gus said. "Ain't gonna be easy, no sir. But we've got good men and we can do this."

Cole turned to him. "Do you really think so? Is it worth it? Bram's dream has been destroyed."

"No it hasn't!" declared Jamie. "My father's dream was more than just the house." He looked to George, and Dianne

539

watched as his uncle nodded in agreement. "His dream was to make a home for his family — to tame the land — to raise cattle. His dream was to live out his life here and make a better way for his children." He looked back on the valley and straightened. "We can rebuild. We are strong, and the Lord will help us."

Dianne knew Koko would have been very proud of her son in that moment. She would have been proud too of George. He had obviously influenced the boy's thinking.

Cole looked to Dianne. "What do you think?"

Dianne wiped tears away with the back of her hand. "I think Jamie is right. We're strong and able. We've seen worse, though not by much." She looked down on the lonely ruins of her uncle's dream. "We can do it. We're Montanans."

Cole grinned and turned to Gus and the boys. "You heard the lady."

Some of the boys gave a holler and headed down into the valley as though they'd been offered Christmas dinner on silver platters.

To Dianne's surprise, Ardith began to ride down toward the house as well. Jamie followed her several paces behind. Only Gus and George remained with Cole and

Dianne.

"Where do we begin?" Cole asked the older man.

Gus rubbed his chin. "Well, we need to make provision for the people and the animals first thing. Won't be a chance to put together much in the way of a real home for some time — probably not until spring."

"We've got at least four weeks — maybe more — until it turns cold," George said. "I would have said by the signs before the fire that we will have a mild winter — slow in coming."

"I agree with you," Gus said. "I think that will be in our favor. Still, we need to get cabins up. There isn't much good lumber left in the area, and hauling in logs from beyond the fire is going to be difficult. We'd need good freight wagons and plenty of help."

"Zane!" Dianne exclaimed. "Zane has the freight business. Maybe we can enlist his help."

"Good idea," Cole replied. "I was thinking it would probably be best to have you and the children winter in Butte with him while I worked down here. But maybe he can send some of his wagons and men."

Dianne shook her head. "My place is with you."

All three men looked at her. "You're going to have a baby in the middle of winter. You can't be doing that without a warm house and help," Cole began. "I know it's hard to think of being separated for a time, but honestly, we need to be wise about this."

"Then set us up in Virginia City. Find a place for all of us there. We're familiar with that place at least. Butte is far away and much too rowdy for the boys. Besides, I doubt Koko and George would be welcomed."

"She's got a good point," Gus admitted. "There's a whole lot of folks in Virginia City. Chinese, a few Mexicans, and probably some other half-breeds. They could probably live there without notice. The town has been failing ever since they moved the territorial capital to Helena. Folks are more worried about surviving than what color skin their neighbor has. Not only that, but because the population is drifting to larger towns, we might be able to pick up something cheap."

"We can check into that," Cole said. "That would put everyone close enough to visit more often. However, the winter months — even if they're mild — are going to keep us busy with the stock."

"I figure we should sell off a good number

of the herd," Gus said. "I think for the sake of rebuilding and because of the poor pastureland, we'd be smart to free ourselves up."

"That's what Dianne and I discussed. It seems we could certainly sell a good number of the horses to the army. They'd pay less because they aren't broken, but they're good animals. We can always build another herd."

"How do we support ourselves in the meantime?" Dianne questioned. "If we aren't raising cattle or horses, the money we get when we sell off is only going to last so long. Then what do we do about replenishing the stock when the time comes, if we don't have a way to make a living?"

"That's something we definitely need to figure out," Gus said.

"Maybe we could take some of our money and expand on Zane's freight business. After all, we're going to need a way to get supplies into the valley for those who are remaining."

"But few people have anything left. Not everyone was doing as well as we were. You said yourself that a good number of people will give up their homesteads and leave for better pastures," Dianne replied.

"And we can't cut wood and sell it,"

George added. "There isn't any wood to be had."

"Well, we know two things," Gus began. "Those who stay will need supplies, and that new train line ain't gonna cut a swath through the valley. At least not yet. Cole may have the best solution. Maybe we need to start by talkin' to whoever is already freighting in Virginia City. Might be we could buy them out."

"That's a good idea, Gus." Cole looked to Dianne. "We could even continue to work out of Virginia City and make it that much easier to come home from time to time."

The idea of seeing her husband on a regular basis comforted Dianne. "All right, then," she said with a smile, "it sounds like we'd best plan a trip to Virginia City and send out telegrams to the army and to Zane."

Joshua had made up his mind to leave, but first he knew he had to talk to Elsa. Since the fire and the announcement that Mara had betrayed them, Elsa had come to him more and more. She wanted to know what the future would hold, but Joshua had no answers for her. Even now, knowing that he would leave Montana — at least for a time — Joshua could give Elsa no real information as to where he would go and what he would do.

Elsa sat peeling apples in the kitchen, seemingly oblivious to the world. But Joshua knew better. Her mind was constantly at work.

"May I interrupt?" Joshua asked.

"Come to say good-bye?"

He startled at her blunt question. For a moment he thought of edging around the comment but instead faced her head on. "Yes, but I also wanted to talk to you before I left."

Elsa shrugged. "If that's what you want."

Joshua turned the kitchen chair around to sit on it backwards. Leaning against the back, he tried to figure out what to say. He'd played this out in his mind so many times, but now it seemed the words wouldn't come.

"Where are you going?" she asked, putting down the apple she'd been peeling and picking up another one.

"I don't know. I figure to go east. I want to go to college and get a good education. Or I might try to apprentice with someone and learn a trade. Maybe then I'll know what I'm supposed to do with myself."

"Will you ever come back?"

"Of course. Fact is, I plan to talk to Mara

as well. If I can secure a decent living, I would like to send for both of you. Would you be interested?"

Elsa looked up, her eyes wide with hope. "Would you truly send for me?"

Joshua smiled. "Of course I would."

She licked her lips and looked back at the apple. "But why? I haven't been very nice to you or Mara. I always figured Pa was right when he called you both weak. I didn't want him to think that of me."

"Father equates weakness with kindness and gentleness. It's not true, you know. Meanness doesn't equal strength, but some folks can't figure that out. I just want you to know that I care about you, Elsa. It doesn't matter what happened in the past."

Elsa looked up. Her soft brown hair was plaited on either side of her face, making her look much younger than her fifteen years. She searched his face as if trying to understand the meaning of his words. "I'm afraid. I don't know what's going to happen when Portia comes back. Pa won't be happy that she's been gone so long."

"I know. I don't know what will happen then either. I can't figure where she's gone or why. Seems she was pretty happy bossing folks around right here. But either way, don't worry. I'll come back for you or send for you as soon as I can. I promise."

"And maybe then you'll have some answers for me."

"Answers?"

"About what happens when we die and whether heaven is real."

Joshua realized the girl was still thinking hard on the issue of death. "I'll try to learn those answers for you, Elsa. That's my second promise to you."

She smiled. "Nobody's ever made me promises before."

"Well, now you have two."

Later that day Joshua rode to the Blackaby ranch. He assumed the Selbys were staying there with the other ranchers whose homes had burned. After asking around, he was finally directed to an encampment of several tents and wagons.

Joshua dismounted and stood awkwardly holding the reins of his horse, wondering what to do next. He knew Cole Selby by sight — he'd seen him in church and a couple of times in town — but he wasn't sure he'd recognize the other members of his family. But to his good fortune, Mara came bounding out of one of the tents, humming a song and carrying a bucket. To Joshua she looked happier than she had in years.

"Have you time for a talk?" he asked.

She looked up, her eyes wide. "Joshua!" She dropped the bucket and ran to him. He hugged her tight, raising her off the ground. Putting her back down, he pulled back.

"You're sure a sight. I don't think I've ever seen you this happy."

"I don't think I've ever been this happy. Here I am living in a tent and doing chores, and yet it's all so much better than what I had at home."

"So they're treating you well?"

"Oh, they treat me better than well — they treat me better than my own family did," Mara declared. "No one yells or screams at me. No one shouts at anyone. You know, I honestly thought all families acted the way ours did, but even the black family here doesn't act like ours."

"I've never been around black folk much. Are they . . . well . . . are they like white folks?"

"Just the same. We all eat the same and dress the same. Faith and Malachi are real nice folks. Faith has been showing me some things about cooking."

"You were already a pretty decent cook."

"Yes, but I knew nothing about cooking outdoors. I feel like I am learning so much. Miz Charity is teaching me about making clothes without a pattern, and Dianne has taught me how to build fires and care for horses."

Her animated voice was a strong indication of her pleasure in each of these tasks. Joshua felt a sense of relief, knowing that what he had come to tell her would be much easier to take in the midst of such joy.

"I came here today to tell you something," he finally said.

Mara sobered. "You're leaving, aren't you?"

He shoved his hands into his trouser pockets. "Yes. I wanted you to know, however, that if I can secure a decent living, I'll send for you. I promised Elsa the same thing."

"Elsa? Why would she even want to go?"

"We had a nice talk the night the fire destroyed Madison. She was really scared and she wanted to know about life after death and what I believed."

"And what do you believe?"

Joshua shook his head and looked to the ground. "I don't know, and that's why I need to go."

"You don't have to go away to learn the truth about that. The Selbys and their friends have that pretty much figured out.

They've really been helping me to understand."

Joshua's head shot up. "What do you mean?"

Mara smiled. "They strongly believe that God exists and that He sent His Son, Jesus, to die for our sins. They believe that the Bible is true and that we only have to believe in God and repent of our sins and that God will forgive us and we'll have eternal life."

"The very things the preacher talked about at church."

"Yes. Ben Hammond, the preacher, is their good friend. Miz Charity is his wife. There's a lot to learn, but I'm feeling better about it every day. And I'm reading the Bible."

"Well, maybe that's what I'll do too. But I still have to go. I want to try to go to college and study something besides ranching."

"Well, I plan to stay with the Selbys. We're going to Virginia City in a few days, so you can write to me there in care of them."

"Virginia City," Joshua repeated, committing it to memory. "I'll send you letters as often as I can."

Mara hugged him again. "Please be safe. I love you so very much. You were the only person who ever really cared about me."

"I'll never stop caring about you."

"Mara, is everything all right?" a voice called from behind them.

"Dianne, this is my brother Joshua. He's come to tell me good-bye," Mara said, motioning the woman over.

Dianne smiled sweetly at him. "Joshua, I've seen you a few times in church, and once or twice in town."

"I never went regularly to either place. Pa always manages to keep me busy, and he doesn't think much of church."

"Never mind that. Where are you heading?"

"I figure to go east. I want to get an education — secure a decent job — then send for my sisters. They've always been miserable on the ranch, just as I have been."

"I don't mind the ranch," Mara admitted. "For me it was the company and misery of my family that I didn't like. I'm sorry to say it, but I've never felt like I belonged. I always felt that because I didn't see eye-to-eye with our father, he had no time for me. Mother was just as bad. She was hardened by Father and therefore if we girls showed softness, she hated us for it."

"Mara tells me she's going to stay with you. I'm much obliged."

"We're pleased to offer her a home. She's

been a great help with the boys and around the camp. Did she tell you that we're heading to Virginia City?" Dianne questioned.

"Yes. She mentioned that. I promised to write her there." He turned to his sister. "I don't know how long it will be before I send a letter, so please don't fret."

"I won't. I'm just glad you're getting away from Jerrod and Roy . . . and our father."

"Well, I'd best be going. I have a long ride ahead of me." He hugged Mara one more time, then quickly mounted lest his emotions get the best of him. He wondered if he'd ever see her again. At least he had the peace of mind knowing that she'd be better off with the Selbys than at home. He only wished the same thing could be true for Elsa. "If you get a chance to help Elsa," he said as he turned the horse for the road, "please do so. She's changed, and I hate to think of her living there alone without anyone to help her."

"I'll do what I can," Mara replied.

He smiled. "I'll see you soon."

The house Cole managed to secure in Virginia City for the family was a massive structure owned by a former politician. The man had been trying to sell the property for some time, but no one needed a house that large — nor could they afford it.

With six bedrooms on the second floor and a variety of other rooms on the first floor, the house would suit their needs nicely. Cole assigned rooms to everyone as they toured the house.

"We'll take this room at the head of the stairs," he told the group. "It's a smaller bedroom with a sitting area that will make a good bedroom for the boys. The next room would suit Ardith and Winona nicely. It's fairly small but big enough for the two of you." Ardith grinned as Winona went dancing off into the room.

"Look how pretty it is!"

Cole smiled. "Apparently she's pleased." He moved them on down the hall. "This next room across the hall will suit Koko and her family. It's very large."

"George can stay with us," Koko announced. "That way you won't have to worry about a separate place for him." George nodded in compliance.

"That will work well," Cole said. "Thank you. The place directly down from yours is similar to ours, but the sitting room has an entry to the hall. I thought Ben and Charity could stay in the large bedroom and Mara could use the sitting room. Will that work?" He turned to the crowd of people gathered in the hallway and searched for Ben and Charity.

"We're just grateful for a place to stay," Ben said. "It suits us fine."

"That leaves the rooms across from the Hammonds and Mara, and those will be Malachi and Faith's rooms. The two rooms adjoin, and one can be for the children and the other for the adults."

Faith peeked inside. "Our first cabin wasn't even half this size. This will serve us nicely."

"Good. Then I suggest we get unpacked. Then the women can start making us a list of household goods we'll need. We are fortunate that this place already has quite a bit of furniture. We'll buy whatever else we can. There are several places around town where I've been told we can secure beds. So let Dianne know what you can use and we'll go from there."

Everyone scattered to their assigned spots, all talking at once and discussing the possibilities for each of their families. Cole came to Dianne and sighed. "Looks like we'll do all right here."

"For the time," Dianne said. "But already I miss the feel of grass under my feet and my lovely mountains and peaceful river. Virginia City reminds me of so many things

— mostly sad."

He put his arm around her. "I know, but we can't let it discourage us. This isn't going to be easy. It may well take us years, but Dianne, I know God will bless our efforts. I feel strongly that He has already made provision. Look how well it's gone with the freighting business. We've already acquired one of the businesses here in town, and the man was desperate to sell. God knew what we'd need before we even did."

"I know. I'm grateful for all He's done. He's kept you and the boys and all of our loved ones safe." She paused and shook her head. "Well, not Levi."

"But Levi loved the Lord. If he's gone as we fear, then we know we'll meet him again on the other side. For now, we must look to the future and put aside the past and the pain it represents."

"I know you're right. I want to be strong, and with you and the Lord, I feel I can do anything — everything required of me."

Cole smiled and kissed her lightly on the lips. "I couldn't have said it better, for I feel the same way about you. I think we'll be happy here. No, I know we'll be happy here. We're together and that's all we need."

Dianne leaned against him and sighed. "This isn't the way I figured things would be, but I know even in this, God is leading the way. I can rest in that."

February 1882
"Push, Dianne. Push hard," Koko ordered.

Dianne bore down with all her might. The baby was coming quickly and with relative ease, but the pain was fierce. Panting, Dianne felt the child emerge from her body. Koko quickly cut the cord and hung the child upside down.

"It's a girl!" she declared as she smacked the baby's bottom to get her breathing.

"A daughter!" Dianne sighed and fell back against her pillow. "I have a daughter."

The baby wailed in protest of her abuse. Koko laughed and immediately handed the baby to Charity. "She's got a good set of lungs. Perhaps she'll be as strong willed as her mother."

"No doubt," Faith said as she brought Koko a stack of clean towels. "That's what she'll need to get her through life in this territory."

"That and a strong faith in the Lord," Dianne agreed. Nothing had ever sounded as good to her as the cry of her new baby. Exhaustion washed over her and suddenly all Dianne wanted to do was sleep. "Please let Cole know about our daughter."

"I'll go get him right now," Faith said.

Koko finished cleaning Dianne up and readied her for visitors. While Faith went for Cole, Charity brought the baby to Dianne. "She's ready to meet her mama." Dianne reached up and took the child in her arms.

"She's a real beauty," Koko said, leaning over to view the baby.

"Oh, she's perfect." Dianne gently touched the copious amount of brown hair on the baby's head. The infant had stilled and looked up at Dianne as if in awe of the world and everything in it.

"Hello, little one," Dianne cooed. "Oh, you're my little beauty."

"What will you name her?"

"Athalia," Dianne said without hesitation. "Mr. Cohen at the dry goods store told me it's Hebrew and it means 'the Lord is exalted.' "

"How perfect," Charity declared. "Athalia."

Cole knocked and peeked in. "Is it all right to come in?"

"Come ahead," Koko said and waved him in. "They're waiting for you. Both of your gals."

Cole came to the bed and smiled. "So you finally got the daughter you wanted."

"And just look at her — she's perfect."

"She takes after her ma," Cole observed.

Dianne lifted the baby up. "I think she looks like her papa."

Cole took the baby in hand, looking most uncomfortable. "She's kind of on the small side."

"Most babies are," Koko teased. "If I remember right, your boys were all about that size."

"Well, she seems a whole lot smaller."

Charity came to his side. "No, but she will be a weight of responsibility. Girls are always much harder than boys. I've heard it declared so more than once."

"I know it to be true," Koko said in agreement.

"Well, our little Athalia will be loved no matter what," Dianne said as Cole handed the child back to her. "Athalia Hope Selby will be the symbol of our new beginning. A symbol of God's love."

Everyone commented in agreement, and Dianne could only bask in the blessings that God had bestowed. Her life had known its moments of despair and darkness, but always God had brought her back around to dream anew.

ABOUT THE AUTHOR

Tracie Peterson is a popular speaker and bestselling author who has written over sixty books, both historical and contemporary fiction. Tracie and her family make their home in Montana.